DEDICATION

This book is dedicated to Nellie Jane Gray, who founded the annual Washington D. C. March for Life in 1974.

Nellie passed away in August 2012 at age 88 and was known as the "Joan of Arc of the Gospel of Life."

CONTENTS

ACKNOWLEDGMENTS

First, I want to thank my husband, Charlie, and my four children: Xavier, Blaise, Jude and Seraphina. You are my *raison d'être*. Second, I want to thank my best friend and "brother from another mother," Jorge Cruz. I could not have published this book without you. Finally, I would like to thank the eight people who believed in the idea of <u>The Bloodstone Legacy</u> before it was written: Dr. Peter and Shirley Arnold, my loving parents and first readers; Carl A. Anderson, the Supreme Knight of the Knights of Columbus; the most Reverend John J. Myers, the Archbishop of Newark; Monsignor Richard J. Arnhols, the pastor of Saint John the Evangelist; Greg Tobin, author and my editorial consultant; Saint Padre Pio of Pietrelcina, my inspiration; and the blessed Virgin Mary as she appeared to Juan Diego, Our Lady of Guadalupe, the Patroness of America and the Protectress of the Unborn.

"You will know the truth,

and the truth will set you free"

(JOHN 8:31).

PROLOGUE

The special place Cassy knew so well from her childhood was in her dream again last night. She walked through a forest and came upon an immense backyard. There was a large, black wrought iron fence that separated the backyard from the forest. Cassy walked through the fence and stood amid an open, grassy field. She could feel the soft grass under her bare feet.

The backyard was at least three acres wide with a gigantic pool in its center. Everything looked expensive and glamorous, the pool's water fountain casting iridescent shades of purple into the air. Cassy walked slowly past the pool toward a beautiful red brick driveway that wound around from the front of the house to the main road off to the left. Dispersed every two feet, the drive was lined with black lanterns with rich, green ivy spiraling up the poles.

In her dream, Cassy walked along the inside of the fence past beautiful climbing roses in shades of pink and red elegantly looping around the black metal poles. She followed the trail to the center of the backyard forest to the special spot where the big gray stone was conveniently placed by Cassy only days before. She remembered frantically digging the hole, upturning the roots of gray–green grass, then feeling the cool clay earth in her fingers.

All the while, Cassy knew the purpose for that hole. She knew about the evil thing she would discard. She knew the importance of it, the value, the power of it. She knew and didn't care. Cassy wanted it away from the house and away from her. The horrible and powerful thing would once and for all be implanted and cast back into the depths of the earthen hell where it belonged. Cassy dreamed that she could feel the earth tremor with excitement as if it, too, knew the magnitude of power immersed within.

Cassy woke with a start. In her dream, the plan was conceived, but today the plan would be carried out. Today, she would summon all her courage to be rid of the evil that had vexed her mother for so long.

Cassy climbed out of her luxurious silken bed, slipped on her robe and slippers, and walked quietly down the long corridor that led to the grand staircase. She felt for the evil thing she had taken from her mother's jewelry box and hidden in the right pocket of her robe the night before. It was heavy and when she lifted her leg to walk, the evil thing hit her on the top of her thigh. She grimaced over her hatred for this thing.

Today, she would be rid of it for good, and this made Cassy smile.

She tip–toed down the long corridor passed the closed nursery door on the right where her little sister, Deborah, slept. Deborah was only six months old and the sweetest and most innocent plaything Cassy had ever held.

Cassy usually created so much noise that she would hear little Deb begin to stir by now. She would stroll into the nursery to lift Deb out of her crib and take her to the rocking chair with the baby on her lap. The two sisters would sit contentedly gazing into each other's eyes. Cassy would touch Deb's ample, rosy cheeks. They were so velvety. This would make Deb giggle with delight.

But today, Cassy had important business at hand, and this business was for little Deb's protection. It was for Cassy's and her mother's protection, too.

Cassy quietly descended the winding staircase. When she reached the bottom, the grand foyer was still as dark as the night before with tiny hints of early morning light. There was a chill in the air as Cassy walked to the double doors at the front of the house. She disengaged the alarm, unlocked the doors and stepped out onto the cold, damp front steps.

A few stairs down, Cassy quickly made her way across the circular drive toward the front lawn. She made a quick left toward the backyard and headed in the direction of the black fence toward the spot at the edge the forest. Light was coming up over the horizon, and Cassy hastened her pace even more. In a half–run, she skirted past the pool fountain and headed toward the secret place.

Luckily, the evil thing was in a black velvet bag, and Cassy didn't have to look at it when she took it from her pocket. She set it down next to the large, gray stone near the fence. Cassy lifted the stone to gain access to the hole. She picked up the bag and for one fleeting second she felt the awkward heaviness of it. There was a power in this evil thing—a power so intense it almost vibrated the bag.

Cassy's body shook as tears welled in her eyes. "That's it," she said. "I won't let myself give up now."

Cassy dropped the bag in the hole and covered it with the small pile of dirt she had left under the fence. She lifted the large stone again and placed it on the loose mound of dirt. Cassy turned to go, but not before she heard an unforgettable sound come from the evil thing under the stone. The sound sent shivers down her spine. It sounded like something Cassy had never heard before, like nails on a chalkboard or teeth gnashing back and forth. It sounded ugly and low and hellish.

Cassy turned on her heels so fast she almost fell, but she regained her footing and ran back toward the house. She sped with all her might past the fountain, across the front yard, and up the front porch steps. Cassy opened the door, stepped inside, and as she closed it behind her, she let out a great sigh of relief. The only sounds in the house were Cassy's sharp, quick breaths.

Later that day, in the great parlor downstairs, Cassy innocently played with her dolls. She heard her mother, Elaina, rush down the stairs toward her. Cassy pretended to busy herself with conversations of dances to attend when her mother came up from behind.

"Cassy, you didn't see my bloodstone cameo necklace, did you? The one with the double clasp at the back?" her mother asked.

"No, Mother. You told me never to go into your special jewelry box. Only the one with the fakes."

When Cassy's mother turned to go, Cassy had never seen such a look of terror in all her young life. She knew she had done wrong, but all Cassy could think of was her immense need for protection.

It would not be long before Cassy's mother would discover her guilt and choose the power of the bloodstone over the safety of her two young daughters.

*

Late that same night, Cassy's panic–stricken mother called a meeting as if death had called her from afar, and she was fending it off like a lioness caught in some tightly constrained lair.

Shortly before midnight, Cassy's mother gathered all the female members of the Taninsam family. Cassy's mother, Elaina, had lost her most valuable possession, and she needed everyone to help her locate it.

What Cassy's mother did not know was that the guilty party who had done the terrible deed she was so diligently bidding to correct was hiding in the coat closet off the back of the dining room. Cassy had stowed herself away in that tiny little closet, her teeth chattering away with fear, her little fingers hooked together so tightly they were beginning to numb.

At midnight, women of all ages descended upon the Taninsam dining room. There was a great oak table in the center of the room, and each took a seat with Elaina at the head of the table looking withdrawn and pale.

Aunt Beatrice, actually Great Aunt Beatrice, was seated to the right of Elaina. Beatrice was wearing too much makeup; her face was a mask of white with two large, blue circles for eyes and one great puckery half–moon for lips. Aunt Marian and Aunt Martha, Elaina's two sisters, were seated beside Beatrice, both wearing their usual black dresses and black hats. Across from them were Elaina's cousins: Jackie, Raya, Connie, Danielle, and Lisa. They all looked very young and beautiful, done up in tailored suits and dresses of silk.

Finally, Dad's younger sister, Aunt Jessica, was seated farthest from Elaina at the end of the table. Cassy's father had died when Deb was first born. His death was sudden, and Cassy assumed it was a heart attack. Cassy had never known her father. Deb had never met him at all. Jessica was by far the prettiest of the Taninsam clan, her hair golden blonde and done up in a braided bun. Cassy couldn't help but notice Jessica's necklace, a beautiful bloodstone cameo clinging to her fleshy breasts, her dress a low–cut floral print.

Cassy stared at Aunt Jessica in her ethereal beauty. She gazed at these women, marveling at their feminine mystique. They all had outward youthful beauty and they all wore golden, glittering necklaces around their necks.

Cassy became more nervous than ever at what she had done to her mother's cameo necklace, for there was one great similarity that united these women beyond physical beauty. They all wore fantastic bloodstone cameos around their necks. Each cameo was a deep green jasper stone with dots of red quartz spattered in different designs on top of the green. Each was also imprinted with a picture of a young woman as innocent as the heavenly Madonna. The bloodstone cameos were a different color or design or size, and all were images of women unique and fitting to the particular person wearing it.

All wore cameos. All, except Elaina.

Cassy's cameo–bearing relatives were assembled around Elaina uttering words of woe and betrayal.

As Cassy stood in the closet watching and listening, she kept asking herself whether she had done right or wrong.

Beatrice spoke first, "All right, ladies. Let's quiet down now. We have much work to do this evening. Raya, dear, please dim the lights. We will join hands and begin the calling process now."

Raya responded quickly and the lighting in the room became mere shadows.

"Thank you, Raya," Aunt Beatrice said. "All right, we have all joined hands and felt the soaring. Yes, this is good. Marian, could you please sound the initial pitch?"

Marian's clear, solid soprano voice made a chiming sound that resembled a single ray of light streaming through crystal. At once, all the women in the room sounded out their own version of that single clear pitch. A chorus of angels emerged from a single crystal ray, and there was an entire rainbow of harmony.

What lovely sounds they all made.

Cassy could barely keep herself contained inside the closet. Her hand found its own way to the door knob, but she quickly pulled it back in fear. Cassy yearned to join them in their beautiful musical creation, but she reminded herself of the horrible danger if she were to be seen. Still, the music was so delicate and delicious to her.

Just as Cassy's hand went to open the slatted door, Marian increased her volume and pitch to levels that were almost piercing. Everyone was increasing at the same rate using their voice as the direction, the illustration—except these were no longer women's voices, but animals' sounds—cats and dogs and wolves and birds all at once, and then out of nowhere came screams of the wild that echoed off the ceiling. There were loud, shrill shrieks and then laughter and crying all together.

Every dimension of emotion was emitted at once.

Cassy laughed and cried inside herself. She felt completely out of control. It felt as if their cries were like an erupting volcano spewing molten ash from its throat. Cassy could feel the knob of the door growing hotter and hotter in her hand. She felt she had to open it now.

The knob turned quickly, and Cassy realized she stood among them. They didn't notice her, though. They were too caught up in their own ecstasies, as Cassy stood watching them.

Aunt Beatrice sat back in her chair with her rich, dark hair spilling out of her usually coiffed bun, her head bobbing back and forth, her mouth distorted with growling sounds too low to make out.

Cassy noticed Aunt Jessica in all her insurmountable pleasure. Her beauty was normally of one dimension, but tonight her cheeks were blushed with euphoria, her blue eyes glittering with excitement, her breasts heaving with every uncontrollable breath.

Cassy was so completely caught up in all of them. She stood laughing and crying as tears streamed down her face. It was more excitement than her eight–year–old body had ever known.

Marian climbed on top of the table, her screams echoing throughout the room so violently Cassy knew a window must break. Marian swayed back and forth making up imaginary beats to accompany her dark cries. Everyone remained on the floor standing, following Marian's direction with their own attempts at dance, whatever movements suited each best.

There was a complete mixture of such emotion and every gamut of emotion; some laughing and cackling, others crying out as if from torture.

It was more than any human being could stand, yet Cassy stood and watched and felt it all. It was tremendously loud in that room, too loud, much too loud for any human ear, yet Cassy could not escape the sounds.

And then silence. All at once and much too suddenly, not a sound was heard but the echo still resounding off the walls and ceiling. That silence filled Cassy's ears with such a force of pressure, it was as if she had dropped hundreds of feet in a matter of seconds. There was a ringing, a terrible ringing in her ears. Cassy's ears began to throb uncontrollably.

Then all began to fade. All traces of noise were gone. All traces of emotion had vanished. All shades of color had disappeared. Cassy was left with nothing—only blackness.

Beatrice was panting rapidly, drops of perspiration sliding down her raven cheeks. "Raya, turn back on the lights, will you?"

Raya looked completely spent. Her breathing came in little gasps as she slowly made her way to the switch. The chandelier glared on so harshly, Cassy's pupils stung in blindness. Her focus came back slowly as she tried to make out the scene and then with horror she realized what it had meant.

They were staring intently at Cassy's mother, looks of satisfaction having emerged on their smug faces. Elaina's necklace was back in its position, sitting idly in mock innocence at the nape of her neck.

How had it occurred? It was more confusion and emotion than Cassy could handle in one night. She took one quick, careless step backwards, her ankle giving way, and crashed to the floor with a loud, horrid bang. The sound brought all eyes from Elaina to Cassy, and it took only one instant before the look on their faces changed from gratitude to anger.

All at once, they knew. They knew the truth. They knew that Cassy was the traitor, the one who had stolen the necklace. At this moment, it was as if one great hex had been put upon her. Cassy became the enemy. The life she knew before, the life she had with her mother and Deb would now be lost forever.

CHAPTER ONE

Twenty years passed, and Cassandra Taninsam grew into the kind of voluptuous woman men loved to adore and women loved to call, "overweight." She had hair the color of autumn–turned leaves on a bright October day, and she kept it long and straight, cascading down the center of her back like glistening strands of an ornate piece of fabric. A simple blouse, skirt and pumps were all she wore; the blouse made of coffee–colored silk, and the skirt, black suede.

Today was September 5, and Cassy drove to her last appointment with Dr. Bernard Lanton, the psychiatrist she had been seeing for two years.

Cassy parked her black BMW on Linwood Avenue in Ridgewood, New Jersey. She grabbed her purse, locked her car and walked to the circular drive that led to the office building. The drive was made of the same dark red brick as the building and stairs. Green ivy grew in abundance along the surface of the building's facade.

As Cassy climbed the stairs that led to the entrance of Dr. Lanton's outer office, she thought about how far she had come since her first visit. Two years ago, at age twenty–five, Cassy began to sense that someone was following her. Sometimes it would be on a dark street, and she would hear heavy footsteps behind her. Most times, she'd turn to see who was there, but she saw no one. Other times, she'd catch a glimpse of a tall dark–haired man wearing a heavy black coat, but as soon as she caught his eye, he would vanish. Cassy felt she must be losing her mind.

*

At age eight, Cassy was sent to live with her Aunt Jessica who was only sixteen years older. Her mother said it would be in her best interest to have Cassy and Deb move out just in case Deb followed in Cassy's footsteps, and began "poking around in places where she didn't belong, too."

For the first two weeks, Deb lived with Cassy at Aunt Jessica's, but for reasons Cassy did not understand, Deb and Cassy were separated. Cassy was not told where Deb was taken; only that she would be much safer if she lived separately from Cassy. Jessica told Cassy that it was for Deb's well–being that both did not know the location of the other, and that perhaps someday they would be reunited.

Cassy lived a comfortable life with Aunt Jessica. While Cassy went to school, Jessica studied medicine at New York University. After school, they would meet back at Jessica's cozy two–bedroom apartment on the Upper West Side of Manhattan and both would study until dinner.

Sometime after Cassy turned nine, Aunt Jessica stopped wearing her bloodstone cameo. Cassy felt instant relief when she no longer had to look at the evil thing. At first, Cassy missed her mother, but after Jessica stopped wearing her cameo, Cassy felt ashamed that she did not miss her mother at all.

Not a day passed, however, when Cassy did not miss Deb. Cassy would cry into her pillow every night at the thought of her beautiful little sister. Every night, Cassy thought about their special times together: Cassy tickling Deb until she giggled in delight,

Cassy caressing Deb's cheeks and feeling her soft skin.

The only thing Cassy could do to comfort herself in the absence of Deb was to fall asleep with a special down–filled pillow with a satin cover. This was Cassy's comfort pillow, and the only way she was able to fall asleep each night.

Cassy's other comfort was her love of music. Cassy loved to listen to classical music when she and Jessica sat together consumed with homework, or when she laid in bed each night falling asleep. Aunt Jessica thought it best that Cassy take up an instrument.

Cassy began violin lessons at age ten, but after two months, she thought the notes were too close together on the finger board and realized it was too difficult to do vibrato from that position. Cassy switched to cello because she loved the melancholy sound of the tenor voice. She began cello lessons and immediately felt at ease with the finger positions and the vibrato. She practiced every day after school. Sometimes, Cassy would practice for three or four hours, so much that her fingers ached with the pleasure of making beautiful string sounds.

By the time Cassy entered high school, she had grown into an accomplished cellist and was first–chair in her high school orchestra. Cassy decided to study music performance at NYU and after receiving her Master's, she auditioned for the New Jersey Symphony Orchestra. She was quite surprised when she received the position of second–chair cellist.

Meanwhile, Jessica became a geneticist and made a very good living as a research analyst and professor of medicine at NYU's graduate school program. Jessica decided it would be more comfortable for the two women to share a home in beautiful Ridgewood, New Jersey, which was only a short train ride into New York City.

A year after taking a job with the NJSO, Cassy met Drew Harrison. Drew became concertmaster of the NJSO at age twenty–eight, four years before, and one of the youngest to ever hold the position of principal violinist for a major orchestra in the country.

Drew was 32 years old, and the most handsome man Cassy had ever seen. He was athletic and tall with wavy dark brown hair that fell to his eye brows, but his most enduring quality was his humble and lighthearted nature. Drew could always make Cassy laugh and, to her, this was the most important quality in a man.

Cassy made eye contact with Drew one day during a rehearsal of Mozart's Requiem Mass in D minor. Vladimir Polzner, the conductor of the NJSO, had a habit of taking Drew's violin every time he felt a passage wasn't done to perfection in order to demonstrate the musical nuances to Drew. Cassy was sure that the maestro wanted to make sure that everyone in the symphony knew that he was the best violinist and conductor in the Northeast.

What Cassy remembered most was the look Drew gave Cassy when Maestro Polzner was going through his weekly show–off ritual. Every time the maestro looked at Drew, Drew gave him a serious expression, but every time the maestro looked away, Drew would make silly faces to the maestro's back. He had the entire orchestra laughing by the end of the demonstration.

Cassy was instantly won over by Drew. She loved his talent, but most of all, she loved the fact that he never took himself too seriously.

At the same time, Cassy began to sense a dark and evil force surrounding her. It was as if there were someone constantly following her: the late night walks to her car after a performance when she heard steps behind her quicken their pace, and Cassy would turn around only to find cold darkness; the practice sessions at Aunt Jessica's apartment when she heard dark voices in her ears only to discover that no one was there but her. These occurrences were nothing, however, compared to what came next.

The car accident that brought Cassy to Dr. Lanton came about quickly as if she had been living her life, blinked for only a second, and suddenly was being whisked away on an ambulance stretcher toward Valley Hospital. Cassy had been broad–sided while driving across a major intersection on her way home. She hadn't seen the other car coming, but the passenger–side impact had pushed her car into the oncoming traffic, and she had blacked out.

Cassy woke in a hospital bed in a private room with Aunt Jessica peering down at her with a worried expression. Cassy could make out Drew in the background, too, his hands pushing into his pockets as if that were the only way to handle his concern for Cassy. Cassy tried to sit up in her hospital bed, but the pain was too severe to move. What happened? Cassy felt as if her swollen lips couldn't form the question she was trying to ask.

Jessica sat down in a chair next to the bed. She took Cassy's hand. "Relax, Cassy. You were in a dreadful car accident. You suffered trauma to the head and chest, but don't worry. It's nothing serious. Thank God for air bags." Cassy remembered Aunt Jessica's warm smile. "Everything is going to be all right," she said.

Cassy heard the door open and she saw Nurse Bridget Monaghan for the first time, the nurse with whom she had stayed in contact for the past two years. Cassy remained in the hospital for a full two weeks before she was permitted to leave. This was the day she saw the man in black again; the man she was convinced had been following her.

Cassy was in the hospital lobby, and Drew had gone to the front entrance to watch for Jessica's car. Cassy saw him, a tall dark figure, coming toward her. She felt fear as she tried to look in the opposite direction, but couldn't. Cassy noticed that his hair was black, shiny, and done in a ponytail in the back. He was thin and tall and wearing a long, black coat with black pants and black boots.

What struck Cassy most were his eyes, a shade of black so dark they appeared inhuman. As the man came toward her, his dark lips turned into a condescending grimace. He raised his right hand as he approached Cassy and pointed his index finger directly at her face.

"You'll do well to remember your name, Cassandra, or next time the accident that landed you here will seem like a walk in the park." The man in black spoke with a hatred so strong it seemed as though venomous poison were coming from his mouth instead of words. As quickly as he had come, he left and disappeared around the corner and out of sight.

After the encounter with the mysterious man in black, Cassy began to think it was just another figment of her imagination. She felt she was seeing things again and needed a professional; a psychiatrist with experience and training. The accident had left Cassy a bit fragile, and she did not want to burden Aunt Jessica or Drew with crazy men threatening her in hospital lobbies or imaginary footsteps and voices in the dark. Cassy decided not to speak a word of this to anyone. She did not want to burden anyone with crazy thoughts. She would handle this professionally.

Cassy saw Dr. Lanton twice a week, and the incidents stopped as soon as treatment began. As Cassy spent more time with Drew, the dark and imaginary episodes became a thing of the past.

Drew proposed to Cassy, and it was a day she would never forget. They were making their way out of the New Jersey Performing Arts Center after completing what may have been the best performance of Carmina Burana ever performed with the Moscow Conservatory. Drew suggested that he and Cassy have a quick bite at Maize's across the street.

As soon as they found a cozy table in the corner and ordered drinks, Drew knelt on one knee and took Cassy's hand. "Cassy, you are the most perfect woman, the most beautiful woman I have ever met, and I want to spend every day with you for the rest of my life. Will you marry me?"

Cassy's eyes filled with tears. "Yes," she said smiling.

Drew leaned forward to kiss Cassy and reached into his pocket to produce a small, black velvet box, which he opened exposing a beautiful diamond engagement ring. Drew took the ring from the box and slid it onto Cassy's left, ring finger.

Cassy kissed Drew and a loud roar of applause emerged from the other diners. Cassy and Drew had no idea anyone was paying attention. They both blushed in embarrassment and Drew stood up and sat back in his seat.

Drew took Cassy's left hand. "Forever," was all he said as their drinks were served.

Cassy and Drew were married at Saint Mary's Catholic Church in Dumont, New Jersey. Drew had grown up in Dumont and spent his grammar school days at Saint Mary's Catholic School. He went on to attend Bergen Catholic High School, but by then, he had already become well known in the orchestral community.

Drew began violin lessons at age five, and by the time he was eight, he had outgrown his local piano and violin teachers. He began violin lessons, exclusively, with a more advanced instructor. Drew's father had graduated from Bergen Catholic in 1971 and knew a fellow graduate who taught violin at Julliard in New York City. Drew auditioned at age eleven and was accepted into the "Young Gifted Artist" program. By the time Drew was twelve, he was competing in statewide competitions, and by his sophomore year in high school, he had won the national competition for "Best Young Soloist."

Drew attended Julliard on full scholarship and received his Master's in music performance by the age of twenty–one. He traveled abroad performing in various renowned orchestras and became concertmaster for the NJSO at age twenty–eight.

On the day of Cassy and Drew's wedding, the pews were filled with hundreds of family and friends who knew the couple as two great artists who had come to share the eternal nuptials of wedding bliss.

Saint Mary's Church was a large and stark building with beautiful stained glass windows and a center aisle more than a block long. On the day of their wedding, Drew stood in front of the altar with June Abad, his best friend and best man from the Philippines. Standing in the center of the aisle was Drew's friend, the priest and pastor of Saint Mary's Church, Father Raphael Diego Ruiz Trujillo, from Puebla, Mexico.

Drew looked up at the large organ in the center of the choir loft as the organist began to play the traditional, "Bridal March." When Drew saw Cassy standing in white organza at the back of the church ready to make her entrance, he would forever have her image emblazoned in his mind. This was the happiest day of his life. Nothing would ever come between them; not on this day.

During the reception at the Rockleigh Country Club, Drew and Cassy were having their pictures taken as the sun was setting behind them. They were standing in front of a garden terrace with red climbing roses growing up either side of the white lattice silhouette.

Jessica made her way to the couple through the intricate maze of walkways that lined the large fountain pools in the center of the grand courtyard. When she reached Cassy and Drew, Cassy asked the photographer to give them a minute, and she and Drew stepped off the garden platform to greet Jessica. They embraced in a circle of three.

"I have news, actually a gift that I would like to present to the two of you." Jessica handed Cassy a thin white envelope.

Cassy opened it and tears filled her eyes. "It's the deed to the house in Ridgewood. Aunt Jessica has given us her beautiful home."

Cassy and Drew exclaimed their gratitude, and then Cassy looked up perplexed. "But where will you live?" she asked.

"I just received word from the University of San Francisco. They would like me to head the research department of the Division of Medical Genetics. I'll be moving to California next week."

Cassy threw her arms around Jessica. "Congratulations, but I'll miss you!"

These were the only words that escaped Cassy's mouth through tears of love and the knowledge that her beloved aunt had become more like a mother to her.

*

Cassy stepped onto the landing in front of Dr. Bernard Lanton's grand, oak door and rang the buzzer. She waited for the familiar click of the lock release and stepped inside.

"Hi, Cassy." Gayle Werther, Dr. Lanton's secretary, gave Cassy the same friendly smile she had seen week after week.

"Gayle, how are you? Can you believe this is actually my last one?" Cassy couldn't contain her smile.

"I know. I know. Don't remind me. We're all going to miss you here." Gayle gave Cassy a quick kiss on her cheek.

"Thanks, Gayle. I'm going to miss you, too." Cassy could feel her stomach tighten with nervousness and excitement.

"You can go right in. Cassy? Are you okay?"

"Yes, thanks. I'm sorry. What did you say?"

"Dr. Lanton says you can go right in and have a seat. He'll be with you in a few minutes."

Cassy smiled cheerily and opened the door to Dr. Lanton's inner office. She closed the door and walked directly to the brown, leather chair she had grown accustomed to during her visits.

Cassy fixed her gaze on the books that Dr. Lanton kept on a shelf to the right of his large mahogany desk. All were large medical and psychiatric books with leather covers except two: a small, worn, hard–cover copy of Kahlil Gibran's _The Prophet_ and a soft–cover copy of the New American Bible with little tab markers sticking out of the side.

Cassy decided to look at the Bible to see which passages Dr. Lanton had marked. She took it off the shelf and turned to the last marker first. To her surprise, a small white note floated down to the floor. Cassy picked it up and her eyes opened wide with disbelief. In Dr. Lanton's large script was written, "Check Leviticus and Kings. Also Zephaniah. Let Elaina know I now have all I need to put the Taninsam ties together." It was dated August 7, 2011, almost a year after Cassy started to see him.

Cassy could not believe it. Did Dr. Lanton really have ties to her mother? Could Dr. Lanton have used information from Cassy's visits to blackmail Elaina? The thought sent Cassy's mind into a spinning frenzy. She had to remember what she had confessed to Dr. Lanton over the past two years. Her mind went reeling back to the night her mother had found her bloodstone necklace, all those years ago…

*

Cassy saw her mother's face hovering over hers; Elaina's eyelashes were thick with glossy, black mascara brushing against her cheek.

She heard Aunt Beatrice in the background. "No, Elaina. She's just a child. She didn't know."

Cassy was shaking with fear when Aunt Jessica turned toward Elaina who was still holding Cassy's shoulders.

"Elaina, no harm has been done," Jessica said. "No harm at all. The necklace was returned to you. Everything is back to its normal state again." She spoke in a reassuring tone, as if she were speaking to a child. Jessica stood protectively behind Cassy.

Elaina let go of Cassy, but her face grimaced like she was straining to contain a miserable beast from inside her. She lunged out her claw–like hand and caught Cassy's hair in one solid grip. Animal sounds escaped her lips as she pulled her daughter's hair.

Cassy screamed in agony, "No, Mother, no! Please, you're hurting me!" Cassy sobbed in pain and fear.

Just then, Beatrice struck a blow to Elaina's extended arm that would have broken the bone of a normal, human being.

All at once, Elaina dropped her arm and lost her grip on Cassy's hair. Cassy quickly stepped back toward Jessica who instantly swept her arms around the shaking child. She clung to her kind aunt breathing audible moans into her bosom.

Cassy heard Aunt Beatrice in the background. "No, Elaina! You must remember the law of the stone! No harm must come to any female member! Not one! If you choose, she can leave, but no harm must come ever!"

*

Cassy was instantly brought back to reality when Dr. Lanton entered his plush office. She secretly placed the small note in the right pocket of her skirt and closed the Bible with a loud thud. She decided to confront Dr. Lanton head on.

"Dr. Lanton, can you please explain the note inside of this Bible to me? Have you been in contact with my mother, Elaina?"

Cassy opened the Bible back to the last marker, but Dr. Lanton snatched it out of her hands and placed it in the left drawer of his desk before he sat down.

"Cassy, the only relationship I have with your mother, Elaina, is through you. There is no note with your mother's name on it. There is no note having to do with you or any of the Taninsams. The only notes I keep in my favorite Bible are those having to do with the Bible Study classes I've been taking.

"Look, you have come to trust me for good reason. We've spent the last two years together in a very amicable, professional relationship. I have been here only to help with your mother and that imaginary 'person' you've always spoken about. Isn't there a chance that you could have imagined your mother's name on a note, too?"

Cassy sat back slowly and looked straight into Dr. Lanton's dark brown eyes. An odd, queasy feeling suddenly came over her.

"I feel like I've come so far from when I first walked into this room," she said. Cassy knew that Dr. Lanton was lying, but she would keep it to herself. "Perhaps you're right. Perhaps I'm just imagining things." Cassy smiled in spite of the situation.

Dr. Lanton smiled, too. "Cassy, you've made so much progress in the past two years. You never complain about imaginary voices or imaginary 'demons' anymore. I think that is worth a thousand toasts."

The psychiatrist stood up and went to a cabinet where he pulled out a small bottle of champagne and two glasses. He opened the bottle, which popped with such force champagne streamed down the sides in little clouds of foam. "Excuse me while I get a towel." Dr. Lanton disappeared inside his private bathroom and emerged with a small hand towel, which he placed around the bottle.

"Let's toast to your good health. Cassy, you are truly in control of your life now. I see no reason why one tiny episode like this imaginary note should hinder your two years of progress." He poured champagne into two glasses and handed one to Cassy.

Cassy hesitantly took the glass. "Thank you," she said. She took a small sip of champagne, but set it down on the doctor's desk with no intention of finishing it.

"Look, Cassy. You can still trust me. Cheers." Dr. Lanton stood up and tripped on the edge of a thick, Persian rug in front of his desk. He tried to steady himself, but he dropped his glass and it shattered on the wood floor below.

"Are you okay?" Cassy asked.

"Yes, yes. I'm sorry, Cassy. I had meant for this toast to be a good thing. A chance to say good–bye."

"No. It was a very nice gesture." Cassy stood and gave her doctor a farewell embrace. When she felt an odd coldness come over him, she quickly pulled away. "Dr. Lanton, can I ask you just one more question?"

"Absolutely."

"What is the connection between Leviticus and Kings and the Taninsam name?"

Dr. Lanton gave her the coldest stare she's ever seen. "I told you. There was no note," he replied.

Cassy hoped that after their two–year relationship her

psychiatrist would come clean and own up to the note. "You're right. I must have only imagined it," she said.

Dr. Lanton's gaze turned from cold to warm in one instant. "Good–bye, Cassy. I'll miss you."

Cassy left Dr. Lanton's office for the last time and walked down the bright, airy corridor that connected his office to the rest of the hospital. Note or no note, she wanted to bid farewell to the hospital staff and that was what she planned to do. Cassy made sure the note was still inside her pocket, as she continued down the hallway.

There was always such a remarkable difference between this corridor and the rest of the facility. Cassy walked through a hallway of renaissance paintings and Persian rugs into a large room with stark, white walls and yellow and white tiled floors. There was no doubt that Cassy had entered the outer wing of Ridgewood's Valley Hospital.

As Cassy walked through the hospital entrance, a strange feeling came over her. She felt the room begin to spin in darkness as if her whole world were a cave under the ground. A cave with no air. Cassy was suffocating. She was gasping for every breath; her mind spinning out of control.

Had Dr. Lanton put something in that champagne to harm her? She felt like she might faint at any moment. She took hold of a chair that stood against the far wall of the entrance.

"Are you all right, Cassy? Can you hear what I'm saying? Cassy?" Nurse Bridget ran toward Cassy who stood with one hand on her stomach and the other holding onto the chair for balance. Cassy sat down heavy as if she could no longer hold her weight while Bridget knelt trying desperately to revive her. Cassy's eyes looked blank.

"No, Mother. No, please," Cassy mumbled as she leaned forward in her chair. She slumped forward so steeply, she looked like she might fall to the ground at any moment.

"Cassy? It's Bridget. Are you all right, dear? What happened?"

The nurse held onto Cassy and tried to prop her up.

"I feel like I'm going to faint. My mind is so dizzy…" Cassy held onto Bridget for support.

"Okay, dear. Your husband, Drew, can I reach him at home?" Just as Bridget spoke, she lost her grip and Cassy fell to the floor unconscious.

"Oh, my God. Claire? Claire, come over here right now while I call Dr. Andrews."

Cassy was caught between the realm of subconsciousness and consciousness, and there was no way of knowing how to push the magic button that would distinguish reality again. She had no choice but to allow her body to remain flaccid and uncontrolled, separated from her mind, driven by some force other than her own will.

Dr. Steven Andrews received the message from Valley the following morning when he returned from a medical convention on the West Coast. He was surprised to hear Bridget sound so agitated when she took his call.

"Dr. Andrews, I don't know how to break this to you gently, so I'll just have to say it straight out. Cassy's back in the hospital again, but I'm afraid it's much worse this time. She's in the ICU, apparently in a coma."

"What? She was seeing Lanton for the last time yesterday. What happened?" The doctor was so consumed with worry, he couldn't think straight. He had become very close to Cassy over the past two years.

"Cassy had some kind of seizure yesterday in the lobby. She's in a coma and spent the night in the ICU." Bridget was anxious to get back to Cassy to check on her. "Please get here as quickly as you can."

"Yes, of course. I'll be there in twenty minutes." Steve hung up and decided to put in a quick call to Bernard Lanton.

"Dr. Lanton's office," Gayle answered.

"Gayle, it's Dr. Andrews from Valley. I received a call from

Nurse Bridget at the hospital, and she just told me Cassy had some kind of seizure and is apparently in a coma. Do you know anything about this?"

"Oh, my God! No, I didn't hear anything! She left yesterday after her appointment, and everything seemed fine!"

"Can I speak with Dr. Lanton?"

"He stepped out yesterday after Cassy left, and told me to cancel his appointments for the rest of the day. He seemed very flustered and hasn't come in yet today. I don't think he's ever been late or missed a day since I started working for him."

"Okay. Listen, Gayle, please have Dr. Lanton call me as soon as he arrives." Dr. Andrews hung up the phone, grabbed his keys and rushed out his front door.

CHAPTER TWO

David Bloodstone sat in his Manhattan apartment alone staring at his reflection in a long mirror that hung on an ornate wall in his library. David's hair was jet black, smooth and tied in a ponytail at the nape of his neck. He wore only black: black jeans, black boots and a black silk shirt. The first three buttons of his shirt were unbuttoned, exposing mounds of black curly chest hair over large pectoral muscles. The gleam of a golden bloodstone cameo necklace could be seen dangling against his dark skin.

David was perched on a stool in his library; a large, airy room with high ceilings and tall bookcases that stood against two adjacent walls. Books, old and new, were scattered about the room. There were large, hardcover books neatly lined on shelves, and stacks of books piled high on either side of the cases.

David sat in front of two large windows with long, sheer beige curtains draped elegantly, billowing to and fro in the breeze of the opened windows. In one corner of the room, an elaborate entertainment center stood with racks of CDs on either side of it. David had selected Brahms' "Adagio for Strings," which was churning out a very melancholy and dissonant blend of violin, viola and cello.

"Oh, to play again! To feel the tickle of the vibrato against my fingers!" David exclaimed with fire and passion, as if newfound vitality were energizing him, filling him with excitement.

David smiled at his reflection in the long and elegant mirror. It had a gold, brocade trim that looked old enough to be of a different time. He spent many evenings in front of this mirror admiring his reflection: looking this way and that, raising one eyebrow at a time, peering into his reflection with rehearsed intensity, lifting the sides of his mouth into a seductive smile.

David rose from the stool and paced back and forth from one side of the room to the other. He had acquired numerous priceless paintings over the years and was studying them as he paced. Some were Renaissance. Some Baroque. Some modern, but all were painted by famous artists of the day and worth more than any single private collection in the world.

After three turns, he stopped halfway and gazed upon his latest acquisition, an 1868 painting by Rubens. The blonde woman in the painting appeared to look at him intimately as if there were no other person in the world. He had been to an auction at Christie's and paid more than he bargained.

"But it was worth it," David said. "It was worth it."

The blonde of the woman's hair reminded David of her. She had been there at the auction. She had wanted the Rubens more than he did, but he bid more than she could afford. And then he invited her to dinner. The dinner would include an intimate discussion of other impressionist paintings and end with a private viewing of the painting in his apartment.

David was very excited about seeing this woman. Normally, he didn't bother with wealthy women. Normally, he paid for a woman's services just like any other service. David paid for her, had his way with her, and disposed of her in the most convenient location available to hide a rejected corpse.

David walked back to the stool for another look in the mirror. "Oh, the poor woman," David said as he continued to gaze at his reflection; a very serious expression on his face. He felt pity for the woman. And then, David's pity turned to evil laughter as he gazed at his exquisite smile in the mirror.

*

Diana Norwood was dressing for a memorable night on the town. Dinner, dancing and perhaps a night cap at David's apartment. She was standing in front of her bedroom mirror, scrutinizing her appearance, wondering if she were overdressed for the occasion. Diana wore a beaded black gown with thin shoulder straps and a long sheer scarf that draped down her well exposed back. The black pumps she selected were higher than she typically wore, but she remembered that David was well above 6'4", and she wanted the capability of kissing him good night.

"Now, isn't that a lovely thought?" she asked as she smiled at her reflection.

Suddenly, the thought of kissing David became the thought of David standing in front of an altar dressed in a tuxedo; her veil softening the church lights as she made her way down the aisle toward him. She stood before him as he lifted her veil and peered into her with his dark, luminous eyes. And then he would pull her close to him, their lips almost touching.

Diana noticed the clock on the wall as it chimed the half hour. "Oh, my God, it's 6:30 already," she thought. Diana had only thirty minutes to meet David across town at The Manhattan Club. She fluffed her long blonde hair, applied a light coat of sheer pink lipstick, and grabbed her bag and keys while she ran for her apartment door.

*

"David!" Diana exclaimed when she strolled into The Manhattan Club's lobby at 6:30 precisely. She spotted him leaning against the bar, his right hand holding the gold railing, his left, a large vodka and tonic with a twist. He turned and flashed a smile that made her go weak at the knees.

"Diana, please have a seat." David pointed to the seat directly next to his. "I'm so happy you decided to join me."

Diana sat and he bent down to kiss her hand. When David looked back up into her eyes, she couldn't help but notice the large gleaming cameo around his neck.

"Your necklace is so beautiful, David. Where did you get it?"

"It's been in my family for years." David's eyes caught Diana's, and she felt a sense of panic come upon her like an animal caught in a trap sensing impending doom.

David felt Diana's apprehension. He put his hand on hers. "When I saw you for the first time today, I thought I was looking at the most ravishing beauty on the face of the planet."

Diana looked into David's eyes and felt a wave of excitement that enveloped her entire body. She couldn't help but blush and when the warmth of her embarrassment darkened her rosy cheeks, David bent over and kissed each one.

Diana smiled sweetly and realized that her fear was completely irrational. "David is a very sincere and honest man," she thought.

"Let's have a drink, a romantic dinner, and then I'd like to show you the painting we both admired today; the painting I admire almost as much as you."

If Diana had misgivings before, they had vanished entirely in the warm glow of David's gaze.

*

John Adams lived on the Upper West Side of Manhattan and always did his morning jog at six o'clock in Central Park. He was able to run five miles in thirty–five minutes and hoped he might even be ready for his first try at the New York City Marathon. John worked as a New York City police officer and his wife, Stacey, was a nurse at Columbia Presbyterian, which meant he knew

Central Park like the back of his hand.

"All right, John. You can do this," he said as he stretched the back of his legs one at a time while leaning on a large rock just inside the park. "Here we go." John put the headphones of his iPod in place, turned on some hard hitting rock music, and began his run at a brisk pace. The weather was cool and crisp and his stride felt particularly good this morning, each step of his sneakers hitting the pavement with a bounce.

John was nearing his fourth mile, and he turned a corner that led to the same path through the park each morning. The rock music was blaring through his headphones, but he heard a rustle through the trees to the right that made him turn his head. "Must be some animal," he thought as he looked in the direction of the sound. What John saw sent a shudder up his spine. He stopped short.

John saw the bare leg of a woman sticking out through a pile of leaves between two large oak trees. The foot of the leg was beautifully manicured with bright red nail polish. John carefully made his way over to the leg. When he reached it and could see up close, it looked as if there was likelihood that an entire body would be attached to that leg and was lying underneath a pile of rust–colored leaves.

"Oh, my God!" John felt a pang of fierce emotion, anger, and depression all at once. He reached down to remove the top leaves so that he could uncover the body. After five clumps of leaves were removed, John was able to peer into the unseeing eyes of a beautiful woman. She was in her early thirties with long blonde hair and blue eyes. Her neck had ligature marks, indicating strangulation. John reached down to remove more leaves, but when he discovered that she wore no clothes, he put the leaves back into place to cover her naked body. He reached into his pocket, pulled out his cell phone and called headquarters.

*

When Dr. Steven Andrews arrived at Valley Hospital, he found Cassy in the Emergency Room with a series of doctors and nurses trying to resuscitate her. Cassy's heart stopped sometime in the early hours of the morning following her collapse in the hallway. Once stabilized, she spent the night in the Intensive Care Unit.

Drew slept next to her bed, slumped over in a chair with his head resting by her side. He fell asleep with the steady beats of the monitor, but when the beats stopped, the monitor made a loud hum that woke Drew and sent him into a panic. A flurry of doctors and nurses rushed in, and Drew was told to wait outside the room.

Dr. Andrews rushed into his scrubs as quickly as possible and half ran to Cassy's side.

"What happened?" Steve was questioning Dr. Greg Wilson, the doctor on duty and the one holding the defibrillator in an effort to shock Cassy's heart back into action.

"Heart attack? Seizure? I don't know. Cassy collapsed and went into cardiac arrest."

Dr. Wilson lifted the defibrillators again and applied them to Cassy's chest. Her limp body was pulled from the table in an attempt to bring her heart back to life.

Both doctors looked at the monitor in hopes of seeing her vital signs appear on the screen.

Nothing.

"Mind if I try?" Steve Andrews looked at Dr. Wilson in pleading.

"Not at all." He handed the defibrillators to Steve.

With as much effort as Dr. Steve Andrews could muster, he positioned the defibrillators once again. This time, the shock to Cassy's heart caused her body to propel itself off the table and into the air. Both doctors looked again at the monitor and when nothing appeared, they could audibly hear each other's sighs.

A full five seconds passed, and a faint glimmer of a heartbeat was seen pulsing across the monitor. Everyone in the room, the nurses, the technicians, Dr. Wilson and Dr. Andrews, let out an exclamation of joy.

"Thank God!" Steve felt his eyes well with tears.

When Cassy's condition seemed stable again, the two doctors walked out of the ICU and lowered their surgical masks.

"Steve, I need to tell you something of concern." Greg Wilson laid a hand on his colleague's shoulder. "Bridget Monaghan told me something really strange. Apparently, Cassy kept saying that she'd been poisoned."

*

Later that day, when Nurse Bridget walked into Cassy's dimly lit hospital room, she noted how pale Cassy appeared lying under the starched white sheets of the bed. Cassy was hooked up to an IV that trickled tiny dots of fluid she needed to stay hydrated. The monitor that flashed red lines of rhythmic pulses beat steadily to the sound of her heart.

Bridget continued around the bed to the empty chair between Cassy and the window. She suggested that Drew take a break and grab a bite to eat. She would stay with Cassy. The nurse looked out the window and discovered that it had begun to rain on a day that started with sun.

"Drat. The darn rain," Bridget said. "And to think I don't have enough to think about with my poor Cassy in a coma." She laid her hand on Cassy's; the white of Cassy's skin blending in with the white of the sheet.

"Hold on there, dear. Hold on to the little bit of life you've got left. I know you have it in you. Hold on there, dear girl." Nurse Bridget leaned forward to kiss the hand she was holding and thought she felt just the slightest little pressure on the palm of her hand.

"Could she be coming out of it?" Bridget gazed at Cassy as she slept, willing her to open her eyes.

Bridget watched the up and down movements of Cassy's chest,

the even flow of breathing that came faintly, yet easily. She waited for something more, some movement of the hand, some recognition of life in her face, some breath heaved out of turn, but no. There was nothing.

"You come around for us, dear. I am only a few steps away from you." Bridget held Cassy's hand and brought it gently back to the bed before she got up to go.

In her coma, Cassy heard footsteps going further and further away. She heard a door being opened and closed as if in a distant dream.

In a state of subconscious slumber, Cassy became agitated. She needed more time to figure out what happened to her. She needed more time to discover the meaning of Dr. Lanton's note and why he wanted to harm her. Cassy's body was betraying her. How could she escape this eternal interlude of sleep? It was like a gray cloud of haze was intentionally poisoning her vision.

Cassy had to get control of herself. She had to force herself to think clearly. She had to find her way back to the surface. Cassy had to concentrate on the immediate. She had to take back possession of her body.

Cassy could feel the muscles in her eyes twitch when she squinted. Her eyelashes fluttered as she tried to open her eyes.

"It's all right, Cassy. You can do it. I feel the strength within you."

At once, Cassy's eyes opened as if she had been awake all along. She did not know the stranger's voice and felt a sense of fear so sharp, she was immediately brought back to reality.

"You don't know me, Cassy, but I know you. I have been watching you. Looking out for you."

The beautiful man in front of her had long brown, flowing hair and brilliant blue eyes; his beard well–groomed around his full, red lips. His shirt was white and silky and billowed out at the elbows with rich, lacy cuffs elegantly cascading down his long fingers.

When Cassy lifted herself off the hospital bed and walked to his side, she looked down at the bed and could still make out her comatose body; her chest showing life with each breath she took, her vital signs beeping rhythmic pulses in the background.

How could Cassy be standing over her own body? How could she be witnessing her own subconscious state?

"Am I dead?" Cassy asked innocently.

"No. Your physical body is lying in a bed in a coma. Your spiritual body is standing next to me. Don't be afraid, Cassy. You can do important work this way, faster."

The man took a step toward Cassy and held his long arms open for an embrace. "Come here, my dear. Let me hold you."

Cassy readily did as she was told and threw herself into his arms.

He held her long and hard against his muscular chest and rocked her back and forth as if cradling an infant.

Cassy studied the man's innocent face when he let her go. His beauty was so entirely magnificent, it was almost ethereal.

"I am here to guide you through what needs to be done."

"I...I don't know what you mean?" Cassy was startled by the seriousness of his words.

"Oh, but you do, Cassy. That is why you took the necklace, remember? All those years ago, you were so very young, but yet you knew. You knew all along how wrong and evil it was. And now I am here to help you."

"Help me? I don't even know who you are."

"You will, my dear. For now, just call me Paolo. Whenever you utter my name, I will come to help you, to protect you from any danger."

"How did you know about the necklace?"

"I know all about the Taninsams."

Cassy took a step back. "I'm afraid," she said. "I'm afraid of Dr. Lanton. I'm afraid of my mother. Most of all, I'm afraid of the man in black. I'm afraid he'll find me again."

"Cassy, I will do everything in my power to protect you, but

I'm going to need your help. Elaina knows that Dr. Lanton has discovered the truth. She will do everything in her power to keep it hidden. You see, it wasn't his idea to give you the poison. It was hers."

Cassy took another step back and let go of Paolo's hands.

"Are you saying that my own mother, my own flesh and blood, is trying to kill me?"

Paolo touched the side of Cassy's arm. "You have become a serious threat to your mother, Cassy, and she knows this. She knows that you hold the power to destroy the curse of the bloodstone. Your aunt, Jessica, and your sister, Deborah; together, the three of you hold the power to destroy the curse."

"You know about Jessica and Deborah, too?"

"I am not the only one who knows Jessica's location and, more recently, Deborah's location. Your mother knows. And so does the man in black."

"No." Cassy sat down hard in the chair next to the bed.

"Cassy, there's more." Paolo knelt before Cassy. "At this very moment, your sister, Deborah, is in grave danger."

CHAPTER THREE

Debbie Romano lay on one of the two twin beds closest to the window of a small room located in the Milwaukee Psychiatric Institute, a private mental health facility. Only twenty–one years old, she appeared younger because she was so thin and frail. Debbie wore jeans, a blue long–sleeve sweatshirt, and her long, straight black hair cascaded down along the pillow on either side of her head. She needed no makeup to highlight her intense green eyes, finely contoured cheekbones and ample red lips. Her feet were bare and even they looked sleek and refined.

The girl heard footsteps approach her room. She sat up, hoping it was her mother and father come to visit, but it turned out to be her roommate, a girl of seventeen who liked to be called, "Lucky" Richards. Lucky was a high school drop–out who had spent time on the streets when her parents and younger brother were killed in an apartment fire three years ago. On the streets of Milwaukee, Lucky had discovered drugs, alcohol and "love" in a backstreet alley where she lost her virginity at age fifteen. When the boy decided to leave her for another girl two years later, Lucky tried to kill herself by ingesting an entire bottle of sleeping pills. Lucky was, in fact, lucky to be alive.

"You have a visitor," Lucky mumbled to Debbie. She peered

around the door dressed in her usual goth style complete with black hair, black eyeliner, and black fingernail polish. Lucky chewed gum between her words and blew a bubble so large, it looked like it might pop at any moment.

"Do you know who it is?" Debbie sat up.

"No. Some tall guy with long, black hair." Luck's bubble popped on her face with a loud smack.

Debbie's eyes grew wide with instant fear. She rose and pulled Lucky into the room before closing the door behind her.

"Do me a favor, okay? Go out and tell Jean that this guy is dangerous and should be put on the 'No Visitor' list. Do it quietly, so he doesn't hear you. Tell Jean she should tell him that I'm no longer here—that I've checked myself out. Please, Lucky. This might be the most important thing you've ever done in your life."

Lucky crossed her arms over her chest. "I don't know. I've done a lot of important things already. Remember the time I saved my parents and my little brother from the fire?"

Lucky's psychiatric troubles stemmed from the emotional trauma of the loss of her family and the protection she needed through blocking out the reality of her loss.

Debbie decided it would be best to play along with Lucky's story. "Yeah, Lucky. I remember. This favor will be almost as important as that."

A gleam came into Lucky's eyes. "Okay. I'll do it."

When Lucky left the room, Debbie closed the door behind her and bolted it shut.

*

Jean Barnes, R.N., was trained to work with psychiatric patients and had extensive experience to accompany her training. She was also a mother of five, and the maternal nature she employed in child–rearing was the same that she used on all her patients. If one of Jean's patients was a danger to himself, or if a visitor was a potential threat, she would stand in the way like a mother bear protecting her cubs.

Jean peered out over the entrance desk toward the waiting area where the man in black was standing. Lucky had privately taken Jean aside in the back office and told her about Debbie's plea. Jean did not like the way this man looked—too arrogant, too polished, and too old to be visiting a 21–year–old girl if he was not a family member. Jean did not need to be a rocket scientist to figure this one out. He was probably the typical unmarried rich guy preying on pretty, young girls. Jean stoically stood and made her way to the waiting area where the man in black sat on a gray upholstered chair.

"Good afternoon. I'm Jean Barnes. The head nurse at this facility. May I help you?"

The man presented his hand, "I'm here to see Debbie Romano. I'm a distant relative."

Jean shook his hand. "Distant relative, my foot," she thought. "Nice to meet you, Mr.?"

"My name is David Bloodstone."

"Unfortunately, Debbie has just been released…this morning. She no longer resides here." Jean looked directly into David's eyes, and a shiver of fear went up and down her spine.

"I see. You don't happen to know where she's gone?" David held fast to Jean's hand, his grip growing more and more firm.

"No. I am not allowed to divulge that information."

David released her hand and looked around at the other visitors in the room. "If you happen to speak with Deborah, I mean Debbie, please let her know that David stopped by." He emphasized the word, "David."

"I'll be sure to do that."

David gave Jean one last look with his black eyes and walked to the elevator.

She watched him leave, then immediately made her way to Debbie's room and knocked on her door.

"Who is it?" Debbie called.

"It's Jean."

Jean heard the bolt release, and the door opened to reveal Debbie, looking paler than Jean had ever seen her. Lucky excused herself and shut the door behind her.

"Do you want to tell me about David?" Jean asked. She had that worried mother look written all over her face.

*

At six months old, Deborah Taninsam had been whisked from her mother's home, to her Aunt Jessica's apartment, and then on to live with Pietro and Lucia Romano, who were friends of Jessica's. Pietro and Lucia were originally from Rome, Italy, but after immigrating to the United States more than thirty years before, Pietro took a job as a professor of medicine at New York University and had become one of Jessica's teachers. Jessica often had dinner with Pietro and Lucia in their modest Brooklyn apartment.

On one of these visits, Jessica was extremely agitated and told Pietro and Lucia about her brother, Samuel's, unexpected death and her sister–in–law, Elaina, a dangerous and evil woman. She told them that both girls were in danger and that she needed to separate the girls immediately for their protection.

Jessica would raise Cassandra on her own, and she hoped that Pietro and Lucia would adopt Deborah. She remembered that the couple had been trying for a child of their own for years with no luck.

"I have legal custody of both girls and can arrange custody of Deborah to go to the two of you. I would only request that her name be changed from Deborah Taninsam to Deborah Romano." Jessica held Pietro's and Lucia's hands. "I have grown to love you as my own family. I trust you completely with all my heart, and I know you would make wonderful parents to my beloved,

Deborah."

Joyful tears escaped Lucia's eyes at the thought of a new baby in their home. She embraced her husband and her dear friend, Jessica, at the same time.

One week later, Lucia held the tiny infant in her welcoming arms. Deborah was a beautiful baby with curly black hair and rosy, chubby cheeks. Lucia couldn't resist touching the child's glowing face and her little fingers, the only two body parts visible through the pink velvet blanket swaddling her tiny body. Lucia tickled under Deborah's chin and the baby giggled with delight.

Jessica saw that the green of Deborah's eyes matched the green of Lucia's, and the black of Deborah's hair matched the black of Lucia's. "It is truly amazing how much the baby looks just like you!" The resemblance between Lucia and Deborah was more than mere coincidence. God had inspired this match.

*

Deborah Taninsam officially became Debbie Romano at age one. She was reared by Pietro and Lucia in Brooklyn until she turned five when Pietro was offered a position as Director of the School of Medicine at Marquette University in Milwaukee, Wisconsin. They moved to a small suburb of Milwaukee called Oak Creek where Debbie attended grammar school at Oak Creek Elementary.

When Debbie turned fifteen, Pietro and Lucia decided to retire in a beautiful resort town an hour southeast of Milwaukee called Lake Geneva. They bought a modest house a block from the lake and a mile from Badger High School. The move took place in August, which was convenient since Debbie wanted a chance to be able to swim in the lake and get to know some of the other kids her age before school started.

After a week of helping her mother unpack boxes, Debbie asked her mother for a ride into town to spend the day at the beach. Lucia dropped Debbie off at the local pier front property adjacent to the beach area called the Riviera, and Debbie immediately headed straight back through the "Riv" where she could get a better look at the ferry boats that waited to take passengers on guided tours around the lake.

When Debbie reached the piers, she noticed a round, blue sign that read, "Walters' Marina." Directly under the sign, was a small boat house with a young girl selling boat tour tickets. There was a long line standing in front of her window waiting to buy a ticket for the next tour. The girl looked like she was Debbie's age and had beautiful red, wavy hair that flowed well past her shoulders. The girl noticed Debbie and gave her a huge smile with bright, shiny white teeth.

"Hey you! Back there! Could you give me a hand with something?" she asked.

Debbie pointed at herself and shrugged her shoulders as if to say, "Who me?"

"Yeah, you!" The girl working at Walters' Marine gestured for Debbie to come forward.

Debbie walked through the line of people and went directly to the window where the girl was working.

"Hi. I'm Linda Walters. See that silver pole down there connected to that rope? Can you please do me a favor and stand it back up? The wind constantly knocks it over and then these people have no clue where to stand."

"Sure." Debbie placed the pole back into position and realized the line was supposed to curve around the side, but went straight back into the Riviera blocking tourists who were trying to walk along the sidewalk. Debbie repositioned the poles and gestured for the line to follow along the inside of the ropes now assembled around the side of the boathouse. "Is this okay?"

Linda stood up and saw the new line that was formed. "Perfect! Say, if you ever need a job, just let me know. My family owns this marina. What's your name?"

"Debbie Romano. I just moved here from Milwaukee."

"No kidding. What grade are you in?"

"I'll be a freshman this year at Badger High School."

Linda swung her long hair around to the back of her shoulder. "No kidding! So will I, but I'm from here, so I can introduce you to pretty much everybody!"

"Thanks. Making new friends isn't exactly my strong suit."

The elderly couple standing behind Debbie coughed to get the girls' attention.

Debbie noticed the couple and the long line of people. "I'd better get going. I was going to check out the beach for the first time since we moved here." Debbie smiled and waved good–bye. "See you at Badger!"

"Hold on, Deb. I get off in a half hour. How about a boat ride?"

Debbie walked over to the cream–colored sand to wait for Linda who emerged a half hour later wearing a bathing suit with a fuchsia cover–up and white boat shoes. "Ready?"

"Sure." Debbie walked back toward the pier behind Linda and expected to be boarding one of the large ferry boats on her right. Instead, Linda turned toward the far left pier where a series of elegant wooden speed boats floated with ropes and water skis.

"We're going in one of those?" Debbie couldn't believe her luck.

"Actually, this one right here!" Linda stepped into the boat and put on a bright, orange life vest. "Come on in!" she yelled to Debbie at the top of her lungs.

Debbie sat on the edge of the pier and put her feet in the boat unsteadily. A wave blasted the left side, and Debbie lunged forward toward Linda. Linda caught Debbie, helped her regain her balance, and threw another orange life vest her way. In one quick instant, Linda untied the boat and sat in the driver's seat.

"Here we go!" was all she said and Debbie was thrown back into the passenger's seat.

This day began the friendship of two girls destined to be

brought together by something greater than mere fate.

*

On Debbie's first day at Badger High School, she sat next to Linda on bleachers in the newly renovated gymnasium. Linda fanned herself with a program of the day's events.

"I'm so hot I can't stand it!" Linda lifted her hair above her shoulders and circled it into a bun at the back of her head.

"Me, too. Don't worry. It will be over soon." Debbie looked around to see if there was anyone she knew from the lake. Over the course of the last weeks of August, it seemed Linda had introduced her to the entire Class of 2008.

Debbie caught a glimpse of a boy named Rick out of the corner of her eye. She had seen him only once before on the beach after a full day of water skiing. Debbie was particularly attracted to his long, beach–blonde hair. Rick noticed Debbie looking at him and smiled. He was one year older than Debbie, but since he had to repeat the sixth grade, he was also a new incoming freshman. As soon as Debbie noticed Rick looking at her, she turned her head in the opposite direction.

*

That same night, Badger High School held an annual bonfire to celebrate the start of the new academic year. The celebration gave the new freshman class a chance to get acclimated with the new high school routine. The party began at sundown and took place in a large grassy field to the left of the football field next to two tall silver bleachers. The high school band dressed in uniform and beat a loud drum that could be felt through rhythmic vibrations that pulsated off the ground.

All of the freshman class took part in the initial festivities, but different groups of kids broke away from the main crowd to form the various clicks that had already emerged. Debbie and Linda stood among the group known as the popular crowd; those students known as the "jocks" who were mostly football players and cheerleaders. The football players seemed particularly animated, feeling the excitement of the new season upon them. The cheerleaders, a mix of both boys and girls, were extremely competitive and could form pyramids three stories tall. The boys understood the precision, timing and athleticism of the cheerleading sport. They also understood the chance to hold beautiful girls on their shoulders who wore short skirts and matching bikini briefs.

Other groups of kids that sectioned themselves off according to various classifications were: the brains, the nerds, the thespians, and the burnouts. Debbie noticed Rick with the burnouts. He stood in the back of one by the bleachers with a group of kids that looked like they wanted to keep hidden. Occasionally, Debbie saw Rick take a puff off a cigarette and drink from a large bottle in a brown bag.

Debbie needed a chance at adventure and decided to make her way to Rick and his brand of friends. She walked across the field and reached Rick's side.

"Hi. I'm Debbie. I saw you at the assembly today."

"Yeah? I'm Rick." He took one last hit off his cigarette and threw it down to the ground where he made a circular motion with his foot to put it out. "So, Deb, how come I haven't seen you around before tonight?"

"I just moved here from Milwaukee. My dad retired from Marquette, and he wanted to spend some time by the lake." Debbie pulled the bottom of her sweatshirt down over her jeans and the sleeves over her hands. "You want to hang out closer to the fire? I'm getting cold."

"Yeah, all right."Rick turned to his friends, "Hey guys! I'm goin' by the fire. Steve, watch this for me." He handed his friend the bottle in the bag.

"Rick, don't you think you've had enough of that?" Steve was Rick's caretaker more than his friend. He thought Rick needed an older brother since Rick was the youngest of four and the only boy. And since Rick's dad left his mom over the summer for some younger woman he met at a Pell Lake bar, he drank more and smoked dope.

"Steve, lay off, buddy. I've got it way under control." Rick put an arm around Debbie's shoulder and winked at his friend.

He and Debbie walked over toward the bonfire. As soon as they reached it, Debbie put her hands up to the fire to warm them.

Rick turned toward Debbie, "So, Deb, can I tell you that you are one amazing girl?"

Debbie felt her cheeks blush. She smiled and turned toward Rick. "I was kind of thinking the same about you. Only instead of amazing girl, I was thinking amazing boy." Debbie leaned in close to Rick.

"Hello, Debbie and Rick!" Linda came up from behind to surprise them.

"Hi, Linda. We're just talkin'." Rick cocked his head drunkenly and glared at Linda.

"Listen, Rick. My friend Debbie's new here, and I don't want anyone messing with her." She leaned in close to Rick and whispered harshly in his right ear. "It smells like you've been drinking, too, and that's underage drinking!"

"What? Are you my mother? Leave us alone!" Rick was inebriated enough to slur his words, but he said the word "alone" so loudly, some of the classmates around the fire took notice.

Linda took a step backward to get away from his yelling and the foul beer odor that emanated from Rick's mouth. "Debbie, I'll be right over there if you need me. Okay?" She pointed toward the football crowd to her left.

"Thanks, Linda. I'll be all right."

Rick took Debbie's left hand in his. "Deb, let's go for a walk for a second...get some fresh air." He led Debbie by the hand past the bonfire and down a small hill. There was a large field in the distance that was bordered on the far right by long rows of corn. About a hundred feet straight ahead, there was a large black forest with tall dark trees.

Debbie and Rick continued forward still holding hands, but Debbie stopped as soon as she realized they were alone. She felt uncomfortable because Rick was stumbling, and she was afraid to be near him when he was so drunk.

"Listen, Rick, maybe we'd better get back to the bonfire. I'm starting to get cold again."

Rick was so drunk his eyes rolled up into the back of his head. "What's the matter, Deb? You don't like me anymore?" He was slurring his words so badly, spit was gliding out of his mouth like a worn hose with a slow leak.

"Please, Rick. Let's get back to the bonfire." Debbie looked for Linda out of the corner of her eye. She spotted her over the hill a great distance away standing next to Steve, Rick's friend. Debbie began to walk toward her.

Rick caught the back of her sweatshirt and yanked it backward. It was hard enough to hurt, but not hard enough for anyone to notice. "Keep walkin'. I wanna talk to ya' alone." He grabbed her waist and squeezed her right side so hard she felt like the jolt of a needle was piercing her side.

Debbie walked in the opposite direction toward the forest. She figured if she couldn't get to the protection of the group, she'd seek the protection of the forest. Debbie felt tears stream down her cheeks as she was led away from the group against her will. She was so afraid a chill ran up her spine making her shudder.

"Whas wrong, Deb? How about jus' one small kiss?" Rick let go of Debbie's side for a brief moment and she ran as fast as she could toward the forest. Rick caught her from behind and pushed her forward with such force, she fell down hard onto the dirty ground.

Rick fell with all his weight on top of Debbie and forcibly

pulled down her jeans and underwear. Despite his drinking, he managed to pull her arms above her head with his left hand and pull his own jeans down with his right. He entered her hard and rough with a desperateness that only long hours of guzzling too much beer can produce. She felt the burning pain of someone ripping open the most private and intimate part of her body, which produced a feeling of violation like nothing before.

In Debbie's shock and horror something internal erupted—an inner sense of defiance and rage, which she had never experienced in her young life. She felt a power well up from within, and she knew what to do. The rage was fierce and strong. Debbie grabbed Rick by the hair with her right hand and pulled him off her in one quick gesture. She pulled up her jeans and ran into the forest as quickly as her legs would carry her.

Debbie found a large oak tree to nestle against. She felt more protected next to the lone tree than she had all night. She cried softly and her tears released feelings of violation and betrayal so strong, she thought her heart might fall to the pit of her stomach. How could this have happened? How could she have been so stupid?

Suddenly, Debbie heard rustling through the crisp dry leaves of the forest. She stood up quickly and ran deeper into the woods. Her escape stopped short, however, when she ran right into a tall man with long black hair. He immediately took Debbie into his arms.

"Are you okay?" The man looked down with a reassuring smile.

"Yes…I…a boy hurt me." Debbie let out an uncontrollable sob and the man embraced her paternally. Debbie didn't care that this man was a complete stranger. She needed to let out her harbored anguish.

After what seemed like hours, Debbie stepped back and wiped her eyes on her sleeve. "I'm so sorry. I can't believe I let myself cry like that."

The man in black took a step back, too. "Is there anything I can do for you? Do you need me to call someone for you?"

"No, I can't bear to hurt my parents with this. Besides, it's my fault. I put myself in this situation. I can deal with it on my own."

The man stepped forward and knelt down to retrieve something from the ground. He picked up a gleaming gold necklace and held it up for Debbie to see.

"Did you drop this?" he asked innocently.

"No. I've never seen it before." Debbie stared at the necklace, and her curiosity got the best of her. She took it in her hands and held it up to see. It was a beautiful cameo necklace with an elegant woman carved on an intense green stone.

"It looks like it was made for you. Here, let me help you put it on." The man in black placed the necklace around Debbie's neck and fastened it in the back.

Debbie felt lightheaded. There was an intense serenity that enveloped her. Suddenly, the night's tragedy felt only like a bad dream. It didn't matter anymore. All that mattered was the kindness of this stranger and the feeling of the exquisite necklace around her neck.

The man lifted Debbie's long black hair to free it from the necklace and stepped around to admire it on her. "You look beautiful, Deborah, just beautiful. I've been anticipating this moment for a long time. I think you know as well as I do what you're meant to do."

"How did you know my name was Deborah?"

"I've known you all your life." The man in black stepped back deeper into the forest and disappeared.

Debbie discovered her true identity. In one instant she was no longer Debbie, but Deborah Taninsam and the forgotten power of the bloodstone cameo was hers once again.

Deborah put the cameo inside her sweatshirt and stepped out of the forest. Linda and Steve were running in her direction, and Rick was pulling up his jeans.

It didn't matter, though. Deborah had lost all memory of Rick. Debbie had come to know Deborah Taninsam.

CHAPTER FOUR

No mention was made of the bonfire night during Debbie's entire high school career. She placed the bloodstone cameo necklace in a drawer and brought it out every now and then to admire its beauty. Debbie avoided Rick and hung out with Linda and the "jock" crowd instead. She and Linda tried out for the varsity cheerleading squad, and they cheered their way to the all–state football championship their senior year.

Debbie's graduation was a blur. She remembered the graduation ceremony in the gym, the red and white robes they all wore, and the aerial photo they took outside with the entire senior class forming a giant "2008." Debbie's parents, Pietro and Lucia Romano, threw her a beautiful surprise party that night at the local Riviera on Lake Geneva. Debbie and the rest of her friends danced until midnight.

That summer flew by as Debbie spent the long days water skiing on Linda's boat and nights hanging out on the beach with friends. In September, Debbie and Linda decided to attend Marquette University together studying history. Debbie's fascination with history began with her interest in the Catholic Church. She thought that the Church was a great mystery with a fantastic history spanning over two thousand years to the time of

Christ's birth.

Debbie and Linda shared a small dorm room together at Marquette and came to love the collegiate life. They attended classes throughout the day, and studied in the large common area of the dormitory at night. They both worked in the cafeteria on campus to make extra money and easily made new friends.

Debbie brought her bloodstone cameo necklace with her and hid it in her top right dresser drawer. Late one night when she took it out to look at it, Linda sat up in her bunk bed watching her friend in the dark.

"What is that?"

Linda startled Debbie so much, she almost dropped the necklace. "Oh, my God! I thought you were asleep! You frightened the stuffing out of me!" Debbie exclaimed.

"I'm sorry. I heard you get out of bed and open your drawer. Where'd you get the necklace?" Linda asked innocently.

Debbie looked up at her friend with the necklace tucked away in her fist. "It's just something my parents gave me for my graduation. Do me a favor and make sure nobody ever touches it. I think it might be worth a lot of money."

Debbie knew she could trust Linda with the necklace. She just didn't trust anyone else.

"Sure, Deb. We'll keep it under lock and key." Linda lay back down in her bed. "You should get some sleep with the big test tomorrow."

"Yeah, you're right." Debbie hid the necklace back away in her top drawer and climbed up into her bunk. "Good night, Linda."

"Good night."

The next night after the big test, Debbie and Linda rented a movie to show on the big screen in the common area downstairs. They invited some friends over from their art history class. The girls wanted to relax after a grueling week of studying, and they felt they'd "Aced" it.

Halfway through the movie, Debbie went into the kitchen to get soda pop. She reached into the refrigerator to get a can when a rattling noise at the backdoor caught her attention. Debbie closed the refrigerator and saw a dark figure standing just outside the door. She walked to the door and opened it.

Debbie recognized the man in black from all those years ago in the forest next to Badger High School's field. He was the one who gave her the cameo necklace.

The man stepped into the kitchen and shut the door. "Where is it?"

There was only one word Debbie could manage through her frightened lips. "Upstairs," she answered.

"Let's go." The man in black took Debbie by the arm and led her through the back of the darkened common area where the group was still watching the movie. They walked to the staircase just beyond the back doors. The man led Debbie up the stairs. "What floor?" he asked.

"Third." They continued to the third floor and walked down the long hallway with dorm room doors on either side of the corridor. "It's around the corner on the right...314," she said.

When they reached the door, Debbie entered the code and opened it. The man held her arm and they both walked into the room. He shut the door hard and turned to Debbie.

"Get the necklace out now!"

Debbie did as she was told and opened up the top right drawer of her dresser. She kept the necklace in a brown wooden box, which contained the most sentimental valuables she possessed including the set of Rosary beads given to her for her first holy communion. She handed the necklace to the man.

"Good. Good. Deborah, I am not trying to scare you, but I don't think you realize the value of this necklace. Do you know that it goes back in your family for many generations?"

"No. Why didn't you explain that to me when we first met?" she asked.

"I thought you would have realized it on your own. You see,

Deborah, there is a particular and special power that is given to the one who wears it. A power you can't even begin to imagine."

The man in black held the cameo in the palm of his hand and moved it closer to Debbie. "Do you see the image of this woman? Very beautiful, isn't she? Looks an awful lot like someone we both know…you."

Debbie peered at the image of the woman and opened her eyes in astonishment. The image carved into the face of the stone was a mirror image of her face.

Debbie's eyes met the man's gaze. "You're right!" She took the necklace from him to study it. "But what does it mean?" she asked.

The man took Debbie by the hand and sat her down at her desk in the back of the room behind her bunk bed. The man knelt next to her and took her pale thin hand in his. "Deborah, you and I are related. Your real name is not Debbie Romano. It's Deborah Taninsam. The man and woman you call 'Father' and 'Mother' are not your real parents. They adopted you when you were just a baby."

Debbie felt a terrible nausea well up in her gut. The room was spinning and she was caught in a horrible whirlwind of a reality she could not grasp.

"I don't believe you," Debbie said.

"Deborah, my name is David Bloodstone. Your mother's name is Elaina Taninsam. Your father, Samuel, died when you were just a baby. If you don't believe me, look it up."

David opened her hand, the one that still held the necklace. "If it weren't true, why was your image engraved on that cameo? That bloodstone cameo was made especially for you when you were born."

David stood and walked to the door on the other side of the room. "With that necklace, the whole world is at your command." He opened the door and left the room.

*

Just as David left the room, Linda noticed him in the hallway. She wondered if he had just left their dorm room, but quickly dismissed the idea. "Must be somebody's father," she thought.

When Linda reached the door, it was wide open and she could see Debbie sitting at her desk with her head slumped over in her hands. Linda could see that Debbie was crying.

"Hey, Deb, are you okay?" Linda pulled her desk chair over to Debbie's and sat next to her best friend. A minute passed and Linda placed a hand on her friend's back. "Debbie, are you okay?" she asked again.

Debbie suddenly jolted upright and stood in a state of fury. "I don't know who you're talking to, but do not ever call me 'Deb' or 'Debbie' again! You got that, Linda! My name is Deborah. Deborah Taninsam!"

Deborah ran out of the room and down the hallway to the bathroom at the end of the hall. As soon as she was inside a locked stall, she opened her fist to reveal the bloodstone cameo necklace. She opened the clasp at the back and hung it around her neck. It felt heavy like the weight of it was more than her thin body could hold up, but it felt warm and comforting. Deborah smiled. David was right. The whole world was hers if she wore this beautiful necklace. It was hers.

Deborah walked out of the stall and stopped at the mirror to admire her reflection. The cameo sparkled with a radiance that dazzled brilliantly off the mirror. She hid the cameo under her T-shirt and left the dorm to get fresh air.

The next morning, Linda woke early to make sure that Debbie was there. Linda had stayed up waiting for Debbie to return, but had fallen asleep sometime around 2 a.m. She looked across the room and saw a long bump under the covers of Debbie's bed. She looked at the clock. It was eight in the morning. She decided to shower and dress before she woke Debbie to make sure she was okay.

When Linda stepped back into the room after showering, she opened the door and was surprised to see that Debbie was already up, dressed and standing next to her dresser with the right drawer open.

"Debbie, are you okay?"

"Yes, thanks. Sorry I was out so late last night. I guess I just needed some fresh air."

"No problem. Can you just answer one quick question, though?" Linda closed the open door to their room. "Can you please tell me why you want me to start calling you 'Deborah Taninsam?'"

"I don't know what you're talking about," Debbie replied as she quickly closed her top right dresser drawer.

*

Linda decided to forget the name, Deborah Taninsam. She figured as long as Debbie didn't bring up the name again and as long as she didn't flip out and act weird again, it was over. As a result, the girls' freshman year ended in triumph: good grades, good friends, and no more mention of Deborah Taninsam.

However, when September came around again for the start of their sophomore year, Linda noticed the same tall man in black she had seen the night Debbie called herself Deborah instead. At first, she didn't think anything of it, but his appearance became more regular during their junior year and Debbie's mood began to fluctuate for the worst every time Linda saw him there.

Linda questioned Debbie one day when they were studying in their dorm room. "Debbie, have you noticed a really tall guy dressed in black visiting here? I thought he might be somebody's father, but I just wanted to find out for sure."

Debbie stopped doing her homework and turned toward Linda. "No, I haven't noticed anybody who looks like that." She immediately resumed her studies.

Linda decided she had to confront the man. She had the opportunity when she noticed him entering the common area one night in early spring. It was the end of March and Linda was downstairs making herself a hot cocoa to combat the chill in the air. He was walking toward the elevators, and Linda decided it was now or never. She would discreetly follow him up to see exactly who he was visiting.

The man stepped onto the elevator and Linda took the stairs. After all, she knew he was getting off on their floor. Linda stepped up onto the landing of their floor and waited for him by the glass door of the staircase entrance. She heard the elevator open and saw him step off; his black hair long and straight and tied neatly in the back with a hair band. Linda quietly opened the door and followed him a short distance behind. The man disappeared around the corner in the direction of the room she shared with Debbie and stopped directly in front of their door.

Linda was in shock. Debbie had been lying to her. She decided to confront them head on and barged into the room behind the man. When Linda entered, Debbie was sitting innocently at her desk doing her homework. Was she seeing things? Linda had to be patient and wait for another opportunity.

Nothing happened and by the end of May, Linda assumed everything was back to normal. Debbie never wanted to be called Deborah, and Linda never saw the mysterious man in black. She began to breathe a sigh of relief until the night before final exams; the last night Linda would see Debbie at Marquette.

Linda had spent the entire day in the library studying. By six o'clock, she was exhausted and starving. She needed to stretch and have a dinner break. The cafeteria was only a short distance away, so she decided to walk there first, grab a bite, and then see how Debbie was doing with her studies in the dorm.

When Linda stepped outside, the air was warm and fragrant with the smell of spring blossoms still hung on trees like glistening white stars in the night. The trees were lined on either side of a wide walkway that ran horizontally through the campus to the large brick building where the cafeteria was located. A small field of grass and more budding trees were located on either side of the walkway. Through the right field, Linda noticed a tall man in the distance standing beside one of the trees. He was dressed in black and was leaning against the tree talking to someone.

As Linda moved closer, she saw Debbie next to him, her long black hair blowing in the breeze. Debbie appeared almost ethereal, and there was something gold glowing from her neck. Linda decided to take a chance and walk to the right through the trees so she could get closer without being seen. She came to a tree that was only about ten feet from Debbie and the man, and Linda hid behind its trunk. She could hear some of their conversation.

"Deborah, I've taught you everything you need to know about our purpose. Now it's up to you to move forward and leave this place." The man was leaning over Debbie with his right forefinger under her chin. He was trying to pull Debbie closer.

"David, I know what you want me to become. I'm just not ready yet. I need more time. I think it's important for me to get this degree." Debbie looked like she was trying to turn away from him.

"Degree? In church history? What a mockery. Don't you see our world is more free without a God who enslaves with harsh rules? Don't you see our world is trying to break free from God's constraints? It's absolute tyranny!" David raised his voice and students turned their heads.

"What about my freedom, David? What about my needs? Don't you see? I have come to love you, David. I have come to realize these feelings, but I will feel that love even more strongly if you allow me the freedom to finish my studies here…with Linda."

"Linda? She will not be able to advance you as I will. She is nothing."

"She is my best friend." Debbie turned to leave.

David grabbed her by the arm, "Deborah Taninsam, you'll do well to remember your purpose. Remember, I'm doing this for your own good." He held Debbie's left shoulder tightly and placed his right hand over her head. David closed his eyes and muttered a strange language under his breath. Suddenly, Debbie yelled as if in pain and dropped to the ground.

Linda ran to Debbie's side and put her arm underneath Debbie's head to try to revive her. Linda looked up as David glared down at her and mysteriously vanished into thin air.

"Debbie? Debbie?" Linda was gently shaking her friend trying to wake her. "Debbie, are you okay?" Linda tried to lift Debbie to a sitting position and noticed the cameo necklace around Debbie's neck as it came out from under her blouse. Linda leaned closer to get a better look.

"Oh, my God," she thought. "The woman in the cameo looks just like Debbie!"

Debbie was completely unconscious when Linda called to other students for help.

*

When Debbie first arrived at the Milwaukee Psychiatric Institute, she was Deborah Taninsam and only Deborah Taninsam. She had no recollection of her past life as Debbie Romano. Pietro and Lucia Romano visited as often as possible and tried to hug their daughter, but Deborah refused to allow them to touch her. Lucia was often brought to tears, and a consoling Pietro comforted her and told her that everything would be okay. The doctors told them that Debbie had suffered a concussion and lost her memory. Through therapy, her past could eventually trigger her memory.

After each visit, Pietro and Lucia returned to Lake Geneva and stopped at Saint Michael's Church where they said a prayer for their beloved daughter in front of the Blessed Sacrament. Their friend, Father Andrew McLaughlin, the pastor of Saint Michael's, came to them to give them spiritual comfort.

On one of their visits to the hospital, Pietro and Lucia brought

Father Mac with them to pray over their daughter and give her a blessing. When they arrived, Jean greeted the three in the waiting area.

"Mr. and Mrs. Romano, nice to see you. Debbie or should I say, Deborah, is waiting for you in one of our private visitor's rooms. Nice to meet you Father. I'm Jean." Jean held out her hand, and Father Mac shook it warmly.

"Nice to meet you, too, Jean. I take it we haven't seen 'Debbie' since 'Deborah' arrived, what was it two months ago?"

"That's correct, Father. I have not had the pleasure of meeting the real Debbie Romano since she arrived. Please follow me." Jean led them down a long corridor to a small private room off the back hallway. The room had a table in the center with couches and chairs around it and a large window with a beautiful view of Lake Michigan.

Jean knocked on the closed door before they entered. "Come in." Lucia recognized the voice. It was a more mature version of Debbie; the girl who now called herself Deborah.

Jean opened the door and gestured for Lucia, Pietro and Father Mac to follow. Deborah was standing with her back to the three looking out of the window toward the lake. She was wearing a black halter top and a black mini skirt with black stiletto heels that made her appear a half foot taller. Deborah turned to greet Lucia and Pietro, but when she saw Father Mac, she let out a loud scream.

"What is he doing here?" Deborah pointed toward the priest with a look of hate on her heavily made–up face.

Jean intervened immediately. "Now, just a minute, Deborah. Pietro and Lucia, your parents, have brought a very good friend with them, someone you used to know in Lake Geneva. This is Father Mac."

Father Mac tried to step forward to greet Deborah, but she grabbed for the door to exit the room. Jean intercepted quickly, shut the door, and stood in front of it to block Deborah's escape.

"Now, Deborah, let's just give your parents and Father Mac a chance, okay? Why don't you sit down and relax. This will not be a long visit." Jean was used to having to take charge of uncomfortable situations.

Deborah let out a loud sigh, walked over to the small couch on the right, and sat down. "Let me just get one thing straight before anything further is said. Lucia and Pietro, you both seem like very nice people, but you are not my parents. I have only one parent and her name is Elaina Taninsam. My father, Samuel, died when I was a baby."

Lucia couldn't help but interject, "No, Debbie, that's not true. Elaina Taninsam gave up custody of you when you were only six months old. Your Aunt Jessica gained custody and wanted Pietro and I..."

"Do not ever call me Debbie again! My name is Deborah Taninsam!" Deborah was leaning so far forward on the couch, a gold cameo necklace dropped out of her blouse.

Father Mac was the first to notice. "Deborah, that is such a beautiful necklace. May I see it?" He sat next to her.

"No. It's mine. It was given to me as a gift by a...friend." Deborah quickly hid the necklace back in her blouse.

"All right, Deborah. That's fine. Lucia and Pietro, why don't you take a seat over here?" The couple sat on the small couch opposite Deborah. Jean sat in a chair beside them.

"Deborah, do you remember the Rosary you received for your first holy communion? The one you brought to Saint Michael's to have me bless? Lucia and Pietro said you didn't want it, so I brought it today to give back to you." Father Mac reached into his pocket and pulled out a long strand of beautifully ornate Rosary beads. He dangled the crucifix right in front of Deborah's eyes.

When Deborah saw the image of Jesus on the cross, she covered her eyes and moaned. "No, please. Take that away from me."

Lucia noticed that Deborah's voice sounded more like Debbie's. Father Mac took out a bottle of holy water and opened it. "In

the name of the Father, and the Son, and the Holy Spirit. Amen."
As he spoke, the priest squirted holy water on the Rosary beads
next to Deborah. Droplets of holy water landed on her head and
hands. As soon as the water touched her, she began to cry
uncontrollably.

Lucia quickly rose and went to her lost daughter. She threw her
arms around Debbie's shoulders and the two women wept. Pietro
remained seated while tears ran down his face. Their daughter,
Debbie, had come back to them.

"She was lost and now she's been found," Father Mac said
smiling.

Jean clasped her hands together under her chin feeling very
good about her job.

Pietro rose and embraced Father Mac. He had never lost hope,
but today Pietro's prayers were answered.

CHAPTER FIVE

Pietro Roberto Antonio Romano was raised just outside of Vatican City in Rome. His parents moved to the city from the country, which was a far cry from being reared by generations of farmers. He was born in 1951 and had four older sisters and one younger brother who he felt might as well have been his twin, they were so close in age. Pietro and his brother fished together at a small stream that ran behind the back of his house; a farm house built on top of a hill that looked over acres of meadow and rich agricultural land. The Romanos grew tomatoes and peppers, but Pietro's father had one special piece of land that produced an annual harvest of ripe, dark Merlot grapes that he planted with the hope of becoming a great wine producer. Pietro and his siblings counted down the days until the harvest eager to get their hands on those juicy, delicious grapes.

Every year, Pietro's father hoped that this would be his year—the year that brought him first prize for best Merlot in the county. Come every harvest, he imagined himself with the blue ribbon for best Merlot, but it never happened. Every year, his father brimmed with anticipation for the harvest and the wine making. Then, when the first bottle of wine was opened, it became a great ceremony, and he rejoiced when he tasted that year's wine.

Pietro's father brought his wine to the county's fair only to be beaten out by some other producer. At first, he responded with anger and resignation that this would be his last year in the wine–making business, but then planting time came again and his father's anger was replaced with hope once again. This was the cycle of his father's life.

Pietro's mother was the nurturer of both her children and her husband. When Pietro's father was excited about his new harvest of grapes, she was excited. When he was disappointed with his loss, she was there to comfort him. Pietro's mother was also the religious one of the family. She made sure that her husband and children attended Mass daily. She led a family recitation of the Rosary every evening after dinner. She was the reason that Pietro felt a calling for the priesthood when he was only ten.

Pietro remembered that day vividly. He stood outside on the porch watching the sunset in the distance after dinner. The winds were gusting and he was hoping for a late summer storm. Pietro always slept better in a rain storm. He looked out over the horizon and caught a glimpse of his mother standing in the distance with her wavy, black hair down long and whipping in the wind. Her hands were clasped together as if she were deep in prayer and her head was tilted down with her eyes closed. Pietro thought he had never seen such piety and beauty in all his young life. His mother was the calming and peaceful presence in his life. It would bring her such joy to know that he was thinking of becoming a priest.

This thought would not emerge again until much later. Pietro was in his last year of high school when his younger brother, his best friend and the one sibling with whom he shared everything, died suddenly and tragically at seventeen after being diagnosed with leukemia only four months before. At the funeral Mass, Pietro sat in the first pew next to his mother who silently held his hand. His father sat between his sisters scarcely able to contain his grief, and Pietro knew at that moment that he wanted to become a priest. He would become the consoler of the family. He would become the rock they could lean on.

Pietro entered the Pontifical University of Saint Thomas Aquinas, also known as the Angelicum, in Rome. He ate little, prayed often and worked on his studies night and day. His mother and father seemed very proud of their son. They were happy with his vocation to the priesthood, and the first four years of his time of discernment at the seminary passed quickly.

At this time, Pietro received a very important phone call from his parents back home. One of his fellow seminarians took the call and brought Pietro to the phone so urgently, he thought it must be a matter of life and death.

"Hello?" Pietro answered hurriedly and hesitantly thinking the worst; something must have happened to his parents or one of his sisters.

"Pietro? Pietro?" It was Pietro's father brimming over with so much excitement, he sounded out of breath.

"Papa? Are you well?" Pietro asked.

"Yes! Pietro, I won! I won the blue ribbon for my Merlot! Pietro, after all these years, I won!"

"Congratulations, Papa!"

"Yes! Pietro, you are to come home immediately! Take a little vacation, my son. We are having a party!"

*

Pietro's father's celebration was so large that even distant relatives attended and stayed with them at their large farmhouse. The night he arrived back home from the seminary, he was introduced to Lucia Maria Luccese, the niece of his mother's cousin. As he held Lucia's hand, Pietro looked into her exquisite brown eyes and knew that he would do God's good work as a happily married man and not as a priest. He and Lucia were married in the country, but decided to move into an apartment in Rome so that Pietro could attend medical school. He received his doctorate and became a professor of medicine.

Not long after, Lucia's mother became ill and they moved to the United States so that she could see an American specialist in New York. Pietro taught medicine at New York University and he and Lucia became close friends with Jessica Taninsam. Lucia's mother passed away the following year from Stage IV ovarian cancer. Years later, when Jessica brought Deborah to the Romanos to adopt, they realized that God had brought them to New York to find Debbie, their beautiful daughter.

*

A miracle occurred the day Father Andrew McLaughlin baptized little Deborah Taninsam who became Debbie Romano. When Father Mac dipped the shell into the baptismal font to bless Debbie "in the name of the Father, and the Son, and the Holy Spirit," and doused the top of her head with holy water, the baby stopped breathing. At first, Pietro and Lucia thought the child had been startled and forgotten to breathe. When several seconds passed and there were still no signs of breathing, however, little Debbie's face turned blue, and she opened her mouth as if she were gasping for breath.

"What's happening?" Lucia shouted to Pietro.

"Call an ambulance!" Pietro turned toward Jessica who immediately took out her cell phone and dialed. Pietro took the baby from Lucia and placed her on the carpet before the baptismal font to check her vital signs. He leaned over her little face and performed mouth–to–mouth on her while applying small amounts of pressure to her tiny chest. When Pietro took a break and looked at his child still not breathing, he picked her up by her chest with one hand and patted her back with the other. More time passed, and there was still no sign of breathing.

Lucia couldn't bring herself to believe that this child, their greatest gift, could be taken from them. She took out her Rosary, made the Sign of the Cross over Debbie's head, and said a "Hail Mary." As soon as Lucia finished, she felt a warm breeze touch her face and noticed the sweet fragrance of lilac. For one split second, Lucia was sure she saw a beautiful woman dressed in blue standing on the altar on the other side of the font. Miraculously and without explanation, Debbie let out a loud gasp and immediately began to cry.

This was the most fantastic sound in the world to Lucia and Pietro as tears streamed down their faces. Every person in the church was cheering and clapping, even Father Mac. If a miracle did occur, no one seemed to care. They cared only that the little child in front of them was declared "fit as a fiddle" by the medics who arrived a few moments later to care for Debbie.

Lucia and Pietro took Debbie to the hospital for tests, which all proved that Debbie was perfectly fit and healthy. Years later, Debbie's parents laughed when she received an award for never missing a single day of school all throughout elementary and high school. They had no way of knowing what Debbie would endure in college. They knew nothing of the bloodstone curse.

*

When Father Mac stood up to leave the Milwaukee Psychiatric Institute, he asked a much more accommodating Debbie if he might borrow the bloodstone cameo necklace to have a look. He promised he would bring it back to her in a couple of days. Debbie readily agreed and began a new process of healing at the Institute. It became a pleasure for Jean to treat the new Debbie and after a few days, she thought that it wouldn't be long before Debbie would return home.

Father Mac, on his word, brought the necklace back to Debbie and his only comment was how strange that the image of the woman should so resemble her. Debbie stuck the necklace in her dresser drawer and forgot about it. An entire month went by and everything progressed along so well for Debbie, she even helped out her roommate, Lucky.

Everything until now. Now that David had attempted to visit Debbie. This was all she could remember to relate to Jean. Jean had asked about David, and Debbie told her everything she could remember.

Jean went to Debbie who sat up on her bed, and put an arm around the frightened young woman. "No worries, Debbie. David's gone and he will not be getting anywhere close to you. Not if I have anything to do with it."

"Thanks, Jean. You've been such a good friend through all of this. I wouldn't have gotten this far without you."

"All right, that's that. Now, why don't you go freshen up? It's volleyball time, and everybody loves volleyball time."

Every night, a group of patients played volleyball in the gym. It was a chance to unwind, have fun and get a little bit of exercise. Jean left the room and Debbie went into the bathroom to splash some water on her face. It had been a tiring experience seeing David and she needed a break. She left her room, and went into the living room to find Lucky for volleyball. No Lucky in the living room.

"Okay, maybe she's already in the gym," Debbie thought out loud.

Debbie walked toward the elevators next to the visiting area, and hit the button to go down. The left elevator beeped first and Debbie noticed the arrow pointing down light up. When the door opened, she saw David standing in the back. Before she could turn and run, he grabbed her from around her neck and pulled her into the elevator just before the door shut.

"Let go!" Debbie screamed. David's grip was so powerful, she felt like she was fighting for her life.

"I thought you'd left, Deborah! Why are you lying to me when I've given you everything?"

"I want my old life back! I know who I am, David, and I don't belong with you!"

David brought Debbie's necklace out of his pocket and placed it back around her neck before she could utter another word. As soon as it was in place, Debbie relaxed and looked up at him with loving serenity.

"David? Where am I?" she asked.

David smiled back at Deborah. He had won.

*

The morning after David Bloodstone visited and she discovered his background, Jean witnessed Debbie's transition back to Deborah Taninsam. Debbie had missed the volleyball game the night before because she told Jean she was tired and went to bed early.

The next morning when Jean knocked on Debbie's door, she heard Lucky's voice on the other side of the door telling her to come in. Jean found Deborah lying on top of the covers dressed in the kind of outfit only a hooker would be caught dead in. Deborah looked like she had fallen asleep without changing; she was still wearing the high heels she must have worn the night before. When Jean caught sight of the gleaming cameo necklace around her neck, she felt odd and queasy. Jean decided to let her sleep through the first session.

An hour later, Deborah walked into the meeting room wearing the same outfit and too much make–up. All of the patients looked up at once.

"Hey, why didn't anyone wake me?" Deborah asked. "What the heck do you guys think you're doing starting without me?" She stood with her hands on her hips and looked like she might hit someone at any moment.

Jean rose from her seat and walked over to Deborah. "Deborah, why don't you sit down and relax. You looked tired this morning and I wanted to give you a chance to rest." She tried to put a hand on Deborah's shoulder to comfort her, but Deborah pushed her away and her back fist struck Jean's collar bone. Jean was thrown backwards and onto the floor.

Jean's assistant, Susan, opened the door to call for help and two tall, burly men dressed in white entered the room within seconds. They took Deborah by her arms and dragged her kicking and screaming back to her room. When they reached the room, the men struggled to place Deborah on her bed and Susan took a syringe from her pocket and injected something that would help Deborah relax. Deborah was back to sleep in one instant, and Susan noticed a cameo necklace on the floor that must have come off in the commotion. She set it on Deborah's dresser.

That evening when Debbie awoke, she saw Jean, Father Mac and her parents peering over her like some black and white sci–fi movie. She sat up quickly. "What's going on?" she asked in a horse whisper.

"You really don't know, do you?" Jean was looking at Debbie like she was a criminal.

"No, the last thing I remember is that I was on my way to a volleyball game."

"Debbie, do you remember putting on this necklace last night?" Father Mac held the cameo necklace up for Debbie to see.

"No. Why?"

"Your personality changed to Deborah again," Jean answered.

"Are you saying that thing has the power to change who I am?" Debbie asked.

Father Mac responded, "We're not saying anything. Let's just keep a distance between you and the necklace for a while and see what happens."

Lucia and Pietro kissed their daughter good–bye, and Father Mac tucked the necklace in his coat pocket.

When they reached the dark parking lot outside, Pietro struggled to retrieve his car keys from his pocket when a loud growl rang out like a howling wolf. The three jumped at once, and

Father Mac called out, "Holy Heaven!" to the darkness.

"Let's get back home," Lucia said under her breath.

They were back on Highway 50 toward Lake Geneva when Father Mac felt in his pocket for the necklace. His pocket was empty save for a stick of peppermint gum.

*

David reached Deborah's door unseen and walked into the darkened room. Lucky had gone outside for a cigarette.

David walked to Deborah's bed and shook her gently. "Deborah," he said. "I brought you something."

Debbie woke quickly and sat up straight to defend herself from David.

He slipped the necklace around her neck before she could stop him.

"There is something very important that I need to ask you," David said as he sat next to Deborah on her bed.

"What?" Deborah asked still dazed from the injection she had been given earlier to relax.

"Has a man named Michael Murray been here to visit you? A reporter named Michael Murray?"

"Yes. Why?"

"He wants the necklace. You see, my darling, he wants the same power you possess. I possess. He wants to steal it from us. Promise me that you will not allow him to visit you again."

"I promise." Deborah lay back down on the bed wearing her bloodstone cameo necklace, and David vanished into the night.

CHAPTER SIX

As Michael Murray drove along Interstate 43 toward Milwaukee, he thought about Lake Geneva, the place where he had grown up. It struck him that most people he met thought being from Lake Geneva either meant you were from Switzerland or the corn fields of Wisconsin. Neither was true. Lake Geneva, Wisconsin, was a resort town with a beautiful, fresh water lake situated between Milwaukee and Chicago.

Michael loved Lake Geneva. He loved to watch seagulls fly overhead as he soaked up the sun on wheat–colored beaches. He loved to gaze at the elegant, red brick building called the Riviera with authentic steamboats and paddle boats ready to take tourists on ice cream socials around the lake. He loved to walk along the shoreline and watch wealthy people live lives of large mansions, private boat docks and enough lakefront property to house a Tokyo golf course. Most of all, Michael loved that you could walk down the street and say, "Hi," to strangers who didn't know you, but said, "Hi," back because that's what it meant to be of down–home, Midwestern breeding.

As Michael steered his hand–me–down black Volvo with more than 90,000 miles logged on the odometer, he thought about the two people he loved most in the world: his father and mother.

"Doc" and Marie Murray were a nice pair. Very Catholic. So Catholic, their best friend was Father Andrew McLaughlin whom everyone called "Father Mac" for short. Father Mac had been the pastor of Saint Michael's Church in Lake Geneva for the past sixteen years. He was the kind of priest who loved being around people more than anything.

The thought of being back home put a smile on Michael's face. It took him years of traveling—a little Europe, a little New York and a lot of D.C. to understand he should never have left. Michael's smile dazzled white with years of drinking milk and visiting Doc who drilled teeth and fixed tooth decay for a living. Doc Murray always said looking at the inside of people's mouths was a little depressing, but somebody had to do it.

"Yeah, and he makes a pretty good living for himself, too," Michael thought. "Good enough to play eighteen holes of golf three days a week."

Michael's friends joked that Doc was really a semi–professional golfer who did dentistry on the side. Michael chuckled at the thought of his father.

It was a rare occurrence for Michael and Doc to argue. Michael could only think of one conversation that may have led to a "potential" argument. Doc had suggested that Michael think about dental school someday so he could take over the practice. Michael knew Doc had always wanted him to follow in his footsteps.

"You know, the practice is all set up now. Got a long list of patients, all new equipment, and heck, you're situated right on the bay, beautiful there."

"I know, Dad, I know. I just don't know if I could 'do' dentistry. I mean it's a great living for some, but you know how my left hand shakes. I could never do any of the detail work." Michael remembered how disappointed Doc had looked. And then, his father's smile had quickly returned. "Want to go to Lake Lawn? Play a round?"

"Yeah, Doc's whole life revolves around golf," Michael

thought. "Man, I sure love that old goat."

Michael Murray became a journalist instead of a dentist. He moved to Washington D.C. where he covered the 2004 and 2008 elections. Michael built up a sizable reputation for what critics called, "his objective journalistic integrity."

The truth of the matter was Michael liked writing about politics more than anything. He could put meat into a story without worrying about putting too much heart into it. "Who worried about getting personal in Washington, right?" Michael thought. Fact was fact. And fiction became fact. And then, the most imaginative, made–up fiction became fact, too. Michael ate it up. For him, it gave creative writing a whole new meaning.

Besides politics, Michael freelance wrote for whatever newspaper, magazine or trade journal he could convince to publish his work. Freelance work was the main "career" reason Michael moved back to Lake Geneva. The area was great for writing. He had Milwaukee, forty–five minutes away, Chicago, an hour and a half away, and pure beautiful countryside for miles waiting for him to soak up and throw back on paper.

The thought of writing brought Michael's attention back to the business at hand. He was on his way to the Milwaukee Psychiatric Institute to interview a girl named Debbie Romano. Debbie was diagnosed as manic depressive with an occasional tendency toward schizophrenia and multiple personality disorder. Debbie told Michael the diagnosis depended on what mood the shrinks were in and which shrink she saw that day.

The most confusing part was Debbie Romano thought she was Debbie Romano one minute and a girl by the name of Deborah Taninsam the next. Debbie was smart and witty, grew up in Lake Geneva, high school cheerleader, attended Marquette University on scholarship, had it all. Deborah was vampy and depressing. She liked to wear tight dresses cut too low on top and too high on the bottom.

Whenever Michael did an interview with Debbie, Deborah tried to seduce him. "Not that she wasn't attractive and all that," Michael thought. "She's just not my type."

The problem was Debbie, on the other hand, was very much his type. "When you turn thirty, you start to think about finding the right girl," he reasoned. And Michael had certainly thought about it more than once when he was in Debbie's presence. He just didn't think he could be with someone he liked one minute and couldn't stand the next. It wasn't that Michael hated Deborah. She was just kind of weird and spooky. That's all. Very spooky.

Even spookier was the person who contacted him to do the story on Debbie. She said she wanted Michael to do a story on Debbie because she was a concerned family member. She said she would direct deposit weekly sums of money in a bank account in exchange for weekly visits. Michael had never actually met this family member in person. Just conversed with her over the phone and extracted the deposits. That was it.

And her last name was not Romano. It was Taninsam. Imagine that. So was Debbie really just some sort of made up personality? Michael spent a half day researching this at the local high school and found out that Debbie really did exist. She was the daughter of a couple named Pietro and Lucia Romano. After moving from Milwaukee, she spent four years at Badger High School in Lake Geneva and graduated in 2008. After that, she spent three years at Marquette University majoring in History and then mysteriously vanished. This was the most interesting part of the story. If Debbie existed, but Deborah belonged to the Taninsam family, how were the two related? Was it possible to have two distinctive personalities within one body?

Finding answers to these questions was the reason Michael had stuck to the story. He had arranged a meeting with Lucia and Pietro Romano and discovered they were actually friends of Father Mac's, too. That was a lucky coincidence because Michael found out that Father Mac had done some investigating on his own. Debbie was in possession of a very unique cameo necklace, which

71

seemed to play an important role in her personality switch to Deborah. Father Mac said the only thing unusual about the necklace was that the woman engraved on the cameo looked exactly like Debbie. However, that necklace did appear to be a significant clue into the link between Debbie Romano and Deborah Taninsam.

The Romanos and Father Mac had expressed concern over Michael's involvement with the Taninsam family, but they were also eager to discover any possible links to the necklace and Debbie's personality switch to Deborah. The three decided that Michael should move along discreetly. As long as Debbie or Deborah remained in the hospital, they figured she was safe. Michael began to feel that this mystery was worth unraveling. He wanted to learn the truth.

Michael would have quit the assignment long ago if it hadn't gotten under his skin so much. Back in Washington, when a story got under Michael's skin, he used to call it "the burn." When he had the burn, he was hot on the trail of a story and nothing could stop him. No amount of hunger or exhaustion or sexual proposition could get in the way of completing the mission. To Michael, the mission was to find answers and discover the truth. In fact, Michael's sole mission in life was to make the world a better place by seeking and living truth. The only problem was most of Michael's friends didn't understand this particular work ethic. One such friend was a buddy named, Joe Crisik. In fact, the two had gone out the night before.

"Come on. Let's go out for a beer. Just one, and then I promise I'll get you home by your 9 o'clock curfew." Joe had already had too much to drink and was beginning to get on Michael's nerves. He didn't understand "crunch–time" and deadlines and having to pay Visa on time. Joe came from Chicago Board of Trade money where Mom and Dad were more than happy to pay their son's bills even if he was going on thirty–one.

Yeah, Michael had his regular friends back and his regular

hangouts where he was always ready for action. Unfortunately, that action didn't always mean the Nobel Prize. It usually meant drinking too much beer and losing too many games of pool.

Last night's bar of choice had been Champs, a hearty little sports bar located in downtown Lake Geneva with a significant selection of games to play—pool, basketball, indoor golf—you could take your pick depending on the mood of the evening. Just the thought of the word, "mood," made Michael want to puke as he continued to drive toward Milwaukee. Last night, he had agreed to meet Joe for one beer and a quick game of pool, and all Joe could talk about was this girl and that girl and anything that walked into the joint that didn't pee standing up. After a heart–wrenching, self–pitying conversation about why women found Joe's money more attractive than his character, one beer turned into six and one game of pool into four.

"God, Joe, can't you talk about anything else? Can't we have an interesting, intellectual, half–way decent conversation about anything other than your sex life?" Michael asked his friend.

"Oh, boy. Listen to Mr. Superman talk here. The guy who has every beautiful babe in the world after him at any given moment. Yeah, right. Sure. And most of the time, you don't even seem interested. You know what, Mike? If you had as much interest in the women who proposition you as you do in your work, maybe, just maybe, we'd both be getting laid tonight." Joe glanced over and pointed to two young, giggly college students who were sitting at a corner table trying to make eye contact with Michael. Joe got down on his knees in front of Michael in a "beggar" gesture, hands held together in pleading.

Michael looked down at his friend and rolled his eyes, "You know what, Joe? Maybe, just maybe, if you had more interest in work, you'd have more propositions. Come on, let's get out of here. I've got an early appointment tomorrow and I've got to get some sleep."

"No, come on. I was just kidding." Joe got up quickly and

yanked Michael over to the pool table. "Let's play one more round. Come on, just one. I'll let you win." Joe, either due to lack of female attention or real talent, had won all four games of pool they had played up to that point.

"That kind of talk could sweep a girl off her feet. All right, rack 'em up." Michael turned to get the stick he had been using when a beautiful redhead in her early twenties grabbed his shoulder from behind.

"Are you Michael Murray, the guy who's doing the story on Debbie?"

"Yeah, I'm the one. Who are you?" Michael couldn't help but look the young woman confronting him up and down. She was gorgeous and had a figure that rivaled any Sports Illustrated swimsuit model.

"I'm Linda Walters. I saw Debbie's picture in the local paper today right next to the story you're doing on her. I know you're looking for people who know her. Well, I know her all right. She is my best friend and roommate at Marquette. We both majored in history. Halfway through her Junior year, she started having issues." Linda stressed the word "issues" and took a deep breath before she spoke again, "Mr. Murray, how much do you believe in the spiritual world?"

*

When Michael first laid eyes on Linda Walters at Champs Bar, he couldn't believe his good fortune. To have information about Debbie gift wrapped in a beautiful package was a dream come true for Michael. "Thank God for good 'ole Saint Justin, the seeker of truth," he thought.

"Linda, do you want to go somewhere a little quieter, like for coffee or something, so we can sit and talk?" Michael asked. "There's a Starbucks right around the corner from here."

Michael was already holding onto Linda's arm, leading her out of Champs when Joe turned from his task of racking up a neat triangle just above the center of the table. When Joe saw Linda standing next to Michael, his jaw dropped so low, Michael began to envision a bulldozer, its crane lowered to scrape up the large pool of drool mounting from Joe's dog–like tongue.

"Sorry, Joe, 'ole buddy. Got to go do an interview. As usual, work prevails," Michael called to his friend as he led Linda through the crowd of pool–playing, beer drinkers and out toward the exit.

Joe watched the two enviously, slowly closed his mouth, and gave Michael his best, "Yeah, sure you gotta work" look. His eyes rolled up to the ceiling as he turned back to the table, "Why, Lord? Why not me, Lord?" Joe thought.

When Michael and Linda reached the local Starbucks café one block down from Champs, they both ordered a small latte, and took a seat at a corner table where they could have a bit of privacy.

Michael turned to Linda. "What kind of issues was Debbie Romano having at Marquette?" he asked.

Linda took a sip of her coffee before she answered, "Well, like I said, we were roommates. One night, she had this totally mysterious man visit her. Kind of weird, too. He was very tall with long, black hair. He was also dressed all in black, very striking. I asked Debbie about him, whether she had a tall, dark stranger visiting her. She denied it, but I didn't believe her because I followed him one night and saw him enter our dorm room, but as soon as I reached the room, he disappeared."

Michael started to think that either this girl's marbles were as loose as Debbie's or she was just a beautiful talking head with nothing between her ears.

Linda seemed to read Michael's mind because she said, "Hey, do you want to know the truth or not?"

"Yes…yes…I'm sorry. It just all sounds kind of unbelievable. Let me ask you an important question before we go on. Why did you ask me about a 'spiritual world?'"

"That's exactly where I'm headed, Michael. When I followed this guy to our dorm room, he entered and I came into the room right behind him, but there was no one there. It's like he had vanished or something. Debbie was just sitting at her desk doing her homework alone."

Michael gave her the I–don't–believe–you–one–iota look once again and this time, Linda got up to leave. Michael, stood up quickly, and took Linda's hand in his. "I'm sorry, Linda. It's just that I'm not that used to talking about things that aren't exactly black and white, you know what I mean? Come on, I'm a reporter from D.C. In D.C., there's nothing but black and white."

Linda realized Michael was being sincere, and she needed to be more patient. After all, she had felt the same way when she first encountered the stranger with Debbie, hadn't she?

Linda sat back in her chair. "Okay, Michael, just please try to keep an open mind when I tell you the story."

Michael sat back down, too. He took a small digital recorder out of his pocket. "Do you mind?" he asked.

"No, I'd do anything to help Debbie."

Michael hit the "Play/Record" button. "Shoot," was all he said.

*

When Michael finally reached the Milwaukee Psychiatric Institute, his nerves grew more tense as he thought about the information he had received from Linda the night before. He entered the hospital and was ushered into a private meeting room where he sat on the edge of a chair waiting for Debbie.

Michael had heard so many wild stories from Linda, he had to work hard to stay focused on his mission. Michael kept repeating phrases in his head. "I have to keep an open mind. I have to keep an open mind," he thought, but the more he said this to himself, the more nervous he became. He had met with Debbie or Deborah before, but he had never thought that she was anything more than confused or plain crazy.

Michael heard a knock on the door and he was hoping and praying that the person on the other side of the door would turn out to be Debbie. "Please God," Michael said to himself.

Unfortunately, the person who entered turned out to be Deborah, the nymph, instead of Debbie, the normal.

Deborah closed the door behind her, and took a seat directly opposite Michael. She sat toward the back of her chair and crossed her legs, her skirt short enough to completely expose her lean, long and fish–net–stocking legs.

"I'm sorry to say this, Michael, but as much as I like you and as much as you really turn me on, I'm not going to be able to see you anymore," she said.

"Why?" Michael asked curiously.

"Because he doesn't want me to," Deborah answered.

"Who?"

"I'm not allowed to tell you."

"Why not?"

"It's a secret." Deborah rose from her chair and walked over to the window with her back to Michael.

"Okay, Deborah," Michael continued. "Let me ask you a quick question about your family, the Taninsams?"

"Yeah, what about them?"

"Does Debbie know them, too?"

"What do you mean, Debbie? My name is Deborah, not Debbie."

"You mean you're not aware of who Debbie is?" Michael gave Deborah his best I–don't–buy–it look.

"I thought you knew, Michael. I thought you knew the whole truth." Deborah slowly turned into Debbie right in front of his eyes as she walked back to her chair, sat down, and cradled her head in her hands.

"Debbie, I know you're in there. Come on. I want to hear it from you." Michael was trying desperately to help Debbie come out of her Deborah state. "I want to know the truth. I met Linda. She told me all about the necklace. She told me all about David."

Debbie began to cry. She cried like a little girl instead of an adult. Debbie sat with her head in her hands, crying years of past hurt out to Michael.

Michael felt dizzy, like an unseen force was working on his mind trying to extract the very information he felt compelled to give Debbie. After an instant, he felt he was floating above the scene six years ago when Debbie was fifteen and first given the necklace. He could picture it all. He could see David through Debbie's eyes. He could see him bend over to retrieve the necklace. He could see him give it to Debbie and in one sweeping transformation, Michael could see Debbie change. He saw her become Deborah, and he knew in one split second that there was no longer any doubt that the necklace placed on Debbie's neck was the reason for her transformation. There was an evil in this necklace that Michael had to discover.

A violent rage flowed through Michael's body that he could not explain. He felt such an intense hatred for the evil necklace that his body was racked with anger. Michael yearned to discover the truth of the necklace's origin. Linda had been right. There was something "otherworldly" about this whole dilemma, and he was going to get to the bottom of it. The truth–seeker was back, and the burn of his reporter days brought him back to the reality of the moment.

Deborah had become Debbie again, and the necklace that had been hidden under her blouse was now dangling from her hands.

"Debbie, can I see that?" Michael was leaning forward in his chair with a compassionate and reassuring smile on his face.

Debbie lifted the necklace and placed it in Michael's hands. He was surprised at how heavy the thing was. He held the cameo up to his eyes so he could see it more closely.

"Father Mac was right," he thought to himself. "The woman on the cameo looks exactly like Debbie."

Michael had felt so much fear, a fear of something inexplicably evil, a fear of something that doesn't belong to this world, but now, he felt nothing. No fear at all. The mysterious evil was a simple cameo necklace lying in his hand. There were no hidden consequences.

"No," Michael thought. "I will not allow myself to be bought off so quickly. I'm at square one and I'll start at square one."

He stood up and laid the necklace on a nearby table. He took his cell phone out of his pocket and turned to Debbie. "Do you mind?" he asked.

"No, do what you need to do."

Michael took two close up pictures of the cameo necklace and returned it to Debbie.

"Listen, Debbie, please remember that I'm here to help. Linda is here to help, along with Father Mac and your parents. I don't know where this guy came from, the guy who gave you this necklace, but I'm going to find out. I'm going to find out the truth."

Later, when Michael pressed the elevator button to return to the lobby downstairs, he sensed that someone was watching him. He looked around and saw two people in the waiting area: a young girl dressed in Gothic black and an older man with a long, gray beard who appeared to be on all fours barking like a dog.

Michael thought, "I'm going to get you out of here, Debbie. I'm going to get you out."

When Michael reached his Volvo in the parking lot, he said in a loud, confident voice, "The burn is on!"

CHAPTER SEVEN

David followed Lucia and Pietro Romano all day. He thought they would have attempted to visit their beloved daughter, Deborah, in the hospital. But the closest they came to Milwaukee was a little town called Delavan to stop for lunch at a Mexican restaurant called Hernández. Then, grocery shopping. Then, back to their little abode to clean house.

David wanted to know exactly what they and their priest friend, Father Nick or Father Mick or whatever his name was, had discovered about Deborah and the necklace. He thought about killing all three of them, but then he knew he would lose his chance of gaining Debbie's trust, and David was much too intelligent for that. By four o'clock, David's patience was wearing thin and he needed to find himself again—to discover his true calling in life. He wanted to find a woman and give her exactly what she needed most.

Lake Geneva was a resort town, so David decided to walk along the beach and search for a lucky lady. He left his rental car, a long, black Mercedes, parked by the lake across from the Hilton and preceded toward a large red, brick building with piers off the back. David continued along the main pier past the back entrance of the Riviera toward the beach.

"Yes," David thought, "now I feel back in control. Look at all these beautiful babes staring at me."

When David reached the end of the pier, he turned right toward the beach and walked through an opened gate that led to the beach. He took off his shoes, stepped into the sand and thought he might as well take off his shirt and enjoy the sun. David looked around and noticed some of the young women staring at his bare chest. "That's right, girls. Take it all in."

David saw a tall, thin blonde lying on a towel wearing a red bikini. She was completely alone. "There we go. She's all mine."

Barefoot, shirtless and wearing only black jeans, David strolled toward the blonde. "Is this seat taken?" he asked innocently when he reached her side.

The red bikini babe lifted herself into a sitting position and lowered her sunglasses. David knew she was interested in him when she looked him up and down and stopped somewhere between his two pectoral muscles. He prided himself on his physique and knew most women loved the combination of muscles, a broad chest, and a long, lean tanned body.

"It's all yours," she said. "Do you have a towel?"

"No, I'm kind of here on…the spur of the moment."

"Here, I have an extra." The blonde reached into her beach bag and pulled out a fluffy pink towel. "Sorry about the color."

"No, I love pink, but not quite as much as I love red." David made a point to admire her red bikini and the beautiful body that was directly beneath it.

"Me, too," the girl giggled. "So, what's your name?"

"David. And you?"

"Kimberly. Call me Kim."

"Kim, how would you like to join me for dinner tonight since I'm new in town? You pick the place."

At first, Kim seemed unsure about going to dinner with a stranger, but David leaned on his side and began to play with the beautiful necklace dangling on his chest. Kim had a sudden urge to take a chance.

"Okay. Seven o'clock. The Geneva Inn. Meet me there." Kim rose up on her knees and leaned in toward David's face. She came within inches of his lips, and then quickly turned to go. "Keep the towel," was all she said as she glanced back with a smile.

*

When David walked into the lobby of the Geneva Inn, Kim was waiting in the lounge. She wore a beautiful black strapless dress that hung just above the knee.

"This girl comes from money," David thought. "What a fantastic match."

David wore an expensive black suit and sashayed up to the bar with his right hand in his pocket. When he approached Kim, he noticed the beautiful view of the lake from the dining room.

"Good choice. Can I buy you a drink? Looks like your first is empty." He smiled down at her, and she began to swoon.

"Let's get the table first. I'm anxious to eat...dinner." She stood up slowly allowing her body to brush up against David's.

"Yes, let's." David led Kim by the small of her back to the hostess, and they sat at a cozy table next to the window.

After ordering, Kim turned to David, "You know why I chose this place, don't you?"

"The great view...the great food?" he offered.

"The great rooms," she replied seductively.

David could not believe his good fortune. This beautiful woman wanted him badly, and she was all his for the night. Too bad it had to be just one night. David couldn't help but smile.

"In that case, I think we should skip dessert."

After dinner, David reserved a room on the third floor. The room was a large lake view suite with an oversized whirlpool tub, a lake view balcony, and a separate sitting room with a wet bar.

Kim chose to wait discreetly downstairs in the lounge, but she knew the room was available. It was her idea to spend the night with David in that room.

Fifteen minutes later, Kim knocked on the door of the suite. She heard David's footsteps as he opened the door. Kim noticed that he had removed his suit coat and unbuttoned his black silk shirt down to the navel. The necklace she had seen him wear on the beach was completely visible and sparkling in the glow of the night.

"Come in, my dear." David extended his right arm, and Kim passed through the doorway into the beautifully decorated room. Inside the elegant living room, she saw a bottle of champagne set up on a low table. The bottle was sitting horizontally inside a clear, glass ice bucket with matching champagne flutes on either side.

David sauntered over toward the bubbly and filled one flute halfway. He handed it to Kim, filled the other and lifted it for a toast.

"To us," David said huskily.

David led Kim through the bedroom and onto a balcony with a beautiful lakeside view. They stood looking out over the lake, the soft light of the full moon casting a long orange reflection across the deep blue water.

Kim turned toward David, set both flutes on the patio table, and kissed him passionately.

David took the opportunity eagerly and readily, hungrily following behind Kim to the bed. They left the sliding glass door open, the breeze fluttering through the sheer white curtains.

Afterward, the two lay side by side spent and panting. David rose up first and headed to the bathroom stark naked. When he returned, he slipped on his pants and picked Kim's black, silk slip off the floor. He motioned for Kim to sit up so he could help her cover her nakedness.

Kim sat up on the edge of the bed and raised her arms up toward the ceiling. David let the slip drape over her head and shoulders and it easily cascaded down her beautiful body.

"What a shame to waste this," David thought as he turned

toward the balcony. When he came back around to face Kim, she was not at all ready for what was about to transpire.

David held out a long, black snake, its head steadied by David's left hand and its tail coiled around his right. Kim let out a small cry of alarm and rose quickly, but David was too quick for her and circled the snake around her neck before she could escape.

Kim realized that David was using the snake as a rope and cutting off her oxygen supply. She was suffocating and there was nothing she could do to prevent it. Kim felt as though she might faint at any moment, and a sudden fear took hold of her—the fear of death—the fear that she had not even come close to accomplishing her life's goals. She was falling down a long dark tunnel and there was no one to save her.

Suddenly, Kim glimpsed a light of white in the distance and the grasp of the snake around her neck loosened. She noticed David's hands had left her and the snake had disappeared. Kim fell backward and collapsed on top of the bed. She felt herself begin to lose consciousness, but not before noticing a tall figure standing before the lake view balcony. He was wearing a flowing white shirt and his long, dark hair was blowing forward in the wind. Kim could not help but notice the flash of light that emanated from his presence. There was a sweet, perfume wafting throughout the entire suite, like a meadow of roses or lilies had descended on the room. She would never forget that smell.

*

Father Andrew McLaughlin was a people's priest. People could relate to him. When they came to confess their sins and before he gave them penance, he spent time letting them know they weren't the only ones with troubles. He told them of similar hardships he had experienced in his own life. Father Mac told confessors that God was compassionate as long as there was remorse.

"Say three Our Father's and three Hail Mary's." Tonight, this was Father Mac's response to one of his favorite altar boys, Josh. Josh was caught stealing a candy bar at the local drugstore.

"Thank you, Father." The boy left the confessional so quickly, the toe of his tennis shoe caught on the edge of the box. He stumbled forward only to land on his knees.

Father Mac quickly opened the door to help Josh, and tried to stifle a chuckle at the sight of the boy on his knees. Josh was in the best adoration position Father had ever seen him do.

"Are you okay?" Father Mac couldn't stop the smile that formed on his lips.

"Yeah, yeah. Sorry, Father. I was kind of in a hurry." Josh quickly regained his composure, standing tall, hip to one side, hands folded across his chest.

"Don't worry. I just wanted to make sure you were still all in one piece for tomorrow's Mass," Father Mac gave the boy his biggest grin.

"Yes, Father. Okay, I'll see you then."

"Now, go ahead, but take your time and get home safe for me, okay?" Father Mac began to chuckle under his breath as Josh continued his fast pace to the back doors of the church.

As Father Mac watched Josh, he thought of his own childhood and how much time he had spent at Saint Anthony's Church in Brooklyn where he was raised. The McLaughlin children had attended Saint Anthony's Catholic School, and both parents had been members of the choir, so the church had become a second home for little Andy, as Father Mac was known back then, and his four siblings. The church was the McLaughlin children's favorite play place, and the five of them had created many fantastic worlds of exploration at Saint Anthony's.

Father Mac smiled as he remembered that he and his two brothers and two sisters had created a world of castles and moats from the choir loft to the upper church, and dungeons and dragons from the upper church to the lower. Saint Anthony's had become a second home. So much so, that he and one of his brothers became priests and his youngest sister, a nun. "Yes, there is no greater place than God's house," he said to himself.

In fact, Father Mac couldn't have imagined a better place in the whole world. Both of his parents were born in Ireland, and even though they had only visited the country a couple of times, he thought Ireland was better than anywhere, but nowhere was better than Saint Anthony's. He and his brothers had all been altar boys just like Josh, and when he reached high school, he had become the sacristan, as well. "No better place," Father Mac thought again as Josh vanished through the doors.

The boy walked out into the night just as a beautiful young woman in a black evening dress was standing at the door to enter. Josh held the door for her as she hesitantly slipped in, and then scurried along.

The woman continued toward Father Mac, her walk slow and graceful. Father Mac immediately noticed her unforgettable charm, her beautiful blonde hair flowing well past her shoulders. As she neared Father Mac, he could tell she had been crying, her mascara had run down her cheeks and her lipstick had smeared.

"Are you all right, my child?" Father Mac could scarcely contain his compassion for what appeared to be such insurmountable misery within this sad creature. The woman did not speak. She continued to sob silently, tears streaming down her face. And then she knelt before the priest and reached out to hold his hand. Father Mac grasped her hand and prayed over her.

After a long moment, the woman raised her head and looked up toward Father Mac. "Someone tried to kill me...a man...tall...dark...tried to kill me. By the grace of God I was saved." These were the only words that escaped the woman's lips before she fell forward and fainted. Father Mac noticed long, red welts around her exquisite neck.

*

Michael arrived at the Museum of Lapidary Arts in Elmhurst, Illinois just after lunch. The grounds were large and well kept with careful attention made to all the arts including the lapidary or cameo–making arts. Michael entered the museum from the left where he found a small "Entrance" sign above the black glass doors. He entered and found an information desk to his left. Michael pulled out the two photos he had taken of Debbie's cameo necklace to show the person working at the desk exactly what he was trying to locate.

An elderly woman with beaming blue eyes smiled up at Michael from her black laptop computer. "May I help you?" she asked.

"Yes. My name is Michael Murray. I'm doing research on cameos—bloodstone cameos, actually. I was wondering where they might be located and whether or not you have someone here who knows about their origin." Michael showed the woman the two pictures he had brought with him.

"Absolutely. You're lucky to be here on a Saturday. Janet only works weekends. I'll see if I can find her."

Michael read Eleanor's name tag before he replied back. "Thanks, Eleanor."

As Eleanor left her desk, Michael turned to view all the beautiful jewelry cases on the main floor. There were so many antiques it was truly remarkable. There were necklaces, broaches, pendants, earrings, and all had beautiful gem stones with a card describing where and when they were made. The walls were dark and the lighting was dim, but each glass case was given its own spectacular recessed lighting to illuminate the individual piece.

"Excuse me. I'm Janet Wesley. Can I help you?"

Michael turned to find a slim, middle–aged woman standing in front of him. She wore no makeup, and her short hair was dark black with scatterings of gray. Janet's light eyes were innocent and inquisitive with a hint of intelligence that gave her an air of wisdom beyond her years.

Michael held out his hand. "Hi. I'm Michael Murray, a journalist from Wisconsin. Lake Geneva, actually."

Janet shook his hand firmly and confidently. "Hi, Michael. Eleanor says you're interested in our bloodstone cameos. They're located upstairs. Come and follow me."

Janet led Michael to a set of stairs located directly behind the information desk. After ascending two small flights of stairs, Janet opened the door on the right that led to another large room filled with illuminated cases. She showed him the case that was against the far wall.

The case held only three pieces. All were cameos. Michael spotted the cameo in the middle first. It was the largest and most unique. The cameo must have been at least five inches in diameter and was surrounded by diamonds, which formed a perfect oval. The gold loop at the top had a beautiful strand of black velvet running through it that attached to another gold clasp at the end.

Michael gazed at the five–inch bloodstone cameo surrounded by diamonds and a sharp shudder ran up his spine. It was a Medusa, her snakelike hair made from the splotches of red that formed in the green stone. Her eyes were made from two large red splotches as if her deadly stare were as striking as a bolt of fire. The other two cameos were smaller forms of the same Medusa bloodstone cameo. They were not as large and beautiful, but they still held the same red, electrifying glare.

"These bloodstone cameos are made from green jasper and red quartz..." Janet was speaking to Michael, but it was as if no words were coming from her lips. First, words like "power" and "lust" seemed to come from nowhere, but they were being spoken to Michael in the slightest of whispers.

"The power is bestowed on those who wear me." Michael saw Medusa's mouth move as if she were speaking to him.

He took two steps back and blinked in disbelief. Michael took the picture from his pocket, the picture of Debbie's bloodstone cameo, and showed it to Janet. "Is the origin of this necklace the same as the three you have on display here?"

Janet took the picture from Michael and studied it. After a few moments she said, "Yes. Absolutely, the same." She returned the photo to Michael.

Michael compared the images himself. He looked, first, at the image of the cameo in the photo and when he looked back toward the three cameos in the display, they no longer appeared hideous. They were images of three elegant women—exactly the same as the one he held in his hands yesterday. Was Michael seeing things? He had to regain his wits or his search for the truth would prove absolutely futile.

Michael took a slow breath. "Janet, can you tell me the origin of the bloodstone?"

"Sure, the bloodstone is considered to be a semi–precious stone. It's used for carvings, cameos like these, seals, men's rings and other ornamental objects. It's properly known as green Chalcedony and it's a form of silica quartz. However, for all intensive purposes, the bloodstone is green jasper dotted with bright red spots of iron oxide. It is commonly found in India, Brazil, Uruguay, Australia and the U.S."

"Thanks. I really appreciate all your help, Janet." Michael shook Janet's hand and turned to look at the bloodstone cameos one last time.

Janet walked back toward the staircase, but suddenly turned around as if she had just remembered something important. "There is one thing I forgot to tell you. The bloodstone is considered to be the 'bible stone.' I don't know the specifics, but I think it has something to do with Aaron's breastplate. The bloodstone is also considered to be the 'martyr's gem' because there's a Christian legend associated with it. The legend says that the bloodstone was first formed when drops of Christ's blood fell to the ground and stained jasper stone at the foot of the cross."

Michael's eyes widened with curiosity. Could this be a clue to the spiritual world Linda was talking about?

CHAPTER EIGHT

Dr. Jessica Taninsam was forced to attend another ridiculous party where all that anyone cared about was who to meet to get ahead. She glanced at herself in the foyer mirror next to the downstairs' landing. Her reflection showed only half of her forty–two years. In fact, she looked younger and more vibrant with more exposed cleavage than would have been allowed by her normal attire. Her navy dress was long and fitted with a low–cut, sweetheart neckline and a back slit that came up to her thighs. Her silky, golden blonde hair was done up in a French twist with little sprigs of hair hanging down on either side of her beautifully sculpted face.

Jessica had been through so much the past few weeks. The stress of her job had been more than she had ever anticipated. She accepted the position as Director of the Institute for Human Genetics at the University of San Francisco only two years before. Jessica had always loved research. There were so many discoveries to be made, so many cures for diseases just on the horizon, so many sick patients to heal. She was thrilled that USF was receiving grants beyond her wildest dreams for human genetics' research.

Jessica developed a sizeable reputation in the area of genetics at New York University and Columbia Presbyterian, and when the Director of the Institute at USF retired, Jessica was hired to replace him. She took the position and moved into a private gated community with beautiful contemporary villas in the Napa Yacht Club, an easy commute to downtown San Francisco. Jessica loved living by the water along the Napa Riviera. She also loved her work, and she had made very good, very close friends through USF and the yacht club.

"Nothing has kept me from worrying about my girls, though," Jessica thought as she finished her make–up in front of the mirror. "God, how I miss Cassy and Debbie."

Jessica worried constantly about her nieces. She knew that Debbie had entered a hospital in order to get psychological care. When Pietro and Lucia told Jessica about the cameo necklace and the mysterious man who had been visiting Debbie, Jessica experienced so much anxiety, she felt like someone had punched her in the gut and she couldn't breathe.

Then, Jessica received news from Drew only days before regarding Cassy's car accident. When Jessica heard that Cassy had slipped into a coma, she almost bought a plane ticket that very day to be able to rush to her side. Drew had told her not to worry, that the doctors were confident that Cassy would come out of it. Still, Jessica had wanted to be there for Cassy.

Jessica's fears had been somewhat assuaged by the strange dream she had recently. A man had come to her in the dream. A man who appeared so holy, his face and hands were illuminated by a light, which could only have come from heaven. The man called himself Paulo, and he told her that he would look after Cassy and Debbie for Jessica. He said she had important work to do at USF.

When Jessica awoke the next morning, she felt a feeling of euphoria that she would never forget. A happiness and tranquility seemed to envelope her entire body. For some strange reason, she thought the dream was an experience that would become reality.

That day, one of Jessica's assistants at USF handed her a note sealed in an envelope with a red wax stamp. Jessica did not recognize the seal, but a strange sign appeared through the wax that looked like the letters "P" and "X" were juxtaposed. When she opened the seal, the letter inside was only one line written in an ancient scroll. It read, "I am here for you," and was signed, "Paulo."

When Jessica saw the note, she began to cry. She didn't know why, but the feeling of something greater than herself, greater than the unsteady world around her was there to protect her. Jessica had always been the protector, but now she had someone to protect her. Jessica placed the note up against her heart, and leaned her head down next to it. She noticed a unique smell. It was a fragrance she had never smelled before, a sweet, flowery bouquet that filled her senses with—the only word that came to her at the time and she would always remember—God.

The grandfather clock in the foyer began to chime just as Jessica finished powdering her nose. She grabbed her bag, locked the door, and climbed into her red Mercedes convertible.

"Get your mind back to the business at hand," Jessica thought to herself. "You are almost there. The grants for your research in human genetics and a new method of DNA sequencing have been pouring in. All you have to do is convince Palmer and you've got the whole staff behind you."

Jessica reached Palmer Braxton's exquisite estate situated on San Pablo Bay. It was located in Sausalito, one of the most beautiful places in the country. From the high sequoias of Muir Woods to the high–tech spark of Silicon Valley, the Bay Area was known as the land of happiness, wealth, and a constant flux of tourists just waiting to take in the beauty of America's richest sheer natural landscape. In fact, the town of Sausalito was known as the "French Riviera" of the West Coast because of its Mediterranean climate, art galleries and exquisite restaurants.

Palmer Braxton was a wealthy man, and the size of his home was all the testimony needed to ascertain this. He was the Director of the entire School of Medicine for USF. There was a large white tent set up next to the house, the location of the dinner portion of the extravagant gala. Waiters dressed in white coats and black bow ties served fresh shrimp and oysters on large silver trays. On other trays were flutes of Verve Cliquot and large strawberries dipped in white chocolate. Jazz music was being crooned out by some sultry, African–American female singer surrounded by bass, piano and drums in the back of the tent. Everywhere you looked, people were dressed to the hilt emulating glitz, décolletage and hard, green cash from their statures. They stood beside their tables because they didn't want to give up their seats or didn't want to sit long enough not to be noticed.

"Jessica, over here!" Dr. Jonathan Lee excused himself from a group of men wearing suits too tight at the neck and walked over to where Jessica stood at the entrance.

Jessica smiled broadly. "Jonny, thank God you're here. I thought you were at the convention in New York."

"Decided not to go. I was too curious about how much Palmer would spend on the digs. Can you believe this? I hear he even flew to Alaska to catch the lobster himself." Jonathan smiled broadly and Jessica noticed his big, brown eyes twinkle.

"You know what happens to me when I eat shrimp, oysters and lobster all at once," she retorted. "I'm gonna blow up like a balloon! Palmer thinks that every human being in the vicinity of San Francisco is a vegan or vegetarian. Where's the filet mignon?" Jessica flashed a smile and rolled her eyes at the moon.

"I don't know. Hey! You want to check out the house? It's something else. I thought I was doing pretty good until I got a look at that!"

"Yeah, I've got to use the little girl's room anyway. After you, Monsieur." Jessica hooked arms with Jonathan as he led the way to the well lit steps on the side of the house.

All Jessica remembered seeing was marble. Marble floors, stairs, railings and statues. "Boy, get a load of the decorating. My guess is he thinks he's Caesar and we'll find him wearing a crown of golden leaves."

Jonathan escorted Jessica up the stairs to the "Ladies Room," a powder room off the master bathroom with hunter green fixtures and a sunken tub with two shower nozzles instead of one. "I think I can leave you here, my dear."

"Oh no, Jonny. Please don't leave me alone. I might be tempted to steal something," Jessica said with a wry smile.

"I don't think it's possible. Palmer has everything cemented to the floor in marble."

Jessica smiled at Jonathan and closed the door behind her. The lock turned easily and she felt suddenly secure. She wasn't sure if the security came from the lock or from Jonathan standing on the other side of the door. All Jessica knew was that she felt safe with Jonathan.

Jonathan waited for Jessica outside the bathroom door. He was an unmarried man of forty, and had loved Jessica Taninsam from the moment he first laid eyes on her two years ago. They were best friends, but he had always hoped they could be more. Jonathan was six when he originally came to the United States from the Philippines and had always found blonde hair irresistible. The fact that Jessica was blonde and the most brilliant woman he had ever met, made her appear like a goddess to Jonathan. He would have done anything for her.

Jonathan realized how empty it was on the top floor. All the noise came from below and on the stairs themselves. A large cocktail cart was set up on the landing between the first and second staircases. He heard Palmer's voice coming from the front door downstairs, which was left open so that guests would get the idea that the party was actually indoors and outdoors simultaneously. There was raucous laughter at what evidently was the punch line to one of Palmer's stupid jokes. "What people do to get ahead," Jonathan thought out loud.

The bathroom door opened and Jessica emerged carrying a jade green porcelain cat, one of the decorations of choice. "Just thought I'd leave with one little memento." She gave Jonathan her best wry smile.

"You take that and we're bound to get booted from USF sooner than we even anticipated. Besides, it's probably Palmer's favorite pet. I just heard our man enter the premises downstairs, so be a good girl, put it back and we'll make an entrance down the stairs. You in that dress, and every man will be gazing from afar. Come on, my princess."

Jessica set the porcelain piece back on the vanity and took Jonathan's arm as they strolled down the staircase. She looked over the railing at Palmer's silver gray head bobbing back and forth in the excitement of the evening. There were at least ten people standing around him in a circle of mock enlightenment. Jessica thought it looked really disgusting. "What am I doing here?" she thought.

Jessica continued ahead of Jonathan. The middle landing of the staircase was large enough to fit a bar, bartender and an array of people lulling about, drinks in hand, creating light conversation over the loud raucous chit–chat emanating from below.

Suddenly, a tall, dark–haired man emerged from behind the bartender and walked toward the last stair before the landing, stopping directly in front of Jessica. She stood and stared into his dark, luminous eyes. A large smile formed on his thick, sultry lips. His stare became one of lost enchantment.

"Hi, Jessica. It's been a long time. Do you remember me?" The tone of his voice was so deep that the floor seemed to vibrate from underneath her.

"Yes." This was the only word she allowed herself to utter.

"You are even more beautiful than I remember." He spoke in a language concealed to the outside world. He spoke thoughts that only Jessica could hear.

"Surely you haven't forgotten what it was like for us all those years ago?"

Jessica responded through thoughts meant only for him. "How could I forget? No one would dare forget about you, David."

A smile formed on his lips as he stood aside and offered his hand. She took it and stepped down onto the landing. Jonathan looked curiously at the man making such strong advances toward Jessica.

Jessica felt the vibrations of David's power over her. A wave of sexual electricity ran up her skirt like a bolt of lightning, strong and powerful, yet delicate and sweet. He wore a black silk shirt, his sleeves ballooned and drawn in at the wrists. His black hair was sleek, long and tied back in a ponytail at the nape of his neck. His hands were long and slender as he reached out to touch her arm.

Jessica almost fainted with the magnitude of feeling that came over her. It was beyond the sexual tension elicited on those occasions when a connection is made between male and female. It was a tryst between like kind and kin that made it so tantalizing. With this realization, Jessica felt the familiar fear of why she had tried so desperately to rid herself of the Taninsam name.

Jessica allowed her body to move closer to his, and when their bodies were almost touching, she turned away quickly, and bolted down the stairs onto the lower landing where she could be hidden, immersed between the guests. Jessica allowed herself one last look toward the upper landing, but David had disappeared. "Thank God," she thought.

Jonathan had passed Jessica during her encounter and come down the stairs to the lower landing before her. He was speaking shallow pleasantries to fellow doctors and their spouses when Jessica came up from behind and whispered in his ear, "Let's leave now."

Jonathan quickly excused himself and met Jessica at the same door they had just passed through moments before.

"Who was that on the stairs?" Jonathan couldn't resist asking about the curious man in black.

"An old...friend," Jessica responded with a feeling of disdain that she could not hide from her best friend.

*

It was not until two in the morning that Dr. Palmer Braxton said good night to the last of his guests. He decided to take a quick stroll along the water of Pablo Bay before retiring for bed. The party had gone exceptionally well with about a hundred guests, good food, good music and, most importantly, good conversation. Palmer thought it particularly good that so much government funding had been coming in for the university's embryonic stem cell research programs. There was definitely momentum in Washington D.C. for more money put into embryonic stem cells.

To Palmer, embryonic stem cell research was not a matter of ethics. It was a matter of good science. Palmer knew there were people out there suffering with ailments that could be cured if good science were allowed to prevail. He had been so frustrated when his efforts were threatened by all those right–wing nutcases who were trying to place a damper on his valuable research. To think all those religious wackos were actually trying to keep him from coming up with important cures for diseases. They were always making claims that adult stem cells produced hundreds of cures while embryonic stem cells produced none. They said adult stem cells were the ethical choice because embryonic stem cells meant killing babies.

"They're just cells, for God's sake!" Palmer thought to himself. "You want to stop good research over cells?"

Palmer had grown up with wealthy parents in Carmel, California. His father had been a publisher, his mother, a doctor, and his parents' careers had caused them both to spend most of their time away from home. Palmer had been raised as an only child partly because his parents had married late and partly because they believed that better birth control made for a better marriage. Palmer spent many days after school alone, save for the nanny, the maid, the cook and the gardener. He attended all private schools and had private tutors in order to keep up a perfect "A+" average.

After all of Palmer's preliminary education, he attended Berkley Medical School and eventually received his Ph.D. in Molecular Biology with a specialization in Human Genetics. He worked his way up the ladder to become head of the Genetics Department and Senior Research Analyst at his alma mater. Palmer eventually became the Director of the Institute for Human Genetics at the University of San Francisco and then head of the entire School of Medicine at USF. There were two reasons for these promotions: first, Palmer was considered one of the best in the area of stem cell research; and second, Palmer partnered with a researcher from the University of Wisconsin by the name of Thomas James who eventually became the first researcher in the United States to successfully remove embryonic stem cells from a human embryo in order to create embryonic stem cell lines.

In 1998, Thomas James and Palmer Braxton received patents for the technique they used to create and grow embryonic stem cell lines and on the embryonic stem cell lines they created. Under these patents, every researcher using embryonic stem cells in the United States was forced to pay a licensing fee. James and Braxton set up a foundation called, "JamBrax." Non–profits and universities were charged $5,000 to gain access to their embryonic stem cells and for–profits were charged $125,000. There was also an annual $40,000 maintenance fee for the cost of potential royalty payments if researchers produced anything which could turn a profit. James and Braxton also sold licensing fees to companies to develop products using embryonic stem cells. These fees were $200,000 to $2 million with clauses that one to five percent of royalties obtained must be given to them. In other words, JamBrax was created to take in as much money as possible and James and Braxton became very wealthy men quickly.

Even after Palmer's promotion to the prominent position of Director of the School of Medicine for USF, Palmer's pride and joy continued to be the Institute for Human Genetics at USF. He was also very content with the person he had hired to fill his position at the Institute. In fact, when Palmer was first introduced to Dr. Jessica Taninsam, he had been very impressed with her credentials, to say the least. Not only had her reputation at NYU and Columbia preceded her, her passion for cures in the field of stem cell research and human genetics had reminded him of his own. Palmer had been more than just instrumental in getting Jessica the position as director; he had made sure that USF hired Dr. Taninsam and only Dr. Taninsam, no matter the cost.

Palmer was fifty–three years old and unmarried. He had dated beautiful and powerful women throughout the years, but no one seemed worthy of becoming the wife of the prominent Dr. Palmer Braxton. Until now. There was another quality about Dr. Jessica Taninsam that had inspired Palmer to hire her as director besides her brilliance—he found her to be the most enticing woman he had ever laid eyes on in his lifetime. Quite frankly, she was the one for him.

That had been the one disappointment of the evening. Palmer had seen her enter his home, but he had not been able to utter one word to her before she had disappeared early in the evening with Dr. Jonathan Lee.

"Why had Dr. Lee ever been hired?" Palmer thought even though he knew that Jonathan was one of the premiere scientists in the field of genetics and stem cell research today. Palmer only wanted to think of Jonathan in the field of genetics. He didn't want to think of him in the field of competition for a woman's interest.

Palmer knew that Jonathan was certainly no match for what he had to offer Jessica. Jessica didn't even know about the work that he did with the Washington elites. After all, not only was he connected to some of the most powerful pro–choice politicians in D.C., he was also connected to the most powerful pro–choice lobbyist group today. Jessica didn't know that he worked for Parenting Services International as their premiere geneticist in the field of embryonic stem cell research, and they paid him like a king for his expert opinions.

"Jessica has no idea how powerful I have become," Palmer thought. "JamBrax and PSI have made the JamBrax Fountain of Youth Spa possible."

Palmer realized that this was probably the most valuable piece of information that Jessica did not know. He had created the JamBrax Fountain of Youth Spa in Barbados after years of dreaming of owning his own exclusive spa. The spa promoted vitality and beauty for anyone wealthy enough to spend a fortune on simple treatments believed to reverse the effects of aging on the body. This dream had been realized through his patents with James and his work for PSI.

"If Jessica knew this, she would surely be impressed," Palmer thought.

After another ten minutes, Palmer decided to turn around and head back to his house. He would need his rest for tomorrow. It was Sunday, but he decided that he would contact Jessica anyway. Palmer wanted to meet with her urgently about some very pressing news on his latest embryonic stem cell research grants. He smiled to himself as he made his way back to his mansion thinking about Jessica.

CHAPTER NINE

Archbishop Gabriel Sanders, Archbishop of San Francisco, did not rise to the level of bishop of one of the largest cities in the United States because he was an ambitious man. He rose because he was a man of the people who knew what it was like to face every kind of hardship God could give him. God had thrown him challenges like a sculptor who used a knife to carve out a saint's character.

Anyone who knew Archbishop Sanders didn't call him "Archbishop Sanders." They called him "Father Gabe" or even just "Gabe." That's what he liked best. Just Gabe. Gabe was short for Gabriel, the name given to him by his mother who raised him all by herself, a single, black mother living in New Orleans. She named him Gabriel after the great archangel, Saint Gabriel, the messenger angel who gave the Lord's mother the most important news the world would ever hear. When Gabe was a little boy, his mother told him that his name would give him the strength to overcome any obstacle.

Gabe remembered when his mother sat him on her lap and whispered these words of strength into his ears. "Mama named you Gabriel because it means 'strong one of God.' Remember that Jesus is the strength for our souls. Don't ever lose him, honey, don't ever lose Jesus. Because with Jesus, you can do anything."

Gabe's mother spoke these words when he was only five. At the time, he didn't know these would be her last words to him. She had been suffering from ovarian cancer and when she placed him on her lap, it was a thin, fragile body that he had sat upon. It was on a hospital bed that she laid, and it was there on that bed, on her frail lap, that he had heard those final words. The next day, his mother had passed on to the next life to remain in the loving arms of her Jesus for all eternity. This was how Gabe would always remember his mother, in the comfort of Jesus' loving arms.

When Gabe's mother passed away, he was left without any immediate family. His father, a professional saxophone player, had left town as soon as he learned that he would have to contend with the responsibility of rearing a child. Gabe's father assuaged his guilt by leaving a note under his mother's pillow before he left.

Instead of being thrown into foster care or an orphanage, Gabe was sent to live with one of his mother's closest relatives—an elderly priest who was parochial vicar of a local New Orleans parish. The parish was called "Our Lady of Victory," and that is exactly what it became to the many folk who came to worship there—a place of victory.

When Gabe turned eight, his maternal great uncle, Father Anthony John Reese, gave him the daily task of cleaning the inside of the church after school. Gabe took great pride in this responsibility. He knew the meaning of the Blessed Sacrament, he knew who existed within the Tabernacle, and he knew that when that candle was lit, he had better act like a young man who was in the presence of Jesus Christ, the son of God, himself.

Little Gabe attended grammar school until the eighth grade at Our Lady of Victory's Catholic School. In fact, it was the school's principal, Sister Mary Ann McLernon, who would make the biggest impression on him; it was Sister Mary Ann who would plant the seed that would grow into Gabe's eventual interest in the priesthood.

One day, Sister Mary Ann came in after school to pray and

found Gabe kneeling before the altar, his hands cupped around his face, his head lowered toward the floor. She came from behind and noticed his little shoulders shaking as if he might be crying. Sister Mary Ann passed him on the right and went to the altar of Mary to kneel and pray. She felt that Gabe needed his time and she might as well use it to pray for him. After a few moments, Gabe came over to Sister Mary Ann and knelt beside her. She could tell he was still upset; he was wiping tears from his cheeks.

Sister Mary Ann turned to Gabe. "You know, my mother passed away, too, when I was very young back in Ireland. Car accident. I was devastated at first, but then I realized I had another mother who loved me very much—Mary. In a special way, Mary is everyone's mother. And you know what, Gabriel? In an even more special way, she is your mother. You see, Mary speaks to me, and she told me that she is watching out for you, Gabriel. You are a special son to her. Just pray to Mary and she will show you the way."

Sister Mary Ann quietly left the church. From that day forward, Gabe said special prayers to his new mother, Mary, every day in the Church of Our Lady of Victory.

Gabe played sports, too, every day after school when his chores around the church were done. By far, his favorite sport was football, and he was very good at the game. It was a community sport for children who attended Our Lady of Victory School and the local public school.

One day at age twelve, Gabe noticed that some of the public school kids were making fun of him at practice. They were calling him names.

He walked up to one of them. "Hey, what's up with the name calling?"

"Listen, we don't know one black kid who goes to your church. Every kid we know goes to our church—the Baptist one on the corner. We think you want to be white and that's why you go to a white church!"

"I don't want to be white!" Gabe responded. "I'm proud to be black! You know what else? I don't think Jesus cares what color we are!" Gabe stormed off the field and ran to the rectory. There were tears streaming down his face.

Father Anthony was sitting in the dining room. He had just finished dinner, and he saw Gabe run up to his room. Father Anthony followed him up and knocked on his door. "Gabe, you all right?" he asked.

The door opened and Gabe stood before the fatherly priest looking at the ground. "The other kids said I belong to a white church...that I don't like being black."

"What did you say?"

"I said Jesus doesn't care what color you are."

Father Anthony smiled. "Good answer. Come on and sit down. I want to tell you a story."

Father Anthony led Gabe over to a small desk in the corner of the room. Gabe used the desk to do his homework, and there was a window seat next to it. Father Anthony pulled out the chair for Gabe, and he sat on the window seat.

"I want to tell you a story about your mother," Father Anthony began. "Did you ever meet your grandparents—your mother's mother and father?"

Gabe shook his head.

Father Anthony continued, "No, I suppose you would have come along after they were already gone. Well, your maternal grandmother, my sister, was a white woman and your maternal grandfather was a black man. So, your mama was a mix of both black and white. Well, your grandparents loved one another very much. Turns out, your grandmother was Catholic, but your grandfather never felt comfortable going to her church. You see, in those days the church she went to was very white and people didn't make your grandfather feel comfortable attending a 'white' church. That was before the civil rights movement changed everything. People like the late Reverend Dr. Martin Luther King made it so people could feel proud of whatever color God made them. Understand?"

Gabe nodded.

"Now, your grandmother loved your grandfather so much, she married him outside the church, but they raised your mama Catholic inside their home. I was lucky enough to baptize her. It was the first baptism I did when I became a priest. One of the best days of my life, too, because it proved exactly what you said to those other kids just now—that Jesus loves everybody the same. You know something else, Gabe? The word Catholic? It means universal. It means for everybody. Your mama was raised Catholic and she wanted the same for you. Your mama looked at her faith as a gift and she loved you with everything she had."

Gabe got up from his chair to give Father Anthony a hug. "Thank you, Father. Thank you."

Father Anthony stepped away from the window seat and moved to the door. He turned toward Gabe with a wry smile on his Italian face. "Besides, I've always known that Jesus was a black man."

By the time Gabe hit high school, he knew he was being called to the priesthood. He attended Holy Cross High School and played quarterback for the Tigers. After graduation, Gabe spent his first four years of college at Saint Joseph's Seminary, and graduated from Notre Dame Seminary's Graduate School of Theology in 1979. He was ordained that May. Father Anthony and Sister Mary Ann were at the ordination, and Father Anthony had wept like a baby at the sight of Gabe lying prostrate on the altar of the cathedral. He was more proud of Gabe than a father could be proud of his own son. This was the beginning of the fast tracking.

Gabe was only 26 when he became a priest, and he was a brilliant student. Young priests who are gifted with intelligence and communication skills are generally fast tracked to Rome. Father Gabriel earned a licentiate in theology from the Pontifical Gregorian University, and a doctorate summa cum laude in systematic theology, also from the Gregorian, by age 30. Father

Gabe worked at the apostolic nunciature, served on the faculty at Immaculate Conception Seminary in Newark, New Jersey, and was rector at the North American College for seven years. He returned to the Archdiocese of Newark as auxiliary bishop in June of 2000 and was appointed archbishop of the same diocese a year later. Eight years later, Father Gabe was appointed archbishop of the diocese of San Francisco.

Archbishop Gabriel Sanders became a member of the Committee on Ecumenism and Social Relations and the Subcommittee on the Church in Africa for the United States Conference of Catholic Bishops. He was also chairman of the board of directors of Catholic Relief Services, and served as a consultant to the Committee on International Justice and Peace. Archbishop Sanders was a very reputable and distinguished representative of the Catholic Church, and he knew how to shepherd his flock as a man of the people. He liked to be called Father Gabe, not Archbishop Sanders, because he wanted people to know that he cared about them and loved them not as an authority figure, but as a friend and father. In fact, people who knew Father Gabe knew that he could be called upon at any hour of the day or night.

Father Gabe had a fantastic sense of humor, and he was probably one of the only archbishops of the Catholic Church who had earned the respect of the media, even though his viewpoints on certain subjects were completely opposite of the viewpoints of the reporters. A month after Father Gabe was first installed as the new Archbishop of San Francisco, a press conference was held outside Saint Mary's Cathedral. Saint Mary's was the first cathedral constructed in the United States after Vatican II. It was beautiful, contemporary and stood as a beacon against the blue California skies. Father Gabe stood behind a podium directly in front of the cathedral taking questions.

The first reporter began his question by addressing Father Gabe as Archbishop Sanders and was quickly corrected before he could finish. "Archbishop Sanders…"

"No, please, I'd rather be called Father Gabriel. You see, I have the highest respect for the diocese of San Francisco and my position as archbishop, but if I were to address myself or have anyone else address me as anything but a humble servant of God, it just wouldn't seem true to who I really am. I am first and foremost a priest. And as such, I am here to serve the Catholic community as well as anyone else in this great city who finds themselves in need of help. Just look at me as someone who truly strives to live everyday of life as the good Samaritan—I don't always succeed— God only knows, I don't always succeed—but my goal is to be here for you."

When Father Gabe stepped away from the podium to get a drink of water, there was a thunderous applause from the large audience gathered to hear him speak.

The reporter continued, "Nice to meet you, Father Gabriel. I'm Mike Daly."

"Hi, Mike."

"Yes, well, I just wanted to ask what you plan to do first as Archbishop of San Francisco."

"I know one of my first plans is to visit the Ghirardelli Chocolate Factory by the wharf. I'm a big chocolate lover!"

There was a wave of laughter from both the reporters and the audience of onlookers who appeared to multiply every minute.

"No, seriously, Mike," Father Gabe continued. "As you are probably aware, there are too many people in this great city without a place to live, without enough to eat, and without a job to pay for their livelihoods. I hope to work with the mayor and other churches, synagogues and mosques in the area to help provide more shelters and more affordable housing."

After the initial question was answered, a mob of reporters raised their hands at once and Father Gabe stood at the podium fielding questions for the next hour.

Toward the end of the hour, a female reporter in the front row raised her hand. Father Gabe pointed to her. "Yes?"

"Good morning, Father Gabe. I'm Melissa Morgan. CBS News."

"Good morning...may I call you Melissa?"

"Absolutely!"

"Hello, Melissa!" Father Gabe appeared so jovial that every face in the crowd seemed astonished and delighted.

Melissa began her question, "Father Gabe, for some time now the Catholic Church has been unsupportive of stem cell research..."

Father Gabe interrupted, "That's embryonic stem cell research. The Church is absolutely in favor of adult stem cell research."

"Yes. The Church has been unsupportive of embryonic stem cell research. With all of the recent government support of this crucial research, do you feel that the Catholic Church is behind the times?"

"No, and let me stress that emphatically. No. Melissa, let me tell you why I say, 'No.' When I say the end never justifies the means, you know exactly what I mean, right?"

Melissa rolled her eyes in disbelief, but replied back with an unsure, "Right."

Father Gabe continued, "Right. Now let's take this a step further. Do you believe in God, Melissa?"

"Yes! Absolutely!"

"Good. Very good. And would you say that God might be up there right now watching this press conference?"

Melissa looked around her wondering if she were still supposed to be answering Father Gabe's questions. She looked back at Father Gabe and nodded her head. "I think it makes sense that God is up there right now, yes."

"And would you even say that God has control over things that happen to plants and animals and people?"

"Yes, I would say that God has control, but God gave us intelligence for a reason, right? He gave us the means to have brilliant scientists who have done great research and have given us cures for so many horrible diseases."

"That is correct, Melissa. You are a wonderful reporter with a good sense of the world around you."

Father Gabe looked out across the masses of people who had gathered to listen to him speak. He continued, "Gracious people before me, what I am about to say next is very important. God did gift us, we human beings, with reason and intelligence, but God also gave us free will. And with that free will, he gave us a conscience, the ability to know good from evil, right from wrong. The great and Blessed Pope John Paul II once said that science and religion are joined together, hand in hand. He was right, too! With only one, you cannot have the other, and with the other, you cannot have the one! Yes, there is a God, and He is saying right now, 'If you destroy my little ones, I will give you nothing, but if you do not destroy my little ones, I will give you everything.' You see? Don't you think there is a reason that there have been no cures using embryonic stem cells? Don't you think there is a reason that there have been over one hundred cures using adult stem cells? God is in the balance, my good people! God is in the balance, and He is making sure that His will be done!"

When there was only time for one more question, a reporter in the back raised his hand. He was careful to phrase the last question in as delicate a way as possible. He began, "Father Gabe..."

"Hi, Mr.?" Father Gabe liked to get to know each reporter by name.

"Mr. Thomas. ABC News."

"Hello, Mr. Thomas, ABC News."

"Hello, Father. There have been numerous reports of bishops who deny communion to politicians who are pro–choice. Do you plan on denying communion to these politicians, too?"

"Good question, Mr. Thomas. And a direct question deserves a direct response. No. Now you might ask yourself, 'What does he mean, no?' Well, let me tell you what 'no' means. No means that there could be a politician out there who believes that abortion should be a legal and personal choice. That same politician could try to hide behind words like, 'I would never tell a woman how to live her life, but I certainly wouldn't choose that for my wife or daughter.' Then, you know what? That same politician could wake up one morning and have a complete metanoia, a complete change of heart. That same politician could go to his or her priest down the street and confess the sin of supporting abortion and be absolved of that sin right on the spot. That same politician could come to me for communion that very same day, and I would have been right to give that politician communion because that politician would have had a change of heart. You see, Mr. Thomas, it is not up to us to judge others. It is up to us to allow others to have a chance at a change of heart."

Father Gabe stepped back from the podium once more. He was waiting for the next question, but there didn't appear to be any more. He was about to thank the media for their time, when a woman with long gray hair bolted forward from the crowd.

She was within a foot of Father Gabe's podium and she was looking up at him with a hatred he had never seen before. Suddenly, she began to shout, "You priests are all the same! You don't know anything about women's problems! When was the last time you were pregnant and had to bear the burden of an unwanted child? When was the last time you had to deal with the pain of a husband's abuse? You have no right to tell me what to do with my body! It's mine and no one else's!"

Father Gabe stepped forward once again to the mic. "What is your name?"

The woman looked surprised that Father Gabe had taken an interest in her name, but replied, "None of your damn business!"

"No, with all due respect, it is my business. My business is people, and I love people. But I can't stand here and say that I only love certain people. That's not right. Jesus never said, 'I only love certain people.' Jesus loved all people. Even the ones who persecuted him and put him to his death. That's right. Jesus loved all people, even the little ones who have yet to be born."

The woman stormed off and disappeared from Father Gabe's view.

He stepped forward into the microphone one last time. "Thank you all for taking the time to welcome me into my new home! God bless you!"

Little by little, a trickle of applause began to emerge from the audience. Soon, all were applauding the new Archbishop of San Francisco, even the perplexed reporters.

*

The next day, Archbishop Sanders unpacked the last boxes in his office. He was a lover of books, and had already filled two tall bookshelves with writing on every subject imaginable: philosophy, theology, science, art and literature. There were only two boxes left. He opened the first and took out his complete works of Shakespeare, one of his favorites. This book was so large, he had not packed any other book with it. He placed it on a shelf alongside a book of poetry by Robert Frost and another by Maya Angelou.

"Ah, one left," Father Gabe exclaimed out loud. He picked up the last box and opened the cover. Father Gabe turned completely ashen when he saw what was in the box. The dead body of a large rat lay inside. Its eyes were glossed over and its mouth was set in a perpetual snarl exposing pointy white teeth with fangs. Father Gabe looked closer and noticed a white note lying underneath the rat's body. He pulled the note out from underneath the pathetic creature and read the following message written in a typed font:

"We who make the Citizenship Revolution...WILL NEVER ALLOW infiltrated agents from the extreme right, like yourself, to block our path. Remember that accidents happen, remember that accidental deaths occur daily. DO NOT CONTINUE YOUR ANTI–WOMAN CAMPAIGN...death to traitors, death to those who oppose the nation, DEATH OR REVOLUTION."

Father Gabe took the note and placed it back in the box with the dead rat. He covered the box and walked calmly over to the telephone at his desk. Father Gabe picked up the receiver and dialed the San Francisco Police Department.

CHAPTER TEN

David Bloodstone had watched the entire press conference of Archbishop Gabriel Sanders on television. He had traveled to San Francisco to see Jessica, but he figured he might as well remain in town for a few extra days to enjoy the scenery. He was staying at the Palace Hotel in downtown San Francisco, and had enjoyed an evening at the symphony the night before. Now, he was innocently flipping through various news channels and had come upon this freak show.

At first, David had liked and respected this new San Francisco Archbishop, this Father Gabriel, but the last two questions he answered were unbearable. How could this priest, this celibate, this eunuch, have any opinion on the validity of a woman's right to choose? David looked at Father Gabriel with disgust. He turned the television off and threw his slipper at the screen.

The stakes were getting higher lately. David did not like the way the tide was turning. He did not like the way these people were taking in the words of this priest. Yes, the man did appear to be credible. Yes, the man even appeared to be likeable, but he was a priest. What did this man know of the ways of the world?

This priest was probably some disgusting eunuch, born without male anatomy. Or he was one of those priests who did terrible things to little boys in back rooms of churches. David's anger turned into mocking laughter. What was he worried about? The Catholic Church was a thing of the past. No one trusted priests or bishops anymore. They were all horrible eunichs or pedophiles costing the church millions in litigation. The church was being obliterated right before David's eyes. He did not have to worry about doing anything at all.

David walked to the window of the sliding glass door. Was he worried? Were people beginning to trust priests again? With someone like this Gabriel character, people might begin to trust again and David could not have that. David realized this was the time to intervene. He would show this archbishop, this priest, just exactly who was boss. David was a man of power who had many influential people at his disposal to do his bidding: politicians, judges, lawyers, actors, entertainers…he had them all, and he would do whatever was necessary to make sure people knew who was in charge.

God? Please. People did not believe in God anymore, not a God who made life inconvenient for them, not a God who took life's pleasures away. People wanted a God who loved them and told them that the most important things in life were the things that made them feel good. After all, people had a right to feel good.

"Ha! Ha!" David laughed aloud. All he had to do was continue to make sure that his players were lined up exactly where he wanted them. He slid the glass door wide open to get some fresh air.

David suddenly stopped when the door was half open. A final thought took hold of him that he could not get out of his mind, and this realization scared him more than any priest or bishop. A week ago, David had sensed the blinding light coming from the terrace of the suite in Wisconsin. He had let go of his blonde prey and reeled around to find him, a man who appeared familiar, but someone he had not met before. The man had appeared almost regal; the light coming from everywhere, behind him, inside of him, and around him. David had felt his power weaken. There was nothing he could do but disappear from sight.

Was he, David Bloodstone, afraid of this spiritual being? No, he would not allow himself to feel fear. He was, after all, the master of this world, and no priest, bishop or gleamy–eyed Christ figure was going to take this away from him.

David regained his composure and showered and dressed. He looked into the mirror and realized how ridiculous he had been to worry. "Everything is under control," he said to his reflection.

David picked up his cell phone and made a call to the woman who knew him best, the woman who would put his mind at ease, the woman who would make him feel like a man again. He punched in her number and waited for her familiar voice to pick up.

"Hello?" The voice on the other end of the line was smooth and sultry.

"Elaina. I need to see you."

"Now?"

"Now."

David ended his call and left the hotel room.

*

Dr. Bernard Lanton called Elaina Taninsam from a pay phone in a local diner in Fort Lee, New Jersey. He didn't want anyone tapping his phone. He had been staying at a Red Roof Inn on Interstate 4 for the past two weeks, and he just couldn't stand it any longer. He was sick of hiding. Cassy had found the note, and he had acted quickly. After all, Elaina had wanted her daughter dead. Dr. Lanton had tried to kill her, but she hadn't drunk enough of the champagne. She hadn't consumed enough of the poison. Cassy had gone into a coma and he didn't know if she were dead or alive, but he figured a coma was close enough to dead. Besides, he was the one with the information and he had a pretty good case against

Elaina and her multi–billion dollar empire.

"Elaina Taninsam speaking." Elaina's voice sounded more harsh than normal.

"Elaina, Dr. Bernard Lanton." He was so nervous, he was sweating from the palms of his hands onto the dirty pay phone receiver.

"Yes, Dr. Lanton?"

Lanton knew he wouldn't get any information on Cassy's condition from Elaina. "Elaina, I'm sure…uh…I'm sure that news on Cassandra has reached you?"

"Yes, Dr. Lanton, and I thought we had an arrangement regarding Cassandra."

Lanton knew instantly that Cassy must still be alive. "Yes, well, no professional in the area of medicine would consider Cassy able to render any evidence against anyone in her current vegetative condition."

"Dr. Lanton, if I were to look up the word, 'dead,' I'm sure that it would say not breathing!"

"Elaina, I have not been able to return to my office for the past two weeks. Incapacitated by coma or incapacitated by death, I expect to be compensated as promised."

"Dr. Lanton, if I receive a call informing me that Cassandra has passed, I will gladly compensate you. Until then, I wish you good luck."

"Well then, Elaina, I take it you don't care if I contact the media about the information I have on the origin of Parenting Services International?"

"Is that a threat, Dr. Lanton?"

"If I were speaking to you from Aruba with a Piña Colada in my hand, no, that would not be considered a threat. But in the context of my current desperate situation, the situation you have put me in, yes, I would take that as a threat."

"Dr. Lanton, as I have already stated, I would be more than happy to compensate you if the job had been done."

"Elaina, I know who David is…"

There was a long pause before Elaina spoke again. "Excuse me?" she asked incredulously.

"I know who David is." Lanton repeated this information as if he had the upper hand in a poker game.

There was another pause and then Lanton heard a click on the other end of the phone with a loud dial tone. "Shit," was all he said as he hung up the dirty receiver and made his way back to the Red Roof Inn.

On the other end of the line, Elaina sat at her glamorous mahogany desk staring at the gold–plated receiver of her antique phone. She hung up and sat back in her chair with an evil smile.

"Good bye, Dr. Lanton," she said. "Not very intelligent for a doctor."

*

Drew sat by Cassy's bedside. She had been in a coma for two weeks and the doctors were concerned. Her vital signs appeared normal, but her mind was not regaining consciousness. Drew was beyond worry. He had spent the first night in such agony, it was as if the ground beneath him might give way, that he might slip into an abyss of nothingness. He did not know how to go on without the woman he loved. Drew had lost almost ten pounds in two weeks. He barely ate. He barely slept. All he knew was his music. Drew continued his work with the symphony. This is what kept him alive. His music. When he was not working, Drew was at the hospital, next to his beloved wife.

Drew was completely unaware of the other life, the spiritual life that Cassy was leading while her body lay on the bedside next to him. He did not know that Cassy's mind was entirely active as he held her hand in his. Drew gazed at his beautiful wife's face, and did not know that she now had a sense of happiness that he could not begin to understand.

Cassy had been introduced to spiritual travel by Paolo. He had taken Cassy with him on more than one occasion within the past two weeks in order to put her mind at ease regarding the well being of her sister, Debbie, and her Aunt Jessica. She had been to the Milwaukee Psychiatric Institute to visit her sister, and she had been to the University of San Francisco to visit her aunt, but it had been her spiritual body making the journeys while her physical body remained in the hospital.

Paolo explained that this was a form of bi–location, or the ability to travel to a different location spiritually while the physical body remains in its original location. Paolo communicated much to her about the spiritual world in these last two weeks. He told Cassy there was much work to be done to overcome the power of the evil bloodstone. He told her that she, Debbie and Jessica would become very instrumental in the destruction of the curse. Paolo would come to Cassy in her dreams and teach her everything she needed to know, so that she would be ready when she woke from her coma.

"When will I wake?" she asked Paolo on the way back from their journey to San Francisco.

"When you have received all of the necessary information to defeat the evil of the bloodstone."

"How long?"

"I cannot answer in time because time no longer matters."

"Why?"

"Time no longer matters because you now exist in a state of timelessness, in a state of potential eternity."

"Potential eternity?"

"Yes, the possibility of that time before time was created."

"Created by whom?"

"The Creator who gave up everything for love." Paolo took Cassy's hand and lead her to a barren field. "Come, I'll show you."

*

Cassy found herself high up on a cross. Her arms were stretched out wide, her wrists tied to a horizontal board, and her hands pierced by the long nails that were driven through her palms into the dense wood. She could barely hold up the weight of her head and tried to push herself up with her feet, but noticed that her ankles were tied together and pierced through by an even longer nail that went through both feet one on top of the other into the vertical piece of wood at the bottom. The pain was more than she could bear and when she looked to her right, there was a man with long, dark hair and a dark beard hanging on a similar cross. She noticed that further to her right, beyond this man was Paolo, also hanging on a cross. The man in the center was looking up to the clouds overhead and speaking to them in a hushed whisper. He was speaking a foreign language, but Cassy was able to understand his words.

"My God. My God. Why have you abandoned me?"

He continued, but Cassy could no longer hear him. She found herself on the ground at the foot of his cross. She was standing next to Paolo, and another man who was young and handsome. Next to him, were two women, a young woman with long hair past her hips and an older woman who had covered her hair with a veil. Both women were crying and holding one another for support.

The man hanging from the center cross spoke again, "Father, forgive them for they know not what they do." He appeared to be in horrible agony and when it seemed he took his last breath, Cassy heard him declare, "It is accomplished!" She noticed his head fall to his shoulder and his chest became still.

Both women continued to sob, and Cassy wished there was something she could do to comfort them. The young man with Paolo was also crying, and Paolo looked toward Cassy with a tear flowing down his cheek. He was in terrible grief. Suddenly, it occurred to Cassy that this man who had just died was no mere human; this man was the son of God, himself. He was there above

Cassy, dehumanized and crucified up on that cross. "My Lord." The words escaped Cassy's lips without thought.

A soldier came from behind Cassy dressed in Roman armor. A long sword hung from his side. Paolo and Cassy watched as the soldier took the sword and lanced the dead man's side. Cassy witnessed the blood and water, which poured out from the divine wound of the man on the cross. She was struck by the blood flowing from his side. Cassy witnessed his blood fall to the ground without anyone's hastening to gather it up. She noticed that even the ground itself seemed resolved to remain in spirit at the foot of the cross in order to receive the divine dew.

From the wound on his heavenly side, the droplets of blood and water combined and formed pools of a red mixture that fell to the ground below. Cassy saw that the ground was not entirely brown, but that there appeared to be a gleam of green that was interspersed among the brown dirt. The droplets of red were not just mixing into the earth, but were forming little pools on top of the green rock.

Cassy gently tugged at Paolo's hand and led him to the area behind the cross where the blood had fallen on the green rock. As she came closer, she noticed that the mixture of blood and water was not falling on ordinary rock. It was falling on what looked like jasper, a type of rock that shown brilliant and green. The mixture was falling on jasper, and it was not merely sliding off. Cassy could see that the blood mixture was penetrating the jasper. It was forcing itself inside the green rock and forming a new rock that appeared green with little droplets of red inside it. It had formed itself into what looked to be…bloodstone. Bloodstone. Cassy's heart skipped a beat.

She looked up at Paolo, and she felt her eyes swell with tears. One large tear trickled down the side of her face. Had the blood of this man created the bloodstone? Had the curse of the bloodstone originated here? She had to find out who this God–man was immediately.

Cassy squeezed Paolo's hand, and he nodded to her. She felt herself suddenly transported. In the midst of the journey back, she could not wait to have her question answered. "Who was he?" she asked.

Paolo smiled. "The alpha, the omega. The beginning, the end. The Christ, the Son of God. The Savior of the world."

Cassy could not believe what she had just heard. "But how could the bloodstone formed from the blood of the Son of God, someone so holy, be used for such great evil in the future? Did someone evil steal it and use it for his own?" she asked.

Paolo shook his head. "This was not the only bloodstone formed from jasper stone. There was also an evil, counterfeit bloodstone formed from the blood of Satan."

CHAPTER ELEVEN

In 1942, Elaina Taninsam's grandmother, Alexandria, founded Parenting Services International or PSI. Alexandria was a brilliant woman and knew exactly what kind of business façade she would need to create in order to hide the truth of the Taninsam family name. She hid the truth of her family background and the power of the bloodstone behind the marketing brilliance of PSI. She hid the truth of a heritage of witches that had spanned for generations. She hid the reality that without PSI, the Taninsam family would become all but extinct.

Alexandria devoted her entire life to what she called her cause: the international birth control movement through the creation of PSI. She knew that through birth control there would be abortion, and the killing of the innocent was exactly what she needed to fulfill her plan. Alexandria fought the American Judicial System and Christian traditions in her successful effort to strike down laws forbidding the distribution of contraceptive devices and information. As president of the American Birth Control Organization, she became editor of the, "Women's Birth Control Review." Alexandria's drive came from her determination to spread a new ethic where social and economic situations were determined by the inherited ability to survive.

Alexandria was born in New York City in 1879 to parents who were considered ahead of the times. They were both freethinkers and were proud to call themselves atheists. Alexandria had two older sisters: Athena and Annesca. The three girls were raised in an environment where nature was the dominant life force and men and women were subservient to the earth, which was regarded as one living organism called Gaia. The Taninsam family practiced goddess worship, and the female biological functions were accorded the most respected role. The Taninsam heritage was one in which a matriarchal society dominated.

Within the Taninsam family, women were regarded as superior to men because all spiritual worship came from the covenant of the Goddess. All living things were of equal value and humans had no special place. Human beings were not made in God's image. They possessed divine power from within themselves and they considered themselves to be gods or goddesses in their own right. The Taninsam family's personal power was unlimited by any deity, and consciousness could be altered through the practice of rite and ritual.

At a young age, Alexandria became interested in the field of eugenics, and she began to study Darwin's theory of the survival of the fittest. She theorized that nature was thrown out of balance by keeping people artificially alive who would long ago have been eliminated by natural selection. Alexandria concluded that those who should have been eliminated lived in slums and were breeding like rabbits because of their animalistic nature. She thought that they would soon overrun the boundaries of their slum and contaminate the better elements of society with disease and inferior genes.

Alexandria began to connect eugenics to birth control. Social engineers of the times were afraid that birth control would be used by the wrong people, noting that the average number of children of Harvard graduates was either one or none at all. Alexandria began to create famous slogans for the birth control movement like:

"More children from the fit, less from the unfit—that is the chief aim of birth control," and "Birth Control: to create a race of thoroughbreds." She realized that birth control was a mechanism used by social elitists to keep the lower echelons of society from reproducing.

In Alexandria's "Women's Birth Control Review," there were numerous writings by the world's most renowned and respected eugenicists—including scientists, physicians, and psychologists. In fact, a personal friend of Alexandria's, Dr. Langford Wallace, wrote several books with blatant racist statements against blacks and other minorities, and even went so far as to express his admiration for the Germans' method of cleaning up their race problems by sterilizing those who were unfit to produce children.

In 1914, Alexandria married a man from a wealthy family, but after ten years of playing housewife and giving birth to their three daughters Madelena, Isabella and Beatrice, the marriage dissolved. Alexandria felt that marriage was merely a means for women to be contained. She believed that individual sexual satisfaction, not law or tradition, could make marriage holy, and that marriages that were not sexually satisfying for the woman should end in divorce.

In 1924, Alexandria remarried the president of a major American oil company. The marriage changed the thrust of the birth control movement because Alexandria's considerable wealth made her the premier leader of a movement of white, native–born Americans with considerable income and education. Alexandria's "Women's Birth Control Review" featured an article by a doctor and professor of Human Genetics and Eugenics entitled, "Eugenic Sterilization: An Urgent Need." In this article, people from "bad stock" needed birth control and "well–endowed stocks" needed to increase their birth–rate.

In Alexandria's guidelines to rid the world of the inferior race, she provided pamphlets on contraception and abortifacients. If contraception should fail, women could rely on abortion, which was the ultimate goal of Alexandria's creation of PSI. When the world realized the logical consequences of Hitler's heredity–eugenic totalitarian type of government, her birth control movement had to take a step away from eugenical language. Eugenics, under the Nazis, had justified wholesale sexual sterilization and euthanasia for the allegedly unfit and provided the justification for the slaughter of six million Jews. Alexandria and the leaders of the American Birth Control Movement realized if they were going to succeed as social engineers, birth control had to be billed in a more subtle, democratic manner if it were to eliminate human waste.

Alexandria decided the best way to communicate birth control was to remind society of the high cost and tremendous burden of supporting the dependent. She worked to advance the acceptability of abortion by pointing out how much more expensive the welfare costs were compared to the cost of abortion. Alexandria saw birth control and abortion as the best way to eliminate human suffering. She knew she had most of America on her side if she could market her idea of abortion as a business and perhaps even a tax–paid business.

Alexandria's youngest daughter, Madelena, Elaina's mother, carried forward the ideals of the business in the early part of the 1950s. Madelena gave birth to three daughters: Marian, Martha and Elaina. She was a brilliant marketing strategist who brought PSI from a societal necessity to help the poor to a social norm to liberate women. Madelena became president of the Women's National Organization when the sexual revolution hit in the 1960s. She was instrumental in pointing the way to a new morality in which sexual expression and human development would not be in conflict with contemporary society. Madelena challenged the morality of religions where moralists preached abstinence and self–denial. She described these types of moralists as fiends who wanted to stamp their morality on the tensed bodies of men and women who had to suppress their natural sexual impulses. Madelena pointed out that the sex instinct was too strong to be bound by the dictates of the church.

Elaina took over the responsibilities of PSI in the late 1970s. She continued the work of her grandmother and mother flawlessly by championing the cause of liberation for women and their reproductive rights, as well as educating the American culture and abroad of the peril of population growth and world hunger. Elaina knew that if she continued the culture of hedonism and the importance of self, her business of providing abortion on demand would grow. She began programs for sex education among teenagers because she knew that the more rampant the sex among the young, the more rampant the need for abortion. Elaina's empire grew and PSI became a multi–billion dollar industry. No one outside of the Taninsam family knew the truth of this well constructed, multi–generational façade. No one. Elaina even managed to keep this information hidden from her own daughters.

*

Elaina sat in her office, a luxuriously decorated room with Persian rugs laid on a great oak floor. There were floor to ceiling book shelves stuffed with beautifully ornate books that had never been opened, but enhanced the room by adding a hint of the intellectual to her otherwise lavish and excessive tastes. Elaina sat behind a grand mahogany desk in the corner of the room.

Elaina was a very beautiful woman. She had shoulder length, ashen blonde hair and her makeup was always done to perfection. Elaina wore very glamorous and expensive suits with heels that gave her tall frame a sizeable boost. Today, the suit was silver and she complemented it with a white silk blouse that had the same silver piping along the sleeves and neckline. The blouse hung low and exposed her ample cleavage, which she was proud to flaunt since her breasts had been redone twice.

Elaina was unmarried and she lived alone. She had two butlers, one gardener, four maids, one cook, one trainer and two secretaries, but she lived "alone." Elaina relished her independence. She thrived on it and did not need a husband telling her what to do, nor a child burdening her with the unnecessary stresses of motherhood. Occasionally, Elaina thought of Samuel, her late husband, and Cassandra and Deborah, her lost daughters. But not today. Today, she was in a very good mood, and she did not want any thoughts of the past to tamper with her optimism.

Elaina heard a knock on her office door. "Come in," she answered.

The door opened and her butler appeared. "Mr. Bloodstone to see you, Madame."

"Yes, thank you Joseph. Have him come in."

Joseph turned to the side and held out his arm for David to enter. David walked quickly and confidently to Elaina's desk. She stood and held out her right hand. David grasped her hand and bent down to kiss it.

"That will be all, Joseph. Thank you," Elaina said.

Joseph stepped out and closed the door behind him.

"David, it has been too long, my darling. How have you been?" Elaina motioned for David to follow her to a burgundy leather couch between two tall windows with sheer, white flowing curtains. They sat down together on the couch holding hands.

David looked away from Elaina before he answered. "I am not well, darling. Not well. I have stresses and grievances that you cannot begin to imagine," he said with self–pity.

"David, let me set your mind at ease. Everything is going our way. I was just on the phone with Jack Green, our marketing director, and he has just confirmed exactly what we had hoped. The President's new healthcare plan ensures that tax dollars go to fund abortions. The United Nations ensures that women all over the world have access to abortions. You see, David, all of our carefully laid plans are in place. Every day there are more and more abortions, and every single woman thinks this is in her own best interest. That's the beauty! We have women across the globe behind us! We have all of the most influential people in the world behind us!" Elaina exclaimed with a grand smile.

David relaxed and sat back on the couch with his legs crossed. "You see, my darling, this is why I visit you whenever I feel low. You are truly the single most important person in my life. Let me put it to you straight. While in San Francisco, I witnessed a new Catholic bishop speaking to the media outside his cathedral. This man, this bishop, was very convincing about the importance of what he called, 'the culture of life.' In fact, it looked like he might even have some influence over young people."

"Oh please, David," Elaina replied smugly. "You know as well as I do how successful our U.N. Youth Conferences have been. Young people want sex. That's it, and they don't care how they get it. That means more accidental pregnancies and more abortions."

"I know, Elaina, but this bishop did seem somewhat convincing. And...there have been other issues. These issues may be far worse. Issues that do not have so much to do with this world, but the next."

"What do you mean?"

"I've had a run in with someone...someone who appeared to have very strong powers."

Elaina's face turned ashen as she stood up. "Who do you mean?"

"I have no idea. I was with a woman, a young, meaningless woman, and I was trying to do away with her. That is my nature, Elaina. It can't be helped. I was in the process of disposing of her when this man, this figure, came from nowhere and stripped me of my power. I felt as though I could not move, so I fled and haven't seen him since."

Elaina sat back on the couch close to David. "Perhaps you were just feeling tired and only thought you had become powerless." She took David's hands in hers and looked intently into his eyes. "Perhaps you were only imagining this ridiculous figure." She smiled cunningly.

Elaina's look was mesmerizing, and David was instantly caught up in her. David took her in his arms and kissed her passionately over her face and neck. They were interrupted by the phone on her desk.

Elaina pulled herself from David and walked over to her desk. "Hello?"

"Elaina, it's Dawn." Dawn Adams was in charge of media relations for PSI. "I have some news. It seems that they are getting ready to close another one of our facilities in Jackson, Mississippi, and another in Montgomery, Alabama. There's been a group of those anti–choice protestors out again with their graphic and offensive inflammatory signs. You know, the ones that call themselves something like, '40 days for life,' or something. They are doing tremendous harm to our business! Elaina, what do I do about this?"

Elaina sat back down at her desk. She looked over toward David who sat motionless on the couch. Elaina responded to Dawn without taking her eyes off David. "Dawn, don't worry. This is just a drop in the bucket. I'll think of something and call you back. Meanwhile, just keep a level head and do not let any of this go to press until you hear from me."

Elaina hung up the phone. "You may be more right about that grassroots' problem than I first thought," she said to David. "Two more of our facilities just closed in the South. I also know that we are facing various lawsuits across the country—some for unsterile facility conditions, one for wrongful death, one for failure to report signs of sexual abuse, and one for failure to report the rape of a minor."

David stood up with such hostility that Elaina had to catch her breath. He walked to her desk and screamed, "What?!? You told me that everything was moving along perfectly and going our way! You worthless whore!"

Elaina had never seen David this angry. She braced herself with her hands on the side of her desk. David's face turned red as the pupils of his eyes began to enlarge. As David's eyes turned yellow, Elaina watched in horror as he began to resemble a wolf hunting its prey. When he opened his mouth, David's bicuspid teeth had grown long and pointed like the fangs of a vampire.

When David spoke, his words vibrated off the ceiling like a low, guttural growl. "You are destroying this operation, Elaina! You are destroying everything we have worked so hard to create!"

David raised his right hand, and his eyes turned red with anger. He bowed his head and a great magical power came from his outstretched hand.

Elaina's body was instantly propelled up toward the ceiling, as if she were being lifted into the air with David's hand clutched around her neck. David remained on the floor, but his hand felt as if it were strangling her. Elaina's breath had been taken away, and all she could do was hang lifeless in mid–air. She was powerless as her head hung forward. The last thing she saw before she blacked out was her bloodstone cameo hanging out from her blouse exposed.

David saw it, too, and he felt the power of Elaina's bloodstone unite with his bloodstone cameo hanging around his own neck. "This is foolish of me," he thought. "I must not let my anger get the best of me. I need Elaina alive."

Slowly, David released his power over Elaina and her body descended slowly back to the floor. When she reached the ground, she lay motionless next to her mahogany desk. David went to her side, and picked her up in his strong arms. He laid her on the couch and kissed her soft, red lips. She woke, her long, eyelashes fluttering up and down. When she looked at him, her expression was filled with fear.

"Don't be afraid, my darling," David said. "I never should have taken my anger out on you. Please forgive me."

Elaina's love for David surpassed all doubt and fear. She held out her arms for him. After all, this was not the first time she had had to endure David's wrath. And it probably would not be the last. This was the only man she had ever loved.

"Oh, David," Elaina said as she kissed him passionately. "My love..."

CHAPTER TWELVE

Before breakfast, Father Andrew McLaughlin walked across the lawn to the little chapel inside Saint Michael's Church in Lake Geneva. He knelt before the Blessed Sacrament to ask God for strength. He and a group of parishioners were scheduled to pray outside Milwaukee's Parenting Services International. Father Mac knew it was going to be a tough day because they'd have to stand for hours in the bitter cold and take harassment from pro–choice onlookers. But it was all worth it if they could save one life.

Years ago, Father Mac didn't think he would need strength to pray for life. He didn't think a faithful priest would have to worry about harassment. He had been naïve, but then again, he was only thirty–two. As Father Mac knelt, he remembered his first pilgrimage to the Right–to–Life March in Washington D.C. thirty years before.

In 1982, Father Mac and twenty–seven other priests took a bus from the Milwaukee Diocese and traveled overnight to D.C. on January 22nd. They played a couple of old films on the way to pass the time. Father Mac remembered the Hitchcock film "I Confess" with Montgomery Clift, a priest who, like Christ, offered himself as a ransom for the sins of others. Were the innocent unborn similar to this character because they offered their lives for others?

"No," Father Mac thought. "They weren't given any choice."

When Father Mac and the other priests exited the bus at the Mall in D.C., there was a cold, wet chill in the air that hung like a wet blanket.

"Would have been better to snow," Father Dennis Holmes said to Father Mac. "Snow's always better than rain in January."

"You're right." Father Mac was so caught up in the marchers, he hadn't noticed the cold. There must have been thousands. Tens of thousands in the Mall ready to march for life on a cold, January morning. He noticed children with mittens and hats, some small enough to be carried on shoulders or pushed in strollers.

"Ready?" Monsignor Allan Campbell from the seminary led the way to the stage set up in the Mall for pro–life speakers before the march began.

"Yes!" Father Mac thought he must have been the only enthusiastic person ready to march in the bitter rain.

The group of priests followed the monsignor and stood through the peppy rhetoric of pro–life leaders and politicians. The pro–life leaders were there because they believed in the pro–life message themselves. The politicians were there because they wanted to show their constituents that they believed in the pro–life message.

Father Mac listened intently to all the speeches, but the one that stood out most, the one he would never forget, was given by a woman who had been pregnant with a severely handicapped child. Almost every doctor she saw told her to abort the baby because the child would not survive outside the womb. However, there was one doctor at a Catholic hospital in New Jersey who did everything possible to keep her baby alive after delivering him via C–section. Her beautiful son, Matthew, lived for only eight hours before he died peacefully in her arms, but these hours were the most meaningful of her entire life and she would remember Matthew forever.

After the speeches, Father Mac noticed the line for the March begin to move. He saw how genuinely happy the people appeared despite the weather. He saw families patiently wait to gather up children as the elderly infirmed were pushed in wheelchairs. He heard people praise God and sing those praises in song. Father Mac joined Franciscan Friars as they passed his group reciting the Rosary, some friars carrying a large wooden set of rosary beads.

Father Mac felt a euphoria so strong it was as if the Holy Spirit were working in the hearts, minds and souls of thousands simultaneously. There were smiles all around in the large crowd gathered to save lives. Babies giggled at mothers from strollers. Husbands and wives held hands. Priests laughed with religious brothers and sisters, and high school and college students joyfully yelled out pro–life chants. The weather cleared and the cold rain stopped. Father Mac saw a bit of sun peek out from behind a cloud in the distance.

Father Mac's first Right–to–Life March would forever mark his memory as one of the most joyous celebrations of life he had ever experienced. And then it happened. Just at the moment when they rounded the Supreme Court building and he felt so enlightened by the gifts of God's grace, it happened. Father Mac remembered standing next to his brother priests, next to his fellow friars, next to families with little children, when it happened. They were waiting for them. He remembered feeling they were waiting for them.

Father Mac wasn't sure what hit him first. It might have been the shock of the screamed curse words. It might have been the shock of topless women exposing themselves perversely. It might have been the bras and underwear thrown at them literally hitting one Franciscan on the side of the head. Father Mac had not expected any of this. Monsignor Allan had told the group of priests that no matter what was said to them, they were not allowed to say anything back. They were there to march peacefully and prayerfully, and that was all. As Father Mac heard vulgarities screamed at them by topless women hurling underwear, he remembered a line from Scripture when Jesus said, "If you mean yes, say yes. If you mean no, say no. Anything else is from the devil."

Father Mac realized that there had been no response from his group. They had heard and seen, but they remained determined to continue in peace, looking forward, heads slightly bent in prayer. The innocent friar took the bra from his bald and bearded head, dropped it, and kept marching. The other priests focused on the road ahead without a glance at the women sneering at them and kept marching. All of the families stayed huddled together marching, and when one child cried, the friars and priests in Father Mac's group formed an enclosure around the families to act as a protective shield for the children on the inside.

Father Mac would always remember this moment most—what it must have looked like to see priests, friars and other religious shield and protect the innocent from the vulgar and obscene cries of the ignorant. Father Mac found himself on the outer right–hand side of the March, directly behind a young friar with red, curly hair and a long red beard. The friar's sandaled feet must have been freezing in the middle of January in D.C. The friar was wearing a long gray tunic tied with a rope, holding wooden rosary beads in his hand and was so obviously caught up in prayer, he didn't seem to notice the woman on his right bearing her breasts to him.

Father Mac heard her scream, "It's my womb! You can't tell me what to do with my womb, you son of a bitch! It's my womb, you filthy bastard! Go to hell!"

Father Mac was reminded of C.S. Lewis' "Chronicles of Narnia" when Aslan walks to the stone table to be martyred by the evil witch. On either side of Aslan are demons and monsters screaming vulgarities at the innocent, God–like lion. The image of the courageous lion filled Father Mac's thoughts and he began to think of Jesus on his way to Calvary. Jesus was spit on, slapped, scourged and called every horrible name by the wicked Roman soldiers, but he marched on bearing the weight of the cross.

Women on either side of the group of priests and religious continued to hurl vulgar rhetoric at the innocent marchers, but they stood fixed on the road in prayer. Fixed on the way to Calvary. Fixed on the face of Christ. Fixed on God, the Father, whom they would one day meet in heaven for all eternity.

Father Mac noticed the louder the woman screamed into the friar's ear, the louder he prayed the rosary, so Father Mac decided to join the friar in prayer. As soon as Father Mac joined in, the other priests and friars joined in, too. Then, the religious and families joined in, as well. Each "Hail Mary" became louder and louder until no horrible scream could be heard again. Father Mac would never forget the simple red–haired friar with his wooden rosary beads. The memory would give him the strength he needed every time he prayed for innocent life.

Father Mac rose from the kneeler to greet his guests feeling like a battery that had just been recharged.

*

Marie Murray, Michael Murray's mother, was a very active member of Saint Michael's Church. She was president of the Altar and Rosary Society, a member of the church choir and a member of the Pro–Life Committee. Father Mac began the Pro–Life Committee ten years before to educate his parishioners about the dignity and value of all human life from the moment of conception until natural death.

"From the womb to the tomb," Father Mac always said to Marie and Doc Murray over fish fries at Anthony's Steakhouse.

Most parishioners thought the Pro–Life Committee prayed for the lives of unborn babies who were in line to be killed at abortion clinics, but that was only part of it. The committee also cooked and served food at local shelters, performed at local nursing homes and senior–citizen centers, and offered a workshop called "Rachael's Vineyard," which provided support for those who had experienced the pain of abortion and were looking for healing and forgiveness. These were only a few of the services offered by the Pro–Life

Committee at Saint Michael's Parish.

Today, Father Mac was offering a new Pro–Life Committee service at the advice of Marie Murray. She wanted the parish to become involved with a group called, "40 Days for Life." Forty Days for Life had begun only a few years before and had spread all across the United States and abroad to places like Canada and Australia. Forty Days for Life provided an opportunity for people to pray peacefully outside abortion clinics every spring and fall across the country and around the world.

When Marie arrived at the church at seven o'clock that morning, Father Mac was already standing outside holding a tall Styrofoam cup filled with black coffee. There were two young people standing next to him, apparently a newly married couple. They were holding hands and quite obviously very much in love. Marie stopped before the couple and held out her hand.

"Hi. I'm Marie Murray." She shook the woman's hand and then the man's.

Father Mac stepped in to introduce them. "Marie, this is Emmanuel and Rosa Rodriguez. They're new to the parish. In fact, they're new to the area. They just moved here from Florida. They were married in Miami only a year ago, and Rosa is already expecting their first child."

"Congratulations!" Marie exclaimed. "What fantastic role models for today's prayer vigil!"

"Nice to meet you, Marie," Emmanuel said. "Rosa and I are really excited to be a part of this great cause."

Father Mac continued, "Manny and Rosa met at a 40 Days for Life on their college campus a couple of years ago."

"Good. We'll have some seasoned help," Marie responded.

Father Mac finished his coffee and threw the cup away. "Ready to save babies?" he asked.

"We're ready to save babies and mothers and fathers, too," Rosa responded.

"Let's go!" Father Mac led the group to a silver minivan.

When they reached the PSI clinic in downtown Milwaukee, there were already over a hundred people gathered along the pavement holding large, blue and white "40 Days for Life" signs. Some also held "Honk–for–Life" signs, and Father Mac responded with a loud "honk" before he parked across the street. Father Mac, Marie, Manny and Rosa quickly joined the group who had just begun to pray the rosary out loud. As they prayed, Marie was astonished to discover the young age of many of the prayer volunteers. There were young families with children in strollers and a large group of college–aged students. There were also some elderly people leaning on walking sticks or sitting in wheel chairs.

Marie noticed a young boy who seemed more interested in listening to his iPod than reciting the rosary. He looked no more than fifteen years old, and he was standing all alone. Marie took the opportunity to stand next to him. When they finished praying the rosary, she heard the loud "honks" of passing cars to show their support for the pro–life cause.

Marie introduced herself to the young teen standing next to her. Marie loved children of all ages, but especially teenagers. They always seemed more open about the important matters of life, like the reason they were standing outside the PSI clinic.

"Hi. I'm Marie Murray," she stepped up to the teenager and held out her hand.

The boy was shy, but he seemed to appreciate Marie's gesture. He shook her hand as limply and delicately as possible. "Hi," was all he said.

"What's your name?" Marie asked.

"Bobby."

"Hi, Bobby. Nice to meet you." Marie pointed to the white iPod in his hand connected by two white wires that hung from his ears. "What are you listening to?"

The boy's eyes lit up with pleasure. "A rap song called, 'Happy Birthday.' It's a really cool pro–life tune. You wanna hear?" He held one of the earphones out so Marie could listen.

Marie took the earphone and held it next to her right ear. She began to nod her head to the beat. "Cool lyrics!" she said.

Bobby smiled so wide, his grin spread from ear to ear.

Marie smiled back and handed Bobby his earphone. "Let's see if we can play it on the microphone speaker," she said.

"Go for it!" Bobby was so excited he nearly jumped out of his pants.

Marie walked over to Father Mac and whispered her request in his ear. Father Mac looked at Bobby and smiled. He walked over to a tall, young man standing in the center of the group who was holding a microphone next to a large black amplifier. Father Mac introduced himself and pointed to where Bobby stood with his iPod. He asked the man if he could play the song, and the man smiled and nodded his head. When Father Mac gestured for Bobby to come over, Bobby was by their side in less than three seconds. When the song began, the man turned it up so that everyone on the sidewalk could hear. As the entire group clapped to the beat of the music, Bobby's smile looked like it was permanently frozen on his face.

Marie saw a couple of PSI employees open the blinds inside the clinic to peer out at the group making the noise. They immediately came out to express their obvious disdain for the loud music of the 40 Days for Life group. In anger, they stomped back into the clinic to call the police. A few minutes later, two police cars pulled up to the sidewalk and four uniformed police officers walked over to the tall man in charge of the group. Father Mac, Marie and Bobby were still huddled in the center next to the man.

"Good day," one of the police officers said to the tall man.

"Good day, officer."

"Can I ask what your business is here, today?" the police officer asked.

"Absolutely. My name is Tony Adams and we've organized a peaceful prayer vigil outside this abortion clinic through a 40–day–long event called, '40 Days for Life.' We're here to pray for the women who are going into the clinic to seek an abortion because they think this is their only option. We're praying that by some miracle, by some grace of God, they may change their minds."

The police officer asking the questions looked at the other officers and smiled. The other officers smiled, too. "Well, I don't see any problem with peaceful prayer. You're standing on public property. You're not disturbing anybody. You go right on ahead and keep prayin'." The officer patted Bobby on the head before he turned to go.

Bobby spoke up, "Officer, our music wasn't too loud then?"

"Not at all, son. Not at all. You all just carry on your God–given work. We'll let the employees know at the clinic that you are right within your legal rights to remain on public property. Keep it up and let us know if you need anything further." The officer tipped his hat to Bobby and Tony and led the other officers to the doors of the clinic.

The crowd stood silent in disbelief as the officers walked toward the clinic. The music was still playing, the car horns were still honking, but you could have heard a pin drop in the midst of the crowd's jubilation. As soon as the police officers stepped inside the clinic, the group erupted into a loud roar of delight. They had just witnessed their first miracle of support.

Marie and Father Mac were holding up their hands and cheering, when Bobby saw a large, black SUV turn the corner and speed toward the group. Bobby pulled on Tony Adams' shirt sleeve and pointed to the vehicle.

Father Mac and Marie noticed the SUV when Bobby pointed, but it was coming up on them so fast, they did not have time to think of the consequences. The SUV had huge wheels and was disproportionately riding high above the ground. The windows were tinted and made it impossible to see the driver. It was accelerating quickly and only seconds from smashing up onto the pavement. The SUV was headed straight for the group, and they did not have any time to take cover.

When the SUV was only a few feet from the curb, the driver hit the brakes. It was obviously a scare tactic conjured up by some pro–choice fanatic, but the driver could not stop in time. The SUV had accidentally struck someone in their 40 Days for Life group, and it was not someone that Marie and Father Mac did not know. The SUV had struck Rosa and hit her from the side as she stood pregnant and holding a small "Pro–Life" sign in her hands. She instantly fell into the arms of her husband, Emmanuel. The black SUV quickly backed up and sped away, and Marie noticed the four police officers running out of the building toward them.

*

Marie felt as though the SUV had hit her instead of Rosa. The wind had been knocked out of her at the thought of something terrible happening to Rosa and her unborn child. She could see Manny in the distance looking ashen and shocked as he bent over his beloved young wife. It took only seconds for Marie and Father Mac to push through the prayer volunteers to get near Manny and Rosa, but it seemed like they were characters in a movie being played in slow motion.

It all happened so fast that Marie felt like she was a character in a real–life documentary. The invisible camera inside her brain was recording all that transpired in slow motion. One of the four police officers was speaking into a police radio, obviously reporting the accident and calling for an ambulance. Father Mac and Tony Adams were giving an account of the accident to the other officers. Bobby looked at Marie with a wide–eyed gaze, and drops of tears trickled down his innocent cheeks.

The ambulance could be heard in the distance coming around the corner for Rosa. Marie saw Manny holding his wife's hand as she lay across the sidewalk with one leg twisted badly and obviously broken. Rosa was in a great deal of pain, but it looked as if she and the baby would be okay. Marie breathed a sigh of relief and smiled down at Rosa's angelic face.

One of the officers knelt down on the other side of Rosa. He reached for Rosa's hand to check her pulse. After a few seconds, he looked at Manny and the rest of the group and smiled, relieved that her pulse was still strong. Marie felt tears of relief flow as she placed one hand up to her mouth to stop the sob that had escaped her lips.

Father Mac placed his arm around Marie's shoulders as the sound of the ambulance came closer.

The movie Marie was living in was now playing in real time, and she was impressed with how quickly the EMTs worked to place Rosa on a gurney and into the ambulance with Manny at her side.

"The three of them are going to be just fine," Father Mac said as the ambulance sped toward the hospital.

Marie knew Father Mac was right. God took care of His helpers.

CHAPTER THIRTEEN

Linda Walters received a call from Michael Murray when he returned from the cameo museum in Illinois. He told her there was definitely something odd about the bloodstone cameos he saw at the museum. Michael said the image of the beautiful woman on the cameo changed into an ugly beast right before his eyes. He photographed the cameo with his cell phone and sent the picture to her e–mail, but the beautiful image was unchanged. In fact, all three bloodstone cameos were unique, but they looked exactly the same as Debbie's bloodstone cameo—just an image of a beautiful woman.

Linda decided to research the origin of the bloodstone cameo on her own. After all, she was a history major. Most interesting to Linda was Michael's comment about the bloodstone being considered the "Bible stone." He said it had something to do with Aaron's breastplate.

Linda picked up her Bible and searched through the Book of Exodus to the passage that described Aaron's breastplate. In Exodus 28, it said there were twelve stones on the breastplate in four rows of three stones each, but Linda did not see one mention of a bloodstone. She googled Exodus on her computer and still, there was no mention of a bloodstone.

Linda copied down all of the different stones on Aaron's breastplate just to make sure she wasn't missing anything. The first row was a sardius, a topaz, and a carbuncle. The second row was an emerald, a sapphire, and a diamond.

"Expensive breastplate," Linda thought.

The third row was a ligure, an agate, and an amethyst; and the fourth row was a beryl, an onyx, and a jasper. Linda thought that jasper sounded familiar, like she had heard that stone mentioned in the Bible before. Hadn't Michael said something about a jasper stone from his trip to the museum?

Linda decided to drive to Marquette University, so she could utilize their library to do more specific research. When Linda entered the main floor, she found a book on cameos with a significant array of pictures taken from the same museum Michael had visited.

"This is interesting," she thought.

She flipped through page after page of cameos, but it wasn't until the last page that she came upon a bloodstone cameo. Linda's eyes widened when she saw the image of the bloodstone cameo. It was not the typical woman she was so used to seeing from Michael's photos and Debbie's cameo. This woman looked exactly like Medusa. She had snakes for hair, and her right ear did not look human. It was that of a wolf or a dog, and it was large and pointed. It could have been the ear of a large gargoyle for all Linda knew. The red dots of the bloodstone looked like blood trickling down the sides of Medusa's face.

Linda read the description that accompanied the picture: "A bloodstone Medusa was a potent amulet against harm and sickness in ancient Roman times. The eighteenth–century cameo pictured is a striking example of the matching of subject to stone material."

Michael said he might have imagined it, but this cameo looked exactly like the one Michael described. Could this Medusa image be the one Michael saw at the museum? Could this be the image that "spoke" to him?

"How long have they been carving these bloodstone cameos?" Linda whispered out loud.

She looked up the term, "bloodstone," and on page forty–nine, she found her answer. It said that "bloodstone was a favorite of early carvers, especially for modeling the head of Christ wearing a crown of thorns. The red splotches in the stone were made to represent drops of blood. According to an old legend, bloodstone was formed by the drops of blood of the crucified Jesus following the thrust of a Roman soldier's spear; the drops supposedly fell upon the green jasper on which the cross was standing. When the blood penetrated the stone, bloodstone was formed."

Linda sat back in her seat. "Aha!" she said out loud. "The jasper stone in Aaron's breastplate is really bloodstone!"

A couple of students turned toward Linda and gave her a loud, "Shh!"

"Sorry," she said under her breath.

Questions reeled in Linda's mind as she began to understand the magnitude and significance of the origin of the bloodstone. Was the jasper stone on Aaron's breastplate actually bloodstone? Could bloodstone made from jasper stone and the blood of Christ be used for evil? Or could bloodstone only be used for good?

Linda knew that the only way to find answers to her questions was to write everything down in chronological order. She loved research, and her methodical way of thinking enabled her to make the Dean's List every semester. Linda was pursuing a degree in history for a reason—she loved to research the past to discover how the present came to be. If people could modify the present based on past problems, a better future could be created.

Linda took out a notebook and pen and wrote down all she knew in the proper Biblical order. She used arrows to draw how each past event led to the next. First, the jasper stone was the twelfth stone on Aaron's Breastplate. Second, jasper stone was the type of stone that was found at the foot of the cross. Third, bloodstone is a combination of jasper stone and Christ's blood.

Linda made "Aaron's Breastplate" and "Christ's Bloodstone" into two different headings. Under Aaron's Breastplate, she wrote, "Jasper—12th Stone." Under Christ's Bloodstone, she wrote, "Jasper + Christ's Blood = Bloodstone." The only common element Linda could find in the two columns was jasper.

Linda walked downstairs to the computer lab and googled "Aaron's Breastplate 12th stone." All that came up was information she already had on jasper, but there was a link to an interesting site called, "Precious Stones of Sacred Scripture." Linda clicked on it and when she scrolled to the twelfth stone, jasper was not the only thing that came up. She saw the name "Benjamin" and the name "Peter" listed below the term, "Jasper."

"Okay," Linda thought. "Benjamin must be the Old Testament link to jasper, and Peter must be the New Testament link. This makes sense."

Linda read further to the descriptions of Benjamin and Peter. It said that Benjamin's stone, jasper, was placed in the twelfth position on Aaron's breastplate because Benjamin was the twelfth tribe of Israel. Here, the source said to look at Genesis 49, for the order of the tribes. The source said Peter was the first apostle to Christ and to look at Revelation 21.

Linda picked up a Bible and turned to Genesis first. Chapter 49 was called, "Jacob's Testament," and it was, in fact, a list of the sons of Jacob or the twelve tribes of Israel. Benjamin came last. He was the twelfth and was called the "ravenous wolf" who would "devour the prey" and "distribute the spoils." She wrote "Jasper–12th Stone" and "Benjamin, the ravenous wolf who devours prey and distributes spoils" under the "Aaron's Breastplate" column.

Next, Linda turned to the Book of Revelation. When she turned to Chapter 21, something profound caught her eye under the verse called, "The New Jerusalem." It began, "One of the seven angels who held the seven bowls filled with the seven last plagues came and said to me, 'Come here. I will show you the bride, the wife of the Lamb.' He took me in spirit to a great high mountain and showed me the holy city Jerusalem coming down out of heaven from God. It gleamed with the splendor of God. Its radiance was like that of a precious stone, like jasper, clear as crystal."

"Wow! Jasper is everywhere in this passage," Linda thought.

She read on, "The wall of the city had twelve courses of stones as its foundation, on which were inscribed the twelve names of the twelve apostles of the Lamb. The wall was constructed of jasper, while the city was pure gold, clear as glass. The foundations of the city wall were decorated with every precious stone; the first course of stones was jasper, the second sapphire, the third chalcedony, the fourth emerald, the fifth sardonyx, the sixth carnelian, the seventh chrysolite, the eighth beryl, the ninth topaz, the tenth chrysoprase, the eleventh hyacinth, and the twelfth amethyst."

The first thing Linda thought was that the wall sounded exactly like the inverted order of Aaron's breastplate. This time, jasper was first and in the same position as Peter, the first apostle. She wrote "Jasper–1st Stone" and "Peter, the rock on which I will build my church" under the "Christ's Bloodstone" column.

Linda went back to the page on Aaron's breastplate to see if there was anything she missed. The page came up, and she scrolled down to the section called, "Hebrew Scripture." It said that according to the Hebrew Bible, "stones used for 'an' Urim and Thummim were kept in the breastplate of Aaron, the brother of Moses."

"What does Urim and Thummim mean?" Linda googled Urim and Thummim and the first reference was a Hebrew translation. It meant "lights and perfections" or "revelation and truth."

There was more beneath. Linda scrolled down. It read, "The earliest reference to Urim and Thummim in the Hebrew Bible is that Aaron carried them with him as High Priest. Many scholars believe Urim and Thummim were originally stones that resided in the breastplate of the Jewish High Priest ceremonial clothing when he officiated in the tabernacle or temple. Others believe that Urim and Thummim is another name for the casting of lots, rather than a device or stones used as a medium. In either case, Urim and Thummim is not mentioned specifically in Biblical text in regard to this calling."

"So, the Urim and Thummim was a medium used to call upon God for answers," Linda thought. She scrolled down to the bottom of the page and saw the word "witch" printed there.

"That's strange," Linda thought. She noticed a link for someone called the "Witch of Endor." She clicked on the link.

The picture of a beautiful woman with a wicked expression came up. Above it, the heading read, "The Witch of Endor." Below it, the copy read, "In the Hebrew Bible, the Witch of Endor of the First Book of Samuel 28: 4–25, was a witch, a woman 'who possesses a talisman,' through which she called up the ghost of the recently deceased prophet Samuel, at the demand of King Saul of Israel. After Samuel's death and burial with due mourning ceremonies in Ramah, Saul had driven all necromancers and magicians from Israel. Then, in a bitter irony, Saul sought out the witch, anonymously and in disguise, only after he received no answer from God from dreams, prophets or the Urim and Thummim as to his best course of action against the assembled forces of the Philistines. The prophet's ghost offered no advice but predicted Saul's downfall as king. The Witch of Endor may be seen as a survival of archaic Canaanite religion, similar to a sibyl."

Linda took a closer look at the picture of the woman. Her eyes widened and her heart raced at what she discovered. This woman, this "Witch of Endor," was wearing a bloodstone cameo around her neck—the same kind of bloodstone cameo she had seen around Debbie's neck.

"Oh, my God! Oh, my God!" Linda sat back in her seat so quickly, the chair made a loud squeak. She was breathing so heavily it was audible. Linda noticed her fellow students staring at her like she was some kind of idiot. She had to get control of herself.

"Don't let your emotions get the best of you," she thought.

"Okay, you have to think rationally or you'll never make any headway."

Linda had so much information to add to her diagram under the "Aaron's Breastplate" column, she wondered if it would all fit on one page. She jotted down everything she had just learned when her cell phone rang. Linda looked at her phone and was surprised to see that it was Michael. She was going to call him and give him an update on her research as soon as she finished.

"Hi, Michael! You will not believe what I just found out about the origin of the bloodstone cameos!" Linda exclaimed.

"Great! Listen, Linda. I have some really horrible news. It's about Debbie. She's missing. She didn't come down for breakfast this morning, and the people at the hospital have been searching all day for her on the premises, but she hasn't turned up. Linda, Debbie's been missing all day and no one has any clue where she is."

CHAPTER FOURTEEN

Paolo came to Cassy in the middle of the night. Drew had already left to try to get a good night's sleep at home. Paolo walked to Cassy's hospital bed where she had spent the last four weeks. She remained in a coma, but Paolo knew that her brain was entirely active. He reached out and touched her forehead with the back of his hand. Her eyelids slowly opened. Cassy gazed at Paolo and a smile spread across her lips. She admired him greatly and a genuine friendship had begun to form between the two. He held out his hand for her and she took it, but not with her earthly body. She took it with the body that had become her spiritual double.

There was a translucent aura to her spiritual body. Cassy grew accustomed to seeing her physical body sleep peacefully as she journeyed with Paolo. He was not only a teacher, but a spiritual advisor—the one who guided her and gave her the strength she would need when she awoke. Cassy knew she would have to face her worst fears when she woke. She would have to face her mother, no doubt, but she would also have to face David. Cassy knew that through Paolo, she would gain the strength needed to face him. At that point, Cassy would no longer need to feel fear.

As Cassy walked down the hall of the hospital corridor, no one noticed her or Paolo. They were like ghosts in the middle of the night. Cassy wore a long, white silk nightgown with a matching robe. Her feet were bare, but she felt nothing of the cold floor. Paolo wore a white ruffled shirt and black trousers. He, too, wore nothing on his feet. There was no need. Their spiritual bodies were lighter than earthly ones and their feet did not touch the floor at all. They moved along as if floating in mid–air. For Paolo and Cassy, there was no need for doors. They could walk through them.

When Paolo and Cassy walked through the front entrance of the hospital, he took her by the hand and they lifted up into the night like birds flying through haze before dawn. Cassy felt the soft breeze against her face, and she noticed that her long hair was floating behind her in the wind. Paolo's hand gripped hers gently, but with a manly power that was strong and confident. As they flew higher, there was a light in the distance like a sunrise without the intensity of burning heat. They flew toward the light, and when it seemed they could not ascend any higher, Cassy saw a patch of green grass and she and Paolo landed in a field. There were beautiful flowers throughout the field, and the sun had just risen on the dawn of a new day. However, it was not a day in the present. It was a day in a time gone by hundreds of years before.

There were bushes clipped in perfect square borders that made foot paths around beautiful gardens. In the distance, toward the back of the garden was a great castle built for a king. Near the castle, Cassy saw a man with light brown hair dressed in king's clothes with a crown of ivy on his head. As Cassy and Paolo moved closer, the king was speaking to another royal dressed in vibrant colors. His hair was jet black and worn in a ponytail at the nape of his neck.

The man with the ponytail addressed the king. "Nero Caesar, O good emperor, I, Simon, am no mere magician. I am the son of God come down from heaven. Until now I have endured Peter calling himself an apostle. Now the evil is doubled, for Paul also teaches the same things. If you do not destroy them, it is very plain that your kingdom will fall."

Nero Caesar looked concerned and ordered Peter and Paul to be brought before him. The two men were brought forward by guards from the right side of the castle wall into view. They were elderly with beards and one was completely bald on the top of his head. Their garments were worn and frayed.

Simon pointed toward the two poor men. "These are the disciples of the Nazarene. They have come from among the Jews."

"What is a Nazarene?" Nero asked.

"There is a city of Judah which has always been opposed to us, called Nazareth, and the teacher of these men came from there," Simon answered.

"God commands us to love every man. Why, then, do you persecute them?" Nero asked.

"This is a race of men who have turned all Judea away from believing in me," Simon replied.

Nero turned to the man named Peter. "Why are you unbelieving, according to your people?"

Peter addressed Simon instead of Nero. "You have been able to deceive many, but me never," he said. "Those whom you deceived, God has through me saved from their error. Since you have learned by experience that you cannot defeat me, I wonder how you praise yourself before the emperor, and suppose that through your magic you shall overcome the disciples of Christ?"

"Who is Christ?" Nero asked Peter.

Peter turned to Nero. "He is what this Simon the Magician claims to be. But Simon is a wicked man and his tricks are of the devil. O good emperor, if you wish to know what happened in Judea concerning Christ, read the writings of Pontius Pilate sent to Claudius, and you will know all."

Cassy turned to Paolo, but he had disappeared. She noticed that Nero was giving instructions to one of his Roman soldiers. The soldier disappeared inside the castle entrance and returned with Paolo dressed as a Roman nobleman with an ancient scroll in his hand.

Paolo turned toward the assembly and unwrapped the scroll. He held the scroll up to the light. "Pontius Pilate to Claudius, greeting. An event recently occurred in which I myself was involved. Many, through envy, have brought on themselves, and those coming after them, dreadful judgments. Their fathers had been promised that their God would send them his holy one from heaven, who according to reason should be called their king, and he had promised to send him to the earth by means of a virgin. He came into Judea when I was procurator. They saw him giving sight to the blind, cleansing lepers, healing paralytics, expelling demons, raising the dead, subduing the winds, walking upon the waves of the sea, and doing many other wonders, and all the people calling him Son of God."

Paolo cleared his throat and continued, "Then the chief priests moved with envy against him, seized him, and delivered him to me; and telling one lie after another, they said that he was a wizard, and violated their law. I, having believed that these things were true, gave him up, after scourging him, to their will. They crucified him, and after he was buried, set guards over him. But, while my soldiers were guarding him, he rose on the third day. And to such a degree was the wickedness of the people inflamed against him, that they gave money to the soldiers, telling them, 'Say his disciples have stolen his body.' But the soldiers, having taken the money, were not able to keep silence. They have testified that they saw him after he was risen, and that they received money from them. I have reported these things that no one should falsely speak otherwise, and that you should not suppose that their falsehoods are to be believed."

After the letter was read, Nero turned back to Peter, "Tell me, Peter, were all these things done by him?"

Peter responded, "They were, O good emperor. For this reason Simon is full of lies and deceit, even if he tries to appear to be what he is not, a god. In Christ there is victory through God and through man, by an incomprehensible glory that came to men through a man. But in Simon there are two parts, man and devil, who through the man endeavors to ensnare men."

Simon walked to Nero full of conceit. "O good emperor, I wonder that you listen to this man, an uneducated man, a poor fisherman, with no power in word or rank. That I may not long endure him as an enemy, I shall order my angels to come and avenge me upon him. Do you believe, O good emperor, that I who was dead, and rose again, am a magician? Order me to be beheaded in a dark place, and there to be left slain. If I do not rise on the third day, know that I am a magician; but if I rise again, know that I am the Son of God."

Nero ordered this and Cassy and Paolo watched as Simon, by his magic art, managed for a ram to be beheaded instead of himself. In the dark, the ram appeared to be Simon, but the executioner realized that it was the head of a ram. The executioner did not say anything to the emperor, for fear that he would be punished.

On the third day, Simon pretended that he had risen. He went before Nero and said, "I have been beheaded, and as promised, I have risen on the third day."

Nero turned to Paul. "Paul, why do you say nothing? I think that you have no wisdom, and are not able to accomplish any work of power."

The man named, Paul, the one with no hair and a long beard, came forward to Nero. "Why should I speak against a desperate man, a magician, who has given his soul up to death, whose destruction will come quickly? He should speak, who pretends to be what he is not, and deceives men by magic art. If you consent to hear his words, you shall destroy your soul and your kingdom, for he is an evil man. As far as he seems to raise himself towards heaven, so far will he be sunk down into the depth of Hades, where there is weeping and gnashing of teeth. But about the teaching of my Master, of which you asked me, none attain it except the pure, who allow faith to come into their heart. This teaching was given to me, neither from men, nor through men, but through Jesus Christ who spoke to me out of heaven. He also has sent me to preach, saying to me, 'Go forth, for I will be with you; and all things, as many as you shall say and do, I shall make just.'"

"What do you say?" Nero asked Peter.

"Everything that Paul said is true. There were before us false Christs, like Simon, false apostles, and false prophets, who, contrary to the sacred writings tried to destroy the trust," Peter answered.

Simon stepped forward to defend his actions. "O good emperor, take notice that these two have conspired against me. I am the truth, and they propose evil against me."

"There is no truth in you; everything you say is false," Peter declared to Simon.

"Do you expect me, O good emperor, to argue with these men, who have come to an agreement against me?" Simon asked Nero.

"Simon, as I see it, you are being carried away with envy, and you persecute these men. There seems to be great hatred between you and their Christ. I am afraid that you will be defeated by them, and involved in great evil."

"You are led astray, O emperor," Simon retorted.

"How am I led astray? What I see in you, I say. I see that you are manifestly an enemy of Peter and Paul and their master."

"O good emperor, these men have depended on your mercy and have bound you."

"My will is my own. I am not sure about these men, and I am not sure about you either."

"Since I have shown you so many great deeds and signs, I wonder why you doubt me," Simon said to Nero.

"I neither doubt nor favor any of you."

"I no longer answer you," Simon retorted.

"On this account, I perceive you to be a liar in everything. But why do I say so much? The three of you show that your reasoning is uncertain. In all things you have made me doubt, so that I find that I can believe none of you."

"We preach one God and Father of our Lord Jesus Christ, who has made the heavens and the earth and the sea, and all that is in them, who is the true King; and of His kingdom there shall be no end," Peter responded.

"What king is lord?" Nero asked Peter and Paul.

"The Savior of all the nations," Paul answered.

Simon came forward and spoke, "I am he of whom you speak."

"May it never be well with you, Simon magician full of lies," Peter and Paul said together.

"Listen, O Caesar Nero that you may know that these men are liars, and that I have been sent from the heavens. Tomorrow I go up into the heavens, that I may make those who believe in me blessed, and show my wrath upon those who have denied me."

"You, called by the devil, hasten to punishment," Peter said.

"Caesar Nero, listen to me. Banish these madmen so that when I go into heaven to my father I may be very merciful to you."

"And how shall we prove this, that you go away into heaven?"

"Order a high tower to be made of wood, and of great beams, that I may go up upon it, and that my angels may find me in the air; for they cannot come to me upon earth among the sinners."

"Tomorrow, I will see whether you will fulfill what you say."

Nero ordered a high tower to be made in the Campus Martius. He commanded that all the people and the dignitaries be present at the spectacle. Paulo transported Cassy through time, and she saw that the multitude Nero had commanded was already present and that Nero was ordering Peter and Paul to come before him.

Nero said to them, "Now we will see what is the truth."

"We do not expose him, but our Lord Jesus Christ, the Son of God, whom he has falsely declared himself to be, will expose him," Paul said. He lowered his head in prayer.

"Accomplish what you have begun for both your exposure and our call is at hand. I see my Christ calling both me and Paul," Peter added.

Nero looked up and saw nothing. He turned back toward Peter with disbelief. "Do you also then intend to go away to heaven?" he asked.

"If it is the will of Him who calls us," Peter responded.

Simon came forward. "O emperor, that you may know that these men are deceivers, as soon as I ascend into heaven, I will send my angels to you, and will make you come to me."

"Do at once what you say," Nero answered.

Simon climbed up upon the tower and crowned with laurels, he stretched forth his hands and began to fly.

Nero saw him flying and said to Peter, "This Simon is true, you and Paul are deceivers."

"Immediately shall you know that we are true disciples of Christ. You shall know that he is not Christ, but a magician, and an evildoer," Peter declared.

Then Peter, looking at Paul, said, "Paul, look up and see."

Paul, full of tears, looked up and saw Simon flying and said, "Peter, why are you idle? Finish what you have begun for already our Lord Jesus Christ is calling us."

Nero smiled, "These men see themselves defeated already and have gone mad."

Peter turned to Nero, "Now you shall know that we are not mad."

Looking steadfastly at Simon, Peter said, "Angels of Satan, who are carrying him into the air, that you might deceive the hearts of the unbelievers, I order you, by the God that created all things, and by Jesus Christ, who on the third day was raised from the dead, no longer keep him up, but let him fall."

Immediately, being let go, Simon, the magician, fell quickly and forcibly to the earth below. He hit the ground with such force, Cassy was horrified to witness his body separated into four parts by the powerful impact of the fall. She moved closer to the ground where Simon had perished and noticed that there was a tremendous amount of blood that was streaming from his dismantled body. A green sparkle on the ground underneath Simon's body caught Cassy's eye. This was the same jade green she had seen on the ground underneath the cross on which Christ, the Son of God, had been crucified. She turned to Paolo who was standing behind her with his hand on her shoulder.

Paolo answered Cassy before she had the chance to ask her question. "Yes, Cassy, this is how the evil Bloodstone was created, by the blood of Simon, a messenger of the devil."

"Is this the bloodstone that was used to make my family's bloodstones?" Cassy asked hesitantly.

"Yes."

"What happened to Peter and Paul? Did Nero realize their innocence?"

Paolo shook his head. "Paul was beheaded and Peter, crucified."

Cassy bowed her head in despair for the two holy men she had learned had been faithful followers of Christ. "What became of Nero?" she asked.

"The people of his kingdom revolted against him and when he learned of it, he fled into the desert. Through hunger and cold he died and his body became food for wild beasts."

Cassy let out a deep breath. She asked Paolo one last question before their return to the present. "Will my family receive the same fate as Nero if they continue their evil?"

"Yes," Paolo answered. He took Cassy's hand in his, and their spiritual bodies ascended into the air.

CHAPTER FIFTEEN

One of the first recollections Father Raphael had of his childhood was a trip his family took to the Basilica of Our Lady of Guadalupe. The Basilica was located about three hours west of his home in Atlixco, Puebla, on the outskirts of Mexico City. Raphael was eight years old, and he and his six siblings, five boys and two girls, traveled with his father, mother and grandfather in a large white van. The closer the van came to the Basilica, the faster Raphael's heart began to beat.

Raphael sat next to his older brother, Juan, who acted like he was in charge of Raphael's every move as soon as he turned ten. Juan was poking Raphael in the side and shouting in his ear, "Hey Raffa, what do you have in your hands?"

Raphael was holding a beautiful set of blue rosary beads. "My beads from Tío," he said. He had received the rosary from his mother's brother who was a priest in Puebla.

"Hey, let me see those." Juan tried to pull the beads out of Raphael's hands.

"No, they'll break." Raphael held tightly to the crucifix of the rosary while Juan pulled at the strand of beads.

"Yeah, I want to see them, too." Jorge, Raphael's eleven–year-old brother, tried to pull on the strand of beads, too. The strand was

159

so strained it looked like it might break at any moment.

In an instant, Pedro, Raphael's oldest brother who was fifteen, turned and grabbed Juan and Jorge by their ears.

"Ow! Ow!" Juan and Jorge let go of the rosary beads simultaneously and rubbed their ears to ease the throbbing.

"Those beads were a gift to Raphael from Padre Miguel! They are very special to him, and if I see you touch them again, you'll be rubbing more than just your ears!" Pedro stared Juan and Jorge down sternly until they turned forward with their hands in their laps. Afterward, he gave Raphael a loving wink.

Raphael smiled back shyly at his big brother and quickly stuffed the blue rosary beads back in the front pocket of his jeans.

"We're here! We're here!" Raphael's father, Carlos, yelled so loudly, his face turned red. He looked like an excited child as he sat in the driver's seat bouncing up and down.

"Yeah! Yeah!" Raphael's youngest siblings, Miguel who was four and Maria who was two, shouted almost as loudly as their father.

Anna, Raphael's fourteen–year–old sister, placed a loving arm around Miguel and Maria and kissed each child on the top of their heads.

"Well, that was not a bad drive at all," Raphael's grandfather, who everyone called, "Pappa," said in a condescending tone. The drive had taken over four hours with the congestion through Puebla and the traffic on the toll highway.

Raphael's mother, Rita, turned toward her father. "Carlos did his best to get us here as quickly as possible, Pappa." She was giving him a critical look, but her glare quickly softened. Rita was known as the one who kept everyone happy, and everyone loved her for her peaceful disposition. She was a striking woman with long black, flowing hair.

Raphael looked at his mother in the reflection of the rearview mirror and smiled. He loved his family more than anything, and he had a very special bond with his mother and father. When he was younger, he felt the closest to his mother. He would always remember her hugs and kisses and the way she smelled. She had a sweet fragrance that he loved when he went to her for comfort after a bump or bruise or fall off his bike.

In the past year, Raphael had come to love and admire his father more than any human being on earth. They fished together, swam together, hiked together and when Juan and Jorge were causing trouble, and Miguel and Maria needed their mother's attention, Raphael and his father cooked together. Their specialty was chicken with rice and beans served spicy hot with jalapeño peppers mixed into the sauce.

Raphael paid particular attention to the way his father treated his mother. He watched the contented look on his father's face when he gave his wife a break from household chores or the loving look on his face when his mother gave him a grateful kiss. Raphael watched his father laugh when he picked up Miguel and Maria in both arms, and hugged them with all his might. Carlos was a loving husband and father, and Raphael looked up to him like no other.

Raphael smiled and looked out the window as his father parked the van near the Basilica of Our Lady of Guadalupe, otherwise known as "La Villa de la Guadalupe." Raphael could feel his heart beat so fast, he thought it must be protruding from his shirt. He stepped out of the van and followed his family to the plaza that housed the famous massive structures of Our Lady of Guadalupe. Raphael had to pinch his arm to remind himself that he was really here and not just living in a dream. He looked to the left and saw the Nueva Basílica built between 1974 and 1976 by the Mexican architect Pedro Ramírez Vásquez. It was very flamboyant and looked more like a stadium than a church.

Raphael pointed to the large, round structure. "Look, the Nueva Basílica! That is where the Tilma is!" He ran to the building and left his family to have to follow him. When Raphael entered the Basilica, he saw the image of Our Lady of Guadalupe on the apron that had once belonged to Saint Juan Diego hanging from a glass case next to the altar. With awe and admiration, he knelt next to the entrance. Pedro ran in behind Raphael, but Raphael was already on his way to Mary's famous image on the altar.

As Raphael stood admiring Mary, he remembered the history of Our Lady of Guadalupe. According to tradition, Saint Juan Diego was walking between his Aztec village and Mexico City in 1531 when the Virgin Mary as Our Lady of Guadalupe appeared. She told him to build a church at the site. When Juan Diego spoke to the Spanish bishop, the bishop did not believe him and asked for a miraculous sign. Although it was winter, the Virgin told Juan Diego to gather flowers, and Spanish roses bloomed right at his feet. When Juan Diego presented these to the bishop, the roses fell from his apron, which was called a Tilma, and an icon of the Virgin was miraculously imprinted on the cloth. The bishop ordered a church to be built at once, which would be dedicated to Our Lady of Guadalupe. The shrine of the Virgin of Guadalupe became so popular that millions of indigenous Aztecs converted to Catholicism. She became the patron saint of Mexico City in 1737 and the patron saint of all of America in 1946.

Raphael heard a loud, "Aah!" come from behind, and he turned to see his little sister, Maria, point to the Holy Mother. The rest of his family had gathered around him at the foot of the image of Mary on the Tilma. They were so caught up in the presence of a miracle that they had forgotten to be mad at Raphael for abandoning them earlier.

Something in a glass case caught Raphael's eye and he turned to take in the bent brass crucifix that was displayed on a cushion. Raphael could not believe that someone would have tried to destroy the Tilma with a bomb. On November 14, 1921, a factory worker placed a bomb a few feet from the apron. The explosion demolished the marble steps of the main altar, blew out the windows of nearby homes and bent the brass crucifix, but the fabric of the Tilma suffered no damage. Since 1993, the apron has been protected by bullet–proof glass.

Raphael said a quick "Hail Mary" and exited the Nueva Basílica to see the original Basilica of Our Lady called the "Antigua Basílica." This was the original church that had been built in the time of Juan Diego in 1536. Outside, when Raphael came face to face with a statue of Juan Diego, he felt a sense of pride that the first indigenous saint in the Americas was Mexican. He had been named "Raphael Diego Ruiz Trujillo" after Juan Diego. Raphael had also been named after the great archangel Saint Raphael. That's why his mother insisted that his name be spelled "Raphael" instead of the more Spanish "Rafael" used by most Mexicans.

Raphael heard little feet running up behind him near the statue. He turned and saw Miguel and Maria coming toward him. Raphael bent down to give each one a warm hug. When he stood back up, his mother and father looked at him scolding.

Raphael's father spoke in a criticizing tone, "Raphael, I know you are excited about being here, but you must stop running and take your time to wait for us. Pappa is having a difficult time keeping up."

Raphael's mother turned to look for her father who had not yet caught up with the group in front of the statue. After a few minutes, they saw Pappa appear outside the door of the Nueva Basílica.

When Pappa saw his family waiting for him, he purposely slowed down to show Raphael that he was having a hard time keeping up with him. Pappa reached the statue and turned to Raphael, "Remind me to paddle you later when I finally regain my breathing again." He looked at Raphael sternly and put a hand on Carlos' shoulder. "As I have often said, my son, the apple does not fall far from the tree."

Rita took her husband's hand, squeezed it, and looked up to the sky in exasperation.

Pappa walked over to the statue of Juan Diego and looked up. "Who is that?" he asked, and then he winked at Raphael and continued to the stairs that led to the Antigua Basílica.

Raphael gave both his parents an apologetic glance and quickly caught up with his grandfather on the stairs. He looped his hand in his and they continued slowly up the stairs together. When they entered the original Basilica, a feeling of serenity was felt by the entire family. This was the church that had been built by the Holy Virgin Mary, the Mother of God. The Trujillo family walked to the front of the Basilica and sat in the first pew bowing their heads in respect for Mary's beloved house of God.

When they finished their prayer, Raphael could not wait to get outside to the beautiful waterfalls of Tepeyac Hill where Our Lady of Guadalupe had first appeared to Juan Diego before the Basilica was built. It was well known that this hill provided the best view of The Guadalupe Basilicas. Raphael decided to ask his parents' permission before he made a calculated run for it. He wanted to get there and have a peaceful look around before Juan and Jorge created chaos.

"Mommy and Poppy, can I please go outside to see Tepeyac Hill? I wanted to have a moment alone to pray in the footsteps of Juan Diego." Raphael thought he had his best chance if he gave credence to the great saint who shared his family's name.

"Of course and thank you for asking this time," Raphael's mother answered. His parents were looking at him as if he had just become the golden son.

"Thank you, Poppy! Thank you, Mommy!" Raphael ran out before anyone could follow. He found the steps to Tepeyac Hill and quickly ran up. When he got to the landing, the waterfalls were cascading down beautiful rock formations. He was alone.

"At last!" Raphael thought to himself. He felt elated. He looked up to the top of the hill and was about to make his way up another flight of stairs when he noticed a woman in the distance standing on top of the hill. She was dressed in a long, light–blue dress that flowed in the wind. She was smiling at Raphael. Raphael noticed a fragrance in the air that he would never forget. It was the fragrance of lilacs, and it filled the air with a heavenly sweetness. Raphael felt as if all his boyhood cares had vanished, and nothing else mattered. Nothing mattered but his gratitude toward God for so many wonderful blessings. He was in the presence of something divine.

Raphael was so excited he took the next flight of stairs two at a time and reached the top of the hill as quickly as possible. He looked out to the place where the woman had stood in the light–blue dress, but there was no one there. She had vanished. As quickly as she had appeared to Raphael, she was gone, but the lingering scent of lilac still hung in the air.

Raphael turned to see the beautiful view of the Basilicas below. They were magnificent. Up close, he could see the colorful offerings of other admirers of Our Lady of Guadalupe. There were flowers, rosary beads, prayer cards and pictures, all as gifts left for Mary. Raphael stood by the little shrine and looked down. He saw his family walking toward the stairs below, and he smiled. Raphael knew that Mary had come to him on this hill, this Juan Diego hill, in order to bring him a message from God. Raphael knew that he had been called to a life of holy service. He knew that he had been called to the service of the priesthood.

*

This was not the first time Raphael had a vision of Mary or smelled the fragrance of lilac. The next time was not in the comfort of Tepeyac Hill, however. The next time was in the hills of the rural countryside of Huaquechula where he was visiting his cousins. Raphael was twelve and Pedro had already gone off to university to study medicine at the National University in Mexico City. The rest of the Trujillo family was visiting Carlos' sister and her family in Huaquechula, a quaint, rural town known for its churches built by Spaniards in the 1500s.

Raphael, Juan and Jorge decided to join their cousins Rudy and

Manny on a day–long hike in the hills. It was a mountainous and arid region, and a great place for a young boy to discover nature.

"Raffa! Hey, over here!" Manny, who was Raphael's age and a really skilled climber, called Raphael to meet him on the top of a hill where the five boys could take a break and have lunch. Rudy, Juan and Jorge, who were a little older and needed to prove their age, were already at the top. Manny was waiting for Raphael half way up a worn path that led to a look–out on top of a big white rock.

"Thanks, Man! How did I know the other three wouldn't wait?" Raphael caught up with Manny, and they both ascended the hill together. They heard noises and peered around the corner to see Rudy, Juan and Jorge standing on the rock playing air guitars in a non–existent band.

"Hey, look at me!" Juan was calling out to the other two and jumping up and down with his air guitar. The three were all laughing at the same time.

"Juan, you'd better be careful. There's a huge drop on the other side of the rock and I'm telling you—you won't survive that fall. No way," Manny warned Raphael's brother who was always the biggest dare devil of the group.

Rudy jumped off the rock and looked up at Juan. "It's time to have lunch anyway guys. I'm starving."

Juan and Jorge followed suit and jumped down, too. "Yeah, I'm starving, too," they said in unison.

Manny and Raphael were each carrying large backpacks stuffed with food. They were selected to carry the two sacks because they were the youngest. Simultaneously, they opened the packs and brought out large wrapped corn tortillas stuffed with meat and beans.

"Let me have one!" Juan and Jorge shoved each other forward so they could be first. They both grabbed a tortilla and a Coca–Cola and sat on the side of the rock.

Rudy came forward to get a tortilla and a Coca–Cola, too, and sat next to Jorge.

Manny and Raphael took out the last two tortillas and Coca–Colas and sat on the other side of the rock a couple meters from Juan.

The five ate in silence. When they were finished, Manny went back to his sack and pulled out homemade caramel candies that his mother had made especially for their outing. He handed them out and sat back down next to Raphael.

Raphael could hear audible sighs from the boys as they let the delicate, rich sweetness of melting caramels tantalize their taste buds. They finished and all five decided to take a nice, relaxing siesta on the rock with the afternoon sun shining on their faces. Raphael was wearing a baseball cap, but he took it off so he could put it over his face to cover his eyes. He laid down flat on the rock next to Manny with the cap over his face. Since he was wearing shorts, Raphael let his bare legs hang out over the sides to absorb the warm sun.

Raphael thought the afternoon could not have been better when he felt a horrible sting on his right ankle. It burned so strong and hot, he sat up on the rock and let out an audible, "Aah!"

"You all right, Raffa?" Manny sat up quickly to make sure his cousin was okay. The other three followed suit and sat up.

"Oh, my God! I've never been stung like that in my life! You got some huge wasps flying around here, cousins!" Raphael tried to rub his right ankle, but the pain was too intense.

"Hey, let me see that!" Manny got off the rock and saw a yellow scorpion race back under the rock. "A scorpion!" he yelled.

"Oh, man! Where?" Rudy jumped off the rock at a speed that would have rivaled lightning as soon as he heard the word "scorpion."

"Where?" Rudy peered underneath the rock to try to get a glimpse of the scorpion. "What color did you say it was, Man?"

"Yellow!" Manny shouted as if this were the worst possible color a scorpion could be.

"We got any ice in those sacks?" Rudy maintained his calm and took control of the situation.

Manny ran to the sacks and quickly looked inside both. "No! No ice!"

"Raphael, let me see your leg!" Rudy exclaimed.

Rudy had never used Raphael's real name in his life, so Raphael immediately determined that this must be serious. He turned his leg so Rudy could get a better look and noticed that it was swelling more quickly than he would have anticipated.

"We got any medicine for the swelling in the sacks?" Rudy asked.

Manny looked again and saw nothing. "No!" he resounded.

"Oh! Oh!" Raphael groaned and a good amount of spit came from his mouth and slid down his chin. He laid back and held his stomach like he was in terrible pain.

"What are we gonna do? What are we gonna do?" Juan and Jorge had come to their brother's side and were wringing their hands with worry.

"We gotta make it to a local hospital as quickly as possible!" Rudy was back in charge and over on the rock next to Raphael. He put his arm under Raphael's shoulder. "Raphael, can you get up? We gotta get you somewhere for help quickly." Rudy pulled Raphael up from the back, but when Raphael got up to a sitting position, he immediately vomited all over his shorts and legs.

"It's okay, Raphael. It's okay. We gotta get you someplace fast and quick!" Rudy pushed Raphael's back forward and when he was standing, he steadied him from underneath his left arm, and Manny went around to his right arm to steady him on the other side. "Juan, Jorge, get the sacks and let's go!" Rudy and Manny were already helping Raphael down the path in a half walk, half run.

By the time they made it back to the local road, twenty minutes had passed and Raphael was beginning to drag his right leg.

"You okay, Raphael?" Rudy looked over at Raphael's leg and

saw that the ankle had now ballooned to over twice its size. He knew they had to work quickly. Raphael looked like he was having an allergic reaction, and Rudy knew they only had so much time to get Raphael the help he needed.

They walked down the road toward the local town and its medical clinic. Another ten minutes passed, and Raphael lost control of his legs completely. The weight became too much for Rudy and Manny. Raphael slid through their grasp and fell to the ground on his face. The boys had never known so much fear in all their lives, but Rudy had to stay in control or he knew Raphael wouldn't have a chance.

"Juan, Jorge, drop the sacks and come over here! You grab your brother's legs and we'll grab his arms! We're going to carry your brother to the clinic no matter what it takes! If we hear a car, we run into the road to stop it! We do whatever it takes, got it?"

"Yeah!"

They all worked together to grab Raphael's limbs. Juan and Jorge grabbed his legs, and they noticed that he must have lost control of his bladder because the smell of urine was permeating the air. It didn't matter, though. The only thing that mattered was getting Raphael to the clinic as quickly as possible. They all muttered prayers to Jesus and Mary as they heaved Raphael's body down the local, dirt road.

Another thirty minutes passed, and they felt they might not be able to carry him another minute. It was getting dark and they were so scared and exhausted, they thought their bodies would not be able to walk another centimeter. Suddenly, they heard the sound of a car coming from behind, its headlights making long rays of light on the road. Juan and Jorge immediately let go of Raphael's legs and ran in front of the car yelling. The car stopped quickly and a man in a farmer's hat got out of the car.

"Hey, you crazy or something?!?" He was so angry, he was looking at the boys like he wanted to tan their hides.

"Señor! Thank God, Señor! My brother has been stung by a

scorpion and we need to get him to the clinic! He cannot even walk any longer!" Jorge was crying and yelling with all his might.

"Get in the car now!" The man opened the back for them as quickly as possible. Rudy and Manny dragged Raphael over and pushed up his torso to get him in the back seat. Jorge and Juan ran around to the other side and slid Raphael across the seat by his arms. When Raphael was lying in the back, Juan and Jorge got in next to Raphael while Rudy and Manny climbed into the front. The man got into the driver's side, quickly shut the door, and sped along the dirt road.

"Thank you, Señor," Rudy exclaimed when they were on their way. "You are a messenger from God."

To Juan, Jorge, Rudy and Manny, this was the longest ten minutes of their lives. They were completely silent and when Rudy turned back to check on Raphael, he realized that Raphael was unconscious. Rudy checked his chest to make sure that his cousin was still breathing. Raphael was breathing, but his breaths seemed short and raspy like he was laboring hard for every breath.

When they reached the clinic, the driver stopped his car with a loud jolt directly in front of the hospital doors. The boys worked quickly and took Raphael out of the car from the left side. The man held the door and they half–dragged Raphael inside where an attendant knew instantly that it was a medical emergency. A gurney was pushed over to Raphael, and the boys lifted him onto it in a hushed flurry.

The attendant looked at Rudy and asked, "Scorpion?"

Rudy stared back and said, "Centruroides," and Raphael was whisked away toward the emergency room.

When Raphael woke up three days later in the presence of his mother, father, grandfather, brothers, sisters, and cousins on his way to a full recovery, there was only one memory of the scorpion incident that would last forever—the woman in light–blue who had come to visit him every night in the clinic and the smell of lilac that accompanied her.

CHAPTER SIXTEEN

By the time Raphael entered his last year of high school, he was determined to become a priest. Raphael thought it would be best to enter the seminary in Puebla where his Uncle, Padre Miguel, was a priest and pastor. When he announced his decision to his parents, they were so excited that they threw him a party, and all his family and close friends attended. Pedro, already twenty–five, was finishing his last year of residency and would begin practicing medicine that fall. Anna had become a grade school teacher, and Jorge and Juan were studying computers at the university. They wanted to follow in their father's footsteps and run the family's computer business. Miguel and Maria were enjoying their remaining years in grade school.

The Trujillos were happy, but adding another priest to the family was the icing on the cake. In Mexico, it was considered an honor to become a priest, and Raphael's parents took that honor seriously on the night of the party. Carlos and Rita were glowing with pride from ear to ear. Raphael stood on the backyard porch and admired his mother's party decorations. There were strings of colorful lights and lanterns hanging from the ceiling of the porch and from poles in the yard. Friends of the family were playing live Mariachi music, and there were so many people dancing, Raphael could not even count the number.

Raphael felt a hand on his shoulder, and he turned to see a beautiful girl named Carmelita come up from behind. They graduated together and would probably remain friends for a lifetime.

"Carmelita!" Raphael put his arms around Carmelita's waist and kissed her on both cheeks.

"Hola, Raphael and congratulations!" Carmelita embraced her friend, and the two stood arm and arm watching the dancers. She turned back toward him and took both of his hands in hers. "You know, we always knew that God was saving you for something special—everyone in school—we always knew."

"That means the world coming from you," Raphael said as he peered into Carmelita's eyes.

"Where will you go to study?" Carmelita asked.

"Puebla."

"Good. That is not too far away and I can visit."

"I would not have it any other way."

Carmelita let go of Raphael's hands and hugged him tightly. "Raphael, I would have been jealous if you were celebrating your engagement to someone else tonight, but marrying our Mother Church makes me so happy for you my heart feels like it might burst."

"Carmelita, if I were not marrying the Church, I would surely be marrying you. Now I hope that you will remain in my life as my best friend." Raphael smiled, his teeth straight and white, his black wavy hair surrounding his handsome face. "Someday you will meet the man of your dreams and I will be the rugged, handsome priest who marries you and baptizes your little niños!"

Suddenly, Raphael and Carmelita heard a loud scream come from one of the dancers. Rita was frantically screaming and crying as she looked down at the ground where Carlos was lying, his body unmoving. Raphael and Carmelita rushed down the porch steps to the commotion around his father.

"He's fainted! He's fainted!" Rita kept screaming over and over. Raphael put an arm around his mother while Pedro knelt to check Carlos' vital signs.

*

When Carlos was diagnosed with stage four pancreatic cancer, the Trujillo family was devastated. He went through chemotherapy and radiation treatments like a hero. When six months passed and the cancer miraculously disappeared, the family attributed it to Raphael's prayers at the seminary in Puebla. He went into the chapel every night and knelt in front of the Blessed Virgin asking that his father be saved and rid of cancer. Raphael had read that whatever Mary requests of her son, Jesus does not refuse. Blessed Pope John Paul II also said, "Through Mary to Jesus." Raphael's family knew of his prayers to Mary and when Carlos went into remission, they sensed that Mary had worked a miracle for the Trujillo family.

Raphael spent his first year studying philosophy and began his coursework in theology for the next two years. He was a remarkable student, and his professors knew that he would make an excellent priest.

One day while Raphael was in the chapel praying, Padre Miguel asked to take him to lunch. His uncle told him that the United States was in need of Spanish speaking priests. Padre Miguel had connections to a seminary in New Jersey called the Immaculate Conception Seminary School of Theology. He knew several graduates of the seminary from Mexico who had been ordained priests through the Archdiocese of Newark. This might be an excellent opportunity for Raphael, and his service to the Church in the United States would be greatly appreciated.

"Perhaps Mary is calling you to the United States, Raphael," Padre Miguel said.

Raphael immediately began the process to enter the Immaculate

Conception Seminary School of Theology—a school dedicated to Mary, the Immaculate Conception. Within one month, Raphael entered a community in Puebla to begin his introduction to the English language. After six months, he interviewed for the American seminary and was immediately accepted. Raphael was granted a visa and moved to the Emmaus House in Newark. He spent one year studying English at Rutgers University and after passing his MATs, he began his seminary studies at Immaculate Conception Seminary. Four years later, Raphael Diego Ruiz Trujillo graduated from the seminary with a Masters in Divinity and a Masters in Pastoral Ministry.

On May 15, 2000, when Raphael had just celebrated his twenty–seventh birthday, he was ordained a priest through the Archdiocese of Newark at the Cathedral Basilica of the Sacred Heart. Raphael's entire family sat in the first pew of the great cathedral looking upon their son, brother, grandson and nephew with the greatest admiration and respect. Raphael had found his calling in the house of the Lord, and the happiness that gleamed in his eyes was something from heaven itself. The last memory Raphael had of this fantastic celebration was the look of joy in his father's eyes when he turned to face the congregation as Padre Raphael. Raphael had never seen his father cry until that day.

*

Father Raphael's first assignment in the United States was as parochial vicar at Saint John's Church in Bergenfield, New Jersey. St. John's was a large suburban parish with four thousand families, and there were five priests assigned to the church—an American pastor, a Filipino, a Colombian, an Italian, and now a Mexican. Saint John's had a large Hispanic community, and there were special Masses said in Spanish every Sunday. Many of these Masses were said by Father Raphael, but his specialty was working with the youth of the parish. Teens loved "Father Raffa," as he became known, for two simple reasons: he was young, and he loved being a priest. During his four years at Saint John's, there were many young men who thought about the priesthood because they wanted to be like Father Raffa.

When the Archbishop of Newark needed a new pastor at Saint Mary's Church in Dumont, he asked Father Raphael to take the position. He was only thirty–one. With 2,400 families, Father Raphael was given two parochial vicars: Father Rudy from the Philippines and Father Francisco from Colombia. Three years went by and the parish began to flourish with the many different activities that went on at Saint Mary's Church. There were four Masses every weekend and two Masses every week day. Father Raphael was well–loved and made himself available to his parishioners as often as he could. He missed his family in Mexico, but he was able to stay in contact with his family through e–mail.

This was how Raphael found out about the return of his father's cancer. As soon as his mother sent an e–mail, he took a flight to Puebla and drove a rented car to his hometown of Atlixco. Raphael's father was home from the hospital, the cancer winning its battle against his body. Carlos preferred to die at home.

Raphael walked into the house where he had grown up and saw his mother sitting alone on the couch in the den. She looked completely ashen, paler than he had ever seen her. When Rita saw her son, she let out a hushed cry and ran into his arms. Raphael's mother stayed like that for a long time, crying into the shoulder of her handsome son who had now become her spiritual pillar—a beacon of light shining out in her darkest hour.

When Rita felt she could not cry any longer, she pulled back from Raphael's arms. "He will be so relieved to see you," she said in a low voice. "He is fighting it. He is fighting death and is afraid to go. You should go and give him the comfort he needs."

Raphael walked up the stairs toward the bedroom that his mother and father had shared for forty–two years. When he saw his father lying on the large, king–sized bed, Raphael almost did not recognize him. The muscular, burly figure of his father had vanished and the weakened, emaciated resemblance of him was lying in the center of the bed, his head propped up by a stack of pillows, his body covered by a quilted comforter. His father's eyes were closed, and his chest was moving haltingly, as if he were struggling to catch every breath. Raphael looked around the room and saw Anna sitting in a rocking chair next to an open window. Her head was propped against the back of the chair and her eyes were closed as if she, too, were catching a quick nap.

Raphael's mother came up from behind and whispered, "Anna's been here almost every night for the past week staying up with him so that I could get some sleep. Pedro's been here, too, to make sure his pain does not become unbearable. He's on a morphine patch. That has been helping."

"Where is Pappa?"

"Out on the porch with Miguel and Maria and their families. Your grandfather has been so wonderful. I always knew how much he loved your father, but now even Carlos knows."

"How about Juan and Jorge? Are they at work?"

"Yes. They have been taking care of the business for Dad."

Carlos began to wake. When he saw his son standing before him in his priestly collar, his eyes lit up and he smiled broadly.

"Raffa...my son," he said in such a low voice, Raphael could barely hear his father.

Raphael walked to the side of the bed and knelt to embrace his father. Anna woke and smiled when she saw her brother. The two women left the room so that Raphael and Carlos could be alone.

"How do you feel?" Raphael asked his father.

"I've had better days." Carlos tried to sit up, but he did not have the strength. "I think God is calling me home, but..." His voice trailed off and he seemed like he didn't want to finish his thought.

"Are you afraid?" Raphael asked.

"I don't want to leave your mother."

"But you will only be apart until she rejoins you. Just think of it as paving the way for her so that one day you can be reunited in the kingdom of heaven."

"I know, but what if I'm not invited…into the kingdom of heaven?"

"You know Jesus loves you, right? That you are God's son?"

"Yes, but I have been a sinner."

"No more than any of us are sinners."

"I don't judge others. I just know my own faults." Carlos looked away from his son and over to the door leading into the room.

"Would you like to say your confession to me? It might make you feel better about the situation."

"I do not think I can say my sins to my own son."

"Do not look at me as you son, Father. Look at me as your priest."

Father Raphael remembered the bond that was created that afternoon in the dimly lit room where his father lay dying. Throughout his father's last confession, Raphael kept recalling one particular phrase—that our sins are washed as white as snow in the blood of the Lamb—this was what it meant to confess to a priest.

Later that evening, the Trujillo family was congregated in front of Carlos' bed while he struggled with the reality of his oncoming death. Raphael took out his crucifix and told his father to gaze upon it as he held the beautiful figure of Christ before his father's eyes. It was somewhere between 7:30 and 7:45 when his father expelled his final breath surrounded by his wife, father–in–law and seven children. The spouses and grandchildren of the family were out on the porch and in the backyard.

Before his father's passing, Raphael felt God's grace when he anointed him with holy oil and gave him final absolution. The Trujillo family recited the Apostles' Creed together several times during Carlos' final minutes. Raphael held the crucifix before his father and told him not to take his eyes away from Jesus. He told him to have courage and follow where Jesus was leading him.

Carlos died gazing at the crucifix his son held before him. Raphael looked over toward his mother. When he saw the look of love in her eyes, Raphael smelled the fragrance of lilac for the third time in his life.

CHAPTER SEVENTEEN

Drew Harrison stood by Cassy's hospital bedside gazing down at his wife who slept peacefully. Six weeks had passed since she fell into a coma, but Cassy still looked young and beautiful, her lips red, her cheeks pink, and her body still filled with obvious vitality.

His eyes filled with tears as he bent down to kiss her.

"I pray to God that you will wake soon. I pray that you and I will live a long life together forever." Drew stroked Cassy's long, auburn hair with the back of his hand.

Just then, Dr. Andrews gently knocked and entered Cassy's room.

The doctor shook Drew's hand, and the two men smiled warmly at one another. They had become genuine friends who shared a strong common goal—to see Cassy regain her health as soon as possible.

"She looks better every day I visit," Drew said.

"I agree," Dr. Andrews replied as he noticed the obvious color in Cassy's cheeks. Her chest was rapidly rising and falling and her pupils were darting back and forth underneath her eyelids as if she were in the midst of a dream. Cassy's mind was extremely active.

"I wonder what she's dreaming about," Drew said as if he had read Dr. Andrew's mind.

"Whatever it is…it looks like she's getting a great workout," Dr. Andrews said smiling. "Look, Drew, I know you're hopeful, and I really do believe that Cassy's going to come out of this. Her scans look completely normal, and there doesn't appear to be any brain damage, but I want to make sure that we remain cautiously optimistic. There is every reason to remain optimistic, but we also need to be cautious in our optimism. That way, if anything should happen, it won't be such a shock."

"No, I understand. I think cautiously optimistic is exactly where I am right now." Drew turned toward the window and peered out through the dampness of an autumn shower. He turned back toward Cassy's doctor, both hands dug deep into the pockets of his gray slacks. "I won't lie to you, Dr. Andrews. There are times I'm so hopeful, I think Cassy's going to jump up off her bed and come running toward me. Then, there are other times, I think she's never going to wake up ever, and I'm left to make some horrible decision about whether or not to keep her on life support…"

"Let's not let our minds go down that path, Drew, the negative path. When I said, 'cautiously optimistic,' I meant always positive. Always positive and hopeful. Always positive and optimistic. That means keep the optimism, and just let it stay controlled."

"That's good. I like that," Drew replied. "A controlled optimism."

"Right." Dr. Andrews held up Cassy's wrist to take her pulse. Everything appeared normal, and he gently lowered Cassy's wrist. "Listen, Drew. Along that optimistic path, I need to tell you something that I think is extremely promising and positive, but it's also a bit…difficult to explain."

"Yes?" Drew asked.

"The physical therapist came in yesterday to work on Cassy's legs to make sure that her muscles remain active, so there's less chance of atrophy…"

"Yes?" Drew asked again.

"The physical therapist said that Cassy's muscles appeared

healthy, and that it looked like she'd been getting daily workouts since she's been in a coma."

"What?" Drew was having difficulty understanding what the doctor was trying to explain.

"I know this seems completely implausible," Dr. Andrews replied. "The physical therapist said it looked like Cassy was getting regular exercise in her sleep. There is no real medical reason for this, but it's obviously good news. The only plausible explanation is that perhaps her brain has become so active, she has begun to have control over muscle activity, like the saying, 'mind over matter,' except this is more of a literal lesson in behavioral kinesiology, the study of mind over matter."

"Is this evidence that Cassy is getting ready to come out of her coma?" Drew asked.

"This is evidence that Cassy's mind is alive and well. Perhaps more than some who are completely awake," Dr. Andrews answered.

"That's great."

"Yes, and there's one more thing, Drew. This is the more bizarre of the physical therapist's findings, and I have no explanation whatsoever for this."

"Yes?"

"She said that Cassy's feet were completely covered with dirt and grass stains."

Drew stared at Dr. Andrews with a bewildered expression on his handsome face.

The doctor's only reply was to shrug his shoulders. He had no reasonable explanation to give Drew. The only explanation was completely ludicrous. Dr. Andrews honestly believed that the only way Cassy could have grass–stained feet was to run through grass fields in the middle of the night, which was absolutely impossible given her condition.

*

When Dr. Andrews left Cassy's room, Drew sat in the chair next to the window. He could not help but remain curious about the physical therapist's findings.

"How could Cassy's feet be dirty if she can't walk?" Drew thought. "Perhaps her feet were dirty because she hasn't had a real bath in six weeks. Perhaps the therapist saw shadows and mistook them for dirt."

Drew rose from his chair and pulled Cassy's sheet up so that he could see her feet for himself. The bottoms of her feet appeared white and clean.

"They must have cleaned them," Drew thought.

Drew's mind raced for an hour as he paced back and forth in front of Cassy's bed. He looked at his watch and realized he should have dinner before his concert later that evening. Drew kissed Cassy's forehead before he turned to go. In the outside corridor, he said good night to the nurses on duty and walked to the two large elevators at the end of the hallway. He pushed the down button and waited for the doors to open. Drew was surprised to see Nurse Bridget carrying a box of clothes as she stepped off one of the elevators.

"Mr. Harrington," she said. "I was just going to Cassy's room to hang her things in her closet. They were misplaced in a locker downstairs."

"Thanks, Bridget," Drew said.

"Would you like to take them with you? Or would you prefer to have me hang them in her room?"

"Hang them, Bridget. She'll need them soon."

"Yes, Mr. Harrington."

Drew stepped inside the waiting elevator. "Thanks!" he called to Nurse Bridget while the doors closed in front of him.

Bridget walked to Cassy's room with the box in her arms and stepped inside. She looked over at Cassy who slept peacefully. Bridget continued to the closet and began to hang Cassy's blouse and skirt. When she lifted the skirt onto the hanger, a small white sheet of paper fell out of one of the pockets and fluttered to the floor. Bridget picked it up and looked to see if it was something to keep or throw away.

The note said, "Check Leviticus and Kings. Also Zephaniah. Let Elaina know I now have all I need to put the Taninsam ties together."

"That's strange," Bridget thought. "What would Cassy want with secret notes in her pocket? And who's this Elaina person with Taninsam ties?"

Bridget realized it wasn't right to eavesdrop. She folded the piece of paper and put it back into Cassy's skirt pocket. She would let Mr. Harrington know about the note the next time she saw him.

*

Dr. Bernard Lanton's body was found floating in the Hudson River near a pier in the financial district of New York City. The man who had poisoned Cassy six weeks earlier was discovered dead two weeks before Halloween.

Sal Trentino walked toward the pier practicing lines he had been rehearsing that morning when he noticed the body. The last thing Sal thought he'd find near his investment banking firm was a dead man floating face down in the Hudson. He had come here to celebrate the first anniversary of meeting the girl of his dreams— the girl he was scheduled to meet in a few minutes, on the very same day at the very same time he had bumped into her accidentally on his way to work a year ago.

When Sal discovered the body, his first reaction was to feel for the black velvet box that held an exquisite two–carat diamond ring, as if seeing a dead body had anything to do with whether or not it would still be there. Sal had planned to put the ring on her finger as soon as he knelt down and asked her to marry him.

"What do I do now?" Sal asked himself.

This wasn't going to be the romantic setting he had imagined so often since he bought the ring. Not with some dead guy floating next to the pier. Sal realized he'd better call the police while he waited. He didn't want to seem irresponsible to the girl he wanted to make his wife. She'd think it was terrible if he didn't call the police and report this fish–floating dead buffoon who was really messing up his perfect plan.

"Maybe I can just walk her away from the body so she won't be able to see it, and then I can call the police after I propose," Sal thought. "He's not going anywhere. He's dead."

Sal's guilt got the best of him, so he decided to make the call before the body floated out to sea. He realized his cell phone was in the same pocket as the ring. He wanted to get it over with as quickly as possible before she arrived, so he pushed his hand into his pocket and grabbed hold of his phone. Sal pulled out the phone and realized, too late, that the black velvet box was on top of the phone and coming out of his pocket hard and fast. Before he could do anything to stop it, he watched as the box flew through the air and into the water, landing only about five feet from the dead body. The velvet box with the engagement ring floated for a second and then sunk deep into the murky muck of the Hudson River.

"What the hell!?!" Sal screamed out under his breath.

Just then, Sal felt someone's hand on his shoulder.

"You okay, Sal?"

Sal turned from the river and saw beautiful Susan, his Susan, looking into his distraught eyes with worry. He felt completely dumbfounded and no explanation of what had just happened came into his mind.

"You okay?" Susan asked again.

Without giving it any more thought, Sal got down on one knee and took Susan's hand in his own. "Susan..." he began slowly. "I came here today to ask you to be my wife because I love you and I want to spend the rest of my life with you. Now, if you look behind me you're gonna see a dead guy floatin' in the river. When I thought about how I'd propose, I never thought in my wildest dreams there'd be this dead guy there, but there is...and I had this all planned out. I had the most beautiful ring, but now...the ring flew out of my pocket when I was trying to get my phone to call the cops and it landed smack dab in the Hudson, and now it's probably sitting in the belly of a fish swimming underneath the floating body of that dead guy!"

Sal had spoken so fast, he hadn't even taken a breath. He stopped for a second and looked up to see Susan's expression.

Susan looked sick and pale, her eyes darting back and forth in disbelief. She looked past Sal's head toward the water. As soon as she caught a glimpse of Dr. Bernard Lanton's body floating above the engagement ring she would probably never see in her lifetime, she let go of Sal's hands and took a step backward.

Before Sal could get back on his feet again, Susan was lying on the ground passed out cold. He looked down at his phone and realized he had already hit "911," to alert the police before Susan arrived. Sal pushed the "send" button and waited to report, not one, but two disasters. He knew the police were never going to believe this one.

CHAPTER EIGHTEEN

By the middle of October, Michael and Linda had become fast friends in their effort to find Debbie and discover the truth of the bloodstone legacy. They were both very concerned because Debbie had been missing for two weeks. Lucia, Pietro and Father Mac had done everything in their power to try to locate her. Debbie had been last seen at the Milwaukee Psychiatric Institute, and every employee had been interviewed and had gone out of their way to help with the investigation.

Lucia and Pietro had also contacted the police, and every law enforcement officer in the southern half of Wisconsin was busy investigating Debbie's disappearance. The Romanos felt confident that Debbie would turn up soon, but a sense of fear kept them from speaking the truth out loud. They knew deep in their hearts that the person who had kidnapped Debbie was the man in black, the man who had visited her at Marquette and the hospital. They had given this information to the police, but not a word had been spoken about him since, not by any member of the group.

Linda, Michael and Father Mac had spent the evening at the Romano's home discussing the case over a lovely Italian–style dinner. Lucia was a fantastic cook and went out of her way to prepare a feast of lasagna, fresh–baked bread, salad and home–

made tiramisu.

After dinner, they sat in the living room around a large, glass coffee table. There was a marble fireplace with a long oak shelf that ran above the hearth where pictures of the Romano family were displayed in ornate frames. On top of the coffee table were books on cameos and a large, leather–bound Bible.

The Romanos sat on a rose–colored loveseat where Lucia looked visibly nervous. She was wringing her hands in her lap, and Pietro put a loving arm around her shoulders to console her. Father Mac sat in a recliner with his pipe, and Linda and Michael sat in matching arm chairs holding notebooks crammed with research they had both compiled.

Michael had gathered detailed information on the mysterious man in black. "Before we discuss our research," he began, "I think the most important thing is to try to think as objectively as possible about the facts of Debbie's disappearance. If we allow emotion to play too big a role, we might miss out on an important detail, something that might help us find Debbie."

Michael looked directly at the Romanos before he continued.

Pietro put a hand on his wife's knee and smiled reassuringly. Lucia nodded her agreement before Michael continued.

"Okay, then. All evidence regarding Debbie's disappearance points to the tall, mysterious black–haired man Debbie has been seen with on numerous occasions. Linda witnessed the two together at Marquette, and Debbie's roommate and the staff at the hospital witnessed him visiting on several occasions. Debbie was seen with this man just prior to her disappearance. There also seems to be a connection between this man and the bloodstone cameo necklace that we have seen Debbie wear. In fact, every time this man was seen with Debbie, she was wearing the bloodstone cameo necklace; the same necklace that Father Mac believes has some sort of magical, demonic power. Therefore, we have no choice but to deduce that this man, the man who calls himself, 'David Bloodstone,' has a connection to the bloodstone cameo and a connection to demonism."

When Michael said the word, "demonic," Lucia made an audible gasp and lowered her face into her hands. Everyone waited while Pietro placed his hand on her shoulder and whispered comforting words into her ear.

Lucia regained her composure, lifted her head, and apologized to Michael.

Michael nodded and continued, "I think we should divide our evidence regarding Debbie into three categories: first, the bloodstone necklace; second, David Bloodstone; and third, if I may, Debbie's biological mother, Elaina Taninsam, and any possible connection she may have to Debbie's disappearance."

Michael looked at Lucia apologetically, and she smiled back to let him know there was no need to apologize. "No need to worry, Michael. Please, go on," she said.

Michael nodded, "First, we know something about the bloodstone necklace, and second, we know something about David Bloodstone. However, what do we know about Elaina Taninsam? We know nothing in relation to Debbie. She's had no contact with her daughter since she was a baby. The only thing we know about Elaina is that she is president of PSI or Parenting Services International. This corporation was created by Elaina's grandmother, Alexandria, and has nothing to do with bloodstone cameos or necklaces or anything magical whatsoever. It's funded, in part, by government subsidies, in part, by private donations, and, in part, by the services they provide."

"What services do they provide?" Pietro asked.

"Women's health services, birth control…but they make most of their money performing abortions," Michael answered.

The room grew quiet, and no one spoke for a full minute.

Finally, Father Mac broke the silence. "Well, it's wonderful to know that Debbie's biological mother has chosen such a splendidly moral profession for herself," he said sarcastically. Father Mac turned to Lucia and Pietro, "The best thing that ever happened to

Debbie was when you two entered her life. Thank God for the both of you."

"Thank God for Debbie," Lucia responded.

"Yes, and we are going to find her. I have all the faith in the world," Pietro added.

Next, Linda had finished a very detailed diagram on the origin of the bloodstone, and was holding a thick spiral notebook on her lap. "Michael talked about three categories: the bloodstone necklace, David and Elaina. When we researched David and Elaina, we came to a quick dead end. However, when I researched the origin of the bloodstone, things began to get interesting. I also want to clarify that some of the findings on the origin of the bloodstone are fact and some are fantasy, so try to keep an open mind because I think that some of the fantasy may actually become fact, as well. Let's start with the facts: one—jasper stone was used to make bloodstone when the blood of Christ fell on jasper stone at the foot of the cross during the crucifixion; two—jasper stone was the twelfth stone on Aaron's Breastplate; and three—jasper stone was used in several instances in the Book of Revelation when John spoke of the holy city coming down from heaven with radiance like that of jasper, and the wall was constructed of jasper and the first course of stones of the foundations of the city was jasper. Father Mac, could you fill in the Scriptural blanks for us?"

Father Mac smiled and nodded. "When Michael visited the Museum of Lapidary Arts in Elmhurst and sent pictures of bloodstone cameos to Linda that looked exactly like Debbie's bloodstone cameo, I didn't think the research would lead anywhere new. However, when the curator at the museum told Michael that bloodstone was considered to be the Bible stone, it's just as Linda explained. All of the facts point to one specific stone—jasper. I never thought there was any importance or relevance to a seemingly unprecious stone like jasper. We could all go to the museum right now and purchase a piece of jasper for a small amount of change. But then I realized that when it comes to

Scripture, jasper has significant value. Look at it this way, the Bible begins and ends with Genesis and the Book of Revelation, and jasper is mentioned in significant places in each book."

Father Mac picked up the Bible, "First, there's Genesis, which speaks of Benjamin's tribe as the twelfth tribe of Israel, and Benjamin's stone as jasper, which is placed in the twelfth position on Aaron's breastplate. Then, there's the Book of Revelation where Christ chose twelve Apostles to proclaim his teachings to all the nations, and Christ is said to have looked upon like a 'jasper.' Again, jasper is mentioned, but so is something else. I have always believed that Biblical numerology is important, and the important number to consider here is the number, "twelve." In other words, the twelve foundations for the Church are the twelve tribes of Israel and the twelve Apostles upon whose teachings the Church was built."

Father Mac sat back in his chair and took a moment to think. "First, Bible numbers are very significant because they speak to us on multiple levels. They make the meaning of the number transcend into a fuller, deeper language. This is the reason jasper is so significant. It appears as the first stone of the foundation of the New Jerusalem, which represents the first apostle, Peter, who became the 'rock on which the church was built,' and it appears twelfth on Aaron's breastplate, which represents Christ and His Church in total. Jesus had twelve disciples, and there were twelve tribes of Israel. In Revelation, 24 elders and 144,000 are multiples of 12. The New Jerusalem city has 12 foundations, 12 gates, 12 thousand furlongs, a tree with 12 kinds of fruit, 12 times a year eaten by 12 times 12,000 or 144,000. The Biblical number 12 implies supremacy and the only stone to be mentioned so supremely in every context and given the importance of being first and last, or first and twelfth is jasper. It is no wonder that God chose to create bloodstone from jasper."

Lucia pulled herself from her husband's arms and asked, "Do you mean my daughter was wearing a special Biblical necklace with powers from God?"

"Yes and no," Father Mac answered. "Yes, it does appear that her necklace had special powers. I'm just not altogether sure that the powers came from God."

"But bloodstone was created from Christ's blood, right? It's a holy stone," Lucia sounded like she was pleading for Father Mac to change his mind.

"Lucia, Debbie is a good girl," Father Mac began. "She is a daughter of Christ. But perhaps when the bloodstone is put into the wrong hands, it can be manipulated to do evil. When Debbie was wearing the necklace at the hospital, she was not acting of her own will. There was an evil force acting upon her."

Pietro sat up in his seat, "In terms of this evil force, Michael, I need to ask you a question. I know that when you and the authorities tried to find the woman who first contacted you to do the story on my daughter that you came up empty handed. The number she used to phone you was a dead number. I also know that Elaina Taninsam had no apparent ties to Debbie since she was a baby. But what about David Bloodstone? Father Mac, is he the evil force you are speaking about?"

Father Mac decided to take this opportunity to discuss Debbie's disappearance. "Michael, if I may...I would like to discuss this evil. We all know the mysterious man who was visiting Debbie at the hospital...the man named David Bloodstone. We know that the bloodstone cameo necklace that Debbie wore had some sort of magical power, but we also know that this man, this David Bloodstone, is the one who created the evil in the bloodstone. I know in my very depths that David Bloodstone is evil and he bears the name, 'Bloodstone.' There is no coincidence here. David Bloodstone is the manipulator. He used his evil to turn the bloodstone into an evil device, and I am quite certain that he is the man who kidnapped Debbie."

Pietro stood up as soon as he heard David Bloodstone's name. "We gave every single police officer in the state of Wisconsin a description of David Bloodstone," he exclaimed. "What I'd like to ask is how a tall, thin, striking frame of a man standing at 6'4" can just disappear into thin air? Forget the origin of jasper or the origin of bloodstone. How about the origin of David Bloodstone?"

Linda glanced at Michael and Father Mac and smiled reassuringly at Pietro. "That's exactly what I want to cover next. Mr. Romano, remember when Father Mac and I spoke of Aaron's Breastplate? Well, I came across information connected to jasper and bloodstone that might shed some light on David Bloodstone. It's called the Urim and Thummim."

"The Urim and Thummim?" Michael asked surprised.

"Yes," Linda replied. "No one really knows what the Urim and Thummim was. It could have been the breastplate itself or something hidden inside the breastplate. The only thing anyone really knows for sure is that the device was used for casting lots, for telling the future, for speaking with God."

Father Mac chimed in, "The Urim and Thummim was used by Aaron and King Saul. In the Hebrew Bible, specifically the First Book of Samuel, after Samuel's death and burial, King Saul sought the guidance of the Urim and Thummim as to his best course of action against the assembled forces of the Philistines. When he received no answer from God, he sought out the Witch of Endor for guidance..."

"The Witch of Endor?" Michael interjected.

Linda looked at Father Mac before she answered, "We think David Bloodstone may be a descendent of a long line of a family of witches. Specifically, a descendent of the Witch of Endor."

"I have a meeting tomorrow with an old friend of mine," Father Mac added. "He's a local rabbi in Milwaukee who might be able to shed some light on the Urim and Thummim and the Witch of Endor. We think this might be our clue to find David Bloodstone."

CHAPTER NINETEEN

The following day, when Father Mac met with Rabbi Joshua Levine, Linda and Michael took advantage of a warm October day on the waters of Geneva Lake. It was the last day to sail before Linda's family pulled their boats from the lake for the fall and winter months. Geneva Lake was one of the most beautiful deep, inland freshwater lakes in the country with crystal cold clear water that shined dark blue. The lake was nine miles long and three miles wide with three prosperous towns situated along the coast: Lake Geneva on the east, Fontana on the west, and Williams Bay in the middle of the two.

The Walters were members of the Lake Geneva Yacht Club, and Linda's family owned several sailboats including a small, 20–foot sailboat called a C–Scow that her family raced in the Yacht Club C–Class every Wednesday and Saturday.

Michael and Linda finished Sunday brunch with her parents and stood on her private pier looking out over the water. The wind blew hard enough to produce waves with white caps on the top of the dark blue water.

Michael looked at Linda while the wind blew through her red hair. "Great day for a sail," he said.

"Awesome day," she responded. "It must be blowing at least

twelve knots."

Linda walked over to the shore station next to the pier and turned the crank wheel to lower the sleek, white C–Scow named "Mindy." It was nestled in the station like a baby sleeping peacefully in her cradle.

Mindy was lowered into the water by a hoist, a job made easy when the racing boat weighed only 650 pounds. When the boat was settled in the water, Linda took the bowline and she and Michael walked Mindy around to the front of the pier.

"What a beautiful boat!" Michael exclaimed.

"Yeah, we do all right with Mindy," Linda responded heartily. "Dad and I have won a lot of races with her. I'd be in big trouble if anything happened to her, but I know you're an experienced sailor, too."

"Yeah," Michael said a bit unconvincingly. He hoped the few times he'd gone out sailing with friends would prove helpful. He knew that a C–Scow was difficult to keep upright in winds above ten knots.

Linda held the boat steady so Michael could get in first. He wasn't quite as graceful as he would have liked, but he managed to stand upright and hold onto the pier to steady the boat for Linda. She hopped on like a prize stallion jumping over a fence.

As soon as Linda was on board, she hoisted the main sail up into the wind. Michael noticed that there was no jib, a sail that worked in conjunction with the main sail to capture more wind.

"No jib, huh?" Michael asked.

"A C–Scow doesn't need a jib," Linda replied.

Linda trimmed in the main sail, and the sleek sailboat accelerated quickly as they made their way up the lake from Lake Geneva toward Fontana. The boat was fast and took the wind well. When it began to heel, Linda gestured to Michael to hike out over the water on the high side of the boat. Michael was used to a sailboat with a heavy lead keel on the bottom, which automatically balanced the boat when it heeled from the force of the wind, so he knew exactly why they needed to hike out on the high side. This would create their own personal keel to counterbalance the tipping force of the wind.

Michael watched as Linda slipped her feet into the hiking straps and half her body was quickly outside the boat. He was impressed at her strength and admired her tanned, muscular legs. Michael strapped himself into position, too, and carefully hiked out next to her. Linda was still holding onto the main sail sheet with half gloves on both hands that made her look like a professional sailor.

Michael hadn't remembered feeling this free in ages. They were traveling southwest and making their way toward Fontana quickly.

"How fast are we going?" Michael asked.

"If I had to guess, we're doing about seven knots," Linda responded with a huge grin. She had tied her hair back in a ponytail before they left the pier, and Michael could see Linda's face in the sun. She had eyes the color of aquamarine and there were a few freckles lightly spattered on her nose and cheeks. Michael felt his heart race from the thrill of sailing with such an exciting woman.

Linda told Michael that they were beating up the lake and would need to tack soon. She pulled the main sheet to uncleat it and moved the tiller for the tack. The bow of the boat moved left through the wind onto a starboard tack as they sat in the boat. As soon as they felt the boat begin to heel, they hiked out on the starboard side.

Michael felt the wind over his right shoulder. It felt incredible and completely exuberating. He looked at Linda and noticed how beautiful she looked. She was so comfortable on the water. He watched as she expertly handled the main sheet and tiller with hand and foot working simultaneously.

"Thanks so much for having me over today, Linda. This is really incredible—the lake, the boat, everything. I always felt lucky to live in Lake Geneva, but it must have been even better to live right on the lake."

Linda turned to Michael and smiled, "Yeah, but I don't get to enjoy it quite as much as you might think. My parents had to work really hard to get where they are today, and I think I work just as hard as they ever did. I've been working since I was twelve, and before that I was always around the marina while my parents worked. I was probably already learning the business before I learned to walk."

Linda spoke with sarcasm, but Michael could sense the immense pride Linda had for her parents and their business.

"So, why did you decide to pursue a degree in history?" Michael asked.

"Good question. I always had a curiosity about the past, you know? How we got to where we are today, the good and the bad. I mean, why was there ever slavery? Why was the freedom of millions of innocent, African people taken away? Thank God for Abraham Lincoln and the other people who came forward to abolish it. And what about the Holocaust? How could Adolf Hitler get away with so much evil? Why did millions of innocent human beings have to suffer like that? From an historical perspective, that's what I care about the most—the destruction of innocent human life.

"You know what, Michael? I look at abortion the same way as those other atrocities. The destruction of innocent human life. I look at our country, and I know it shouldn't be legal to murder innocent human beings. It's considered okay to kill. And that gets me. It doesn't make any sense. It's not okay to shackle innocent human beings because of the color of their skin. It's not okay to gas and murder innocent human beings because of their ethnic heritage or their religion. And it's not okay to kill innocent human beings at their first stages of life just because they're an 'inconvenience.' These are the reasons I decided to study history."

Michael could see tears welling in Linda's eyes. He touched her arm. "Linda, listen. I'm totally with you. And you know what?"

Linda smiled warmly. "What?" she asked.

"You have to meet my mother, and I have never said that to any girl before."

Linda laughed heartily. She felt the wind change and realized they needed to tack to port.

They had been out for nearly an hour, and Michael felt like a regular pro. In the distance, he saw another sailboat and a couple of power boats to his left. One speed boat, in particular, looked like it was heading toward them, but Michael knew that sailboats always had the right of way over power boats.

Michael and Linda were hiked out on the port side when Linda turned to Michael with a worried expression. "Michael?" she asked.

"Yeah?"

"I'm worried about Debbie. I mean, I know everyone's worried about Debbie, but I'm worried about her in a spiritual way. You know what I mean?"

"You mean you're worried because your best friend might have ties to a family of witches, and has just disappeared with a supernaturally–powered freak who is possessing her with a 2,000–year–old bloodstone cameo?"

"Yeah, that's exactly what I mean." Linda couldn't help but smile at Michael's wry sense of humor.

"I'm worried, too," Michael answered seriously.

Linda decided to tack back to starboard. She let out the sail and moved the tiller to start the tack. When they were in the middle of the tack, Michael noticed the speed boat again, the one that was headed toward them. It was still pointed toward their C–Scow, but this time it was much closer. There was only one person in the boat.

Michael pointed at the boat. "Linda, is it correct that sailboats always have the right of way?" he asked.

Linda noticed the speedboat, too. "Yeah, that's right. Probably some out–of–towner who doesn't know the rules." She finished the tack and steered the boat to the right to maneuver the C–Scow out of the way of the speed boat.

Linda and Michael hiked out on the starboard side.

They had sailed to an area of Lake Geneva called Black Point, which was located near Majestic Hills across from Williams Bay. Black Point was more than half way to Fontana, and they'd only been on the lake for an hour.

The two sailors were looking toward Fontana when Linda heard the sound of a speed boat so close to the port side of their C–Scow that her senses went on automatic heightened alert.

"What the…" Michael heard the sound, too, but it was too late.

The impact of the speed boat hit the C–Scow at the bow hard and fast. There was no way to see the boat coming because it had been hidden by the tall, main sail. The C–Scow tipped all the way over, and the main sail was left floating in the water with the boat on its side.

At the moment of impact, Michael and Linda were catapulted up into the air and landed on top of the main sail. They were left unhurt, but very shaken. The speed boat continued its momentum through the front of the C–Scow, and Michael and Linda caught a glimpse of the driver. Without a doubt, it was the very same person responsible for Debbie's disappearance.

Michael and Linda bobbed in the water as they watched the beautiful C–Scow sink into the depths of the dark blue lake. They had no thought of the loss of the boat, however. Their only thought was the image of the man in black as they watched his long, black ponytail fly in the wind, his speed boat turning around to come back toward them.

*

Michael and Linda were still a half mile away from land when the speed boat came racing back toward them. Their only thought was to go underwater and hide from the hideous demon who was trying to kill them. They looked at one another as the boat approached and took a huge gulp of air before they immersed deep within the waters of Geneva Lake. A few feet hidden under the dark blue of the water, Michael and Linda looked up to see the bottom of the speed boat overhead. Michael pointed south toward the shore of Black Point, which was over 140 feet and the deepest part of the lake. He and Linda kicked off their shoes and swam hard and fast in the cold water. Sixty–five–degree water on a hot October day could revitalize the body enough to swim faster than normally possible. Linda felt revitalized, too, but it was fear that made her swim so fast. When they could not go any further without coming up for air, they swam toward the surface to make sure there was no sign of the speed boat overhead. Everything looked clear.

As soon as their heads cleared the surface of the water, Michael and Linda looked around frantically to see where the speed boat had gone. They noticed it several feet away, southeast of where the two were rapidly treading water. The man in black was looking down at the water trying to spot them underneath.

Michael looked at Linda. "Let's go," he whispered.

Linda nodded and the two dove down again and swam deep and hard toward the shore. Every time they needed a breath, they came up frantically searching for the boat, and every time, the boat seemed further and further in the distance.

When they saw the shore in sight, Michael and Linda breathed a sigh of relief, but the sound of the speed boat brought back instantaneous fear. They looked up to see the man in black racing toward them again. Michael and Linda were both strong swimmers, but they were so exhausted in the cold water that they bobbed like floating beacons frozen with fear.

Michael and Linda saw the speed boat come closer and closer, and then it suddenly veered off in a northern direction toward the opposite shore. They realized why the man in black had given up pursuit. There was a water safety patrol boat in the distance with its lights flashing and its horn wailing. It was coming toward them—it's motive clear—this boat was coming to their rescue. Someone must have seen the accident from the shore and called for help. Michael and Linda felt more relief in that one instant than they thought anyone could feel in a lifetime.

CHAPTER TWENTY

Father Mac reached for the door to Rabbi Joshua Levine's office with a bit of trepidation. He didn't want to give his friend the wrong impression. If he started talking about demons that kidnap young girls or bloodstone cameos with mind–controlling powers, Josh would think he was crazy. Father Mac needed information on the Urim and Thummim from a Hebrew perspective. That was it. He knocked on the closed door.

"Come in," Rabbi Levine answered confidently.

When Father Mac walked into his old friend's office, there were books strewn all over the room. Every inch of wall space was hidden by rows of shelves filled with books turned on their sides and stacked on top of one other. There were large, leather–bound books with beautiful gold embossing. There were multiple copies of paperbacks intended to go to members of the rabbi's synagogue who requested information. There were pamphlets, CDs, DVDs, and copies of articles and papers. The rabbi had piles of books and papers piled so high on top of his desk that Father Mac could barely see his friend even after he stood.

"Is that you, Josh?" Father Mac half joked as he walked forward to shake his hand.

"Come in! Come in!" Rabbi Levine had always been

exceptionally jovial to Father Mac. The two had met ten years before at an interfaith gathering in Milwaukee.

"Thank you for taking the time to see me," Father Mac said.

"Of course, of course." The rabbi pointed to a chair in front of his desk.

Father Mac cleared a large pile of books off the chair and sat down.

"How are things at Saint Michael's?" Rabbi Levine asked.

The rabbi was on staff at the seminary in Milwaukee to teach Hebrew and Judeo–Christian courses. He had a keen understanding of the Holy Trinity and the Blessed Virgin Mary. In fact, Rabbi Levine taught a class on Mary, and some students could not understand that Mary was the Immaculate Conception because she was the only human being who had been born without sin. It was obvious to the rabbi that the virgin mother of the son of God had to be without sin and he couldn't understand his class's inability to comprehend this concept.

"How can you be Catholic and not understand that Mary is the Immaculate Conception?" Rabbi Levine exclaimed to his class. "Mary had to be without sin and a virgin who had not come in contact with a sinner in order to bear the son of God!" He put his hand to his heart and looked up at the ceiling, "Oy–yoy–yoy, I'm Jewish and I understand it!"

Father Mac and Rabbi Levine exchanged information regarding their church and temple before they got down to the business at hand.

"What can I do you for?" the rabbi asked.

"Well, it's just this. I'm really curious about the Jewish perspective on the Urim and Thummim. You know, what exactly is the Hebrew translation and interpretation of the Urim and Thummim?" Father Mac wriggled in his seat as he tried to find the right way to ask his question.

"The Urim and Thummim, ay?" Rabbi Levine was squinting at his friend over his modern, black metal reading glasses.

"Yes, the Urim and Thummim. You know, Aaron's Urim and Thummim." Father Mac shifted uncomfortably as he waited for his friend's response.

"Why?" Rabbi Levine asked candidly.

"Several of my parishioners have been asking me about the Old Testament, I mean, Hebrew Scripture, and one particular fellow asked me about the Urim and Thummim."

"You came all the way here just for that?" Rabbi Levine's office was almost two hours from Lake Geneva.

"Hard to believe?" Father Mac asked uncomfortably.

"Yes, I've seen you twenty or thirty times in the last ten years, and I think only one was spent here."

Father Mac wrestled with his decision to be less than forthcoming or risk looking like a complete nut case. The truth finally won out and he envisioned himself in a straightjacket before he continued. "Okay, okay. I need information on the Urim and Thummim because a family of witches known as The Taninsams might be distantly connected to the Witch of Endor."

Rabbi Levine sat for a full minute laughing before he settled down to address Father Mac seriously. "So you're really here to get information on the Witch of Endor?" he asked.

"Yes, I mean no." Father Mac realized he had to explain everything he knew about Deborah, Elaina and David before he could ask any more questions. "Let me start from the beginning," he said.

*

When Father Mac finished telling Rabbi Levine about the Taninsams, David Bloodstone, and their link to witchcraft and the power of the bloodstone cameos, the rabbi sat motionless with his jaw dropped to the edge of his tallest leather–bound book. He finally cleared his throat and sat forward in his chair. "Can I get you some water?" Rabbi Levine asked the priest.

"No thanks. I'm fine."

"Okay, I'll be right back," the rabbi rose from his desk and walked to his office door. "I'm in desperate need of liquid and I don't, in fact, mean water."

"Fine. Then count me in," Father Mac said with a wry smile.

When the rabbi returned, he was carrying two glasses with a clear brown liquid poured over ice. He gave one to Father Mac and they toasted one another. "To our shared God and His denial to protect us from the meshugana of this world." Rabbi Levine sat back down at his desk and downed the entire glass in one sip. He smiled, "Ah, much better. So you want to know about the Urim and Thummim?"

Father Mac took one small sip of the brown liquid and nodded his head.

"I'm assuming you already know that Aaron was said to have carried the Urim and Thummim with him inside his breastplate. I'm sure you also know that the Urim and Thummim was considered a plural thing and that the translation of the words is 'lights' and 'perfections.' And you may even know that the Urim and Thummim could have been used to cast lots, to find out the future and to communicate with God, right?" the rabbi asked.

Father Mac nodded again.

Rabbi Levine continued, "Okay, it's important to know that only a high priest could use the Urim and Thummim, which was a mode of communication different than Moses' because Moses spoke with God directly. Moses did not need a device to speak with God. Aaron was the first of the high priests to carry the device. Now, you might ask me, what did this device look like?" Rabbi Levine asked rhetorically. "No clue. However, there are some theories. One theory, I have come to believe in wholeheartedly."

The rabbi stood up before he continued. "You want another?" he asked.

"No, thanks. I'm still nursing this one," Father Mac held up his unfinished drink and set it on the edge of the desk before reaching for a notepad and pen.

When Rabbi Levine returned, he was carrying his drink and a laminated photocopy of a long scroll with ancient writing on it. The rabbi sat and downed his second drink before he opened the scroll. "You've heard of the Dead Sea Scrolls, but I'm not sure if you know that there have been scrolls recently discovered that pertain to the Holy Grail. I know that Christian legend has always assumed that the Holy Grail was the cup used by Christ at the Last Supper. This particular 'Holy Grail,' though, the one written about in the Dead Sea Scrolls may, in fact, be the Urim and Thummim." Rabbi Levine looked up to see Father Mac's reaction.

Father Mac looked stunned and took another sip of his drink.

Rabbi Levine continued, "This Holy Grail or Urim and Thummim has also been linked to legend. According to the story, it gave all earthly desires to its keeper in abundance. So, it was more than an oracle. More than a communication line to God. It was the most powerful object on earth. With it, you could acquire anything you wanted. With it, you could probably rule the world. But in the wrong hands, I don't know. I mean, it stands to reason that you would have to be a believer in the one true, God. Otherwise, the object could bring utter ruin to that individual. In the wrong hands, it would most likely bring death and destruction."

Father Mac took another sip of his drink, but it went down the wrong pipe and Rabbi Levine had to wait for his friend to finish coughing before he continued.

"The Holy Grail was thought to be a round glass ball filled with water and held in a tree–like stand," the rabbi said. "These were said to be Jewish objects or Urim and Thummim. Whether made of stone, metal or earth, or a combination of the three, there is little doubt that the Urim and Thummim existed, and was used by Jews with the proper authority who lived at the time from Aaron to Solomon."

Rabbi Levine picked up the laminated scroll. "According to the scrolls, the object known as the Holy Grail or Urim and Thummim was buried along with the Ark of the Covenant in a cave system somewhere in Jordan. The literal translation for this Holy Grail or Urim and Thummim is 'the stone that came down from the stars' or 'a pure stone exiled from paradise.'"

Father Mac cleared his throat, "Are you telling me that the Urim and Thummim or the 'Holy Grail,' as you put it, was cast out of heaven and landed somewhere on earth?"

"That's exactly what I'm saying," the rabbi replied. "According to the Dead Sea Scrolls, the Holy Grail or Urim and Thummim was thought to be a stone similar to agate. It says, 'I will make as agate all your pinnacles.' In another translation it is a stone with 'tongues of fire' where it says, 'the stone, just as (the Lord commanded...) (and your Urim shall come forth) with him, with tongues of fire.' The writings speak of the stone, 'He shall make you mighty by His Holy Name, so that you shall be as a lion among the beasts of the forest.' These writings give us some clue as to the visual description of the Holy Grail or Urim and Thummim."

"Where is it now?"

"Don't know. I've looked back through the course of historical events in Holy Scripture to try to decipher its present whereabouts. Like this, Mac. You start with Aaron and you know it was passed through the High Priests of the family of Levi until the death of Eli. Then, you realize it probably went to the Prophet Samuel, and passed to Abiathar who gave it to David. This is when it gets a little cloudy. It was either kept by King David or transferred to Zadok in the time of Solomon. That's all I know."

"Was there anything written in the scrolls to give any clues?" Father Mac asked.

"As a matter of fact, the Hosea prophecy, which speaks of its absence until the latter days, is repeated almost exactly word for word as in Holy Scripture, except...except for one thing." Rabbi Levine took out his reading glasses and put them on. He picked up the copy of the scroll and brought it close. "I will quote from the Hebrew text that is a duplicate text of the original readings of Hosea, 'For the children of Israel shall abide many days without a king, and without a prince, and without a sacrifice, and without an image, and without an ephod, and without seraphim. Afterward shall the children of Israel return, and seek the LORD their God, and David their king; and shall fear the LORD and his goodness in the latter days, those days which shall come to pass in the time of the LORD's Keepers of His Church and His Elect, in the time of the unity of our LORD, and in the time of Divine Authority.'"

Rabbi Levine looked up from his scroll over the top of his reading glasses. "Any thoughts?" he asked.

"If the Urim and Thummim still exists, it doesn't give us much of a clue about its location," Father Mac replied.

"No, I don't think this scroll tells us where to find it. I think this scroll tells us when we're going to be able to find it."

"When does it say?" Father Mac asked.

"Your guess is as good as mine." Rabbi Levine rose again to refill both their drinks.

*

As Father Mac drove back to Lake Geneva on Highway 43, he glanced down at the copy of the Dead Sea Scroll that his friend had made for him. Neither of them was able to calculate when the Urim and Thummim was going to make its reemergence into the world. If the clue were connected to a certain date, he would have to figure it out on his own.

"Thank goodness I remembered to bring up the picture of the cameo before I left," the priest thought.

When Father Mac rose from his chair after visiting with Rabbi Levine, he reached into his pocket for his keys and pulled out the picture of the cameo that Michael had taken at the Museum of Lapidary Arts.

"Josh, I almost forgot to mention this." Father Mac unfolded the picture of the cameo and gave it to his friend. "Do you know anything about this woman? I mean, is this a picture of the 'Witch of Endor?'" Father Mac asked.

Rabbi Levine took the picture from Father Mac and held it close to his eyes, but realized he needed his reading glasses. He grabbed them off his desk and put them on. As soon as he saw the photo, Rabbi Levine's eyes widened and his mouth opened in shock. "That's Lilith," the rabbi said disgustedly. He handed back the photo as quickly as possible as if he couldn't wait to get the filth off his hands.

"Who's Lilith?" Father Mac asked.

"You know Satan?" Rabbi Levine countered.

"Yeah, of course."

"Same thing."

*

Michael and Linda sat on one of the iron benches at the Riviera in Lake Geneva waiting for the police to arrive. They sat with blankets around their wet bodies and were still wearing the soiled boat clothes from the accident. The water safety patrol boat had fished them out of the lake after Linda's C–Scow sunk and had dropped them off at the Riviera. They knew that the man in black had crashed his speed boat into them in an effort to kill them, but they were too scared to mention this to the police.

The loud sound of police shoes on pavement brought Michael and Linda to attention. They sat up straight, prepared to answer questions. The two officers who had been dispatched to the scene had already spoken to the water safety patrol.

"How're you guys doing?" one officer asked.

"We've had better days," Michael replied with a wry smile.

"We'd like to find out exactly what happened to the two of you," the other officer asked.

"Sure," Linda spoke up first. "Michael and I took out my parents C–Scow from my private pier in Lake Geneva. We were headed to Fontana when a small speed boat plowed into us just west of the Bay toward The Geneva Inn. We were tacking and the main sail obstructed my view of the boat, so it surprised us and we were not able to maneuver our boat out of the way of the speed boat. The C–Scow sunk and we made an attempt to swim for shore. That's when the patrol boat came and rescued us. Thank God!" Linda seemed content to talk about the accident as if the man in black did not exist.

"Did you see what the driver of the speed boat looked like?" the first officer asked.

"Not really. I could only see the back of his head. I think he had dark hair. Hard to say. He was also very thin and tall if that helps." Linda finished and looked toward Michael.

"Can you add any information, sir?" the other officer asked.

"His hair was long and in a ponytail," Michael responded. "And he definitely was wearing all black."

Both officers were writing up individual reports. When they finished, they looked through their notes with a puzzled expression on their faces.

"Didn't you think it was odd that the boat that hit you fled the scene?" the first officer asked Linda.

"Yes, as a matter of fact, we did, but we were both underwater, so maybe he figured that if he couldn't see us, he should go for help," Linda answered.

"The officers on the patrol boat said that it looked like the two of you were in a race toward shore. They said it looked like you were trying to get away from the speed boat," the second officer added.

"Did you two know the person driving the speed boat?" the first officer asked suspiciously.

"No...no...never saw him before in my life," both Michael and Linda spoke up at once. They knew they were dealing with an inexplicable reality, and nobody outside their little circle wanted to believe in something that was so unbelievable.

"Is there any reason why someone might have purposely attempted to destroy your boat, Miss?"

"No, absolutely not," Linda responded confidently.

"No reason someone would be trying to hurt you?"

"No, I know of no one," she said again.

"How about you, sir? Anyone out there who might be holding a grudge? Anyone who might want to hurt you and make it look like an accident?"

"Thank, God. No," Michael said a little more unsteady than he would have liked, but the officers seemed to buy it because they both let up.

"Here's a card just in case you think of something you might have forgotten to mention." The first officer handed both Michael and Linda a card and they walked off. "Take care of yourselves," he called over his shoulder just loud enough to hear over the police shoes.

Michael and Linda looked at one another and smiled mischievously.

"They wouldn't have believed us anyway," Michael said finally. "Let's go change into dry clothes and find out if Father Mac has any info yet."

When they got up from the bench, they realized they needed to get a ride to Linda's house where Michael had originally parked. One of the Walters' Marina employees untied a beautiful redwood antique boat from the Marina pier. Michael and Linda climbed aboard and they sped toward her house. The employee pulled the boat up to Linda's pier, and she and Michael jumped off and waved "Good–bye."

Michael followed Linda across the pier and up a flight of stone steps that led to a beautiful back patio with sliding glass doors into the house. She hit a couple of buttons on her house security system keypad and pulled the door open. Instantly, a large, colorful laminated flier with something stuffed inside fell to the floor. It must have been stuck in between the doors by someone outside.

"What is this?" Linda asked more to herself than Michael. She picked up the flier and opened it. It was a full–color picture of the Milwaukee Museum of Modern Art, otherwise known as the "Calatrava," named after the Spanish architect. Linda noticed a small piece of paper bunched up into a little ball and taped inside. She opened the ball and found a key.

"Who's key?" Michael asked.

"Let's see," Linda held the key up to the light to see if there was anything written on it. Nothing.

"Don't know," Linda answered. She studied the Calatrava flier and noticed a New York City address written on the last page. "Michael, look at this." She handed the flier to him.

Michael read the handwritten address out loud, "311 West 34th Street, NYC." He studied the other pages of the flier before he gave it back. "Can I see the key?" he asked.

"Sure." Linda handed the key to Michael.

Michael held it up to the light. "Looks like an apartment or house key," he said.

"You think it might be some kind of clue? Something that might lead us to Debbie?" Linda asked.

"If it's a clue, we're going to take it in steps. First, we'll find out what information Father Mac has for us. Then, we'll find out if the Romanos have heard anything. I also want to know why this person was at the Calatrava. It might sound paranoid, but I can't help but think there might be some sort of connection between the boat accident and this clue."

Michael was geared up to discover the truth of the bloodstone legacy more than ever. He realized this was the most intense "burn" he'd ever felt in the game of following a story. The only problem was this was proving to be a very dangerous game.

CHAPTER TWENTY–ONE

This time Paolo did not wait for night to fall when he came to take Cassy. It was the full of day sometime in the beginning of November. Two months had passed and Cassy still lay on the same hospital bed, her beautiful auburn hair flowing over her pillow like a golden–brown halo surrounding her angelic face. Her cheeks had regained some of their color, her lips remained pink and full, and her eyelids covered darting eyes, as if she were living a dream. This was the only indication that there was still life in her motionless body, but her spiritual travels remained private knowledge known only to Cassy and Paolo.

Cassy had grown accustomed to the wind that struck her face as she flew through time and space to the history lesson Paolo chose to teach his yearning pupil. In her travels, Cassy felt free. Perhaps more free than she had ever felt in her lifetime. This freedom came from a great love that had embraced her since her coma sleep. Through Paolo, Cassy sensed the love of God. God's love was so immense, so infinite, that Cassy did not have the capacity to understand it, but she could feel and savor it and that was all that mattered. God had allowed her to taste just a sample of His great love, and Cassy would allow herself to trust in the freedom of the gift of this great love.

When Paolo and Cassy reached their destination, she stood on the marble floor of a great temple in front of a vast altar next to Paolo. There were men on the altar before them dressed extraordinarily in ancient Israeli garments. They wore long robes made of fine white cloth with black silk cloaks and each wore glorious white headdresses. The men carried metal urns that hung by chains and spilled out gray smoke of burning incense. They moved the chains back and forth in a rhythmic pattern intended to incense the entire altar and make holy that which was already filled with celestial wonder.

One man stood in the center of the others. He appeared to be the most elderly, his beard as white as snow. The man stood on the altar holding the incense in his right hand, his head tilted toward the ornate ceiling, as if he were pleading with God. The man's left hand was palm up, so that God knew his gesture implied humble obedience. He chanted in ancient Hebrew, all the while moving the incense back and forth in a circular pattern.

Then, from the back of the temple far beyond the altar, Cassy saw another man emerge from the shadows of heavy veils. He carried something gold and shining in his arms. The man with a beard of white appeared elderly, but his years seemed to vanish as soon as he appeared in the light of the altar. He was the most angelic man Cassy had ever seen, and as he walked closer to the man in the center, she noticed a strong resemblance.

"Moses," was all Paolo whispered into Cassy's ear.

Cassy's eyes widened in astonishment as she gazed at Moses. She knew that the men could not see her. She and Paolo were like invisible ghosts. Cassy turned her attention back to the elderly man in the center.

"That's Aaron, Moses' brother," Paolo said.

"And the rest?" Cassy asked.

"Aaron's sons," Paolo replied. "Naheb, Abihu, Eleazar and Ithamar."

"Why are they gathered? What is Moses carrying?"

"You will see," Paolo answered.

Moses lifted the golden garment up toward the light and it sparkled like nothing Cassy had ever seen. The dazzling garment was made of gold with rows of jewels displayed in its center. The glorious breastplate had an embroidered coat, mitre and girdle to match. Moses placed the garments ceremoniously on Aaron's body one by one. The ephod was selected first, which was an apron hung from the shoulders by straps and tied at the waist with the loose ends of a belt. The shoulder pieces attached to the ephod and the girdle, and there were gold chains that attached all the pieces together. The breastplate was held up and strapped on last.

Cassy noticed the colors of the breastplate as it was fitted onto Aaron's torso. It was a glorious mixture of gold, blue, purple and scarlet, and all made with the finest of linen. On the front of the breastplate there were three rows of four stones each and every stone sparkled magnificently. Every stone except the last, which showed a small hole where the twelfth stone should have been.

"Where is the twelfth stone?" Cassy asked Paolo.

"You will see," Paolo replied.

Moses took a beautiful, gleaming jade–green stone from the inside of his robe. He held it up to the light, and it sparkled more brilliantly than any of the others. When Moses placed the sparkling stone in the twelfth position of Aaron's breastplate, a sound like thunder cracked through the air and a delayed ray of light hit the entire breastplate. The light glowed out horizontally from either side of the breastplate and through the East and West sides of the temple walls.

The light was so blinding, Cassy had to cover her eyes with the back of her hand. She squinted and moved her hand up to see the breastplate gleam with a spectacular, mystical light.

Cassy looked at Paolo and he answered her before she could ask.

"It's jasper," Paolo said. "The very same stone used to make bloodstone. Jasper is the one true heavenly stone."

"Why is the breastplate glowing?" Cassy asked.

"That is Aaron's breastplate promised to him by God through his brother, Moses. It is the mark of the priest. The very first high priest. It contains the Urim and Thummim, the light, the wisdom, the completion, the perfection. The very oracle of God."

"Can jasper stone be used to communicate with God?" Cassy asked.

"Jasper stone is used to symbolize the creation of life, itself," Paolo replied.

"So, the bloodstone became a symbol of life, too?"

"Yes and no. The bloodstone that was made from the blood of Christ, the one true Bloodstone, became a symbol of life. The bloodstone that was made from the blood of Satan, the cursed bloodstone, became a symbol of death. To this day, it has been used to kill millions of innocent human beings. It needs to be stopped. It needs to end, Cassy, with your help. It is difficult, yes, but it is also possible. Only the power of the one true Bloodstone contained in the Urim and Thummim can stop the evil of the cursed bloodstone, and only you, Deborah and Jessica, with your combined strength, can wield its power."

Cassy felt the weight of the world upon her shoulders as Paolo spoke.

*

Father Derek Ekwonye looked at his watch and realized he had just enough time to grab a quick gelato before his meeting with Father Gabe Sanders at Saint Mary's Cathedral. The handsome priest lived in the Italian section of San Francisco, just a couple of blocks from Saints Peter and Paul Church, the church he was assigned a pastorship five years before. He crossed the street toward his favorite gelato place and stepped inside.

"Hey, Ellen!" Father Derek said to one of the clerks behind the counter.

"Father Derek, it's been too long." Ellen pretended to look at her watch. "I think approximately fourteen hours? You're early."

"Yeah, I know. Got a meeting to attend and I need a little something to keep the mind sharp." Father Derek smiled broadly while he tapped his right temple.

"Okay, but don't say I didn't warn you. I mean, wearing black is supposed to make people look thinner, but I have to be honest, Father. The calories are starting to show."

"Yeah, you're right, but guess what? I'll start thinking about that tomorrow."

"Remember, I warned you." Ellen got off her high stool and opened up the freezer with scoop in hand to fill a large cup with one half chocolate and one half coconut gelato, Father Derek's favorite.

Father Derek paid Ellen for the gelato and left with a smile and a wink. As he walked, he took a bite of his gelato and savored the sweet taste as it melted on his tongue. As usual, memories of what it was like for him and Evee came flooding back into his mind.

"If you're desperate for food in this country, you can go to a shelter," Father Derek thought. "We had miles of wasteland with no food in sight."

Father Derek's thoughts of hunger were still painful beyond words. How strange that he should overindulge in the decadence of gelato when so many in this world were still facing the ravages of hunger today.

Derek and his sister, Evee, had grown up in the midst of a dictatorship, and it was the greed of an evil leader that had produced a poverty–stricken country. In Nigeria, he and Evee had lost both parents to a violent death when Derek was only seven and Evee, four. Derek had become a father to his sister in those first weeks after their parents were killed. He had become accustomed to a harsh and violent world early on. That's why he needed to protect little Evee. Derek knew he would have given his own life for hers if that's what had to be done. There were days when Derek and Evee went without any food, and he remembered trying to get by with anything he could get his hands on. It didn't even matter if it was insects.

The beat of Father Derek's footsteps reminded him of the beat of his seven–year–old fists in the hot African sun to imitate the patter of rain. He summoned the ants out of their little dry hills so he and Evee could scoop them up to eat them. When they felt so thirsty they couldn't stand any longer, Derek prayed to God Almighty and discovered a newly formed spring to satisfy their thirst. These were not days of indulgence. These were not days of sweet gelato on the tongue. These were days of survival, and if he had to go with nothing so that little Evee could have a little of something, so be it. Until Father Zac came along.

Father Derek entered the cathedral rectory, threw away his gelato container, and grabbed his Blackberry and car keys.

Father Zac had saved their lives. Just when Derek felt he and Evee could go no further, they found a Mission deep in the heart of a violent and oppressed Nigeria. At first, Derek thought the Mission was just a mirage, but God Almighty had never left them stranded, and Derek and Evee were given the greatest gift that day.

There was a small church in the center of the Mission community. When Derek saw the golden cross on top of the church steeple in the distance, it was lit up by the sun and pointed to heaven like a shining star. There was a little school at the Mission run by nuns and overwrought with children in dirty uniforms and no shoes. The first thing Derek and Evee saw were children playing and laughing outside the Mission school. These children didn't look rundown and starving with protruding bellies. These children looked happy and content.

Sister Felicity, the school principal, was the first one to see Derek and Evee. Evee was so weak and emaciated that she couldn't stand on her own. Derek had carried her for the last mile on their quest for food. When he saw the look on Sister Felicity's face, Derek remembered the way his mother had looked the last day he saw her.

Sister Felicity walked over to Derek in silence and took Evee into her loving arms. She turned toward a little building, the Mission's hospital, and Derek felt instant relief as he followed closely behind the nun.

While Derek and Evee regained their strength, Father Zac visited them and over time, the two looked at Father Zac and the other missionaries as family. They attended school and church and slept in netted tents to protect them from dangerous insect bites. Derek and Evee had found a family in the Mission just like the other orphans who had come to know one another as sisters and brothers.

Derek celebrated his first Christmas at the Mission. He attended every Mass he could and sat in the front pew so he could watch Father Zac on the altar as closely as possible. Evee usually stayed with her classmates, but on Christmas day, she joined Derek for the last Mass celebrated at twelve noon. The Mass was so joyful, it had lasted until well after two.

Father Zac looked tired and parched, but when several of his parishioners asked if he would bless the nativity they had constructed a little ways down the road, the priest nodded his weary head and smiled.

Father Zac, Derek, Evee, and twenty parishioners marched down the dusty, hot road in search of the unblessed créche. When they reached it, Father Zac took out a small bottle of holy water. The priest told Derek to hold it for him while he opened up his little black–leather Bible to the scripture passage he wanted to read for the blessing.

Derek was so happy to be such an important part of the Christmas blessing. Evee gave Derek a pinch on his arm to let him know she wanted to be part of the action. Father Zac read the passage from Luke, but when he raised his hand to bless the créche, he stopped and looked around for something that seemed desperately vital to the nativity.

"I see Joseph and the baby Jesus in his cradle," Father Zac said looking at the manger scene with shepherds, angels and little creatures that looked like donkeys. "It's all so wonderful, but I don't see Mary, the Mother of God."

One of the older gentlemen stepped forward and respectfully removed his hat before the gracious priest. "Father," the man began quietly, "we did the best we could, but we just could not find a Mary statue anywhere." The man pointed to the cradle with the baby Jesus. "The only Mary we could find is right there in the cradle."

Father Zac peered into the cradle, and Evee pulled on Derek's shirt so she could see, too. There was, in fact, a picture of the best Mary Father Zac had ever seen anywhere. It was a color picture of Marilyn Monroe torn directly from an American magazine and taped inside the créche next to the baby Jesus. Father Zac reached for his holy water and Derek held it out to him as the priest blessed the beautiful and original nativity with a broad smile spread across his face.

*

Father Derek continued toward Saint Mary's Cathedral and caught a glimpse of the Golden Gate Bridge out of the corner of his eye. Perhaps it made sense that he had wound up in the city of Saint Francis and his famous bridge. After all, it had been a bridge that had saved Father Zac's Mission.

Derek and Evee had known violence, but when it crept back up on them the day after their first Christmas at the peaceful Mission, they were not at all prepared. The dictator's soldiers were firing at the innocent Christians, and Father Zac received word that two priests and an entire village community down the hill were killed. The soldiers were headed for the Mission to kill all of them and anyone in their path along the way.

Derek was helping Father Zac clean the Christmas vestments

and clothes in the sacristy. When Father Zac received the terrible news warning him of the soldiers, the priest handled the situation calmly. He told Sister Felicity to alert the other sisters at the school to round up the children as quickly as possible and send them over to the church. Derek knew that Evee would be heading over to the church with the other children. He also knew that she would not handle the news well.

Everyone filed into the church while Father Zac set up for a prayer vigil on the altar. Derek helped Father while he waited for his sister to arrive. Suddenly, he saw a small form enter quickly and loudly with tearful sobs and cries. Derek knew it was Evee and watched as she ran up onto the altar and into his arms. Her crying was so loud, all Derek could think to do was lift her and pat her back. He knew that his sister had already faced too much fear and death.

Evee squirmed uncomfortably in Derek's arms. As soon as he let her down, she ran to Father Zac and pulled on the priest's arm. "Father, please no more dying," Evee cried out painfully. "Please, Father, give me poison! I want to die before they come. Please, no more killing."

Father Zac knelt down and picked Evee up in his arms. He carried her off the altar and into the sacristy with Derek close behind. Father Zac closed the door and motioned for Evee to sit. Derek sat next to her and put his arm around her while Father Zac disappeared inside a small back office. When the priest returned, he was carrying two large candy canes and gave one to each child. Evee wiped her eyes with the back of her hand and stared at the red and white striped cane with awe. She and Derek had never had candy in their lives.

"Do you know what this is?" Father Zac asked.

"Candy!" Evee yelled out with a smile on her face. She had seen pictures of candy in her school books, but never tasted the sweetness before.

"Yes, but do you know what it means?" Father Zac asked again.

"Good and tasty!" Evee exclaimed.

"Yes, but do you see what letter this is?" Father Zac turned the cane around in the children's hands.

"It's a 'J,'" Derek answered excitedly.

"'J!'" Evee repeated.

"Do you know what 'J' stands for?" Father Zac asked.

"Jesus," Derek answered.

"Jesus!" Evee repeated, looking up at her brother.

"Yes," Father Zac said. "The white was for Jesus' life and the red was for Jesus' death. You know what that means, right?"

Derek looked down toward the floor and answered Father Zac as quietly as his voice would sound. "That dying isn't always bad," he said.

"What was that, Derek?" Father Zac asked.

"That dying isn't always bad," Derek repeated.

"Yes. And why is that?" Father Zac asked Derek.

"Because Jesus died so we could live forever."

Evee got off her chair and gave Derek a hard hug with her little arms around his neck. Afterward, she drew back, looked into Derek's eyes, and put her hand on Derek's cheek. When Evee sat back down next to her brother, she quickly unwrapped her candy cane and put the "J" end into her mouth as far as it would go.

Father Zac smiled at Evee. "Feel better, Evee?" he asked.

Evee took the candy cane out of her mouth and licked her lips before she answered. "Yes, Father. I'm not afraid of dying anymore," Evee answered thoughtfully. "That just means I get to be with Jesus quicker."

Derek carefully opened the top of the candy cane wrapper, and the peppermint sweetness hit his lips for the first time in his life.

During Father Zac's prayer vigil, the bridge that led to the Mission was destroyed, and the dictator's soldiers had not been able to reach them.

*

Father Derek pulled into the cathedral parking lot just as his Blackberry started to ring. When he looked at his phone, Evee was calling. She had recently moved to San Francisco from New York.

When Father Zac was transferred back to London after five years at the Mission, Derek and Evee were adopted by relatives of the priest who lived in England. Father Zac was eventually relocated to New York, and Derek and Evee traveled with him to the United States to attend college as foreign exchange students. Derek entered seminary school in New York, attended graduate school in Rome, and was ordained a priest shortly thereafter. Father Derek took his first pastorship in a small parish in Los Angeles, and eventually became pastor of Saints Peter and Paul Church in San Francisco.

Evee graduated from art school in New York where she made a name for herself as a painter, but moved to San Francisco to be near her brother when Father Zac passed away. She lived in a posh apartment building near the San Francisco Museum of Modern Art with two white fluffy Siberian cats named "Zac" and "Felicity." Her latest paintings were set to be shown at the SF–MOMA that weekend.

"Evee?" Father Derek answered as soon as he put his car in park. "I was just thinking of you."

"Derek, can we meet for dinner tonight?" Evee sounded anxious.

"Sure, Evee. You okay?" Derek hadn't seen Evee in weeks. He knew she was busy getting ready for her first exhibition, so for her to call directly before one of the most important days of her life was completely out of character.

"Yes, I'm okay," Evee answered cautiously. "Well, I was okay until this morning. Some guy came into my studio…I mean my private apartment studio this morning without a key."

"What?" Derek asked concerned.

"Yes, Derek. This guy came in without a key and started

harassing me about my art like he was some sort of critic or something. He said I had no business as an amateur appearing in a professional market. Derek, I was really angry, but then something happened that really scared me. He gave me this horrible look, Derek, like some sort of devil or something. His eyes were glaring at me, and he was so tall and gaunt. Like a skeleton. Like I was being stared at by death itself."

"Evee, why don't I come over there right now? Make sure you're okay?"

"I'm not at the apartment. I'm at the museum. As quickly as he came in is as quickly as he left. It was so unreal I thought I had only imagined it, but then I just noticed something strange in my bag…" Evee stopped, unable to finish.

"What did you find?"

"I found a little piece of ripped parchment paper with a warning scratched in red quill ink. It has a pentagram symbol on top. Below the symbol it says, 'I'll cease playing the critic when your brother and his friend cease playing God.'"

CHAPTER TWENTY–TWO

Father Derek walked up to the rectory of Saint Mary's Cathedral, but Archbishop Gabriel Sanders opened the door before he could ring the bell.

Father Gabe greeted his friend with a big smile. "Derek! How's it going? You all right, man?" Gabe noticed the worried expression on Derek's face.

"Yes, well, no. Evee just called. Somebody's threatening her because of me, actually, because of us."

"What? Come in and tell me what's going on." The archbishop led Father Derek through the foyer to the study.

Derek continued as soon as they sat down. "Some guy entered her apartment studio without a key to criticize her art. Then she found a note in her purse threatening her brother and his friend to stop playing God."

"How did he get in without a key?" Gabe asked.

"She said she didn't know."

"Where is Evee now?"

"At the museum. She's safe there," Derek answered.

"Good, 'cause right now we have other problems. You know the meeting you came for? The one with Father Shenan J. Boquet from Human Life International and Father Frank Pavone from

Priests for Life? Canceled. Just got the call. They had to put out yet another demonic fire. Seems a whole slew of gang members burned down a pregnancy shelter in New York. And that's not all. There are pentagram symbols all over the walls painted in red using blood from discarded fetuses."

"Gabe, listen, Evee said her note had a big pentagram symbol on it, and it was also written in red..." Derek stopped mid–sentence, took out his cell phone and dialed Evee's number.

*

It was a beautiful, sunny Sunday afternoon in Sausalito, California, and Jessica Taninsam was enjoying a well–earned day off with Jonathan Lee. They were aboard Jessica's Aphrodite 101, a sleek, Danish 33–foot keelboat. The sailboat was large enough to sleep four and fast enough to win the most competitive races in the bay.

Jessica and Jonathan made a tack to starboard, and felt the warm November California sun on their faces while the cool bay breeze blew through their hair. Jessica sat with the tiller in one hand and a Heineken in the other while Jonathan cleated the jib sheet. He sat next to her on the high side and picked up his Heineken from the drink holder next to the seat cushion.

Jonathan turned to admire Jessica. She had her blonde hair in a ponytail and she wore a white canvas visor to block the sun. Jessica wore a white v–neck sweater with navy trim and white capris. Her skin looked tan against the white.

Jonathan longed to kiss Jessica, but he was afraid that she would not return his affection. He had always been a bit shy, and he was not used to feeling confident around women. Jonathan had serious relationships in the past, but he had never thought about marriage before he met Jessica. She was the most brilliant woman Jonathan had ever met, and this was one of the reasons he had fallen so completely in love with her.

"Jessica, look at that sunset! When I see something as beautiful as that, I know there's a heaven!" Jonathan pointed toward the bright yellow sphere that was glowing fiercely in the sky. There was no way to look at it without seeing dots of black in their field of vision.

Jessica looked up at the sun burning on the horizon. "You're right, Jonny. This is definitely a picture perfect day," she replied whimsically.

"You all right, Jessica? I mean, with the family situation?"

Jessica looked at Jonathan with tears in her soft blue eyes. "Yes, yes. I suppose there's not much I can do from out here, but I'm worried about my girls...both my girls...you know? I was never really their aunt. I was more like their mother. I had to take care of them. I wanted to take care of them. And then they were separated and Debbie was adopted by the Romanos. Thank God for them. And Cassy found Drew. Thank God for him, too. He loves Cassy more than any human being could ever love another."

Jonathan laid a hand on Jessica's shoulder to comfort her. He squeezed her shoulder, but quickly took his hand away. Jonathan looked as if a light bulb had just turned on above his head.

"What?" Jessica asked.

Jonathan hesitated for a moment and then blurted out the question that had just come to him. "Jessica, do you think there's a reason all of this happened at once? I mean, to both Cassy and Debbie at the same time?"

"Jonny, I don't see how it could be connected. I've thought about a possible connection, believe me, but I think Cassy and Debbie have two completely separate perpetrators. When Cassy collapsed at the hospital and slipped into a coma, her doctor believed she was poisoned, but the person who saw her last was her psychiatrist who mysteriously disappeared. I'd say that makes him the likely suspect. Debbie's disappearance is most likely associated with someone entirely different..." Jessica's voice trailed off before she could finish her thought. Her face had turned completely ashen.

Jonathan leaned forward and put his hand back on Jessica's shoulder. "What is it, Jessica? Tell me."

"I don't suppose I've ever mentioned the name, David Bloodstone, to you before." Jessica's voice took on a robotic tone, and she turned her head back toward the amber horizon.

"Someone from your past?" Jonathan interjected.

"Past and present." Jessica emphasized the word "present" with such disdain, it was obvious she wanted nothing to do with him. "He was the one…the one at Palmer's party," Jessica began.

"The one I asked you about who stopped you on the landing of the stairs." Jonathan had sensed the power and danger of the man when he saw him that night. "Why didn't you want to tell me?"

"I don't even want to mention his name," Jessica spoke with such venom, her jaw was set in a snarl. "Picture the worst person on earth, the sort of person who is so gruesome, you would not want to share the same continent, let alone the same room at a dinner party…that is David."

"And you think this is the person who kidnapped Debbie?"

"I know it."

"Why?"

"He was visiting her at the hospital where she was getting treatment."

"How did he find her? I mean, she had been adopted and given a new identity."

"With David, anything is possible."

"What do you mean?" Jonathan was genuinely puzzled.

Jessica looked down at the floor of the sailboat. She was searching for the right words to explain a very complicated and mysterious past. When Jessica lifted her head again, she seemed anxious. "We'd better head back," she said quickly and pulled the tiller toward her as she eased the main. They were headed back to the Sausalito Yacht Club where she moored her boat.

When the main sail and jib had caught ample wind, Jonathan

cleated off the jib sheet and sat directly opposite Jessica. "Jess, you trust me, don't you?" he asked.

Jessica smiled warmly. "Jonny, I would trust you with my life."

"Then, tell me what you've been too afraid to tell me."

Jessica looked deep into Jonathan's loving eyes and placed her hand on top of his knee. "Jonny, I am not who you think I am. I was born into a very difficult situation from which I knew I had to escape. All of my early years passed by with a sixth sense that there was a great evil which existed around me. At this point, I left everything behind that I had ever known. I took Cassy and Debbie with me. Their mother had lost any sense of loving them, if she ever loved them at all, so I knew I had to protect them. I protected Cassy and Debbie from this great evil. I protected myself from this same evil. And for the first time in my life, I felt free. Free of waking each morning to dread and fear. Free of the sense of loathing and hatred that I had for my life. Free of feeling that I was being controlled and manipulated by some outside force."

Jessica took a second to breathe deeply before she began again. "I thought I was free, but I knew in my heart that he was following me. I think at some point I realized I would never be truly free because he would never let me go. You see, I've been pretending…pretending that I live this different life…this normal life…but the truth is I am one of them, and no matter how much I try to rid myself of the past, I will always be one of them because he will never let me go."

"He meaning David?" Jonathan asked captivated by Jessica's every word.

"He meaning David," Jessica replied.

"But he's just one human being…and one human being cannot have control over another human being."

"David is not 'just one human being,'" Jessica said sternly.

"Are you telling me David is not human?"

"That is exactly what I am telling you," Jessica responded frankly.

"Jessica, please, I know for a fact that there are no such things as ghosts or phantoms or devils or whatever else you'd have me believe." As soon as Jonathan spoke, he felt a sense of guilt. He had told his friend to open up and tell him the truth, and now he was saying he did not believe it.

Jonathan reached out to take both of Jessica's hands in his. "Jessica, I'm sorry," he said. "I should not have come on so strong. I really want you to tell me everything, and it's my responsibility to believe what you have to say."

Jessica smiled at Jonathan, partly because she admired his willingness to listen and partly because she realized how much she loved him. "Jonny, trust me, I know how unbelievable this all sounds. Let me put it into some sort of context. Do you remember reading Bible stories when you were growing up—those that spoke of demons and possessions?"

"Yes," he replied, still a bit unsure.

"Those stories?" Jessica began. "Those stories were written about someone who now calls himself, David Bloodstone."

Jonathan knew instantly, more from a feeling in his gut than a sense of the rational, that Jessica was telling him the absolute and undeniable truth.

Jessica's sailboat neared the Sausalito Bay and her blonde ponytail fluttered in the breeze as she steered the boat into the wind.

Jonathan felt as though he had just caught a chill. He felt a shudder run down his spine and sat completely still as he tried to fathom who or what David was.

*

When Veronica Johnson was sixteen years old, she was living in a one–bedroom apartment with her mother and two younger brothers. The run–down apartment was located in a housing project in the Ironbound section of Newark, New Jersey. Her father had left her mother when Veronica was eight and her brothers, Adam and Moses, were four and two. Fortunately, Veronica's mother, Sarah, was not the type of woman to feel abandoned by any man, so she quickly found a job working as a housekeeper at a local church only a few blocks away.

Sarah didn't own a car and couldn't afford daycare, so the job was considerably convenient because she could walk to work and take the boys with her while Veronica was in school. Father John O'Brien allowed Sarah to bring Adam and Moses to the rectory while she cooked and cleaned. Sarah was also a very spiritual woman and the job at the church gave her a chance to pray whenever she took her breaks. Sarah was raised in a Baptist family, but it didn't matter to her that she prayed in a Catholic church—the only thing that mattered was being in the presence of her Jesus. As long as she had him, she knew she could get by.

That's why Veronica knew her mother would be terribly disappointed with her if she found out the bad news. School was finished for the day, and Veronica lay on the couch waiting for her mother to come home. Sarah was picking up Adam and Moses from basketball practice after work and that's why she was later than usual.

"That's okay," Veronica thought to herself. "Gives me a chance to figure out how to explain this mess I'm in."

Veronica got up off the couch and went into the cramped bathroom down the hall that her family shared with two other families who lived across the hall. The bathroom was vacant, but it was so filthy she had to clean the toilet seat before she could use it. When Veronica finished, she went to the sink to splash water on her face. She dried her face with her T–shirt and looked up at her reflection in the mirror.

"Do I look different?" Veronica thought as she brought her face closer. She was so close up, she could peer into the whites of her eyes. Veronica pulled herself away from the mirror and studied her face from further away.

Veronica was a beautiful young girl with skin the color of milk chocolate and exquisite dark brown eyes with natural long lashes. Her long, black hair was braided down both sides of her shoulders. Veronica's lips were dark red and when she smiled, she showed perfect white teeth.

"If I thought a baby would make me look different, I was wrong," Veronica thought as she left the bathroom and walked back down the hall to her mother's apartment. She stopped at the door with her hand resting on the wooden knob. Veronica looked down at her stomach and put her hand on top of her abdomen.

"Yes," Veronica thought. "You can't tell a thing. My stomach feels the same. My face looks the same. I can get rid of it, and no one will ever have to know. He can pay for it. He did it. End of problem and no one has to know. A done deal."

*

By the time Veronica finished high school, her mother, Sarah, had been working at Saint John's in Newark for over ten years. Sarah had grown to love the parish, the parishioners, and most of all Father John O'Brien. Saint John's had become a home away from home, and Sarah chose to have Veronica, Adam and Moses baptized into the Catholic Church. Veronica did not know it, but becoming Catholic meant that her life would change forever based on one event—the night she attended a Saint John's Parish function where she met her future husband. The event was called, "Youth 2000," and his name, Tom Blake.

Youth 2000 entices young people to gather and pray in front of the Blessed Sacrament all night long. Youth 2000 retreats arc sct up so that the Blessed Sacrament, the consecrated host which is the true body of Christ, is displayed in a monstrance, a highly ornate, gold circular case. Hundreds of small rugs are set up around the monstrance, so that teens can kneel before the body of Christ in prayer. To most teens, a night like this sounds totally boring. To some, however, the experience is completely earth shattering, like no night they will ever have again.

The night that Veronica Johnson and Tom Blake met was New Year's Eve and the dawn of a new decade. Veronica was made to attend Youth 2000 by her mother. Tom, a deeply devout Catholic of his own choosing, wanted to attend even though the rest of his friends on the football team were at some senior classmate's house "boozin'" and "gettin' some."

"You gonna miss out, man." That's what Tom's friend, Dez, had told him. Dez was the team captain, the quarterback, and the only white guy on East Side High's football team.

"I got a previous engagement waitin' for me," Tom replied moving his eyebrows up and down as if some girl were waiting for him at that very moment.

"Oh, I get you, man! I get you!" Dez held up his fist and Tom bumped his fist into Dez's. "All right, man, so I'll see you around." Dez walked to the old, beat–up rusted Chevy waiting for him, crammed with a bunch of teens.

"Later!" Tom Blake called out to his friend.

"Later!" Dez shot back before he got in the car. He sped off and left a dark trail of rubber down the busy urban street.

A half hour before midnight on New Year's Eve, while all his friends partied, Tom Blake knelt in front of the precious body of Jesus Christ. The monstrance that held the consecrated host looked more beautiful to Tom than words could describe. There were hundreds of kneeling teenagers praying instead of partying this New Year's Eve. Tom wasn't the only one.

As a faithful Catholic, Tom joined the youth group at his church two years before. He felt compelled to help feed the homeless at soup kitchens in the local area. Tom's parents thought it was a good idea. They thought it would look good on his resume when he graduated from high school in six months and came looking for a football scholarship. Tom arrived at the local soup kitchen with his parents' full support.

There were two other teens who showed up with Tom that day ready to help the Sisters of Charity prepare the food and serve it to the homeless. They attended Mass with the sisters and followed them into the kitchen to prepare food.

One of the sisters said God always gave them enough to provide for the needy. "Even when it's an hour before we're supposed to serve and we don't have enough to feed the hungry, some local bakery mysteriously drops off a hundred loaves of bread, and then we have enough. God always provides," she told Tom.

Tom stood in front of a counter cutting up vegetables to put in a huge pot of stew. Then, he and the volunteers served the stew to the people, families and children included, who were waiting in a long line with plastic bowls and spoons in their hands.

Tom saw a young woman in the middle of the line dressed in jeans and a T–shirt. He thought this woman could have been his older sister. She was African–American, just like Tom. She was also tall, just like Tom. Then, something profound struck him. Behind her, walked four young children, three boys and one girl. The girl was the youngest and looked like she was only two years old. The children were all dressed in dirty jeans with T–shirts, except the girl. She was wearing worn shorts with a shabby undershirt.

Normally, shorts would have been fine, but since it was the middle of January and there was snow on the ground, Tom knew this little girl would freeze when she went back outside. The little girl was carrying a blanket like Linus in her hand and it was dragging along behind her. Tom couldn't take his eyes off the little girl as she came nearer to him in the line. When she lifted her bowl for Tom to fill it, their eyes met for one brief instant. That instant would change Tom's life forever. Jesus was calling him to do his good work.

Every chance after, Tom Blake did some sort of service for the Church. Every spare moment he had outside of school, he volunteered to work the soup kitchens, the nursing homes, and the homeless shelters. And Tom did all of this without any of his friends or family knowing. To them, he was at the library doing homework, the gym pumping iron, or with some nonexistent girl, like tonight. Tonight, Tom was surrounded by other young people just like him—those who gave God praise because of their great love for Jesus Christ.

At about quarter to twelve, Tom got up and walked over to the window to look out into the night. There was a light snowfall and each snowflake caught the light from the street as it descended down from the sky to the ground.

"I would have appreciated it more if it snowed a week ago. Then, we would have at least had a white Christmas. Now, it's just one big inconvenience," Veronica said from behind Tom.

Tom quickly turned to face a beautiful, slender girl his own age looking up at him with a sad intensity. "Hey," Tom said.

"Hey, back," Veronica replied hesitantly.

"Senior?" Tom asked.

"Yeah," Veronica replied. "You, too?"

"Yeah. Which school?"

"Lincoln High," Veronica answered. "You?"

"East High."

"Oh," Veronica stepped forward to peer out the window at the falling snow. It was coming down in big, soggy flakes. She was suddenly glad that her mother would not have to make the trip to come get her in the bad weather.

"What's your name?' Tom asked from behind Veronica.

"Veronica," she replied as she continued to gaze at the winter storm.

Tom walked to Veronica's side to gaze into the night next to her.

"What's your name?" Veronica finally asked.

"Tom."

Veronica looked at Tom and their eyes met. For Tom, there was an instant attraction. For Veronica, only fear. She did not want to get close to any boy again. Not now. Perhaps not ever.

When Tom and Veronica looked out the window again, it was only a few minutes before the beginning of the New Year, and they could hear the loud noises of celebration outside. Inside the gym of the Youth 2000 retreat, not a sound could be heard but the whispers of hushed prayer.

Tom turned to the clock that hung above one of the basketball hoops. Both hands pointed north. It was exactly midnight, the dawn of a new year and the dawn of new dreams.

Tom turned to Veronica. "Happy New Year," he said.

"We'll see," Veronica replied. She walked toward the monstrance and sat on one of the open rugs. Tom followed close behind.

CHAPTER TWENTY–THREE

On the night of Veronica Johnson's and Tom Blake's college graduation celebration, Veronica realized that Tom held the key that would open the lock to her hidden and tormented past. She realized that what she was trying to hide all these years was screaming to get out. Every single one of her psychology courses made Veronica realize that the guilt she harbored would never be forgiven until she allowed someone to open the lock and unleash the pain.

Tom, in all his beauty and love, had become the one who held the key to unlock her past. As the two strolled arm and arm along a darkened street in Newark after the party that Tom's parents threw, Veronica's pain unexpectedly gave way like rushing waters from a collapsed dam. Tom held Veronica and let her sob into his shoulder. Veronica stood with her arms wrapped tightly around Tom's shoulders, the tears streaming down her cheeks. She had never shed one tear, not one, over the guilt and pain she felt when she ended the life of the once living being inside her womb.

Now the pain of all those years was unleashed in one moment, and when it hurt more than her gut could bare, Veronica fell to her knees on that lone dirty street and clutched her stomach with both hands. Tom knelt down next to her to try to absorb her pain. He had always sensed that Veronica was hiding something from him, like some secret part of her had been shattered in a tragedy. Something had always kept her more guarded. Something had stopped her from loving him completely. And now it was coming out. It was coming to the surface and spilling out before him. It hurt Tom to see Veronica in so much pain, but he instinctively knew that she needed this. She needed this chance to purge herself of whatever skeleton she had hidden in her closet all these years.

When Veronica regained her composure and stood up, she smiled through her tears because she realized that everything would be all right. With Tom, everything would be all right. She had found healing in his selfless love.

Veronica wrapped her arms tightly around Tom's neck, and when she whispered, "I love you," in his ear, the story of a sixteen–year–old girl spilled forth and she no longer felt the need to hide her past. The remorse had been overwhelming, but Veronica came to realize that Jesus had forgiven her with the gift of Tom's love. God forgave Veronica and Veronica forgave herself, and the symbol of this forgiveness became two glorious children gifted to Veronica and Tom after eight years of marriage.

*

Veronica and Tom Blake had a boy named Peter and a girl named Grace. Tom became the marketing director of a financial institution in New York City, and when Peter and Grace were old enough for full–time school, Veronica became the director of a local pro–life pregnancy shelter called, "Turning Point," in Bergenfield, New Jersey, where they lived. Peter was eleven and Grace, seven, and the children attended Transfiguration Academy, a Catholic parochial school a block from Turning Point.

The Blakes attended Mass at Saint Mary's Parish in Dumont, one of the parishes that made up the co–sponsored school, and Veronica became a great friend of Father Raphael Trujillo, the pastor. They often lunched together at an authentic Mexican restaurant called, "La Batalla," which was only a five minute walk from the shelter.

One cold, gray day in November, Veronica and Father Raphael walked into the double doors of Turning Point laughing about Father's hair which had been completely disheveled in the wind.

"Oh, my goodness!" Father Raphael exclaimed joyfully. He was always the first to poke fun at something, especially when the "something" was himself.

"What am I going to do with you?" Veronica asked as soon as she stepped inside and threw her coat on her desk chair. She tried to smooth down Father Raphael's wavy black hair. Veronica noticed strands of gray on either side of his ruggedly handsome face. "You know, Father, gray hair usually comes in coarser. That's probably why your hair gets so messy in the wind." Veronica stepped around the side of her desk, sat down, and looked up at her priest friend with a grin.

"Yes, and I don't even have the stresses of raising children to blame for my gray hair!" the Mexican priest said.

Veronica's expression turned serious. "I know for a fact that's not true, Father. You have more children than anyone could imagine. Spiritual children, that is."

Father Raphael looked at Veronica and nodded. Many of the people who worshipped at Saint Mary's felt the same way about the young priest. That's why Veronica and the Blake family had become parishioners of Saint Mary's when they moved to Bergenfield ten years ago. Father Raphael had been assigned to Saint John's in Bergenfield and when he became pastor at Saint Mary's, the Blakes moved with him.

"All right, Veronica. All right. As much as I would love to stand here and take your fantastic compliments all day, I have to get back to work." Father Raphael turned to go.

"Yes, that's right, Father. You'd better go before I pump up your head so much it's not going to fit through the door."

Veronica's smile was a mile wide when Father Raphael opened the door and made his descent down the stairs.

"Hasta luego!" the priest shouted from the door.

"Hasta yourself!" Veronica shouted back.

The door shut noisily, and Veronica looked back down at the case files sitting on the top of her desk. She glanced at her watch and wondered how she was going to finish them before she had to leave to pick up the kids from school by three. Veronica opened the first file when she heard the doorbell ring. She looked up to see someone standing just inside the door.

"Come in," Veronica said leaning forward on her desk to try to get a view. Veronica saw a young Hispanic girl no more than sixteen.

"Hola?" the girl said hesitantly.

"Hola," Veronica answered. "Can I help you?" Veronica sat back in her seat and smiled warmly from behind her reading glasses.

"Si, si," the girl stepped forward slowly and carefully closed the door behind her. She walked toward Veronica and stood directly in front of the small metal desk smiling shyly. "I have...problem. I think I...pregnant." The girl's English was very broken.

Veronica could have kicked herself for not keeping Father Raphael just one more minute in the office so that he could have translated the girl's Spanish to English. It would have been nice to have someone around who could speak more Spanish than, "Hola."

"Sit down, honey," Veronica said to the young girl, pointing to one of the two metal chairs in front of her desk.

The girl sat and looked down with a worried expression on her young and innocent face.

"What's your name?" Veronica asked taking a prepared form out of her desk drawer.

"Rebecca Gomez."

Rebecca, can you please give me your address and phone number for my records?" Veronica asked, pen ready.

"No," the girl answered.

"No, you can't give me your address and phone number or no, you don't have an address or phone number." Veronica asked this two–fold question because many women who came into Turning Point did not feel comfortable giving this information. Sometimes there were people within these women's own families who did not want them to keep the baby.

"No, I no have…" the girl responded tentatively.

"You don't have an address?" Veronica asked.

"No address. No phone," Rebecca replied.

"Oh, I see," Veronica put down her pen and took off her reading glasses. "I see," she tried to smile at Rebecca to reassure her that everything would be okay.

"I sorry, I sorry." Rebecca looked down and a tear slid down her cheek to the ground.

"Where are you from?" Veronica asked.

"Colombia."

"How long have you been in this country?"

"Six months."

"Do you have a job?"

"Yes. That why I here. Job. Boss. Baby." Rebecca pointed to her slightly distended belly.

"You mean your boss is the father?" Veronica asked.

"Yes. Boss is father. Boss said baby, no job. No baby, job…but I no choose no baby." Rebecca pulled out a gold cross from underneath her sweater and kissed it. Then she cried softly into her hands, still clutching the cross.

Veronica got up and walked around her desk. She knelt in front of the young girl and gave her a hug. When Rebecca stopped crying, Veronica took a Kleenex from a box on top of the desk and handed it to her.

"Don't worry, Rebecca. Everything's going to be okay. You and your baby. Everything's going to be okay." Veronica sat back down at her desk and picked up the phone to call her friend, Chris

Bell, who was the director of Several Sources, a shelter that housed pregnant women with no home. First thing was first, Rebecca Gomez needed a place to live. Veronica looked up and smiled at Rebecca while she waited for someone to answer the phone. Rebecca, looking reassured, smiled back.

"That's why I love this job," Veronica thought to herself. Every time she could be to some other girl what she had wished someone had been to her all those years ago. That's why she loved this job.

"Hello?" Chris' assistant, Rudy, answered the phone.

"Rudy, it's Veronica. I need a favor," Veronica smiled warmly at Rebecca and nodded her head before she told Rudy about Rebecca's story.

*

Grace Blake stood next to her big brother, Peter, with her hands on her hips. "Tell me, again, why Mommy's gonna be late," she said exasperated.

"I told you she's driving some pregnant girl to a shelter." Peter put an arm around his sister and led her over to a seat at the dining room table of Saint Mary's Rectory. He pulled out two large textbooks from his backpack and began to do his homework. One of the school parents had given the children a ride to the church after school so they could wait at Father Raphael's church until their mother could get them.

"Where's Father Raffa?" Grace asked. She was in no mood to do her homework.

"With Mom, too," Peter replied. "He wanted to help because the girl doesn't speak English very well."

"Oh," Grace said sadly.

"What's wrong?" Peter asked.

"Nothing. I just like it when Father Raffa is here. That's all. If we can't have Mommy, I at least want Daddy or Father Raffa." Grace folded her arms across her chest in disappointment.

"Well, Dad's on a business trip, and Mom and Father Raphael will be back soon. Come on and do your homework, so you don't have to worry about it later," Peter said sternly.

Grace finally conceded. She thought she should at least try to be as good a student as Peter, who had carried an A+ average since kindergarten and was at the head of his class.

"Okay. Okay. I'm doing it." Grace took out her pencil and notebook and began to write a sentence for the word, "angel." She suddenly stopped mid–sentence and looked at her brother. "Peter, what's a good sentence for the word, 'angel?'"

Peter looked up to the ceiling for a few seconds before he answered. "My mother does the work of an angel," he replied.

Grace smiled grandly, "That's perfect, Peter!" She quickly erased what she had originally written and proceeded to write, "My mother does the work of an angel," in the best cursive print she could muster.

*

When Veronica Blake arrived at work the following day, she felt rejuvenated. She was able to find a room at Several Sources Shelter for Rebecca through her friend, Chris Bell, and she and Father Raphael dropped her off yesterday afternoon. Rebecca's belongings were scarce, but Veronica knew that Chris and the ladies at the shelter would provide whatever Rebecca needed. When Veronica and Father Raphael were leaving, they noticed that Rebecca seemed comfortable in the home and was already speaking in Spanish to two other young women seated at the dinner table. Veronica was also happy that today was finally Friday, which meant her husband, Tom, would be back from his weeklong business trip out West.

"T.G.I.F. Praise be God!" Veronica muttered to herself as she opened the still unopened file cases on her desk from yesterday. She had only just begun to open the first file when her door flew open with a terrible force. A short burly Hispanic man of middle age came barreling into the shelter. He looked extremely angry and began to shout in Spanish at Veronica. Two untranslatable sentences were spit from his mouth before Veronica could get a word in to stop him.

"Excuse me!" she said loudly. "I do not speak Spanish, therefore, if you are going to continue to yell at me, sir, I suggest you do so in English!"

The man stopped mid–sentence and shouted, "Where is my Rebecca? I know she was in here yesterday! I saw her go in! Where is she?"

"May I ask your name, sir, and what your relationship is to my client?" Veronica asked.

"She works for me!" The man was so angry, his face reminded Veronica of ripe tomatoes.

"As my client discussed yesterday, she is no longer under your employ," Veronica replied calmly with a smile.

"She quit? Rebecca quit?" he asked rhetorically.

"Yes, that is the information she gave me yesterday."

"Where is she? Where did you take her?"

"I am not at will to give you that information, sir. That is privileged and may only be given to a relative. I assume you are not a relative?"

"I am her employer!" the man half spit, half shouted at Veronica.

Veronica looked at the man from above her reading glasses and calmly removed them before she replied. "Therefore, you are not a relative and not privy to that information," she said.

The man's skin looked like it was turning purple with rage. "You bitch!" he screamed. "You better give me that information, or I will have to make you give it to me!" He rushed toward Veronica's desk with his arms extended, and pushed the files onto the floor as he tried to grab the top file assuming it was Rebecca's.

Veronica instantly shot up from her seat and showed the tiny man the full stature of her 5'11" athletic frame. She easily outweighed him in both height and muscle mass. Veronica had grown up on the streets of Newark and a man without a weapon did not intimidate her. She looked menacingly at Rebecca's boss, and he was instantly silenced.

Veronica spoke calmly, "If you do not vacate the premises immediately, sir, I will be forced to call the police." She emphasized the first syllable of "po–lice" with just the right emphatic "o."

The man seemed to shrink before her and quickly retreated back to the door, his imaginary tail caught somewhere between his tiny legs. He opened the door as loudly as possible and slammed it behind him on his way out.

Veronica sat down and a smile formed on her lips. Before long, she was laughing out loud at the little man with the large ego.

"You go, Rebecca. You go, girl," Veronica Blake called out to the ceiling of Turning Point Shelter. "This is going to be a fine day," she said as she picked up the loose papers on the floor and straightened the files on her desk. Veronica sat down and started the work she had intended to do the day before.

CHAPTER TWENTY–FOUR

The University of San Francisco's cafeteria was completely open to magnificent views of the Golden Gate Bridge with floor to ceiling windows on both sides of a hallway that led to a large, bright room with tables and chairs.

Jessica had planned to meet Dr. Jonathan Lee, her best friend and fellow geneticist, Dr. Todd Smith, an associate in the stem–cell research department, and Dr. Barbara Brown, a trusted friend and research analyst, but Jessica changed the location of the meeting at the last minute to a Starbucks a block away.

Jessica's meeting with her director, Dr. Palmer Braxton, the week before was the reason she wanted to hold today's meeting away from USF's cafeteria. The more Jessica recounted last week's conversation with Palmer, the more it bothered her.

"Jessica!" Palmer exclaimed the day after his party when she walked in wearing only her running shorts and T–shirt. He looked at her long, tanned legs like a hungry wolf.

"Hello, Palmer," Jessica replied, surprised at his request to meet at the last minute on a Sunday. "Sorry about the shorts. I just got back from a run. You made it sound urgent, so I didn't want to lose any time changing."

"Yes, yes. Very good," Palmer replied. "I wanted to make you aware that effective tomorrow, we have acquired some new grants in the field of stem cell research, and I will expect our efforts to more than double at this juncture."

Jessica couldn't believe her good timing. She had wanted to discuss embryonic stem cell research with Palmer for weeks. "I am so happy you brought this up..." she began.

Palmer gestured to one of the black leather chairs in front of his desk. "Please sit down," he said.

"Thank you," Jessica sat and continued. "As you are aware, it is a very difficult process to extract human eggs from women. It involves taking powerful hormones to increase the amount of eggs released. It can also require daily injections for up to two weeks and can require that women stop taking prescription medications. Then, we have surgery with sedation for the eggs to be removed. Not a fun process," she said directly.

Palmer tried to appear as compassionate as possible as he took in every word Jessica said. He gestured for her to continue.

"What you may not be aware of is..." Jessica stopped suddenly wondering if Palmer would be happy with the research she had been doing.

"Yes?" Palmer asked.

Jessica continued with caution, "As you know, there have been so many advancements in adult stem cells...more than eighty cures so far for various diseases. And with embryonic stem cells, there has been nothing. No cures. Possible risks. Patients developing tumors...Patients facing the risk of immune rejection...With that in mind, I have begun more intense experimentation in the field of induced pluripotent stem cells from ordinary human skin cells. They're obviously easier to obtain. There's no risk to the patient, and these cells have the potential to change into any type of tissue in the body."

Palmer cleared his throat loudly and put both hands on his desk to raise himself up. He looked down at the papers on his desk with such intensity, Jessica thought she could see a vein on his forehead ready to burst with anxiety. When he looked back up at her, there was a carefully crafted smile on his face a mile wide.

"Jessica, Jessica, Jessica," Palmer said almost laughing. "Everyone in the field knows that adult stem cell research is going nowhere. Everyone in the field knows that the derivation of human induced pluripotent stem cells is too new to give us any real advantage. Technology is at a very early stage and many fundamental questions still remain. This is not where the research money is. The money is in embryonic."

"Yes, Palmer, I am aware of where the money chain is going." Jessica was not going to back down that easily. "I am merely trying to utilize all options in stem cell research."

"Adult is not where I want to go first," Palmer replied firmly.

"May I be permitted to finish the research I began with the iPS cells?"

"I prefer to put that on hold." Palmer was resolute. "I prefer embryonic and only embryonic, at this point."

After Jessica's meeting with Palmer, she had been more than skeptical. Why was she being cornered into one area of research alone? Something was wrong and Jessica had to find out what and quickly.

The four doctors from USF were gathered at a tiny, square table at Starbucks with flavored coffees sitting in front of each. Jessica spoke quickly and urgently, "Listen everyone. Everything I'm about to tell you needs to stay right here at this table and not anywhere else, okay?"

"Of course, it will stay right here," Barbara said without hesitation. "What in the name of God is going on, Jess?"

"Okay. I had an urgent meeting with Palmer and he wants me off everything having to do with adult stem cell research. Apparently, all the money's in embryonic. He said adult stem cell research is going nowhere fast, and he thinks embryonic is going to solve every disease on the planet. In light of the research I've done, this is sheer fantasy. I have come up with just the opposite results.

Palmer wants me to stop going in a direction I think is right and move in a direction that's completely wrong. Anybody know why?"

"Because he's an asshole?" Todd Smith couldn't help himself. Palmer had a reputation and the well–timed remark fit the bill. Everyone at the table laughed heartily including Jessica.

"True. Any other reasons?" Jessica asked again with a smile.

"He is part–owner of JamBrax, right? The one with the patent." Jonathan was sitting on the edge of his seat with excitement. They all were. The possibility of something underhanded going on at USF having to do with Palmer Braxton was a dream come true.

"You don't think JamBrax is the one providing the research grant, do you? Investing in himself?" Jessica asked.

"That does have some element of truth to it," Todd said pointing a finger at Jonathan. "After all, Palmer does have that huge ego."

"Guys, get serious. You think Palmer's gonna waste his money here when he could be spending it on some new yacht or private jet?" Barbara was looking at Jessica like she couldn't believe the men at the table were fellow doctors.

"Isn't he also doing that research for PSA or PSI, whatever that organization is called?" Jonathan sounded like he was seriously trying to connect the dots to Palmer's livelihood.

"PSI, Parenting Services International. The women's reproductive healthcare clinics," Barbara corrected.

"The abortion mills," Todd interjected.

Barbara gave Todd a "look of death" that caught him off guard. "What?" he asked innocently. "That's what they do."

"So, you think there's a connection between JamBrax and PSI?" Jessica asked.

"I don't know about that, but there might be a connection between embryonic research grants and PSI," Jonathan replied.

"What connection?" Barbara asked hesitantly.

"Destruction of embryos," Jonathan answered.

"What about that other place, too? The one that's called JamBrax something?" Todd asked seriously for the first time.

"What other place?" Jonathan asked the question, but Jessica and Barbara had no idea what Todd meant either.

"I'll look it up." Todd took out his Blackberry, quickly thumb–punched his keypad, and after fifteen seconds, had his answer. "JamBrax Fountain of Youth Spa. Barbados."

All four doctors looked at one another with the kind of nervous excitement that only comes when a big discovery is about to be made.

*

Cassy's mind awakened more and more with each spiritual journey she made with Paolo. Bridget Monaghan noticed it, too. When the nurse made her usual morning rounds at the hospital, she checked Cassy's vital signs and noticed that her patient looked flushed. The motherly nurse placed the back of her hand against Cassy's forehead to feel for a fever. None. When Bridget took her hand away, she thought she saw Cassy's eyes open. The nurse looked again. No. Now her eyes were closed again. The nurse felt she must be seeing things and turned to leave.

"She's fine," Bridget thought. "Fine, but still in a coma." Just to make sure, the nurse turned once more to catch a glimpse of Cassy before she left the room. When she looked back, Bridget saw something that startled her so much, her heart nearly skipped a beat. Cassy's entire body appeared to levitate, suspended in midair about a foot off the hospital bed.

"Oh, my God! Oh, my dear God!" Bridget exclaimed breathlessly. Her hand went to the door knob to steady herself, when she noticed a man standing to the left of Cassy's bed. There was an angelic quality about him as if he were not physically there on earth. Bridget felt as if she were seeing a reflection of the man. As if his body had been formed by watercolors on a one–

dimensional canvas.

The man seemed to sense that Bridget could see him, too. He was very handsome with long, dark hair and striking, blue eyes. His mouth formed a warm smile and Bridget felt a sense of something holy. The nurse felt so much emotion, she tried to stifle a sob with the back of her hand. Her hand was shaking and Bridget's heartbeat was pounding hard enough to become audible. She closed her eyes and said a "Hail Mary" to gain control, but when she opened her eyes again, the man had vanished and Cassy's body lay back on the bed as it had for the last ten weeks.

"I must have imagined it…" the nurse began under her breath. Bridget turned one last time to make sure, her hands still shaking from the scare. She saw nothing, but Cassy sleeping peacefully. "And to think it's only morning," Bridget continued to herself. "I'll be seeing flying donkeys by lunchtime if I don't get hold of my mind." Bridget gently closed Cassy's door wondering if she had gotten enough sleep the night before.

*

Paolo smiled thinking how kind the nurse seemed as Bridget left the room. He touched Cassy's hand, and her eyes opened instantly.

"Come, Cassy. We must go quickly." This time, Paolo lifted Cassy off the bed, and she felt the cool breeze of the open air without realizing they had left the room.

In Paolo's arms, she could sense a foreboding in Paolo. This was something she had never felt from him before. It was as if Paolo were carrying the weight of the world's doom on his shoulders alone.

"Paolo?" Cassy asked with alarm.

Paolo smiled warmly as he carried Cassy like a protective father. "It's time," was Paolo's only response.

"Time for what?" she asked.

"Time to discover the truth."

They had arrived at their destination. Cassy noticed immediately that this was the starkest, most barren land she had ever seen. There was no green. No grass. Only soft, clay dirt lay under her bare feet as Paolo gently set her down on the ground. When Cassy looked up to take in her surroundings, a warm breeze hit her face, but she could smell nothing. There seemed to be no life in this place. There were no trees, plants, animals, or people. Only clay dirt and a lifeless wind.

"Come," Paolo said as he walked forward. Cassy followed behind him and noticed that Paolo made no footprints in the dry dirt. She wondered where they were, but felt it best not to ask. Not yet.

Paolo came to a large hill and proceeded up slowly. Cassy followed and the air seemed to grow hotter and hotter the higher they climbed. She felt drops of perspiration on her brow, and she lifted her arm to wipe the sweat from her forehead. The closer Paolo and Cassy came to the top of the hill, the more difficult it became to breathe. The heat was like fire, and Cassy feared that whatever lay beyond the hill was something she did not want to see. Paolo turned to offer his hand. The climb had become so steep, he wanted to help her reach the top. The touch of Paolo's hand was reassuring, but even he could not hide his despair.

When Cassy and Paolo reached the top and looked over the barren land that lay before them, she saw a tall, bronze statue in the distance. It stood in the center of a barren field of dry sand that blew about in the high heat of a desert sun. Cassy saw tufts of dry weeds float back and forth between sand and wind. There were fires on either side of the bronze statue that blazed from low pits.

Cassy turned to Paolo, her hair swept into her face by the wind. "What is that statue?"

"Baal Hammon," he answered.

"Who?"

"Their god."

Paolo took Cassy's hand. "Come. We'll move closer," he said.

The closer Cassy moved toward the statue, the more she heard the sound of flutes and tambourines coming from the area below. She made out the images of people gathered in front of Baal Hammon. With each step, Cassy heard beautiful music being played for a great celebration. She felt the heat of the flames coupled with the desert sun. She saw the great bronze statue in full. The statue of Baal Hammon extended his hands with his palms up and his arms sloped down to the ground.

"Why are his hands extended like that?" she asked Paolo.

"You will see," he answered.

As the heat of the fire and sun were blown into Cassy's face, she smelled something completely foreign to her. It smelled like rot or mold. It was completely horrible, but she could not fathom what was creating the smell. Cassy saw a little package being placed on the hand of Baal Hammon, but she could not make out what was falling from the hand and rolling down the arm and into the fire. And then it hit Cassy all at once and much too suddenly. This was not the smell of rot. It was the smell of burning flesh. And that wasn't a little package rolling down Baal Hammon's arm. It was an infant. A screaming infant who was crying out in fear. Cassy watched in horror as the child slid down the arm of the bronze god. She winced as the child slipped into the fire pit; a hushed cry escaped his mouth before death.

"Paolo, what is...?" Cassy stopped as she heard screaming come from one of the women near the pit. It must have been the infant's mother. Cassy could not hold back the sob that came from her own throat. She turned to Paolo with tears running down her face. "Paolo?"

"Child sacrifices to Baal Hammon, their god, and Tanit, their goddess," Paolo said. "In times of crisis or calamity, like war, drought, or famine, their 'priests' demanded the flower of their youth. Five hundred children will be sacrificed today."

"Where are we?" Cassy asked.

"Carthage," Paolo answered.

"What year?"

"310 B.C."

Before Cassy could ask another question, she saw a grotesquely costumed priest try to pull another infant from her mother. When the mother did not want to let her child go, the woman's husband slapped his wife so the priest could take the infant. The father ceremoniously handed the child over to the waiting priest, and the child began to scream and cry in the priest's arms. Cassy could see the priest chanting something and then he placed his thumb in a nearby urn and painted colorful chalk on the infant's forehead. The child was placed on the hand of Baal Hammon and the sound of her cry was only half of her mother's as the child fell down into the waiting pit.

"That is what the music is for," Paolo told Cassy.

"What?" Cassy asked between sobs of anguish.

"To drown out the parents' cries," Paolo answered.

"Why have you taken me here?" Cassy asked. "I don't understand."

"Because this is where Moloch was given life," Paolo answered as he took Cassy into his arms to comfort her.

Cassy cried into Paolo's shoulder, and her body shook with grief at the unnecessary slaughtering of innocent children. When her anguish had subsided, she pulled herself from Paolo and looked into his heavenly gaze. "Who is Moloch?" Cassy asked.

"Moloch is the god of death," Paolo replied.

"I thought these children were being sacrificed to Baal Hammon?" Cassy asked again.

"Yes, Baal Hammon and Tanit. Both, false gods."

"False gods?"

"Yes. There is but one God. The God of Israel, Isaac and Jacob. One God," Paolo answered sternly. "These sacrificial practices were rebuked by the one God. As it is written, sacrifice is an abomination to God. Moloch was collecting these sacrifices for himself in order that he might have life…human life."

Cassy immediately sensed Paolo's meaning, and before he could utter another word, she dreaded what he would say next.

"You mean…?" Cassy began with wide–eyed astonishment.

"David is Moloch," Paolo answered.

CHAPTER TWENTY–FIVE

Marie Murray stood outside Milwaukee's PSI Clinic for two hours with Father Andrew McLaughlin and the Saint Michael's 40 Days for Life group when the cold wind began to sneak up the back of her jacket. She and Father Mac were scheduled to visit Rosa and Manny at Columbia Saint Mary's Hospital right after lunch. Thank God, Rosa and the couple's pre–born baby were doing just fine.

The wind was so cold, Marie wished the time would go quicker so they could leave for the warmth of the hospital. She wondered why she hadn't thought to wear her hat and gloves when she saw a young woman with long, dark hair walk toward the clinic from the parking lot across the street. The woman was in her early twenties and had beautiful green cat eyes that pierced through the darkness of her olive skin. She was dressed in jeans with black leather boots and wore a dark leather coat with the collar turned up against the wind.

The woman had to make her way through the prayer group to get to the entrance of the clinic from the parking lot. Marie saw the girl look up to read the sign she held that read, "Women Deserve Better Than Abortion," her green cat eyes taking in every word on the board. When she looked down again, the young woman caught Marie looking at her. The women's gaze caught and hung on with a startling connection as if time were standing still for one instant.

Marie could tell that the young woman was yearning for something. Someone to help her make the right decision. Someone to tell her not to go through with this. A shoulder to cry on. A motherly hug from a stranger she'd never met. Marie wanted to engage the young woman in friendly conversation.

"This girl needs help," Marie thought to herself. She moved toward the young woman.

Suddenly, one of the bodyguards employed by PSI came forward and led the girl away from Marie and 40 Days for Life. In that one instant, Marie felt she had made a connection with someone she would never see again, but would always remember. She watched as the young woman with the long, dark hair and green cat eyes was led into the clinic and wondered if that young woman would always remember her, too.

*

As they drove to the hospital, Father Mac thought this was as good a time as any to let Marie know the latest regarding Debbie Romano since he knew that Michael rarely spoke to his parents about the case. Marie and Doc knew very little about the danger their son was up against.

"Marie, I wanted to let you know that Michael has been given a dangerous mission in his pursuit to find Debbie Romano," he began. "This bloodstone mystery has become very complicated, to say the least." Father Mac was trying to lighten the word, "dangerous," by appearing nonchalant.

"What do you mean?" she asked.

"You know that Debbie was kidnapped by a dark, mysterious man, right?"

"Yes."

"You know that Linda and Michael were in a boating accident recently?"

"Yes."

"Do you know that the boating accident was intentional, and that the person who caused the 'accident' is the same dark, mysterious man?"

The look on Marie's face was complete shock. A full minute elapsed before she responded to the question. "That I did not know," was all she said.

"Yes, and there's just one more small thing." Father Mac waited for a second to let Marie prepare herself. "It looks like the dark, mysterious man may be...well it looks like he may be...somehow...and I know this sounds absolutely implausible...but it looks like he may be somehow connected to...I don't know how to say it so I'll just say it straight out...Satan."

*

Michael and Linda sat in the library at Marquette staring at a computer screen of what seemed like the hundredth picture of Lilith, the woman who Rabbi Levine had likened to Satan.

"If I see one more picture of a naked woman with large snakes circling around her body, I think I'm going to puke," Linda said staring at the image with the name, "Lilith," underneath it.

"That picture's better than the one with the hairy legs," Michael retorted. "Wasn't she half woman/half man?"

"More like ape from the waist down," Linda answered. "All I know is the one where she's half tree in the Garden of Eden is the most freaky."

Michael scrolled back to the picture that depicted Lilith in Michelangelo's "The Temptation of Adam and Eve." Here, Lilith is standing between Adam and Eve with a large snake twisting down the lower half of her body, which disappears inside the tree truck. She is tempting them with the apple.

"I never knew Adam's first wife was a woman named Lilith,"

Michael said.

"You never knew it because it's not true," Linda replied angrily.

"Yeah, you're probably right. Anyway, it looks more like Lilith is the one tempting Eve with the apple, not snaky Satan." Michael was trying to calm Linda down. They had been staring at Lilith pictures so long, they were both getting testy.

"What are we looking for anyway?" Linda asked. She wanted to move on to other research. Linda wanted to start with the Calatrava clue they discovered at her house, but Michael insisted they research Lilith as soon as he heard from Father Mac.

"Father Mac said Rabbi Levine has translations of Dead Sea Scrolls that lead to the Urim and Thummim's discovery date," Michael replied.

Linda looked back at the Lilith picture standing in the Garden of Eden and noticed a link to the Dead Sea Scrolls. "Hey, check this out," she said.

Michael clicked the link and saw references to Lilith found in the Dead Sea Scrolls. "And I, the Instructor, proclaim His glorious splendour so as to frighten and to terrify all the spirits of the destroying angels, spirits of the bastards, demons, Lilith, howlers..." Michael looked up before continuing, "Howlers?" he asked.

"The scholarly use of the word, 'howlers,' is sure to give us a date," Linda retorted rolling her eyes.

Michael laughed and continued, "...smitten by iniquity—not for eternal destruction, but for an era of humiliation for transgression. Taken from 'Song for a Sage (4Q522).'"

"Interesting...really fascinating," Linda mocked.

Michael began again, "Her gates are gates of death, and from the entrance of the house she sets out towards Sheol. None of those who enter there will ever return, and all who possess her will descend to the Pit. (4Q501)."

"Okay, so first, it's just a little humiliation and then it's taken to the Pit forever?" Linda asked suddenly curious.

Michael continued once more, "Her house sinks down to death, and whoever should discover the light of life shall escape the Pit. The UT will destroy the darkness of night and the splendor of new life shall fall back on the righteous. (4Q513)."

"So it sounds like God's giving these people a second chance," Linda said.

"Yes, and the good old UT, or Urim and Thummim, is going to give them that chance," Michael added.

"Right, but when?" Linda asked.

"Don't tell me we're going to do more biblical numerology to figure it out." Michael was becoming just as exasperated as Linda had been only moments before.

Linda gazed at the computer screen. She squinted hard and her eyes widened as she appeared to make a discovery.

"What?" Michael asked.

Linda looked at Michael with a knowing smile. "No, Michael, we will not have to do more biblical numerology," she said. "It's already been done. Look at these numbers." Linda pointed to the scroll citations. Each said, "4Q" and "5" hundred and something. What was different was the "22," the "1," and the "13." "That's a date," she said.

Michael's eyes widened as he made the connection, too. "That's it," he said. "That's our date. 1/22/13. And it's right around the corner."

*

By the time Marie and Father Mac reached Columbia Saint Mary's Hospital on North Lake Drive to visit Rosa and Manny, it was already well past lunch and Marie's stomach was grumbling loudly.

"Do you want to stop for lunch at the hospital cafeteria before we go up?" Father Mac asked.

"Was my stomach that loud?" Marie asked her priest friend as she followed him through the double doors into the hospital lobby.

"Let's just say that everyone on the first floor of this hospital now knows you're as hungry as a bear, which is probably a good thing because it's the only way you could ever get me to eat hospital food."

Father Mac and Marie paid for the salad bar, which turned out to be better than they had originally anticipated. They quickly consumed salads and iced teas, and took the elevator to the neo-natal unit on the second floor. When they found the room, Father Mac knocked on the closed door.

"Come in." Rosa's subtle Spanish accent was clear and distinct.

Father Mac pushed on the door, and he and Marie smiled cheerfully when they saw how healthy and radiant Rosa looked. She was propped up by numerous white, fluffy pillows placed behind her back. Her left leg was in a long cast and suspended in a sling above her protruding and pregnant belly.

"Hi!" Rosa exclaimed with a smile. "Thanks for coming!"

"How are you, dear?" Father Mac asked with his usual fatherly care.

"Good," Rosa began to answer.

"You look wonderful!" Marie couldn't stop herself from getting in a compliment. She was so relieved that Rosa was doing so well.

Both Father Mac and Marie noticed the baby monitor on Rosa's left at the same time. It was visibly and audibly punctuating the quick and steady heartbeat of the baby inside of her.

"How is the baby?" Marie and Father Mac asked at the same time.

The three started laughing simultaneously because they all wanted to speak at once. There was so much excitement in the room.

Rosa cleared her throat and announced that the baby was doing perfectly and he or she would be here to meet them in person in only two or three weeks according to the doctors at the hospital.

"I thought I was still more than a month away, but I guess my original due date was a little off," Rosa said with a smile.

"Where's Emmanuel?" Father Mac asked looking around the hospital room with bright–colored flowers in vases on tables next to the bed and window.

"Manny went downstairs to take a call for work. He should be right back," Rosa answered. "I know he was looking forward to seeing you both."

As if by magic, the door opened and Manny appeared as soon as his name was mentioned. He immediately walked over to Father Mac, shook the priest's hand, and gave Marie a big, bear hug.

"Hey, guys! Thanks for coming! It's so nice to see both of you." Manny was so visibly happy, it looked like he might burst out of his shirt. He gingerly sat on the edge of Rosa's bed and held her hand.

"We are so happy for you two...I mean three," Marie began. She stopped mid–sentence.

Manny's foot was shaking uncontrollably. Underneath his smiling face, Marie could tell that he was really nervous about something. She knew that whatever it was that was making Manny nervous was probably something he was trying to keep from Rosa. Perhaps he did not want to upset her.

"Manny have you been back to work since...coming to the hospital?" Marie did not want to use the word, "accident," because she did not want to bring back any bad memories for Rosa.

"Yes, here and there. They've been really patient with me. I'm even able to bring my lap top to the hospital and work remotely from here."

"Are you able to sleep here, too?" Father Mac asked.

"Yes. See that chair right there? Folds into a bed. Not a very comfortable bed, but better than being apart from Rosa." Manny turned toward his beloved wife and squeezed her hand reassuringly.

"I'm so happy for you two. I can't even tell you," Marie said, again, noticing Manny's shaking foot. She was worried for him.

"Manny, Father Mac wanted to give Rosa a special blessing, and I need to find the gift shop to purchase something. Do you mind escorting me down and showing me where it is?" Marie looked at Father Mac like this was the plan from the beginning.

"No problem," Manny replied. "Okay, Rosa? I'll be right back up."

"Okay, Manny. Thank you, Father." Rosa smiled at Father Mac and kissed her husband on the cheek.

Marie followed Manny out of the room to the elevators. As soon as he pushed the down button, Marie turned to him and placed a hand on his shoulder. "Manny, are you okay?"

Emmanuel looked at Marie with a confused expression on his face. "What do you mean?" he asked.

"I noticed your foot shaking when you were sitting on Rosa's bed. Are you okay with everything?" Marie asked again.

The elevator doors opened to go down and Marie followed Manny inside. When the doors closed behind them, Manny put his hands over his eyes and his shoulders began to shake with sobbing. Marie put her arms around him and he turned to accept her comforting hug. When they reached the lobby and stepped outside, Manny seemed to have calmed down considerably.

"I'm getting these calls on my cell phone," Manny began. "I don't know who it is, but someone is threatening Rosa and me. A man. A man with an evil voice. He says that if we don't stop our picketing outside the abortion clinics…that if we don't stop…the accident with Rosa will seem like nothing. He said he wants to see our baby dead."

Marie stood very still and looked completely calm given the circumstances. "Have you called the police?" she finally asked.

"No."

"Have you told Rosa?"

"No."

"Good. For now, let's keep this between us and Father Mac. I'll let him know on the way back home. Manny, everything will be okay," Marie said comfortingly.

"How do you know for sure?" Manny asked.

"I think I know who's calling you," Marie answered with conviction. "He wants us to be afraid, but I absolutely refuse to give in to fear."

*

It was already almost six o'clock in the evening when Kay Dennis heard her son's footsteps as he hurriedly made his way up the stairs to their two–bedroom apartment. She and Kevin lived in a small apartment complex on Boulevard Avenue in New Milford, New Jersey. It wasn't much, but Kay's income had been reduced drastically from the lavish lifestyle she had once known. Kevin's father, her good–for–nothing cheating husband, had left her for a woman ten years younger after nineteen years of marriage. Kay's budget had been reduced to a modest nursing income. She had traded her extravagant gym membership for a discount grocery card. After all, it was tough making ends meet with a small salary and two mouths to feed.

Kevin opened the door and threw his book bag on the sofa in the living room. "Hey Mom!" he said as he walked into the little kitchen nook and opened the refrigerator.

"How come you're so late?" Kay asked, covering up her worry with annoyance.

"Study group after school. Father Raffa after that."

Kevin worked at Saint Mary's in Dumont as the sacristan for Father Raphael Diego Trujillo. He worked mainly weekends, but sometimes Father needed him to come in on Wednesday afternoons to help re–stock the parish food pantry for those in need who lived in the area. Father Raphael knew that Kevin needed the extra money so he always managed to give Kevin extra food to take home with him.

"What did he give you this time?" Kay asked watching Kevin

put a small bag of groceries into the refrigerator.

"Nothing, just extra stuff they had lying around that Father didn't want to go bad," Kevin said through his teeth. Father Raphael knew that Kay and Kevin were having a rough time paying their bills. Kay worked as a nurse at a women's clinic in Englewood, but the salary was low and the benefits were non–existent.

"We're doing just fine on our own," Kay retorted. "When that good–for–nothing father of yours left, I could have cowered back in a corner and asked for government handouts, you know? But I held my head up high and got a job and a nice apartment. Your father might have taken away my house for his new wife, but he wasn't about to take away my pride!"

Kevin finished putting away the groceries and walked over to his mother. She looked so helpless, Kevin had to comfort her. He put his arms around her and squeezed her hard. Kevin was a sophomore at Dumont High School, but he was already over six feet tall and wore a size thirteen shoe. Kay held her son close and sighed as she felt her sixteen–year–old son's love and protection.

Kevin's father had not wanted custody of his son. His new wife wanted to start fresh and thought that Kevin was "baggage." Kay instantly thought that this was her win and her husband's loss for sure. The whole divorce had been a double–edged sword between good and bad from the beginning: good that Kay never had to deal with custody battles, bad that Kevin no longer had a father to rear him; good that the divorce had been quick and effortless, bad that Kay had lost the only home she'd ever known; good that Kay had been given enough money to send Kevin to college, bad that she still had to cover living costs with a low–pay, no–benefit nightmare.

Kay pulled away from her son, her eyes moist. She had been close to crying, but she had learned to become tough and had prided herself for not shedding a single tear since the divorce.

Kay's parents were killed in a car accident when she was

Kevin's age and she was used to having to survive in tough circumstances. She made it through high school on her own and worked two jobs to pay for nursing school at night. She would do whatever it took to survive and whatever it took to raise Kevin. He was her pride and joy. He was her happiness. Kevin was the one thing that gave her life meaning.

Kevin moved toward his book bag to get out his homework. "What's for dinner?" he asked.

"Meatloaf." Kay answered. "Half hour."

*

Kevin finished half his homework, and he and his mother sat at the dining room table after dinner. It was just before eight, and Kay was clearing the table so Kevin could finish his homework and she could go to bed early.

"You okay, Mom?" Kevin's mother usually turned on the news in the living room before cleaning up the dishes.

"Yeah, fine. I'm just really tired tonight. I'm going to bed early." Kay set the dishes on the kitchen counter and put her head in her hands.

"You sure?" Kevin followed his mother into the kitchen. "You look really unhappy. Is everything okay at work?"

"Yeah, sure. No problem." Kay was so distracted, she scraped food off a plate and opened the cupboard to put it away without washing it. She set the plate back down on the counter and turned to her son. "Kevin?" she asked unsure.

"Yeah. I'm here, Mom. Sit down, so we can talk." Kevin pointed to the dining room chair she had just left.

When Kay sat down, she looked like the entire weight of the world was resting on her shoulders. "What would you say if you were working at a place that lies?" she asked.

"What are you talking about?"

"PSI, Parenting Services International, the place I work at in

Englewood, they lied to this girl today. She was pregnant. Only fifteen years old. They told her the tissue inside of her body wasn't really a baby yet, just a cluster of cells. They said she should lie about her age because the man she was with was thirty–four and if she was only fifteen, the police would call it rape and he would get into a lot of trouble and then she would get into even more trouble. Kevin, they didn't care. They told her that everything would be okay if she said exactly what they told her to say." Kay stopped for a second to give her son time to digest what she said.

Kevin stared back at his mother, a look of horror on his young and innocent face.

"Kevin, in nursing, I've seen a lot of bad things that I would never want to see again, but in all my years of doing this, I've never seen anything as bad as what I saw today."

"What was she doing at the clinic anyway?" Kevin asked.

"She was there because her thirty–four year old boyfriend told her that she could either get an abortion or he would kill her." Kay felt so much despair for the young girl she could feel it in her entire body.

"And apparently the clinic was okay with this?" Kevin was in shock as he asked the question.

"Apparently, more than okay with it," Kay answered disgustedly.

"Then leave the clinic, Mom. Leave it now." Kevin squeezed his mother's hand and went to his room. He left his homework unfinished on the dining room table suddenly not caring about the consequences.

CHAPTER TWENTY–SIX

Palmer Braxton was not at all prepared to meet David Bloodstone at his JamBrax Fountain of Youth Spa in Barbados. Elaina spoke of David so frequently and so highly, Palmer didn't know if he should revere him or fear him.

When David walked through the JamBrax lobby to his receptionist's desk, Palmer was stunned by David's appearance. David was so tall and gaunt, he looked like a six foot five skeleton. Palmer had never seen such a striking man in all his life. David's long straight, black hair was swept back from his face so severely, it looked like David's skin had no creases or wrinkles. David's eyes were so black, Palmer could barely make out his pupils.

David wore black from head to foot: black boots, pants, shirt and jacket. The only jewelry David wore was a gold necklace that lay on his exposed chest. It was an elegant cameo, not the kind of jewelry Palmer was used to seeing on a man, but it seemed to fit him anyway. The cameo had the same feeling about it—the same blackness. Palmer was completely speechless when he looked back up at David's eyes.

Elaina came forward to break the silence and introduce the two men. "Palmer, David Bloodstone," she said.

"How do you do?" David extended his long hand to Palmer and

a feeling of fear came over Palmer so fierce, he had to steady his hand to shake.

"How do you do," Palmer repeated unsteadily. David's hand felt strangely cold to Palmer, as if he were shaking hands with a dead man.

Palmer cleared his throat. "Can I offer you coffee or tea before we begin the tour?" he asked trying to regain his composure.

"Tea would be wonderful," David replied graciously.

"Tea for me, too, Palmer. We're really looking forward to this," Elaina said.

Palmer turned to his receptionist. "Maryanne, tea for three in my office." Palmer gestured for David and Elaina to follow him feeling more at ease as he walked through the lobby filled with palm trees and waterfalls.

Palmer, David, and Elaina looked at colorful marketing brochures of the luxurious health services at JamBrax's Fountain of Youth Spa for more than an hour while they sipped tea. Afterward, Palmer began a tour of the spa, complete with pool, hot tub, sauna, steam room, showers, powder room, messages, facials, manicures, pedicures, and gourmet snack bar, just on the main floor alone. The top two floors held fifty luxury suites with balconies, all with a beautiful view of the azure–blue Caribbean waters.

"Where are the Fountain of Youth rooms?" Elaina asked.

"I was saving the best for last," Palmer replied, glowing with pride.

"Very good," David spoke approvingly.

"Follow me."

Elaina and David followed Palmer into the elevator, and Palmer hit the button that read, "LL," just below the lobby. "Secrets are best kept hidden," Palmer said smiling.

When the elevator opened, there was a long hallway that led to three large procedure rooms at the end of the hall. Palmer opened the door furthest to the left. The room consisted of two hospital beds with an IV drip bag and hanger next to each, and a box of latex gloves sitting on an upright metal tool box. There was nothing else in the room—no resuscitation, automatic external defibrillator or any other type of emergency equipment in case of an adverse patient reaction. There were also no windows in the room, which was very different than the rest of the facility. It was sterile and void of anything luxurious.

David strolled over to one of the IV drip bags and held it in his hand even though it was completely empty. "Where are the contents?" he asked.

"I keep my supplies in a large refrigerated closet at the other end of the hall," Palmer replied. "Would you like to see?"

"No need," David replied. He lifted his hand and Palmer could see that the IV bag now contained the liquid that he normally injected into his patients intravenously.

"But how…?" Palmer's face turned white, and he stood with his mouth open as Elaina looked on disapprovingly.

"Your contents come from the Ukraine?" David asked still looking at the IV bag.

"Yeah," was all Palmer could get out.

"It looks as if the contents are aborted at six to twelve weeks and liquefied," David turned to Palmer with his black, bewitching eyes. "Delightful, Palmer. Simply fantastic."

Palmer's mouth had gone completely dry as he stared into David's black eyes.

"Palmer, how much did you say the patients pay for this 'youth' treatment?" Elaina asked.

"Ahh…$25,000." Palmer wondered how he was still breathing. He felt so parched he thought he might die of thirst.

"You think you could get more?" Elaina asked. "After all, this is state–of–the–art regenerative medicine."

"Yes, Palmer, I agree." David stared at Palmer as if he were trying to take over his mind and body.

Palmer felt himself perspiring with nervousness as David made his way closer to him. Palmer's throat felt so dry, he wouldn't be able to swallow if he tried.

David put his hand on Palmer's shoulder and looked deeply into his eyes. "Palmer, you are on the verge of a scientific breakthrough that is beyond any imagining," David said in a low whisper. "I speak from absolute experience when I tell you that this regenerative medicine, this 'baby puree,' can bring about an unnaturally long and powerful life."

Palmer felt his throat completely close as he stood transfixed in fear.

*

Dr. Albert Townsend viewed himself as a man who was successful because he was ambitious and career minded. He was only twenty–eight when he opened his first Women's Health Clinic in Washington D.C. He married one of his nurses two years later and produced two beautiful children, a boy named Albert, now twenty–eight himself, and a girl named Suzie, now twenty–five.

At forty, Dr. Townsend's first wife divorced him when she caught him in an examination room with an assistant half his age. He married the assistant a year later. She was twenty–six. "Townsend," as he preferred to be called, owned four clinics with his partner, Dr. Gary Melford. When he made his first million after only three years of marriage, he realized his new young wife was more interested in his money than him. They were divorced right before her thirtieth birthday.

Townsend decided to enjoy his money with women he did not necessarily have to call, "wife." At first, he met women when he traveled or attended parties, but Townsend realized he could have them right in his office if he wanted. Townsend's sexual appetite grew to the point of near insatiability. In fact, he and Gary, who was happily married or so he said, found themselves hiring nurses for their clinics based more on looks and bra size than on knowledge or experience. If she was good looking, give her thirty grand a year. If she was great looking, give her forty. And if she was a real knock out, give her fifty plus whatever benefits she wanted.

When Townsend turned fifty–eight, he and Gary owned a dozen clinics spread across the D.C. area, and they had both become multi–millionaires. He continued his affairs with knock–out nurses, and eventually married one who had just turned thirty–three. Townsend's grown children gave him six beautiful grandchildren. As far as he was concerned, he was living the American dream and had every success a man could want out of life.

Townsend's partner, Gary, who had just turned sixty–four, had three children with his first wife, two with his second, one with his third, and none yet with his fourth. She was only thirty–one, not quite half his age, and they had only been married a year and a half. Gary had four homes, one for each ex–wife and a 20,000 square foot mini–mansion he shared with his current wife. He owned four luxury vehicles, two boats, a condominium in the Florida Keys and a vacation home in Aspen. He also had seven grandchildren from age fourteen down to two.

Townsend and Gary each worked only a couple days a week. They employed ten doctors, twenty–four nurses, and some fifty plus additional staff to work the seventeen clinics owned by the two men. They were both mega millionaires and quite content with the life they had established for themselves.

Until last year. Townsend heard about the plane crash on a local news channel and thought nothing of it. He was in the den having a cocktail before dinner when the phone rang. A minute later, his butler looked completely ashen and held the phone out to him.

"Hello?" Townsend heard crying on the other end of the line.

"Uncle Albert? It's Dana." Dana was Gary's youngest daughter. She was crying into the phone as she tried to speak. "Brianna and

Olivia are dead. They went down in an airplane crash. Both of their husbands, Brad and Dan, are gone, too. And all five children. Just like that, gone. Please come now. Daddy needs you."

*

When Townsend arrived at the Melford estate, there were police cars parked inside the gated entrance. He drove through the gate and parked on the circular drive directly in front of the double doors. Townsend quickly ascended the brick staircase, but he didn't need to ring the bell. The door was already open. He saw the police officers inside the foyer. They were conversing with the Melfords and asking questions. Gary had his arms wrapped around his wife's shoulders as she sobbed uncontrollably.

Townsend stood frozen just inside the door. He saw Gary look up, his eyes vacant as if no one were home. His expression was void of any emotion.

Dana came running and crying as she threw herself into her Uncle Townsend's arms. He consoled her, wondering if her father would ever be the same again.

That day, Townsend discovered that the plane had gone down killing two of Melford's daughters, two sons–in–law and five grandchildren along with the pilot and four family friends. The plane, a single–engine turboprop flown by the family pilot crashed into a Catholic cemetery and burst into flames only 500 feet from its landing destination. All aboard were killed.

The cause of the crash was a complete mystery. The pilot, a former military flier who logged over 2,000 hours, gave no indication to air traffic controllers that the aircraft was experiencing difficulty when he asked to divert to another airport. Witnesses reported that the plane suddenly nosedived toward the ground with no apparent signs of a struggle. There was neither a cockpit voice recorder nor a flight data recorder onboard, and no radar clues into the plane's final moments because Baltimore airport was not equipped with a radar facility. Police speculated that the crash was due to ice on the wings, but that particular plane model had been tested for icy weather and experts said ice was highly unlikely as the cause.

The plane crashed in a Maryland cemetery owned by Resurrection Cemetery Association in Baltimore. The Catholic Holy Cross Cemetery contained a memorial for local residents to pray the rosary at the "Tomb of the Unborn." Remnants of the plane were found only yards from the tomb. This information distressed Townsend even more than Gary.

Townsend's paranoia began years ago when he and Gary had purchased enough abortion clinics to make them the largest for–profit abortion chain in the nation. The seventeen D.C. clinics performed more abortions in the state than any other abortion provider—PSI included—and they performed abortions through the first five months of pregnancy. Townsend and Gary reaped the profits of the blood money that came from the tens of thousands of babies killed through abortions performed every year at the clinics they owned. The chain enabled them to afford the private plane carrying Gary's family to their week–long vacation at The Yellowstone Club, a millionaires–only ski resort.

Townsend remembered the first year one of the anti–choice groups had shown up outside of Gary's estate, as well as his own. Young activists stood outside Gary's mansion holding fetal development signs and signs that called abortion "Child Murder for Profit." The same protestors showed up regularly every Thursday afternoon to ask Gary and his wife, Pam, to repent, to seek God's blessings and to separate themselves from the practice of child killing.

One Thursday, Gary told Townsend that he and Pam were warned that, for his children's sake, he needed to wash his hands of the innocent blood he spilled because the bible warned that if he did not hate bloodshed, bloodshed would pursue him. Gary and Townsend and their wives never took these warnings seriously.

They laughed outwardly at the ridiculous nature of the signs held in front of their estates.

They were not killers. They were respected doctors and businessmen. They provided legal and safe access to women who made personal choices about the rights of their bodies. If women were not allowed to obtain services that were legal and safe, they would wind up dead in some back alley after a botched "coat–hanger" abortion had killed them. Gary and Townsend were heroes.

A few days after the accident, Townsend accompanied Gary to the site of the plane crash. They stood against the wind with their hands in their coat pockets looking at the few remnants of metal that still remained on the cemetery ground. Townsend saw one lone tear trickle down Gary's cheek. Were it not for that one sign of grief, Townsend would have thought that Gary felt no emotion at all. Most of the time, Gary stared into space as if he were not present to the reality around him.

Townsend walked down a steep hill and saw a small memorial ten feet from the crash site. When he was close enough to read the marble stone of the memorial, he felt his whole face flush with fear. The memorial was called the "Tomb of the Unborn." It was erected as a dedication to all babies who had died because of abortion. Townsend immediately felt sick and faint. The family of Dr. Gary Melford, the co–owner of the largest for–profit abortion chain in the nation, had been killed in a crash near the location of the abortion victims' memorial.

*

Within one year of the tragedy, Gary and his fourth wife divorced, and Gary moved into a luxury condominium in the heart of Washington D.C. Gary eventually grew comfortable with his new bachelor lifestyle. He dated different women, and he and Townsend's business grew.

They opened four more clinics, and the last was opened on the bottom floor of the same building where Gary lived. Gary's commute was an elevator ride from the penthouse to the lobby. They had enough doctors and nurses to run the other clinics, so they spent most of their time at the new clinic in Gary's building. They lived a bachelor lifestyle, even Townsend, whose wife lived at their estate outside the city. Sharing a bed with nurses and assistants was convenient when you lived in a luxury condo twenty floors above your workplace.

Life was good for Townsend and Gary, but Townsend felt more and more restless with each passing day. The plane crash had made him paranoid, and the paranoia fueled nightmares that came every night.

One night, Townsend dreamt that he had become "Scrooge" in "A Christmas Carol" except that the "Ghost of the Past" did not take him to a lost love. The ghost took him to a time before he was born when his parents were having a picnic in a field and there was a beautiful sunset on the horizon. In his dream, Townsend's parents were making love on a blanket in an effort to conceive him.

The "Ghost of the Present" didn't take Townsend to the home of a poor crippled boy, but to the dumpster that was kept back behind the building of their new clinic. The ghost opened the dumpster and Townsend was sickened by the sight of mutilated bodies of dead babies who had been killed inside their mothers' wombs. In his dream, the things he had never allowed to be human became little babies he had seen and known.

The "Ghost of the Future" was the most peculiar part of the dream. The ghost was not someone who had died. The ghost was Gary still living and enjoying every moment of life. That was the strange thing. Gary did not come to Townsend in a dream with grief and despair. Gary came to him with abundant happiness, as if everything in life were something to celebrate.

This was the most horrifying part for Townsend. He

instinctively knew that he and Gary were headed for an eternal end with no chance for survival. If hell existed, Townsend and Gary were headed straight for it.

*

Townsend woke up with a feeling of fear and paranoia that was completely unbearable. The nightmare had been worse than normal. This time, Gary's grin became an evil sneer, and he turned into some sort of demonic creature that looked like a devil with a snake's tail. In his dream, Gary told Townsend to get up and go to the bathroom, but when Townsend sat on the toilet, there were snakes in the water trying to make their way into his anus. Townsend screamed and jumped up to avoid the snakes, but when he looked down into the bowl, there was blood everywhere. The blood was all over the floor and the seat and in the bowl. Townsend looked inside and saw a living baby inside the bloody water. The baby was looking up at him and smiling horribly as if he were really an adult in a baby's body. Gary became the bloodied corpse baby of one of the unborn children they had mutilated and killed.

Townsend felt sweat pour down his face and back. He walked slowly to the bathroom, and checked the toilet before sitting down, just to make sure. All clear. Just a dream. Townsend moved to the shower and started the water. He got in and closed the shower door. Funny, he thought of the word "baptism" as soon as the warm water hit his back. He felt the stiffness in his back loosen, and he began to feel clean. It was as if this shower were the only shower he had taken in years. He felt so clean, it was almost a renewal. A chance to view life differently. When Townsend finished, he dried himself and noticed, too, that he felt lighter than he had in years. As if the nightmare and sweating had caused him to lose ten pounds overnight.

Townsend dressed, kissed his wife good–bye, and grabbed a

freshly brewed thermos of coffee before he left his estate. Townsend drove into the city and watched the sun rising in the distance over D.C. He had so much to tell Gary, and he knew Gary wouldn't be happy with the news. Townsend wanted out. He was sick of living the life they led. Sick of the killing. Sick of the risks. Sick of fearing death because hell could be right around the corner. As soon as Townsend's nurse and assistant came in, he had them cancel all his appointments for the day. He asked them to call Gary for an emergency meeting.

Gary did not arrive until half past nine. Townsend had been waiting since eight. He didn't care, though. He had already felt better as soon as he'd canceled his appointments. The weight of guilt was off his shoulders for today. Possibly forever. Gary looked clean–shaven and smelled of aftershave when he walked into Townsend's office.

"Townsend! What the hell do you want this early? I don't have anything 'til 11." Gary sat down in one of the leather seats in front of Townsend's desk and crossed his legs angrily.

"Gary, listen. I don't know how to break this to you after all these years, but I…I have to get out. I mean, I'm starting to think about my mortality, and it's not looking very good for me…"

Gary opened his eyes wide and sat up in shock. "What are you talking about? What do you mean? Some sort of mid–life crisis or something?"

"No, not a mid–life crisis. More like an end–life crisis."

"You've got plenty of years in front of you. You're in great health with all the time in the gym and the relaxing vacations all these years!"

"No, I mean, you never know, right? You never know when your turn comes. All I know is if it came today or tomorrow? I'd be screwed!" Townsend got up from his desk and started pacing back and forth behind it. "Look, okay? What we've been doing all these years? What we've been making millions doing? It's not sitting with me right anymore. For God's sake, Gary, these aren't things…little masses of tissue…little blood clots…they're human beings, for God's sake! I can't do this killing anymore! I've got to get out!"

Gary sat still for a full minute with his head down in thought. When he looked back up at Townsend, Townsend thought he was reliving one of his nightmares. Gary was looking at him with disbelief and anger, as if he couldn't believe how insane and ludicrous his partner had just become.

"Townsend, Townsend. Let's talk about this, okay? Let's figure this out together. It's not killing, not at all. It's saving. Saving the life of every single woman who comes into our clinics because they need help and we do not want them going to some bozo of a doctor who just pulled his license out of a Cracker Jack box. We make it so these women get treated with the utmost professional, medical care."

"Yeah, and then we sleep with them upstairs or in the back room if our arousal meters go off."

"They love us! They adore us! We're their frickin' saviors!"

"No. We take advantage of a situation because we've duped ourselves into thinking we can get away with anything we want!"

"Listen, I've given up everything to make myself into the successful doctor and businessman I am today, and I will not let you take that away from me! Go and do whatever you want, but don't you dare drag me down with you!" Gary stood up and pounded his fist so hard on Townsend's desk, he thought it might actually crash to the floor and break into pieces of splintered mahogany.

Townsend walked around his desk and gently put a hand on Gary's shoulder. "Gary, listen to me. This is going to sound really strange. I know. Trust me, I know, but I've been having these dreams, ever since the plane crash. I think the dreams are messages telling us to give this up or something bad is going to happen again. I think the plane crash was a warning. And now that I've had these dreams, I think we're being warned again to get out of this evil business. I really think you need to listen to me and take me seriously. Please, Gary. Let's get out of this together."

Gary was listening to his partner intently, and Townsend thought he might have turned him around. Made him think twice. Gary looked long and hard into Townsend's eyes, and then the anger and darkness crept back in and he pushed Townsend's hand off his shoulder so hard, it banged down and hit the mahogany desk in the same spot that Gary had just struck it.

"Never!" was all Gary said and he slammed the door to Townsend's office on the way out.

CHAPTER TWENTY–SEVEN

Townsend packed his things and walked out of his office for the last time. He smiled at the nurses and assistants and nodded his head, "Good–bye." He wanted to tell them what a mistake they were making. He wanted to tell them something bad was about to happen, but he knew they would look at him like he was crazy. He took the elevator to the first floor and strode out into the cold, windy air.

Townsend drove out of the city and wondered what he would tell his wife when he got home. He wondered if she would leave him because of the money and the lifestyle she would have to give up. When he reached the parkway, Townsend turned on the news to keep his mind off the latest events. It was already twelve o'clock and time for the top–of–the–hour news. According to the announcer, a breaking story had just surfaced of a suspected terrorist attack. A bomb had just taken down a local building in the heart of Washington D.C.

Townsend was stunned but not surprised when the announcer gave the address of the clinic and Gary's condominium as the same building that had just imploded. His mind began to reel. He kept seeing Gary's angry face, Gary slamming his fist on his desk, and Gary's last spoken word, "Never!" replaying in his mind.

Townsend knew that God had given them another warning. He knew that his nightmare was really a premonition, but he hadn't been convincing enough for Gary. The guilt wallowed in Townsend's stomach. He needed to pull over to get some air or he was going to be sick.

Townsend took the first exit and pulled over to the side of the road. He got out of his car and slammed the door as hard as he could. Townsend felt like he might collapse. His mind kept spinning, and he didn't know if he had the strength to continue. He walked around the back of the car to the passenger side and threw both fists down hard against the hood.

"God, help me! I can't get through this alone!" he screamed to the sky. Townsend put his head back down into his arms and wept on his hood on the exit ramp.

Five minutes later, Townsend got back into his car and started toward the U-turn that would take him back over the overpass toward D.C. Townsend decided not to go home after all. He headed straight for the airport and Medjugorje.

*

Cassy lay in her coma state, but her mind and body were recharging and coming to life and she instinctively knew that she must be on the verge of waking. She was becoming increasingly aware of her surroundings. Cassy could sense when Drew was next to her. She could sense voices around her, like those of Dr. Andrews or Nurse Bridget. Cassy could even sense when darker forces were present, and those made her wince in pain. She would fear those more if Paolo were not also present as her guardian and protector.

At times, Paolo left her to her own spiritual travels, and today was one of those days. Cassy felt her spiritual body awaken and lift from her earthly body. In mere seconds, she was airborne and traveling through time and space once more. These journeys would be what she missed most when she woke. The pure air on her face and the weightlessness of holiness would always linger in her memories. Cassy felt in the depths of her soul that this must be a sense of heaven, itself.

When Cassy touched down, she stood alone in the middle of a great Italian square, its ground made of ancient cobblestones. Directly in front of her was a large pink granite obelisk in the center of the square, which stood in the shape of a spear pointing toward heaven. Cassy noticed that the obelisk looked like a great sun dial which was held up by four couchant lions, each with two bodies whose tails intertwined. She placed her hand on the lion in front of her and noticed the Roman numeral "XXII" or "22" on the base directly below the lion. Cassy walked clockwise to the next lion and read, "I" or "1." The third lion read, "MM" or "2,000" and the fourth, "XIII" or "13."

"Interesting," Cassy thought, but realized these numbers meant nothing to her.

Cassy looked up from the obelisk and saw that there were two great fountains of cascading water on either side of the square. As she walked forward toward a magnificent cathedral in the distance, she noticed two large white statues of saints on either side of the entrance to the cathedral, as if these two saints were pointing the way to God. The statue on the left was a bearded man with curly hair holding a large key in one hand and a rolled scroll in the other. The statue on the right was a bearded man with masses of wavy hair holding a large sword and a long scroll.

Cassy ascended the stairs that led to the most magnificent cathedral she had ever seen. The heavenly structure was called, "Saint Peter's Basilica." When Cassy stepped inside, the size and magnificence literally took her breath away. The height of the ceiling and the length of the room were large enough to land a plane. An immense structure rose up from the center that looked like a great stage with four columns pointing upward from each corner, almost as if Cassy were looking at a giant, ornate four–

poster bed. The four columns were constructed to hold up a large dome with beautifully painted fresco ceilings.

Cassy saw a staircase with golden arm rails that led to a lower floor. She descended the staircase and stepped onto the lower marble floor where she saw a golden tomb encased in a room with glass walls. She reached out her hand to touch the glass in front of her.

Instantly, Cassy was transported to a monastery choir loft where she saw Paolo, a young seminarian, joyfully singing Latin hymns in the choir. Paolo's spiritual body came out of his earthly body right before her eyes much the same as Cassy's spiritual body did when her earthly body slept in a coma.

In a blink of an eye, Cassy witnessed Paolo being set down in the palace of an extremely wealthy family. The master of the palace was dying just as his daughter was about to be born. Cassy saw a beautiful and ethereal woman dressed in blue walk toward Paolo, "I am entrusting this unborn child to your care and protection. Although she will become a precious jewel, right now she has no form. Shape and polish her. Make her as brilliant as you can, because one day I would like to adorn myself with her."

"How can this be possible?" Paolo asked. "I am only a poor seminarian and don't even know whether I will have the joy and good fortune to become a priest. Even if I do, how will I ever be able to take care of this girl since I will be so far away from here?"

"Do not doubt me," the woman replied. "She will come to you in the Basilica of Saint Peter in Rome. Her name is Angelina."

*

Cassy felt her body take flight as she passed through time and space to witness Paolo's bilocation years later after he was ordained a Capuchin priest. He sat in the same choir loft of the monastery, and Cassy saw his spiritual body separate from his earthly one as it had on the night of Angelina's birth. She traveled with Paolo to the confessionals of Saint Peter's. Cassy saw Angelina, now a young woman, approach the custodian to see if there was a priest who could hear her confession. The custodian shook his head and walked away, but Angelina caught a glimpse of Paolo, a young Capuchin friar, walk toward her.

"Father, please let me go to confess," she pleaded.

Padre Paolo assented and entered the confessional from one side while Angelina entered from the front door.

Several minutes later, Cassy saw Angelina leave the confessional with a grand smile spread across her beautiful face. She stood for several minutes waiting for Padre Paolo to exit the confessional so she could thank him. No one came out. The custodian approached and told Angelina that the basilica was about to close. Pointing to the confessional, she indicated that the Capuchin father who had confessed her was inside. The custodian knocked on the door of the confessional, but no one responded back. It was no surprise to Cassy that when the custodian turned the door handle and opened it, there was no priest sitting inside. The little room was completely empty.

*

The following summer, Angelina spent her summer vacation with her aunt in San Giovanni Rotondo for the first time to see Padre Paolo. When they arrived, the corridor that connects the sacristy with the interior of the convent was thronged with many people who had come long distances to see him. Despite the crowd, Angelina found herself directly in his path as he passed down the corridor. Padre Paolo stopped and looked closely at her.

"I know you!" he said. "You were born the same day that your father died." He gave her his hand to kiss, which was an Italian custom, and he blessed her.

The following morning her aunt, who had confessed with Padre Paolo, suggested that she do the same. As a result, Angelina waited in line to go to confession.

After giving her his blessing, Padre Paolo welcomed her. "My daughter, finally you have come! I have been waiting for you for so many years!"

Surprised, Angelina replied, "Father, you don't even know me. This is the first time I have ever been to San Giovanni Rotondo. Undoubtedly, you have mistaken me for someone else."

"No," Padre Paolo assured her, "I have not taken you for someone else. You already know me. Last year at the Basilica of Saint Peter in Rome you came up to me. Don't you remember? You were looking for a confessor. Then a Capuchin priest came along and confessed you. I was that Capuchin friar."

Angelina was completely taken aback.

Padre Paolo explained, "Listen my daughter. Just before you were born the Blessed Mother took me to your home, and I witnessed the death of your father. She indicated that through her intercession and the merits of his wife's tears and prayers her father had obtained salvation. After telling me to pray for him, our Lady informed me that his wife was about to give birth to a baby girl and that she was placing this child under my care."

"My daughter," concluded Padre Paolo, "you are my responsibility."

Filled with emotion, Angelina began to cry. "Father, since I have become your responsibility, please tell me how I should direct my life. Should I become a nun?"

"No," Padre Paolo replied, "you should not. At the age of thirty, the year of our Lord's public ministry, you shall enter into marriage. At the age of thirty–three, the year of our Lord's passion, death and resurrection, you shall bring forth new life, the first and only fruit of your faithful marriage. You are to name this child, 'Lucia,' which means 'Light.' She will be given the necessary grace to persevere through a time of darkness—a darkness greater than the world has ever seen. Angelina, my daughter, the Blessed Mother is looking out for you. Your life shall be blessed, and your daughter's life after you. Do not worry and pray often. Come to San Giovanni Rotondo frequently. I will guide your soul, and you will live according to the will of God."

At age thirty, Angelina was married to a pious physician in Rome, and at thirty–three, just as Padre Paolo predicted, she gave birth to a beautiful baby girl whom she named Lucia. Angelina took the newborn to Padre Paolo for the baby's baptism in the summer of 1948, and as the holy friar reached over to bless the child, he stopped for one instant and closed his eyes. After several moments of prayer, Padre Paolo continued his baptism with the holy water from the font of the altar.

"I baptize you, Lucia, in the name of the Father and the Son and the Holy Spirit. May God give you and your husband the grace you will one day need to change the world through the conversion of your adopted daughter."

*

When Tom Blake opened the door for Father Raphael, the priest stood on the porch with a bouquet of assorted colorful flowers.

"Hi Father, for me?" Tom asked with a cynical grin.

"No, they're for your beautiful wife," Father Raphael replied with a sarcastic chuckle.

"Oh, you mean my beautiful and married wife," Tom replied.

"Yes, yes, of course. You see, Tom, she may be your partner in marriage, but she is my partner in petitioning the New Jersey Third Circuit Court of Appeals to reinstate the 'Choose Life' case. In other words, we won, my man, and that is the whole enchilada."

"We won?!? We won?!? Woo!! God is good today!" Tom was so overjoyed, he gave Father Raphael a bear hug and the two men danced in circles around on the porch shouting for joy.

"What in the world is going on out here?" Veronica came to the door with a dish towel in her hands, and Peter and Grace followed behind, all three shocked by the behavior of the two grown men.

Father Raphael and Tom stopped dancing and turned to Veronica and the children. "We won!!" they exclaimed together.

*

As Veronica, Tom, Grace, Peter and Father Raphael sat around the Blakes' dinner table enjoying ham, mashed potatoes and greens, there was a profound silence as they all took in the euphoria of victory. They had come so far in six years when the lawsuits first began.

Veronica and Father Raphael had been working steadfastly with The Children First Foundation to persuade New Jersey State's Department of Motor Vehicles to allow motorists the option of purchasing "Choose Life" license plates. Six years before, the pro–adoption group, Children First Foundation, had submitted a proposal for "Choose Life" license plates, which would raise money for adoption programs in the state. However, the Department of Motor Vehicles rejected the proposal because they said the slogan on the plates was too "controversial" and "political."

Children First Foundation and pregnancy shelters advocating adoption instead of abortion knew the reason they were rejected was not because of controversy. It was because the governor of the state of New Jersey at the time was pro–choice. The Alliance Defense Fund filed a lawsuit on behalf of Children First Foundation saying this was a violation of their first amendment rights. Then, the officials for the Department of Motor Vehicles changed their initial "controversial" and "political" justification to a "constituting advocacy" justification—just another justification to reject the plates. The Alliance Defense Fund's lawyers countered that there were already other specialty plates in the state that constituted advocacy for various organizations.

The case was eventually dismissed, but a federal appeals' court revived the effort three years later. With the help of pro–life groups like Turning Point Shelter and Veronica and Father Raphael, The Children First Foundation submitted 2,500 petition signatures and a check for $12,500 to cover the first 500 "Choose Life" license plates. With a new pro–life governor, New Jersey finally agreed to authorize the life–affirming specialty license plates.

Tom lifted his glass of wine to toast his wife and Father Raphael. "To your hard work and the prayers and petitions of all of the beautiful pro–life people of this great state," he said.

"You know, I think this has more to do with our pro–life governor than we think," Veronica said.

"There is a reason for everything," Father Raphael replied. "God has a plan, and we are here to carry that plan through. That is the whole enchilada!"

"Cheers!" Grace said loudly as she lifted her grape juice and clinked it with Father Raphael's.

Peter swung his arm around his little sister for a brotherly hug. "Cheers with grape juice?" he asked exasperated.

"Excuse me, Peter, but don't you know that wine is grape juice!?!" Grace replied adamantly. She pushed her brother's arms away and rolled her eyes with obvious disdain for his lack of intelligence.

Veronica, Tom, Peter and Father Raphael couldn't hold back their laughter, and soon, Grace was laughing, too.

Not one of the five enjoying a festive dinner could have known the looming war that was beginning to rage between the side of "life" and the side of "choice."

CHAPTER TWENTY–EIGHT

Jessica had driven past the Moscone Convention Center in San Francisco many times before, but she had never actually entered the building. A week had passed since the Starbucks' meeting, and The National Convention for Stem Cell Research was today. Jessica was there on Palmer Braxton's recommendation. He wanted her to learn about the possibilities of embryonic stem cell research compared with adult stem cell research. Palmer wanted to prove to Jessica how few put their money in adult compared with embryonic, but she was not driven by money. Jessica was driven by science and truth. Still, she wanted Palmer to trust that she was on his side. That way, Jessica would be in a much better position to find out what was really going on with JamBrax's Fountain of Youth Spa.

Jessica entered the Esplanade Ballroom and was captivated by all the vendors set up in neat rows with gifts and brochures for the attendees. Directly behind the vendors was a large platform with a monstrous JamBrax logo attached to the wall since JamBrax was the host of the convention. A long table ran across the platform with tall models handing out JamBrax literature. To Jessica, every JamBrax logo stood out like a sore thumb as she noticed the JamBrax colors decorating all four of the ballroom walls. She couldn't see Palmer anywhere near the platform, but she knew he was mingling somewhere.

Jessica decided to start from left to right and move through the aisles as quickly as possible. She was meeting with Jonathan for dinner to discuss the best way to get into Palmer's office and onto his computer without his knowledge. This was the only way to find out what was going on at JamBrax's Fountain of Youth Spa.

The first few aisles held vendors from research facilities at universities and hospitals that were funded by the government. Jessica stopped at some of these booths and was not surprised to find that all of their literature pertained to embryonic stem cell research.

The vendors in the middle two aisles were directly in front of the JamBrax platform. Jessica noticed that Parenting Services International held several booths with the PSI logo broadly displayed in each. There were even red, white and blue balloons flying out from each as if their support for embryonic stem cell research was patriotic.

"Why am I not surprised?" Jessica asked herself as she smiled at the women who "manned" the booths. She knew Palmer was connected to PSI through JamBrax.

"Jessica!" Palmer called to Jessica from one of the PSI booths down the aisle. "Over here!"

"Speak of the devil," Jessica muttered under her breath. She faked a warm smile as she strode up to the booth.

"There's someone I'd love you to meet," Palmer said to Jessica just as Elaina, Jessica's long lost sister–in–law, turned around to face her.

Elaina gave Jessica a steely gaze, but if she recognized her, she did not acknowledge it in her conduct. She merely extended her right hand with an air of shrewd confidence and said, "Nice to meet you, Jessica."

"Elaina, this is Dr. Jessica Taninsam, Director of the School of Medicine at USF. She's in charge of all embryonic stem cell research at the university, isn't that right, Jessica?" Palmer emphasized the word "embryonic" as if it were the most important word in the sentence.

"That's correct," Jessica replied with feigned conviction.

"Yes, and Jessica, this is Elaina Taninsam, the President of Parenting Services International. Say, isn't it funny that you two share the same last name, but have no relation?" Palmer asked as if this were the first time he had noticed.

"Yes, quite funny," Elaina said with no trace of humor.

"Yes, a strange coincidence," Jessica replied with a steely gaze. Palmer seemed uncomfortable with the women's edginess, so Jessica decided to lighten the mood. "Perhaps we are distant relatives and we aren't even aware…" Jessica put on a good act and laughed heartily.

Palmer joined in the laughter and sent Jessica off to gather more information from other vendors.

"Nice to have met you, Elaina," Jessica said before leaving.

"The pleasure was all mine," Elaina replied with an evil glare.

*

Jessica knew that she should have been more prepared to run into Elaina at a function that had to do with PSI, especially when there was now a connection between Palmer's and Elaina's companies.

As Jessica walked down the remaining aisles going through the motions of chatting with vendors and taking brochures, her heart nearly skipped a beat when she thought she saw David in the distance standing just inside the entrance.

"Both of them in one afternoon? What are the chances?" Jessica thought to herself as she looked down to the floor and blinked her eyes hard to make sure she wasn't seeing things. When Jessica looked back up, she felt a sudden sense of relief. David was nowhere in sight. "Thank God," she thought.

Jessica reached the last aisle, and started to breathe easier knowing that she was almost done. She looked at these vendors and realized there was a different mood here than at the other booths. The literature even looked different. It was about adult stem cell research, umbilical cord research, and all of the successes they have had curing diseases with these methods.

"I'm surprised they were allowed to exhibit," Jessica thought to herself. She felt more comfortable in this aisle and engaged herself in conversations with other doctors and researchers on the subject. This was the first time all day that she hadn't checked her watch for the time.

When she made it to the end of the aisle, Jessica noticed some vendors who were even more surprising. On the right was a booth that belonged to the Archdiocese of San Francisco with several pamphlets that defended adult stem cell research and umbilical stem cell research as ethical and denounced embryonic stem cell research as the destruction of innocent human life. Jessica saw other vendors who felt the same way and were making their voices heard. There were booths from American Life League, Priests for Life, and the Association of Pro–Life Physicians directly across from the archdiocesan booth. Jessica couldn't help but feel excited and optimistic about their presence.

"Good day, young lady."

Jessica turned to see where this rich, beautiful voice was coming from and noticed a tall, heavy–set African–American priest in his early sixties standing behind the booth from the Archdiocese of San Francisco. He had such a contagious smile, Jessica couldn't help but smile back. She wanted to meet this affable priest no matter how late she might be for dinner with Jonathan.

"Good day," Jessica said as she walked over to the priest with the big personality.

The priest immediately stuck out his hand. "I'm Father Gabe Sanders from Saint Mary's Cathedral, and I'm here to let people know that ethical science is the only way to go."

Jessica shook his warm hand and felt an instant bond to this priest from Saint Mary's Cathedral with the deep voice and the southern drawl. She smiled broadly and was about to tell him her name when she was interrupted from behind.

"Don't let this guy play games with you. Young lady, I'd like to introduce you to Archbishop Gabriel Sanders, the Archbishop of San Francisco." The man came from behind Jessica and stood next to her. He was also an African–American priest, but he spoke with a British accent, was quite a bit younger, and was one of the most handsome men Jessica had ever seen. "I'm Father Derek Ekwonye," he said. Father Derek smiled warmly and extended his hand out to Jessica.

Jessica went from Archbishop Gabriel Sanders to Father Derek Ekwonye, shaking both priests' hands. "Nice to meet you both. I'm Dr. Jessica Taninsam," she said feeling the guard she had worn all day drop completely.

"What is your specialty?" Father Gabe asked.

"Research," Jessica replied. "And I do favor the ethical kind, but I have to say that the reason I favor it is because it's the one I believe will produce the most results. That, gentlemen, is true science."

"Dr. Taninsam…" Father Gabe began.

"Jessica," she corrected.

"Then, please call me Father Gabe," he began looking at Father Derek for emphasis. "Jessica, you have just hit the nail on the head, my dear, because science is only possible when it's mixed with truth, and one day, you will come to know that ethical science is the only way for human beings to learn truth. And I do mean the kind of truth that could one day lead to the meaning of human existence, itself." Father Gabe leaned his hands on the table in front of the booth as if he were sharing a secret with his new friend, Jessica.

"Jessica, I bet you didn't know that Archbishop Sanders has set the record for longest homilies in the state of California." Father Derek's smile was so broad, she couldn't help but chuckle as he jousted with his fellow priest.

"Listen here, Father Derek, the good doctor here is a friend and a partner in ethical stem cell research, so don't go and ruin our relationship," Father Gabe shot back as he winked at Jessica.

"Actually," Jessica began more seriously, "the man I work for is preventing me from doing research on adult stem cells even though I have made great progress. He will only allow me to go where the money is."

"Jessica, we're here to help, and we're not alone," Father Gabe said looking toward the other pro–life booths in their aisle.

"I appreciate that," Jessica replied. "At this point, though, I'm going to have to take a rain check on that help. I'm in the middle of uncovering something that I think might help us all…"

"Jessica," Palmer came up from behind Jessica and was trying to get her away from the archbishop's booth as quickly as possible.

Jessica looked pleadingly at the two priests she had so quickly befriended.

"Jessica, before you go," Father Gabe began, "let me give you the name of that Italian restaurant I was telling you about by the Wharf. I know your associate will love it, too." Father Gabe retrieved a business card and turned it over to write on. He scribbled something quickly and handed it to Jessica. "Nice to meet you, Jessica. Always good to meet another Italian food lover," he exclaimed with a jovial laugh, as he and Father Derek smiled and waved. "Call me if you get lost and need help finding your way."

Palmer took Jessica's arm and led her back to the JamBrax platform. "That was about an Italian restaurant?" he asked suspiciously.

"Yes. I can't believe he's the archbishop. He's hysterical!" Jessica explained with a grin as she tucked Father Gabe's business card safe inside her purse. Jessica let out a sigh of relief as soon as she saw Palmer smile; he hadn't suspected a thing.

*

When Kay Dennis arrived at the Parenting Services International Clinic in Englewood, New Jersey, she had a sense that something bad was about to happen. She didn't feel comfortable working at the clinic anyway, but there was such a sense of foreboding in the air, it felt like a 50–pound weight was lying on her chest. To make matters worse, the day was cold and dark, and it looked like the freezing rain in the forecast was just about to begin.

Kay entered the clinic in her usual white uniform with nurse's shoes and unbuttoned her raincoat as she made her way through the waiting area. She didn't like to pay too much attention to the women who waited for their procedures. It always seemed like she was prying into their personal lives, and that's not where she wanted to go. She wasn't there to be a counselor. She was there to be a medical assistant, a registered nurse.

Kay greeted her co–workers at the desk, trying hard not to notice the faces of the women who sat and waited. She was almost past the waiting area when Kay heard one of the women crying toward the back. She looked up and saw the woman, obviously pregnant, with a toddler on her lap. A man, probably the child's father, was sitting next to her looking away with his arms folded sternly in front of him. The woman looked like she was pleading with the man, crying and saying something unrecognizable to Kay, but the man looked like his mind was made up and there was nothing she could do. The little girl sat on her mother's lap with a blank expression on her face, as if she had seen this behavior from her parents before.

Kay did not want to get involved with a crisis, and that was what most of these women were experiencing—a crisis, which was unfortunately in the form of a baby they did not want. Crisis pregnancy. That's what they called it, and the clinic was there to help.

"Great way to help," Kay thought to herself disgustedly as she made her way to the nurse's station to check the morning schedule.

When Kay looked at the list of appointments, she was surprised to see ten abortions before noon and another thirteen scheduled for the afternoon. This was definitely more than the normal amount for the day, even for an "Abortion Day," which happened three days a week. The other three days were usually filled with what Kay liked to call "normal" Ob–Gyn services, like doing pap tests or providing pregnancy tests. Kay worked six days a week and had only one day off—Sunday. She needed normalcy, but with so many abortions scheduled, this was by no means going to be a "normal" day.

Kay felt the foreboding again and realized it must have something to do with abortion day at the clinic. That's why she was feeling so uneasy. She had forgotten and now she was reminded. Time to do the job. No emotion. Be the professional.

"Hi, Kay!" Dr. Morris, a pleasant, elderly man came up from behind Kay and startled her with his greeting.

"Oh, Dr. Morris. Hi. Looks like a full day," Kay replied.

"Yes. Ready for Number One?"

Kay found it particularly callous to talk about patients that way, but remembered she was just here to do her job. "Yes, I'll be right in."

Kay washed, put on her scrubs and entered into the "Abortion Room" in the back.

The first three abortions Dr. Morris performed were suction abortions, which were the quickest and easiest. They were done up to fourteen weeks because the fetus was still small enough to be sucked out of the uterus. Patients were given medication to help them relax before they entered. Anesthesia was rarely used.

Dr. Morris used an ultrasound machine to see the location of the baby, and Kay assisted him by applying jelly and holding the transducer on the woman's stomach so that he could see the image.

One time, Kay saw a 12–week old baby suck his thumb on the ultrasound. She couldn't believe that a baby that small could actually suck his thumb.

Dr. Morris inserted a big metal suction apparatus into the uterus and poked around until the fetus was all sucked out. The morning was going quickly when Kay realized the first three patients were done in forty–five minutes.

The fourth abortion was a little more difficult because the baby looked like it was sixteen weeks. This time, Dr. Morris had to dilate the woman's cervix and go in with what he called, "His Spaghetti Tongs," to grab parts of the baby and pull them off.

Kay had only done this procedure one other time. She remembered feeling a bit faint when she saw so much blood because the baby would wind up bleeding to death. It also took more time because Kay had to make sure that all the baby's body parts were accounted for to make sure the uterus was completely cleaned out.

Today was no different. Kay felt faint afterward and needed a short break to be able to continue with the other six before lunch. She went into the bathroom and splashed water on her face. "You will not feel any emotion today," she told herself as she walked back to the Abortion Room. To her relief, the next five abortions were all suction abortions. Kay took a quick bathroom break before the last abortion appointment of the morning.

It was just after eleven when Kay entered the abortion room for the last time. To her surprise, the woman lying on the examining table with her eyes closed was the same woman Kay had seen in the waiting room a few hours before with the toddler on her lap. She was no longer crying, but Kay could see silent tears still fresh on the woman's cheeks even though she lay unmoving, apparently now under anesthesia.

The uneasy feeling Kay had felt earlier came crashing down on her all at once. She told herself not to feel any emotion, but a wave of despair hit her in the face so hard, she felt stunned. Kay wanted to tap the woman on her shoulder to wake her, so the woman could get out of there before it was too late. The woman had obviously wanted to keep her unborn child, and Kay felt it was only fair that she be given the choice to leave if that's what she wanted. Kay realized it was ludicrous to think this way, though. She had a job to do.

When Dr. Morris did the ultrasound, it was determined that the woman was already over twenty–two weeks pregnant. Kay knew the clinic did not perform abortions after twenty–two weeks. She felt inclined to remind him of the clinic's policy, but the doctor did not appear to be concerned. He simply wrote, "22 weeks," on the form. Apparently the woman had already been to the clinic two days before, and Dr. Morris had inserted laminaria to dilate her cervix.

"This will be the most educational experience you've had so far at the clinic, Kay." Dr. Morris said this matter–of–factly, as if he had done it a thousand times before, and Kay would receive the good fortune of his vast knowledge.

With the ultrasound hooked up, Kay could see the baby clearly while the baby's heartbeat "bleeped" on the screen. Dr. Morris went in with forceps and grabbed the baby's legs and pulled them down into the birth canal. He delivered the baby's body and the arms—everything but the head. The doctor kept the baby's head just inside the uterus. The baby's little fingers were clasping and unclasping, and his feet were kicking.

Dr. Morris stuck scissors through the back of the baby's head, and the baby's arms jerked out in a flinch, a startled reaction, like a baby does when he thinks that he might fall. The doctor opened up the scissors, stuck a high–powered suction tube into the opening and sucked the baby's brains out. The baby went completely limp. Kay felt unprepared for what she was seeing. She wondered if she might have to run to the bathroom to vomit.

Dr. Morris delivered the baby's head, and cut the umbilical cord before he delivered the placenta. He threw the baby in a pan, along with the placenta and the instruments he'd used, as if the baby were just another "thing" to discard. Kay caught herself thanking God that the woman was still asleep and hadn't witnessed any of this horror.

"You see how flawless and tidy partial–birth abortions are?" Dr. Morris looked up at Kay with a smile a mile wide. He was obviously proud of his work. "And the patient didn't feel a thing. Anesthesia makes it so much better," he said.

Shortly after Dr. Morris spoke, things went from bad to worse. The woman's pulse was rising quickly and she had begun to shake violently. Dr. Morris and Kay stepped in to try to help their patient, but the woman's head and body were shaking uncontrollably. The woman turned her head to the side unconsciously, and a small stream of blood trickled onto the table from her mouth.

"Looks like a grand mal seizure!" Kay screamed out to Dr. Morris.

"Cardiac arrest," the doctor replied. "And keep your voice down, Kay."

"Yes, Dr. Morris." Kay felt like she was the main actress in some dark murder mystery, and the film was running in slow motion.

Dr. Morris and Kay worked as quickly as possible to begin CPR to try to resuscitate their patient. They had a steady pulse after a few moments, but after a second arrest, the woman became completely unresponsive to additional CPR. They tried for several minutes to revive the woman, but their efforts failed and she died.

The woman who had cried because she did not want an abortion was dead. The woman who had held her toddler on her lap only hours before was gone. Dr. Morris and Kay had failed.

After the police report was completed, Kay left Parenting Services International never to return.

CHAPTER TWENTY–NINE

Father Raphael Trujillo and Veronica Blake were still basking in the glory of their pro–life victory when they ordered tostadas with beans and rice at La Batalla. It was "TGIF" Friday and the weather was absolutely beautiful with the sun streaming into the restaurant after days of dismal rain. Father Raphael and Veronica were almost giddy when they finished. Life was about as good as it could get.

"After you, V." Father Raphael held the door for Veronica. She walked out onto Washington Avenue wearing sunglasses with her coat open.

"Ah, the sun feels so good," Veronica said as she and Father Raphael strolled contentedly back to Turning Point Shelter.

"Sure. Just too bad it's almost winter and not spring." Father Raphael looked at Veronica with a teasing grin.

"Okay. You do have a point there," Veronica responded with a sigh. "Father, I'm doing a conference call later this afternoon with Chris and Suzanne about the March for Life. January 22 may seem like a long way off now, but it's almost December and that means Christmas, then New Year's, then January 22. I want to come up with a plan to meet them once we get there. Do you want me to conference you in, too?"

"I wish I could, but I'm teaching a class at Transfiguration Academy. Then, I have meetings before and after dinner."

"Important guy," Veronica said with a condescending smirk.

When they reached Turning Point, Veronica saw a small brown package on the doorstep with her name on it in bold capital letters and bright red ink. There was a bundle of regular mail next to the package.

"Let me help you with this before I go," Father Raphael offered.

"Thanks."

Father Raphael picked up the mail and package and followed Veronica into the shelter. He set everything on her desk, but picked up the package to examine it before handing it to Veronica. "This looks kind of weird," he said.

"Yeah, let me open it while you're around just in case it's a bomb, and we need to dismantle it." Veronica laughed at her own joke while she grabbed a pair of scissors from her desk. She used the scissors to cut the tape that held the brown wrapping paper in place. Veronica took off the paper and looked visibly surprised to see a beat up shoe box underneath. It looked really dirty with dried brownish–red paint all over the top and sides. "What in the good Lord's name?" Veronica asked rhetorically as she stared at the box without moving.

"Veronica, let me open it," Father Raphael said looking concerned.

"No, Father, I've got it." Veronica was not about to let a man do what a woman could do herself, even if he was a priest. She took a deep breath and slowly raised the cover on the old shoe box half expecting to be blown to pieces with Father Raphael and the entire Turning Point building. With the cover off the box, all Veronica and Father Raphael could see was white tissue paper stained with the same brownish–red paint. Veronica breathed a sigh of relief, but she removed the tissues one sheet at a time with trepidation. Underneath, she saw a perfect, tiny little infant hand lying in the box on top of the remaining tissue. It had been severed from the rest of its body during a late–term abortion procedure. What had looked like brownish–red paint was actually the baby's blood.

Veronica took a step back and covered her mouth with the back of her hand. She could not stop the tears from rolling down her cheeks. How many parents were out there who would have loved to adopt this child? Why not let the baby live and put it up for adoption?

Father Raphael went to Veronica and put an arm around her shoulders. There were no words to console her. He looked back into the box and realized there was a note attached to the baby's thumb. Father Raphael let go of Veronica to retrieve it. The note was folded over once and written in the same bold capital letters and red ink:

"ROSES ARE RED. VIOLETS ARE BLUE. ANTI–CHOICE BITCH. I'M COMING FOR YOU."

*

Cassy had traveled with Paolo on journey after journey through time and space into a realm she had never even fathomed existed. She had been crucified alongside the son of God and witnessed his holy blood as it fell on jasper to create the one, true Bloodstone. She had watched as Simon, the evil magician, fell to his death and the blood from his shattered body had mixed with jasper to form the counterfeit bloodstone. She had been present when Aaron received his breastplate and the twelfth stone of jasper had revealed the eternal power of heaven. Finally, Cassy had learned that jasper was used in pagan sacrificial statues, but she did not know that jasper could become powerful enough to bring creatures of the spiritual world into human existence.

Paolo stood next to Cassy's hospital bed holding her hand. He had not meant for any more spiritual journeys for Cassy. Not yet. Not until it had become absolutely necessary. For now, Paolo wanted Cassy to rest. He conversed with her through her mind's eye as if the two existed in her own personal dream.

Cassy saw Paolo's distant figure. She ran to him and took both of his hands in her own. "Where shall we go today?" she asked.

"I have nothing to teach you today," he replied.

Cassy could not contain her disappointment, but an idea suddenly struck her. "Does that mean I'll wake soon?" she asked.

"I must complete something on my own first," Paolo said.

"Can I come?"

"No. At this point, it's too dangerous."

"What do you mean?" Cassy asked worriedly.

"It's about Jessica. And Deborah. David is working on them both. He knows that I need all three of you to make his death possible."

"His death? Is it possible to kill him?"

"Yes, Cassy. That is why I am here. To protect the three of you so that one day, soon, we will be rid of him."

"Paolo, I've never asked, but please tell me something about you. Where did you come from?"

Cassy's innocence moved Paolo deeply. "Cassy, I know that God has a purpose for all of us. I knew for a very long time that He was readying me for that purpose. Now I know that my life on earth was to ready me for this last mission. This last mission with you. Cassy, I will allow you another journey today, but afterward, you must promise to rest. You will journey alone while I tend to Jessica and Deborah. This journey will give you a chance to gather information which may prove useful. You see, Cassy, this journey will be the story of my life."

*

Cassy felt herself ascend into flight. She felt as though angels were lifting her from either side, and she flew a great distance over space and time. Soon, she was lowered onto an old cobblestone street in Italy. The village was situated 1,150 feet above sea level, and Cassy saw a great baronial castle standing tall in the distance rising over an enormous cliff looking out over a magnificent river. It looked as if the old part of town was built around the castle with the houses attached to the cliff. The entrances of the houses opened out to narrow, winding streets paved with cobblestones. They were constructed of limestone, and their walls were unplastered, their cracks easily observed in the stone.

Cassy walked along the cobblestone street until she came to the oldest of all the houses. She saw the number "27" to the right of the open door and heard the cry of a newborn child from the back of a single room not more than thirty square feet. A man wearing a worn, cotton shirt and dusty pants held up by thread–bare suspenders came into the kitchen area with a pot full of used, wet linens. He was looking for something, perhaps more clean linens, but he couldn't seem to find any. The man hastily grabbed up a white lace cover from the top of the table and ran back to a slender woman lying on a small bed. There was another woman standing at the base of the bed holding a small infant in her arms. The man handed the woman the white lace cover and she looked at him as if to say, "What is this?" and then quickly wrapped the baby in the lace and handed him to his mother.

Cassy saw the mother's face when she was handed the child. Her eyes were filled with joy as tears streamed down her weather–worn face. The man looked down on his wife with pride as she held his newborn son.

Cassy could tell that the mid–wife was also proud of her good work in helping to bring the little infant into the world. She beamed at the baby in his mother's loving arms.

"Peppa," the woman said to the mother, "the child was born wrapped in a white veil, and that's a good sign; he will be great and fortunate."

Cassy knew at once that this was Paolo on the day of his birth. As soon as she made the connection, Cassy heard church bells ringing in the distance throughout the village.

*

Cassy was instantly transported to another location in another time. She stood before a young friar dressed in a long, dark tunic with a hood and an ordinary rope for a belt. There were large wooden rosary beads hanging from the rope, which dangled in mid–air as he knelt before an ancient crucifix.

The young friar held one hand to his side and grabbed his rosary beads with the other. Cassy glimpsed the image of a mystical angel floating in mid–air above the crucifix. The angel was bleeding from his hands, feet and side, and Cassy could hear the drops of blood hit the floor with a loud "plup." The angel floated toward the friar carrying a sword in his right hand. Suddenly, Cassy saw the angel lunge forward and plunge the sword into his left side. The friar cried out in agony and fell to his side in front of the crucifix. Cassy ran to him and bent down to touch his head.

The young friar looked up at Cassy and smiled. He was still holding his side and she saw that blood was flowing out of the wound and onto the floor. She became alarmed at the gravity of the wound and noticed that his sandaled feet and hands were bleeding, too.

To Cassy's surprise, the man put his hand on hers and spoke, "It's all right, Cassy. God is getting me ready."

Cassy knew it was Paolo, but she had never known that he had suffered the five wounds of Christ. "Why would the stigmata be part of God's plan to get you ready?" she asked.

"I need to suffer as he suffered."

"Why?"

"Because millions will suffer an unjust death worse than this." He pointed to his five wounds as he spoke.

"But how can your suffering help them?"

"Because in suffering, we become perfect, and perfection creates miracles."

*

Before Cassy could respond, she was whisked off to another place in another time. She found herself standing among a long line of people. Some were sitting in carriages and some were leaning against the walls of gray, limestone buildings on either side of a wide village road. It looked as if the line went all the way through the village and was as wide as the road. When Cassy looked passed the road she could see that the line extended all the way to a monastery chapel on the far end of town. Since no one could see her in her spiritual form, she decided to make her way through the crowded line.

When Cassy reached the end of the line at the monastery entrance, she could hear people talking.

"I waited for eight days before I got to this point, and I'd wait another eight if it meant Padre Paolo could hear my confession," the man on Cassy's right said.

"My cousin Enrico was completely healed of his illness when his mother confessed to Padre Paolo," another in the line said.

"Did you hear about the woman who carried her dead baby in her suitcase all the way to Padre Paolo's confessional? Padre Paolo brought the boy back to life," a woman said from somewhere behind Cassy's back.

Cassy turned to see two elegantly dressed women in late nineteenth century attire with beautiful matching hats and long brilliant plumes sticking out of the tops. They could not see Cassy and appeared to walk through her as they proceeded toward the entrance of the monastery. Cassy walked through the building's entrance and saw that the line ended right before a room that contained two confessionals made of solid wood. Two men spoke in hushed voices, both dressed in black pin–striped suits and black fedoras.

Cassy was curious about the two men in front of her. She

moved directly in front of them so that she could listen to their conversation.

"I told you already. I'm the one who's going to confess murder. You confess the bank robbery. Either way, we'll prove once and for all that Padre Paolo is a fake and a fraud. Bleeding from his hands! It's probably stage makeup!" The taller of the two was holding the other's arm as he whispered loudly into his ear.

A smile formed on the shorter man's face. His carefully combed mustache rose up so high on either side of his mouth, Cassy was reminded of the evil villain in old silent black and white movies. "At the very least, can't I say I carried a gun and shot someone in the leg while I was taking off with the stolen goods?"

"I don't care what you say as long as it's believable," the taller man replied, his hat sitting smugly on the side of his head.

Cassy turned toward the confessional as the door creaked open. A young woman dressed in fine Italian garments came out with her head down. It looked like she'd been crying, but there was something completely awestruck in her gaze, like she had been touched by God.

"All right. You first." The "murderer" nudged the "bank robber" toward the confessional. The shorter man walked slowly to the door, and looked back toward his tall friend before he went in and closed the door behind him.

Cassy waited and heard a great commotion inside the confessional. The door swung open and the "bank robber" frantically ran to the "murderer."

Cassy saw an elderly Paolo come out of the confessional. He was dressed in a long tunic and seemed to have difficulty walking.

"Out! Out!" he yelled at the bank robber. "Come back when you are ready to make a true confession!"

The short man stopped by his friend before he exited the monastery. He said only two words in his ear, "He knows."

The tall man's long face turned red. He became even more resolute than before and walked to the confessional with angry determination.

Cassy assumed this "confession" would end even sooner and was surprised when nearly thirty minutes passed. When she saw the "murderer" come out of the door, he looked entirely different. He held his hat in his hands and his face was so ashen, it looked as if he had been brought back to life from the dead. The man's gaze was focused on nothing in particular as if he were in some sort of trance. He stopped directly in front of Cassy as if he could see her.

Cassy saw a tear trickle down his right cheek as he smiled knowingly at her. Then, he blinked once and seemed to wake up.

The man went to the two women dressed in fancy dresses with plumes in their hats and grabbed each one by the arm. "He's a saint! He's a saint, I tell you! I went in there to lie so that I could prove he was a fake, but do you know what he did? He read my mind. He told me I was a liar. A betrayer of God! Do you know what he did then? He read my mind again and told me my real sins! He told me my real sins! Don't you see? He's real, a real saint!" The man cried as he spoke and ran back to the entrance of the monastery where his friend listened in shock and bewilderment.

Cassy turned back to the confessional and saw Padre Paolo emerge. There were audible exclamations from those who waited days for Paolo to hear their confessions. Paolo looked directly at Cassy as he stood outside the confessional. His gaze was so intense, it looked as if he were looking through her, as if he could see her both in this time as well as the present.

Cassy noticed that there was something different about Paolo than she had seen in her spiritual travels. Paolo's hands were partially covered with dark cotton gloves, so that only his fingers remained exposed. He wore a dark cassock with a hood and a belt made of rope around his waist with a large set of wooden rosary beads hanging from his hip. It was not Paolo's dress that was so different, however. It was his demeanor. He stood bowed down from the waist as if the weight of the world were upon him. Paolo was hunched over and suffering from physical pain. The wounds of Christ had definitely taken a toll on his ravaged body.

Seeing Paolo's mortal body for the first time Cassy realized that for as long as she had known Paolo, she had known only his immortal body. The body she saw today had not yet been healed, redeemed and infused with the sweet essence of the divine. Cassy had been blessed with a vision of the divinized body. She had taken it for granted that everyone who roamed the earth after death would stand as tall and mystical as her friend, Paolo.

Suddenly, Paolo's gaze moved past Cassy to a man she saw through the crowd carrying something in a black velvet pouch. He was dressed exactly the same as the "bank robber" and the "murderer." The lavishly dressed women looked at him with disdain. Cassy could sense that they were about to speak, but their voices were instantly hushed when they saw the black velvet pouch in the man's hands. It was as if they knew that something important and holy was contained in that pouch.

The man entered the confessional and closed the door behind him. Cassy heard nothing for several minutes. Time and space stood still, and she could tell that even those waiting in line seemed calmer and less hurried.

"Do you have any idea who that is in the confessional?" one woman asked the other.

"How should I?" the other responded back.

"It's just that...look!" the woman pointed toward the confessional with a startled expression on her face.

Cassy saw it, too. There were beams of light glowing through the thin spaces between the slats in the door of the confessional. The light was a mixture of blue, red and white, like colored rays reflecting off the object inside the man's black velvet bag.

"What could it be?" Cassy thought out loud.

She made her way toward the confessional and slowly opened the door to see what was inside. At first, the light was so bright Cassy could not make out anything. Then, after a time, the light began to fade and she could see the object that the man possessed. It was a flat oval stone covered with a sheet of gold. On top of the gold was a tree made of metal with a serpent entwined on the tree's branch. Next to the tree was a couchant positioned lion with its mouth opened wide in a menacing snarl. The eyes of the lion were made of sapphire, and Cassy counted seven eyes in total between the lion and the serpent.

As Cassy stared at the object, she became blinded by the magnificent rays of the stone. The entire base was made of jasper. This was the only object that could have contained the one true Bloodstone, and it had been given to Padre Paolo to protect.

CHAPTER THIRTY

When Michael Murray and Linda Walters discovered the date that the Urim and Thummim would be located, they put the mysterious Calatrava Museum clue on hold and called Father Andrew McLaughlin. They gave him the only information he needed to know so far: 1/22/13. The Urim and Thummim would be discovered on that date. They didn't know how. They didn't know where. They just knew that this would be the day when everything would be revealed.

"Do you know which important event happens on that date?" Father Mac asked Michael and Linda.

"No, but it's only a month and a half away," Michael replied anxiously.

"Wait a second," Linda said. "I know that date. It's the anniversary of Roe v. Wade. The March for Life in Washington D.C."

"Yes," Father Mac sounded worried. "The date that made it possible to legally kill millions."

"Not to mention the millions of unborn killed before and after the date in other countries," Linda added.

"Hold on," Michael interrupted. "Are you saying that there have been millions and millions killed by abortion?"

"Two billion, so far," Father Mac replied.

"So, 1/22/13. Roe v. Wade. March for Life. Two billion killed. Sounds kind of apocalyptic," Michael interjected. "Now all we have to do is find the Urim and Thummim."

"In six weeks," Linda added skeptically. "And we don't even know what it is or what it looks like."

"You're right, Linda," Father Mac answered. "We're going to have to figure out what it is before we can figure out where it is. All it's going to take is a little faith. And faith supersedes all uncertainties."

*

Father Raphael thought New Jersey weather was the strangest phenomenon he had ever experienced. It was right between the end of fall and the beginning of winter, and every day went back and forth between the two seasons. One day it was sunny and fifty, and the next it was snowing and thirty. Today, it was somewhere in the middle—forty, partly cloudy and just beginning to snow.

Father Raphael pulled into the Saint Mary's lot and parked his car in the garage. He smiled as he walked through the rectory's outdoor garden to a large white statue of the Assumption of Mary, the patroness of the church. As always, Father Raphael stopped before Mary and said a quick prayer before he entered the rectory. Today was no exception. He prayed for the man he had just visited at Holy Name Hospital.

Afterward, Father Raphael walked down the small flight of stairs that led to the staff offices in the basement of the rectory. He went through the outside door and heard the familiar sound of the buzzer, which opened the lock of the inner door. He was met by the pleasant smile of his secretary, Clara, a wonderful retired woman who had recently lost her husband and was looking for a job to get her out of her lonely house. Clara had been talking on the phone, but put the call on hold as soon as Father Raphael walked in.

"Good afternoon, Father Trujillo," Clara said. No matter how many times Raphael told Clara to call him Father Raphael, Clara always insisted on using his last name. She said she was raised in a generation when priests used their last names. "Your mother is on the line for you."

"Thanks, Clara. I'll take the call in my office." Father Raphael could hear Clara saying, "One moment, Rita. He'll be right with you." He walked into his small office in the back and threw his coat on a chair before he picked up the phone.

"Mom?" Raphael asked as he sat down at his desk.

"Raffa, Raffa! My darling boy!" He could tell that his mother had been crying. Her Spanish was broken by short little sobs.

"Mom, what is it?" he asked without waiting for cordialities.

"Raffa, my son." His mother was having trouble finding the right words to break the terrible news to him. "It's Carmelita, my son. I just spoke with her mother, Maria. Raffa, Carmelita is dead. She died yesterday."

Raphael caught his breath and felt a sharp pain in his chest that felt like his heart had just been stabbed. He was in shock. Several seconds passed without a word.

"Raffa? Are you there, my darling?" His mother was anxious and worried.

Raphael uttered one word when he felt he could breathe again. "How?" he asked.

"Do you know of her relationship with that young man?" When his mother said "young man," she might as well have said, "poisonous snake."

"Yes, we've spoken about him," Raphael replied.

"She became pregnant with his child. He forced her to end the life of her baby. Drove her to a clinic in Mexico City. Paid for it and left her there. At the clinic, her uterus was accidentally lacerated and they could not stop the bleeding. She was transferred to a hospital, but there was nothing that could be done. She had lost too much blood. They tried to save her, but it was too late."

Raphael could not stop the flood of tears running down his cheeks. He could not stop the audible sobs heard on the other end of the phone by his mother. Raphael and his mother wept for the beautiful girl whom he would have married had he not become a priest.

When the tears had been spent, Raphael told his mother that he loved her and thanked her for letting him know. He told her to give his condolences to Carmelita's parents. He would pray for them.

Raphael wiped away his tears and opened the door to his office. Clara looked at him with a mother's concern as he excused himself and walked back outside to the garden courtyard and the statue of Mary.

Father Raphael had not bothered to put on his coat. He put his hands in his pockets to keep them warm. It was still snowing, coming down harder now and he could feel freezing flakes fall on his head as he walked to the statue. Raphael could not take his eyes off of Mary as he walked. She was his comfort when he needed it most. When he reached her, he noticed white flakes accumulating on her upturned arms as she raised them to heaven. In his despair, he brushed the snow from her arms. He wanted to care for her just as she always cared for him. Raphael brushed the snow from Mary's head and made sure there was no snow on her face. Mary's face looked so holy and beautiful to Raphael. Just as Carmelita's face had looked the night of his party all those years ago.

Father Raphael felt a tear run down his cheek as he stood before the statue of Mary. When he brushed the tear away, he noticed that it looked like Mary was crying, too. In his agony, he must have imagined that Mary was crying with him. Raphael blinked his eyes to clear them, but when he looked back at Mary's face, he saw that she, too, had a single tear running down her left cheek. Raphael moved closer to prove that he must be seeing things, but the closer he came to the statue, the more evident Mary's tear became.

Mary's tear was not clear, though. It was dark red, like the color of blood. To Raphael, it looked like Mary was crying bloody tears.

"Oh, my Mary, the mother of our Savior, Jesus Christ! Do not cry! I am your soldier acting in the name of your Son! I will make things right! I will do everything in my power to end this killing that they have made legal in my beloved country of Mexico. Mary, your priest knows the injustice of abortion, and now my Carmelita is gone!"

Raphael did not feel the need to cry any longer. He was on fire with the power of the Holy Spirit. Mary had given him his mission. He would fight hard for the pro–life cause. He would make his voice heard in defense of the unborn. He would let the truth of the dangerous risks of abortions to mothers ring out. He would let mothers and fathers know there were other options. Carmelita had given him his mission through Mary.

Before Father Raphael went back into the rectory, he wiped away the bloody tear from Mary's cheek with the back of his sleeve. He did not want anyone to see it. He did not want a miracle to be discovered by the media. Mary deserved her privacy. After all, it was almost time for the Vigil Mass, and tomorrow was Sunday. More than anything, Father Raphael wanted to keep the Sabbath holy and peaceful.

*

Sunday was usually Kevin's favorite day of the week, but he seemed completely distraught to Father Raphael. After the twelve o'clock Mass, Kevin tripped on his shoe lace and almost dropped one of the chalices on his way to the sacristy sink in the back of the church.

"Kevin, are you okay?" Father Raphael was hanging his vestments, trying to appear nonchalant.

"Yes, Father. Sorry. Just having an off day." Kevin was looking down at the sink, running his right hand through his hair worriedly.

"Anything I can do to help?" Father Raphael walked over and

busied himself with a stack of loose papers on a nearby shelf.

"It's my mom. She's really doing bad. I don't know what to do." Kevin looked up from the sink and Father Raphael could tell the boy was having a hard time holding back tears.

Father Raphael had never met Kay Dennis. She wasn't a church goer and Kevin usually rode his bike or walked to the church from school. "Can you tell me what's happening?" Father Raphael asked.

"Not really. It's a work thing. She quit her job at a women's clinic in Englewood. She said she couldn't go back there anymore. Not with the things they were doing there."

"I see," Father Raphael said. "It's a good thing she quit then."

"Yeah. That's what I said, but she's really taking it hard, like something bad happened and she's blaming herself for it. She's also worried about money because she doesn't have another job yet."

"She did the right thing. She let her conscience be her guide." Father Raphael stood thinking for a second when a slow smile spread across his handsome face. "Look at me. I sound like Jimminy Cricket," he added.

Kevin gave Father Raphael a closed smile as he began to chuckle under his breath. It was the first time he'd felt like smiling all day.

"She's here," Kevin said.

"Your mom's here at church?"

"Yeah. There's a first time for everything," Kevin replied.

"Good. Let me introduce myself," Father Raphael said with a keen smile.

*

Kay's entire body was shaking when she sat with Father Raphael in the confessional. She had not been to confession since her divorce, and she didn't even know if she would still be able to recite the "act of contrition." Kay had told Father Raphael everything that had happened at the Englewood clinic. She concluded her confession with that tragic final day, the day that Cara Maria Rosina died of respiratory arrest and pulmonary embolism, the day that the life of a young mother of a three–year old girl abruptly ended.

After confession, Kay sat for more than an hour in front of the Blessed Sacrament doing penance and praying to a God whom she had longed to call, "Father," but had never felt worthy. Until now.

Kay left the church feeling renewed with a sense of hope and purpose. She exited from the side of the church closest to the rectory and saw Kevin sitting beside Father Raphael on a bench next to a large statue of Mary. After everything that had transpired, Kay found it ironic that she had not shed a single tear, but when she saw her beloved son sitting next to this wonderful priest, she couldn't stop herself from crying now.

"I have nothing to hide anymore," Kay thought as she let her tears flow freely. When she reached the bench, Kevin and Father Raphael rose to greet her. All Kay could do was hug Father Raphael and then her son. She bowed her head and let herself cry into his shoulder. Kevin had grown into such a remarkable young man, and Kay felt so proud of him. He was God's gift to her, and she knew nothing else mattered.

*

A week passed since the JamBrax convention, and Jessica could not wait another day to get the files on JamBrax's Fountain of Youth Spa copied from Palmer's computer. Jessica enlisted Jonathan's help. There was no one else she trusted more, and he was the smartest person she knew.

Jessica and Jonathan had planned it all out the night before, and there was no detail left out. She would schedule an urgent and unexpected meeting with Palmer for two in the afternoon. She would get there early and wait in his office since she was good friends with his secretary. Jonathan would distract Palmer with urgent business on Palmer's way back up from lunch since it was Monday. Jessica knew that Palmer always took long lunches on Monday, Wednesday and Friday when he played tennis at his club.

Jessica stepped into the elevator with a Starbucks coffee in hand and wondered why she felt so nervous in light of all the preparation. "What could possibly go wrong?" she thought. When she walked into her office, she decided to text Jonathan for reassurance. If there was anyone to put a light spin on their upcoming endeavor, it was him.

"READY?" she texted all in caps. A few minutes passed and Jessica's mind started to reel. "Has Jonathan even made it in yet?' she thought. "What if Jonathan doesn't want to go through with it?" Her mind was going a mile a minute. She almost jumped when she felt her phone vibrate in her hand. Jonathan had replied back.

"ALL READY. THE RING. THE CHURCH. THE WEDDING. JUST WAITING ON THE BRIDE," he texted back. Also, all in caps.

Jessica smiled broadly despite her nerves and texted back, "GOOD. WEDDING WILL START JUST BEFORE 2."

*

At half past one Jessica and Jonathan left their respective offices to get an early start on their plan. Jessica made her way to Palmer's office while Jonathan walked toward the lobby of the USF's School of Medicine building.

Jonathan, who spent most of his time doing research in the university's Institute of Human Genetics' building, did not get a chance to venture into the School of Medicine building very often. He was always completely captivated with the immense size of the lobby. It was like a giant great room with long windows in the front and elevators in the back. The lobby reeked of contemporary décor with black marble floors, a black marble desk for the receptionist, and black leather seats around an oblong glass table. There were ultra–modern paintings hung on the walls that reminded Jonathan of Rorschach Inkblot Tests used by psychiatrists to determine personality disorders.

Jonathan walked over to the receptionist on duty and flashed a big, wholesome smile. "Excuse me? I'm Dr. Jonathan Lee, genetics' research at the institute. Has Dr. Braxton come back from lunch yet? I have some urgent data that I need to run past him." Jonathan held up an important looking folder to show the receptionist he meant business.

"No. He's usually not back 'til two. Do you want to wait?" The girl pointed to the chairs.

"Yes, thanks." Jonathan sat in one of the leather chairs and pulled out his Blackberry to text Jessica. It was already a quarter to two. He texted, "WAITING IN LOBBY."

A couple of minutes passed and Jonathan received the reply, "I'M IN."

*

Jessica thought the most difficult part of getting to Palmer's computer files was keeping him from coming into his office for as long as she needed to copy them. The second most difficult part was obtaining Palmer's password, but she had one thing working in her favor: Jacob, the director of technology for the university was a good friend of Jessica's who hated Palmer with a passion. The password was "JamBrax1022." Palmer's company. Palmer's birthday. Not too complicated. Very self–centered. Totally Palmer.

Jessica sat at Palmer's desk and looked up at the office door to make sure it was still closed. Susie, Palmer's receptionist, had been very accommodating, but if Jessica had a two o'clock meeting with Palmer she only had fifteen minutes to get the files copied. She turned on the computer, entered the password, and began searching for the file on JamBrax's Fountain of Youth Spa in Barbados. Five minutes passed and the search came up completely empty. Nothing on any Fountain of Youth Spa in Barbados.

Jessica could feel her face begin to perspire. Her anxiety was so intense, she could feel a knot forming in her stomach. She glanced down at her phone to check the time and realized it was flashing with a new message. A text from Jonathan. "STILL WAITING," was all it said at ten to two.

"Okay, think, Jessica, think," she said to herself. She decided the best way to find any file or document was to scroll down through all the JamBrax docs by hand. Jessica scrolled through several and then one, in particular, caught her eye. It said, "JamBrax Baby." She opened it and quickly realized she had hit the gold mine. The document was all about JamBrax's Fountain of Youth Spa in Barbados: how it began, its location, what it cost to maintain, how much it made, where they obtained the fetal body parts.

Jessica's heart stopped. "Fetal body parts?" she wondered. She read on and discovered that the majority of the babies came from the Ukraine. Some from maternity hospitals.

Jessica felt almost paralyzed. She couldn't believe it. Fetal body parts taken from maternity hospitals? These weren't fetal body parts. They were newborn babies stolen from their impoverished mothers who were murdered and dismembered. "For what gain?" Jessica thought. She wanted to read on but she knew she had to copy the document before Palmer got back from lunch.

Jessica pulled out her flash drive and inserted it into Palmer's computer as quickly as possible. Just as she hit the button on the mouse to save it, she saw her phone flashing again. It was another text from Jonathan. "STILL WAITING?!!!!!!" it said. Jessica checked the time. Ten after two. That doesn't make sense," she thought. Palmer was punctual to the second and never deviated from his schedule.

Jessica knew she had to get out of there as quickly as possible.

The document was copied. Just as she extracted her flash drive from his computer, Palmer's office door swung open and he entered looking more than a little surprised to see Jessica sitting at his desk. She managed to toss the flash drive and her phone into her purse while she stood up, but there was no time to be able to close the document and shut down the computer. She had been caught red handed. Palmer would know that she had broken into his computer.

"Jessica?" Palmer asked, still stunned that his associate was sitting behind his desk at his computer without his knowledge or consent.

Jessica would have to come up with the best lie of her life to get out of this predicament. Palmer must have deviated from his normal plan and come in from the side entrance to the stairs instead of through the lobby. She decided she would have to play her cards right and use her feminine appeal.

"I'm sorry, Palmer." Jessica walked around the desk and behind Palmer to close the door to his office. "I don't know if you remembered, but we have a two o'clock appointment today." Jessica stood very close to Palmer's back.

"We do?" he said as he turned around to face Jessica.

"Yes," she said in a whisper, her lips so close to his, they were almost touching. "We do."

Palmer's face was flushed and his breathing became heavy.

Jessica put her hand on Palmer's arm and motioned toward his computer. "I also noticed that your computer was on, and I was trying to shut it down for privacy's sake," she said squeezing his arm.

"Thank you," Palmer replied, still captivated by Jessica's charm.

"I was wondering if we could reschedule our meeting for sometime in the evening, perhaps over dinner?" Jessica asked as sultry as possible.

"That would be...that would be fine. This evening, perhaps?"

Palmer asked with a slow smile.

"This evening," Jessica replied and she exited out of Palmer's office and closed the door softy behind her.

Palmer could not believe his good fortune. His advances toward Jessica had obviously been working all along, and now it was all paying off. She was falling in love with him. He knew it. And how could he blame her? He had everything a man could offer a woman—and more. As Palmer walked back to his desk, he felt so elated he might as well have floated over.

"What a wonderful woman to want to shut down my computer for me for privacy's sake?" Palmer thought as he sat down. He moved his mouse back and forth so his screen saver would stop flashing the "JamBrax" logo across the screen. As soon as it stopped, he saw the document that Jessica had opened and copied, and Palmer's face turned from a shade of passion to a shade of rage.

Palmer picked up his phone and dialed Elaina's number as quickly as possible. He knew he was in serious trouble and he needed help fast. First, he needed to vanish. Second, he needed a good lawyer.

CHAPTER THIRTY–ONE

When the girl with green cat eyes was led into the Milwaukee PSI clinic entrance by the bodyguard, she realized she really wanted to talk to the grandmotherly woman with silver hair standing next to the priest. She wanted to tell her she didn't want to go through with this. She thought it was killing, but she was being pushed into it by her mother and boyfriend.

Her father told her that he thought a baby might be good for her. Her best friend said that it might be a sign from God that she should become a mother. After all, she wasn't a teenager. She was twenty–seven years old. Twenty–seven and without insurance. That was it. That's what her mother told her. She couldn't afford to have a baby. Her boyfriend said he didn't want marriage. He didn't want the baby. That's why she was there.

The girl with green cat eyes looked back at the woman with silver hair one last time before entering the clinic. She was reminded of the silver–winged bird she saw outside her bedroom window that morning. She was lying on her queen–sized bed next to the sliding glass door that led to the balcony outside her room.

The girl heard a "thud" against the window and saw a small bird that accidentally flew into the glass. The injured bird was lying on its back on the balcony, every breath coming from the bird's little chest an anguished effort. The girl remained frozen on her bed knowing that she was witnessing the bird's last moments. It was only seconds before the bird's gasps for air slowed, and when the bird expelled its last breath, its little body went completely still. The girl had witnessed, first–hand, the loss of an innocent life, and could not help but wonder if this was a sign from God.

The girl with green cat eyes was ushered through the double doors of the clinic and told to sit down in the waiting area. She saw other women waiting around her. Something about the room made her nervous. Nervousness was in the air. Someone from the front desk gave her a form to fill out, and she was ushered into another room with a white counter and chairs. She took a pen and wrote her name. She was numb and beyond feeling or thinking. She used her real name. Why not? She had nothing to hide. It was a procedure like any other, right? Get it over with and move on with her life. That was the plan. That's what her mother and boyfriend wanted and she was made to want it, too. There would be no guilt. There would be no remorse. Only freedom from what they called a burden.

Is that what the woman outside with silver hair would have thought, too? Would the woman with silver hair standing next to the priest have called this baby a burden?

The girl with green cat eyes finished the paperwork and turned it into the front desk. She was given a bill for the procedure and told to pay before she was given anesthesia. Just a little twilight they had told her. Like you get before you have wisdom teeth pulled. Makes it so you don't remember. You close your eyes and wake up and it's over. That's the way she wanted it. She didn't want to remember.

She was told to follow a woman in a white lab coat to an area in the back with lockers and a bathroom. The woman told her she could use the bathroom to empty her bladder and remove her clothes. She gave her a white hospital gown and said she would wait outside to help her put her belongings in the locker.

The girl with green cat eyes tried to feel nothing. She stuffed her things into the locker and followed the woman to another room with a large reclining chair made of black leather and a rolling cart filled with vials of medication and needles. The girl was told that this was where she would receive anesthesia so she could sleep during the procedure. The girl sat, felt the puncture of a needle, and everything became hazy to her.

The girl woke up on the black leather chair in a large room with sunlight coming through windows. She saw at least half a dozen other women sitting in similar chairs facing one another in a circle with a table in the center. She remembered bits and pieces of the procedure through her twilight state. She saw a male doctor sitting next to her chair with a machine that looked and sounded like a plastic vacuum. The sounds coming from the vacuum resembled a gurgling suction that she would never forget.

The doctor was visibly irritated that she had momentarily wakened from her induced sleep. The girl's legs were spread apart and she vaguely remembered that all of the women in the room lying on reclining leather chairs had their legs spread apart, too. It had not been a private procedure. They were all there as a group with the same goal—to end the life of the innocent child inside of them. That was all that the girl with green cat eyes could remember.

*

"Cassy, you have to wake! Hurry! He has discovered your location, and now it is only a matter of time. Come quickly!"

Paolo roused Cassy, but she knew she must rise and take control of her spiritual body herself. She was familiar with her new way of existence and didn't need to rely on Paolo so much any longer. She could "turn on the switch" and ascend all on her own.

Cassy and Paolo ascended into a familiar world of transcendence, but Paolo seemed more disturbed than ever before and this spiritual journey felt different than the others.

"Paolo, please tell me why you are so agitated," Cassy pleaded.

"Cassy, I think you, too, are beginning to sense his presence."

"Yes, Paolo. I know who you're talking about."

"It will not be long before he comes for you. He will try to take you back to himself. I will be there to protect you for as long as I can, but the three of you will have to protect yourselves. The time will come when I will no longer be allowed to guide you and protect you as I have done. There is still much to be learned. Come, we will need to work quickly."

"Yes, Paolo. Tell me where we are going, and I am there."

"First, you will need to know how the Urim and Thummim was passed down and where it exists today."

"I saw you in the confessional with the man who brought the gleaming oracle that contains the one, true Bloodstone. Was the Urim and Thummim given to you to protect?" Cassy asked.

"The Urim and Thummim was not given to me. It was passed from father to son, but stolen by a traitor."

*

Cassy and Paolo did not touch down on land, but a vast expansion of gray fog moving in every direction for miles. There was no reference point for Cassy, and she became suddenly frightened as if she couldn't remember why she was brought here or who she was. She couldn't see Paolo. The fog had become too dense. Cassy stretched out her arms and tried to reach for Paolo.

"Cassy, I'm here. Don't worry," Paolo said in the distance. "I have brought you to a place that does not exist in time or space. It never has and never will. I have become the fog around you to protect you. It is a place that cannot be seen by the enemy. I mean to give you information and that is all.

"The Urim and Thummim was passed from Moses to Aaron, the first of the High Priests. After Aaron's death, it was passed to the High Priests through the family of Levi until the death of Eli. From there, it was passed to the Prophets Samuel and Abiathar, and then to the Kings. Eventually, it was passed to King David and then to his son, King Solomon. Solomon built a great temple, and that is where the Urim and Thummim rested for many years, in Solomon's Temple."

"Is there a link between David Bloodstone and King David?" Cassy asked.

"No, David Bloodstone wanted to become like King David just as Lucipher wanted to become like God. That is why he took the name, 'David.'"

"Do you mean that David Bloodstone was Lucipher?" she asked again.

"No, I mean David Bloodstone is Lucipher."

"The devil?"

"One and the same."

*

Suddenly, Cassy could see something come toward her in the midst of the dense fog. As it came closer, she saw a woman's face emerge surrounded by long black hair. The woman appeared to float through the fog as if she had no feet. The gown she wore was tattered and covered by a dark gray hooded robe. Her skin was so pale, she appeared to have no veins and her nails were long and pointed like talons. When the woman glared at Cassy through menacing eyes, Cassy felt so much hatred her blood became cold and a chill ran down her spine and into her tailbone.

"Behold, maiden, it is false to proclaim David as the first of Kings for I know that Saul be the King who sought me to bring him Samuel," the woman said in a mechanical tone.

"Cassy, do not listen," Paolo began. "This is the ghost wife who speaks to you. The Witch of Endor whom the long line of Taninsam witches and their curse come from. She is their source and the mother of all lies." Paolo spoke invisibly through the fog.

"Hush! Hush, you beast! You mean to lie to my poor, darling. Cassy, King Saul was tricked by David, murdered by David's cohorts. He asked for my assistance in order to seek his good and faithful servant, Samuel. Samuel was there for him when his God and the Philistines abandoned him. He was left with nothing. Saul told me that no punishment would fall upon me for helping him and that I did."

As the Witch of Endor spoke, she became more fair and Cassy saw her hideous nature vanish.

The Witch of Endor continued, "My poor Saul, in his miserable state, was told by the prophet Samuel that he had forfeited God's favor when he failed to kill the king of the Amalekites. Samuel told him that his reign as king would end the day following. I comforted my beloved Saul and I fed and nourished him. I killed a fatted calf and kneaded a measure of unleavened flour, and I made a meal of veal cutlets and matzah for my beloved Saul. And the next day, he was handed over to those barbaric Philistines, and he and his sons were put to a shameful death!"

The angrier the witch became, the more beautiful she appeared to Cassy.

"They slaughtered him and cut off his head, and stripped off his armor, and my poor Saul was disgraced in death as much as he had been tormented in life!" The Witch of Endor cried, and her tears came out in gobs of brown like sewage from a backed–up drain. The smell was so overwhelming that Cassy felt herself awaken from the induced power of black magic.

Cassy saw the figure of the witch fade into the distance, and the heavy fog faded with her. Relief came quickly as Cassy stood in a grassy field with no sign of witches or fog. Cassy saw Paolo and ran into his arms for comfort.

"Paolo, is it true that King David had Saul killed?" Cassy asked.

"No, the Witch of Endor is the mother of lies, and that is what she wants you to believe. Saul died by his own sword rather than run the risk of an unnoble death by the Philistines."

"Where are we now?" Cassy asked.

"The land of Jerusalem. Near the royal palace of King David," Paolo answered.

When Paolo and Cassy reached the palace entrance, they floated to the top floor to the royal bedroom chamber of King David in the early hours of the morning.

King David had just woken from his slumber and was standing on the rooftop of the king's palace where his bed was placed during the warm seasons of the year. He was looking out over the rooftops of his great city—the city of Jerusalem.

King David was handsome and fair with long flowing reddish brown hair that hung in loose curls to the middle of his back. His face was strong and regal with large brown eyes and red, full lips. He had a dimple in his chin and his cheeks were flushed with the time he spent outdoors. He was tall with protruding muscles in his arms and legs, which were completely exposed through a cream-colored tunic and sandals. To Cassy, King David looked exactly as she would have imagined a king to look.

"Cassy, take notice of the black bird flying next to the screen on the nearby rooftop," Paolo whispered to Cassy. "Remember that things are not always as they appear."

Just as Paolo spoke, King David went to his bed and took up his bow and a single arrow.

"Does he mean to kill the bird?" Cassy asked Paolo.

"Yes, but this is not just the king's plan. It is the bird's plan, as well," Paolo replied.

King David took aim and pulled the arrow back with all his might. It shot and moved quickly toward the bird, but missed and struck a nearby screen instead, knocking it down. A beautiful and naked woman with glorious long golden hair, who was no longer hidden by the screen, could be scene bathing on the rooftop. Cassy and Paolo noticed her immediately. King David noticed her, too.

"Who is that?" Cassy asked.

"Bathsheba," Paolo replied. "Satan wanted King David to notice her, to want her, to take her."

"Had Satan disguised himself as the bird?"

"Yes, Bathsheba is a married woman. She is married to Uriah, one of King David's soldiers who has gone off to fight for him. It is unlawful and sinful for David to take her as one of his wives. Satan knows this. That is why he wants to tempt David. It is the story of the forbidden apple all over again." Paolo seemed very bothered by Satan's plan to tempt David. "For failing to avoid Satan's trap, King David spent twenty–two years as a penitent, eating his bread mixed with ashes and weeping for a full hour each day."

"Because he was unfaithful?" Cassy asked.

"Yes, he didn't want to risk the chance of losing heaven. In the past, people lost sleep over where they would spend their eternity. Would they spend an eternity in heaven or an eternity in hell? That was the only important question of the day. Nothing else mattered. Today, people don't believe there is a heaven or hell, so they don't care."

"What happens to Bathsheba?" Cassy asked as she watched King David summon a servant to fetch Bathsheba.

"She becomes pregnant with King David's son, and the king plans her husband's demise at battle. Bathsheba is brought into the king's palace as one of his wives, and she delivers a nameless child who dies of an illness only a week after he is born. Some say this was an act of Yahweh to punish King David for seeking to bend God's will to his own. It is not all lost, however, for a second son is conceived by David and Bathsheba named Solomon. Thus, the Urim and Thummim is passed from King David to King Solomon."

Paolo placed his hand on Cassy's shoulder before he finished. "Nothing is lost on Satan, however, who is already planning his emergence into the world as the new David and the new king."

CHAPTER THIRTY–TWO

Kay Dennis followed Father Raphael Trujillo through the Turning Point Shelter door hesitantly. A few days before, he had called Veronica Blake for a favor. It had been more than a week since the "brown package" incident, and Father Raphael knew that Veronica never let pro–choice threats get in her way. They had turned in the evidence, filed a report with the Bergenfield Police, and moved on. Father Raphael hoped that Veronica might be able to help Kay find a job, and he was right. Veronica was always willing to help a fellow pro–lifer, especially when the pro–lifer was female.

Veronica had spoken with pregnancy shelters in the New Jersey/New York area and they had created a new position for Kay—a nurse practitioner who would visit the shelters on a rotation basis to care for the women and their unborn children who lived there. Veronica would set up Kay's weekly schedules, and Kay would be paid through Turning Point.

As soon as Veronica saw Kay, she stood up from her desk and embraced the timid nurse. "Honey, you are a lifesaver! Where have you been all my life?" Veronica exclaimed.

Kay laughed nervously at how strange it was to have two people who didn't know you, care about you so much. Her laughter was infectious, and the three were laughing like old friends. This was the first time in a long time that Kay found herself excited to be working as a nurse.

*

When Jessica phoned Archbishop Sanders, she didn't think he'd pick up the phone himself, but he did.

"Father Gabe," he answered.

"Father, it's Jessica, Dr. Jessica Taninsam. The woman you met at the JamBrax convention," she said hesitantly.

"Jessica! Good to hear from you," Father Gabe replied jovially. "What can I do for you?"

"Father, I have important information that I need to share with you concerning the Director of the School of Medicine for the University of San Francisco. It is the most unlawful, unethical and sinister that you have probably ever come across," Jessica leveled as best she could.

"Try me," Father Gabe said and directed Jessica to the very same Italian restaurant he had written on his business card only days before.

*

Pete Cooper did not dress the part of a singing churchman. He rode a Harley Davidson and dressed in black leather boots, jeans and a leather vest with a bold "Harley" stitched on the back emblazoned with gold thread. Pete married his high school sweetheart, and they had two teenage daughters whom he loved beyond comprehension even though they drove him absolutely crazy. Pete felt he had a blessed life and was always finding ways to give back to the good Lord what the good Lord had given to him.

Tonight, Pete was giving back to "40 Days for Life" through Father Mac and Saint Michael's Parish. The peaceful prayer vigils ran 24/7 for forty days, day and night. Most people signed up for day prayer, though, since there were so few who wanted to be out in the cold at night in downtown Milwaukee. Pete figured if they needed him at night, he might as well do it.

When Pete rode his Harley into the parking lot across from the PSI clinic, it was almost pitch black. He loved the cold weather, but hated the lack of daylight hours. Pete was scheduled for the midnight shift. Since it was his first time, he came early to get information from the group praying before him.

Pete parked his Harley and walked his 6'4" muscular frame to the prayer group across the street. It was almost winter, but Pete wore only a turtle neck sweater under his leather vest. He noticed a few familiar faces in the small crowd as he strode up.

"Pete!" One of the women from the choir ran up and practically tackled him as she gave him a bear hug.

"Hey! Save any lives yet?" Pete hugged her back and kissed her on the cheek.

Just then, all of the women in the group yelled out, "Pete! Pete!"

He might as well have taken out a black marker to autograph their 40 Days for Life signs like a rock star.

"Thank goodness, Pete's here! Now I feel safe." One of the women in the group walked through the crowd and stood directly in front of him.

Pete took the woman with long, black hair and tight jeans into his arms and imitated the movie greats with a seductive bow and a long kiss.

As soon as the kiss was over, the woman came up for air and furiously declared, "Well, I never!"

The group laughed heartily at Vickie, Pete's wife, who took the prayer shift directly before Pete and was surprised to see her husband had decided to come early.

"I figured I could learn something from you before I go on at midnight. And then I can take my beautiful wife for dinner before she has to go home and get beaten up by our wild and crazy teenage daughters." Pete looked at his wife with a puppy–dog grin, and she couldn't help but laugh and nod her head in agreement.

*

At 1:30 in the morning, Pete stood alone in front of the Milwaukee PSI clinic. He had already completed two rosaries walking back and forth to keep warm. Pete decided to read some of the 40 Days for Life literature to help pass the time. There were teams of volunteers across the country and around the world who prayed outside abortion clinics to let people know that there were other choices. Hundreds of pro–life shelters and pregnancy–care centers opened their doors to expectant women in need. Women did not have to feel like they only had one choice, like they were between a rock and a hard stone. Pete knew all too well what that was like.

After all, he and Vickie had not always been religious. They had not always gone to church. "No, we revolted, big time," Pete thought to himself.

They pushed the limit at her sweet "16" party, which turned less than sweet when Vickie saw the forbidden "double line" on the test. They had both wanted it. No question, but they weren't ready and at sixteen, you make dumb choices.

Pete had carried so much guilt. Guilt because he had paid for it himself. He had worked his butt off all summer carrying three jobs and he had paid for it with the money he earned. Blood money. That's what it was. Judas money. To this day, Pete couldn't go past the golf course where he caddied or the little dive restaurant where he bussed tables without feeling the guilt of working for dirty money.

Pete and Vickie broke up after that. They went to separate colleges, and then God brought them back together. How else can you explain seeing the love of your life in the back of a church ten years later? When Father Mac renewed their wedding vows last year after their 25th anniversary in the same church, the same beautiful and beloved Saint Michael's where there love was rekindled, how could Pete not be thankful? He and Vickie would not let the joy of a wonderful marriage and two beautiful girls be overshadowed by guilt. No, it should have been three, but God forgives, and Pete had faith enough to know that one day their family of five would be reunited one day in heaven.

As Pete looked over the 40 Days for Life literature, a beautiful passage caught his eye: "The half–lidded moon shines down upon us, thin clouds veiling its cold white light, but the pale yellow light from the street lamps dimly illuminates our faces. The people gathered in the shadows are called to pray, and we know that tomorrow, we will return."

Pete looked up at the moon and realized the poetic passage of all pro–lifers across the country and around the world were joined together by the Holy Spirit in a common purpose. Any of those, like Pete, who were alone and looking up at the "half–lidded moon" were not really alone at all. They were all joined together in prayer.

When Pete looked at his watch, he realized it was already well past two. "Less than two hours left," he thought.

Pete decided to walk past the clinic toward the corner, so that he could get a view of the other side of the building. It was getting chillier, and he shoved his hands in his vest pockets to try to warm them.

As Pete continued in the darkness, he saw a man walk toward him. The man looked about forty years old and wore a pair of dirty jeans with holes in the knees and a plaid shirt with no coat even though the temperature was just above freezing.

When the man reached Pete, he approached him. "What are you doing out here?" he asked, the smell of cheap whiskey on his breath.

"I'm praying," Pete responded earnestly. "See that building

right there? They kill almost fifty innocent babies every week through abortion."

"Boy, looks like any other building from the outside, don't it?" The man seemed genuinely surprised.

"Yeah, it does. Abortion isn't something they want to advertise with fluorescent lights. It's something they try to hide in a plain, brick building."

"You know, I've spent time in a plain, brick building like that. I'm recovering from drug addiction," the man told Pete. "Listen, can you do me a favor?"

"What do you need?" Pete asked cautiously.

The man reached into his jeans' pocket and pulled out a crumpled $20 bill. He handed it to Pete. "I want you to use this to save the lives of the unborn babies."

"I appreciate it…" Pete began thinking the man should use the money to buy himself a winter jacket. "We could use your prayers more than your money."

"No, I insist. Please take it." The man stuffed the $20 bill into Pete's hand and walked off.

Whatever amount of cold Pete felt before was now gone. He walked with renewed vigor to the corner and turned left to get a view of the rear of the building. After a few more feet, Pete noticed a small fire in the distance near an employee parking lot in the back of the building. He inched his way forward and saw a group of chairs set up around the fire with employees from the clinic sitting in each one. Pete placed his body up against the back side of the building to get as close as possible without being seen.

Pete recognized the owner of the clinic from a picture on the inside flap of the clinic's flier. He saw her get up from her chair and walk to the front of the building carrying two containers of a clear liquid. The rest of the group rose from their chairs and followed the owner to the front. Pete realized that if he wanted to see what was going on he'd better move back to the front of the building as quickly as possible. He ran to the sidewalk and raced around the corner back to the prayer vigil area where he had first started the night. At this distance, he was too far away to see anything except a hint of the flicker of fire in the parking lot to the right.

Pete quietly moved to the front of the building and noticed that the owner and the rest of the group were coming toward him from the back parking lot to the front entrance. He quickly moved to the left and hid around the side corner of the building to avoid being seen. Pete could hear the owner chant something unrecognizable and while she chanted, she poured the liquid all around the entrance and the walkway that the 'customers' used to enter. The rest of the group was also chanting while she poured and Pete began to feel a chill run up his spine.

Just at that moment, the owner emerged from the left in plain sight of Pete. She poured more liquid on the sidewalk while she glared at him. Pete instantly ran back to the sidewalk so he would not be arrested for trespassing. He knew that the clinic owner and her staff would like nothing better than to see him behind bars. It was a free country and he was allowed to pray, but he knew that he had to stay a certain distance from the entrance to the building. Pete made it back to the sidewalk and glanced at his watch. It was almost four a.m.

Pete could only see blurred figures with one in the center still pouring liquid and reciting unrecognizable words. However, when the last recitation was finished, Pete saw the owner look directly at him with hate while she poured the remaining liquid from the container. She uttered one last phrase and led the group back to the rear parking lot.

Pete heard car engines start and assumed the clinic workers were headed home for a couple of hours of sleep before they would have to be back at the clinic later that morning. He thought he could hear one car's tires screeching as it pulled around a corner down the street. The sound of the engine grew louder and louder as he stood motionless.

"Oh, my God," Pete thought. He had a queasy notion that the car was actually headed toward him.

The car made a loud, long noise as it picked up speed and switched gears. It was headed straight for him.

Pete braced himself. "Trying to kill me…" was the only thought that entered his mind.

When the car was only two feet from where Pete stood, it made a sudden stop directly in front of him. The driver was intentionally trying to scare him away from the clinic. The car's screeching tires were still ringing in Pete's ears as he tried to recover from the shock. Then, the car backed up and raced down the street in the opposite direction with another loud screech.

"Hey, you okay, Pete?" A woman from the church choir was crossing the street toward the clinic and waving her arms frantically. Pete was still in shock when Sarah approached. "You okay? I saw that horrible driver! What a jerk! You okay, Pete?"

Pete tried to snap out of it, but all he could do was nod his head.

"I see that car all the time coming and going when I get here early in the morning," Sarah explained.

Pete looked up and saw the first signs of morning were just beginning to make their way over the horizon. He turned back to the parking lot to see if the fire was still burning. Pete couldn't see any flame and assumed that someone in the group had doused it before leaving.

"You've seen that car before, Sarah?" he asked.

"Yes, absolutely!" Sarah responded with extra emphasis.

"Sarah, have you ever noticed a fire in the back parking lot over there with employees from the clinic sitting around it?"

"Yes, happens quite a bit," Sarah said.

"Have you also noticed the owner walking around with liquid that she pours on the sidewalk?

"Yes, that, too."

"Do you know what the owner chants while she's performing this ritual?"

"Pete, I can't understand a word of what she's saying. And if I could, I'd probably wish I hadn't been able to understand anyway."

"You know, Sarah, I think there may be some things going on at this abortion clinic that could be dangerous. In fact, I don't think this place seems safe. I really think that you should go home and that I should report this to Father Mac and the police."

"I appreciate your concern, Pete, but I am here to pray for mothers and their babies and I am not going to go anyplace else but here."

"Please, Sarah…" Pete began.

"Pete, when we pray here, in front of this clinic, I know God is with us." Sarah responded. "And if God is with us, then who can be against us?"

"You're right, Sarah." Pete answered. "But I'd feel better about the situation if you'd let me pray with you. Just until somebody else from the group comes along. Then, I'll let Father Mac and the police know what's going on here."

*

Veronica Blake was enjoying her newfound relationship with Kay Dennis. Kay was not only an excellent nurse, but a hard worker who would meet a client anywhere and anytime she was needed. In fact, Kay had just left to meet a young woman who was only sixteen years old and six months pregnant. The girl had been kicked out of her parents' home because she had refused to go for an abortion and was staying at a shelter in Hackensack that was run by Turning Point. Veronica looked at her watch and realized she had better hurry up and close the office if she was going to make it to Transfiguration Academy in time to pick up her kids.

Just as Veronica placed the last file she had been working on in her desk drawer, she heard the door swing open. Veronica looked up just in time to see a very gaunt and tall man enter. He was elegantly dressed in black and his black hair was combed back in a severe ponytail. Veronica stood to greet him and noticed that he must have been at least six and a half feet tall.

"Can I help you?" Veronica asked hurriedly.

"Veronica?" the man in black asked.

"That's me," she replied.

"I just wanted to make sure that you and the good priest received my package," he said with a slow smile.

Veronica felt a cold fear come over her like a plunge into the Atlantic Ocean in February.

"Did you receive my package, Veronica?" the man in black asked again as he walked slowly toward her desk.

"I…did," she managed to say under her breath.

"Good. Very good. Because I just wanted to make sure that we could reach an understanding."

The man in black stood so close to Veronica's desk, she could see the veins through his skin. His eyes were so black, she couldn't see his pupils. "What kind of understanding?" she asked suspiciously.

"You get out of the business of saving babies, I leave you alone," he replied flatly.

Veronica's fear turned to rage, and all those years of guilt and remorse for her own abortion came flooding back into her mind like a tidal wave crashing against a calm shore. Suddenly, Veronica didn't care if this man were Lucifer or the burning reaper. He could go back home to hell for all she cared.

Veronica rose to her full height before she spoke, "Let me say this as simply as possible. No one tells me what to do with my life, you understand? I do not, I repeat, do not care what you do to me. I will never ever give up in the fight to save the lives of innocent babies, their mothers and their fathers!" Veronica felt so much venom for this evil man, her mouth was set in a permanent snarl.

What happened next she would not have wanted to happen to her worst enemy. In one split second, Veronica could not explain how, the man in black came from behind her and grabbed her around the throat.

"Veronica, you may not care what happens to you, but what about what might happen to Tom or Peter or little Grace?" the man growled into her ear as he squeezed her throat. "You might care what happens to them."

Just as quickly as the man in black appeared, he vanished and Veronica almost fell backward with the force of his pull suddenly gone.

For the first time in her life, Veronica was truly afraid. When she picked up Peter and Grace from school her hands were shaking so badly, she was sure the children knew something was wrong. On the way home, Veronica decided to take a slight detour so the three of them could pray the rosary at Saint Mary's. The children did not complain. They knew that Mommy needed this.

The phrase that kept repeating in Veronica's mind as she prayed were the words of Saint Padre Paolo, "The rosary is the greatest weapon to combat the devil. The rosary is the greatest weapon."

On the way out of the church after praying the rosary twice, the three stopped in front of the outdoor statue of Mary. Veronica was sure that she saw the statue come alive in front of her. The image was so vivid, Veronica saw Mary's blue veil flutter in the wind and the smell of lilac permeated the air on this cold December day. She did not want to trouble Father Raphael with what had happened. He would be so worried about her and Tom and the kids. Besides, she had a keen sense that the mother of God was beside her to guide her in the battle for life.

CHAPTER THIRTY–THREE

King David sat in ashes wearing nothing but a common sack cloth. He was grieving and whaling aloud at the great sin he had just committed. To Cassy, the immenseness of the sin must have been terrible for the king to suffer so much.

Paolo turned to Cassy to explain. "King David was required to perform one final act of kingship in his later years. He was asked for a census to determine the population of Israel."

"Evil to do a census?" Cassy asked.

"The ancient Israelites regarded the notion of a census as monstrous because it would only serve to assist the king in imposing more taxation on the people."

"Why would King David want to risk losing the confidence of his people?"

"He thought the census was God's will, but God punished Israel for the census by sending a pestilence which killed seventy thousand," Paolo replied.

"Did God ask for the census?" she asked.

"No. Not likely."

"Who then?"

"I think you know by now."

"Satan."

"Yes. More likely."

King David cried out so loudly that Cassy and Paolo stopped their conversation and looked at the miserable king in his agony.

"I have sinned greatly in what I have done!" King David said over and over, crying out to God in his torment.

Suddenly, Cassy and Paolo saw a ghostly shadow of an angel of death show itself to King David as it hovered above the threshing–floor of a Jebusite named Araunah.

"Lo, I have sinned," David continued begging the angel of death to summon God's mercy. "The sheep of Israel, what have they done? Let thy hand, I pray thee, be against me, and against my father's house instead."

Paolo turned to Cassy. "The Israelites regarded threshing–floors as places of special sanctity, and the God of Israel was known to manifest in these places. The angel's appearance in this spot is a message from God that King David should erect an altar unto the Lord in the threshing–floor of Araunah the Jebusite.

"Cassy, the Angel of Death came to King David as a sign of what was to come. It was a sign of the greatest mass killing known to man—the killing of the innocents through child sacrifice. King David knew what was expected of him. He knew that God wanted a temple to be built—the greatest temple ever as a tribute to Him. King David knew that his successor, his son, Solomon, the fruit that Bathsheba did bear, would be the one chosen to build the temple, the Temple of Solomon. But King David did not know that this threshing–floor was the only place sacred enough to house the Urim and Thummim, the oracle containing the one, true Bloodstone strong enough to combat Satan's abortion holocaust."

*

Paolo was running out of time before David would come for Cassy, and he needed to work quickly to reveal the Urim and Thummim's location from past to present. He took Cassy to the magnificent First Temple of Solomon built in 964 B.C. They stood inside a golden room that was called, the "Holy of Holies," or in Hebrew, the "Kodesh Hakodashim." The room had no windows and its walls and floor were overlaid with gold. It contained two cherubim of olive wood, each ten feet high with a wing span of ten feet from tip to tip, so that the wings touched the wall on either side and met in the center of the room.

The Holy Place was overlaid with gold, and a fine–linen veil of blue, purple, and crimson hung to shield the "name" of God. Paolo said that the color scheme of the veil was symbolic: blue represented the heavens; red, the earth; and purple, a combination of the two, a meeting of the heavens and the earth.

The sacred Ark of the Covenant stood behind the curtain. It was made entirely of gold and two long golden rods appeared on either side to enable it to be carried. There were two beautiful golden cherubim kneeling in prayer on the top of the Ark with the tips of their golden wings touching as they faced one another.

"The Ark of the Covenant contains the 'manna' that rained down on the people of Israel to nourish them as they journeyed throughout the desert for forty years; the staff of Aaron; and the stone tablets of Moses," Paolo explained.

Paolo and Cassy disappeared from the Holy of Holies and entered the bedchambers of King Solomon. As the king slept, he dreamt peacefully, and Cassy could make out what was said in his sleep.

"My Lord, God, give therefore thy servant an understanding heart to judge thy people that I may discern between good and bad; for who is able to judge this thy so great a people," King Solomon mumbled as he slept.

"I have heard thy prayer and thy supplication wherewith thou hast made supplication before me, I have hallowed this house which thou hast built, to put my name there unto time age–abiding, and my eyes and my heart shall be there continually," Yahweh responded to King Solomon.

Paolo continued his lesson to Cassy, "God gave Solomon the gift of wisdom in a woman—a Shulamite woman who came to him from the tribe of Issachar from the city of Shunem. She was a good and faithful wife to Solomon, but Solomon was not faithful to her. Solomon instead loved many strange women. The influence of the Shulamite woman led Solomon to the best and most faithful days of his life, but in the end, Solomon did not do God's commandments and let the evil wisdom of his foreign wives turn his heart from God. Solomon suffered great loss, and was not listed with his father, David, in Hebrews."

When Paolo finished, he turned to Solomon who was experiencing a horrible nightmare.

God was speaking to Solomon in harsh tones, "I summon heaven and earth to witness against you this day. I offered you the choice of life or death, blessing or curse. I offered you life that you and your descendants would live. I offered you the length of days on the soil which were sworn to be given to your forefathers, Abraham, Isaac, and Jacob."

Paolo turned back to Cassy. "You see, Cassy, throughout the ages, we have all been given a chance at life. With every decision, we have been given the option to choose life or death."

Paolo and Cassy returned to the Holy of Holies, but this time the Ark of the Covenant had vanished. The golden room was completely empty save the curtain still hanging to protect the dwelling place of God from the potential wrath of the people.

Paolo continued, "When King Solomon died in 925 B.C., the Ark of the Covenant was hidden away with the Urim and Thummim, and Zadok was told to guard them, but the Temple was destroyed by the Babylonians in 587 B.C. A second temple was built on the same site of the Temple Mount in 520 B.C., but this Temple was destroyed by the Romans in 70 A.D. All the while, the Ark and the Urim and Thummim were hidden in secret tunnels that extended out from the Dome of the Rock, the site of King Solomon's original temple. The Ark of the Covenant and the Urim and Thummim survived the destruction of both Temples for more than a thousand years.

"Eventually, they were unearthed by a group of Cistercian Monks founded by Saint Bernard of Clairveaux and a man named Hughes, the Count of Champagne, in 1110 A.D. in the Al Aqsa Mosque on Temple Mount. Hughes and nine others founded the Knights Templar and renamed the Al Aqsa Mosque, the Temple of Solomon, because it was built on Jerusalem's Temple Mount on top of the ruins of the original temple. After 2,000 years, the Knights Templar decided to move the Ark of the Covenant and the Urim and Thummim to a new secret location."

"Where?" Cassy asked.

"Let's go," Paolo said.

*

Paolo explained why the Ark of the Covenant and the Urim and Thummim had to be moved while he and Cassy flew through time and space. "In the early 1300s, King Philip IV of France blackmailed the Knights Templar for money by falsely accusing them of numerous offenses. Jacques de Molay, the Grand Master of the Knights Templar, moved the Ark of the Covenant and the Urim and Thummim to France and hid them in another secret location for fear that they might be uncovered and seized. Molay was burned at the stake, but not before he knew they were in the safe hands of Charles de Molay, his son. They were brought to the new world in the 1500s, and separated and hidden in two locations by a secret religious organization created by the Huguenots called the 'Keepers of the Sacred Secret.'"

"Where did the Keepers of the Sacred Secret take the Urim and Thummim?" Cassy asked.

"To Canada," Paolo replied. "Samuel de Champlain, who founded the Quebec colony, was a secret agent for the society. The Urim and Thummim was moved to Montreal by the Compagnie du

Saint Sacrement and given to a woman named Marguerite Bourgeoys who was entrusted by God to build the first stone chapel of Montreal called the Notre Dame de Bon Secours. The Notre Dame de Bon Secours was built to house the Urim and Thummim because God would only entrust this task to a person of the lineage of the great high priests of the time of King David. You see, Marguerite Bourgeoys was a distant relative of Zadok, the last of the high priests of Israel and the Temple of Solomon."

Cassy and Paolo touched down on the ground of the cobblestone streets of Montreal. They stood next to 400 Saint Paul Street East where Cassy gazed upon the Notre–Dame–de–Bon–Secours Chapel, its high steeple a beacon to those on boat; its quaint stone outer walls, prayerful serenity for those who lived nearby. Cassy and Paolo entered the chapel and descended the stairs to the basement. The foundation of the basement was broken and old with little grave stone markers showing where Hospitallers had been buried when they contracted disease from the soldiers they treated in 1734.

"Fire destroyed the first chapel," Paolo explained, "but it was rebuilt in 1771. Marguerite knew that the wooden statue of Notre–Dame–de–Bon–Secours would not perish in the flames because it housed the precious Urim and Thummim. It was nearly two hundred years later when Marguerite's ancestor discovered the Urim and Thummim in the wooden statue and brought it to me for guidance. Cassy, you witnessed this man come to my confessional with the Urim and Thummim," Paolo said.

"Yes, I remember. The confessional could not contain the great power and light of the Urim and Thummim," Cassy responded.

"This man and his family tried to keep the Urim and Thummim safe," Paolo began, "but it was only a matter of time before it fell into the wrong hands. Our mission was to keep it safe even if it meant giving our lives. That is just what happened to this family. They gave their lives, and now we have to make sure that their lives were not lost in vain. We must retrieve the Urim and

Thummim before it is too late."

*

When Dr. Albert Townsend descended the stairs of the commuter plane that had taken him from Sarajevo to Medjugorje, he felt the heat of the sun sweep across his face and up the front of his sweat–stained shirt. It had been a long trip to the Federation of Bosnia and Herzegovina near Croatia. Townsend was exhausted, but he felt more free and serene than he had in months. He had come here to pray and ask for God's forgiveness. He had come here to make a life–changing decision.

Townsend retrieved one piece of rolling luggage from the terminal carousel and walked outside to hail a taxi. As he drove through Medjugorje, Townsend realized there must have been a time when the little city had been nothing more than desert and dust fields. Mary, the mother of God, had appeared here and many miracles had ensued causing it to boom into a small city where millions of people traveled to find miracles of their own.

When the taxi pulled up to Townsend's hotel, the Hotel Villa Regina, the white of the building appeared to glow against the blue of the sky. Townsend paid the driver, took his bag, and stepped onto the curb wondering how his life could have changed so quickly in one day. He took in a long breath of warm air and stood in front of the hotel without moving. There was a beautiful white statue of Mary standing in a large courtyard near the hotel.

Townsend couldn't believe he was standing in the middle of one of the most religious centers in the world. If someone had told him thirty years ago when he had bought his first abortion clinic that he would be making a pilgrimage to Medjugorje to pray to the Blessed Mother for guidance, he would have laughed right in their face. It was a funny thought, but Townsend didn't feel like laughing. Townsend checked into his room and splashed water on his unshaven face before he headed downstairs for a drink before dinner. He wanted to try to relax and settle down for a nice meal because he knew it was going to be a long night.

Townsend planned it out the day before. While he waited for his flight, he bought a rolling bag and other essentials for the trip, but he couldn't remember if he had even thought to buy a clean pair of underwear. Townsend packed a large leather–bound bible, a prayer book on how to pray the rosary, and a set of wooden rosary beads with the words, "Made in the Holy Land," of Jerusalem on the back of the crucifix. That was it. He hadn't remembered to buy a razor, and God knew he needed a good shave.

"Who cares?" Townsend thought. "God doesn't care what I look like."

Townsend glanced at his reflection after he toweled off his damp face. He saw a man he didn't recognize anymore. Uncombed and disheveled gray hair. Red puffy eyes. Suit coat and pants wrinkled beyond recognition. This was not the neat and polished Dr. Albert Townsend of Washington D.C. This was not the multi–millionaire father of two, grandfather of six, and husband to trophy wife number three that every man envied.

Townsend set the towel down on the side of the marble sink and leaned over the vanity. He closed his eyes and cried softy into the sink, his body shaking with the torment of the last thirty years.

"Help me, God! I can't do this anymore!" Townsend cried as he pushed his back against the bathroom wall and let his body slide down to the tiled floor. He sat with his head in his hands and cried with awakened conscience and guilty despair.

When Townsend woke from where he had fallen asleep on the bathroom floor, the daylight hours had already passed and the hotel room was completely dark. He rose unsteadily, his limbs completely stiff, his head a cloudy mess from all the crying. His mouth was so parched, he felt like his body had been completely drained of all fluid.

Townsend turned on all the lights in the room, opened the wet bar refrigerator, and pulled out a large bottle of cold water. He

LESA ROSSMANN

drank the entire bottle in one drink, and walked over to the sliding glass doors to a little veranda outside. The fresh air breeze hit his face and awakened him. He felt as if he weren't alone, as if God or Mary were present to help him through his agony.

Townsend left the veranda door open and walked over to his luggage to retrieve his bible, his rosary prayer book and his rosary beads. He brought them over to a couch and coffee table near the sliding glass door. The best way to start a conversation with God was to let God go first. He picked up the bible and said, "God, please tell me what to do." He opened the bible to a random page and put his index finger on a random paragraph.

Townsend had opened to the Book of Psalms, and his finger pointed to the words, "But you are at my side with your rod and your staff that give me courage." He turned a page and read exactly where his finger rested again. "Wash me, and I shall be whiter than snow...Give me back the joy of your salvation." He turned again toward the back of the bible. When he opened it, his finger pointed to one sentence and the words brought more comfort than salvation itself. "Here is your mother. Here is your son."

Townsend knew the words were spoken by the crucified Christ to Mary, his mother, and to John, his apostle. They were intended to unite Mary to the rest of humanity, so that she could become our spiritual mother, and we, her spiritual children. Townsend also knew that God was speaking to him directly. Only God could have known that his mother had died when he was only three. Only God could have known that his father remarried a cold woman who preferred to be called, "Jane," and not "Mother." Until now, Townsend had never known a mother. He never knew that Mary, the mother God, was his mother, too.

Townsend set down his bible and picked up his rosary book and his wooden set of rosary beads. "Please, dear God. Please, Mary. Help me discover the truth. Help me learn that abortion is wrong. Give me the strength to give it up, to sacrifice the money, to find a career more worthy. Please, dear God, help me, please."

When Townsend picked up the rosary book and beads, he meant to say just one rosary, but it was near morning when he realized he didn't have the strength to pray any longer. He had said nearly ten rosaries: the "Joyful Mysteries," the "Sorrowful Mysteries," the "Glorious Mysteries," and the "Luminous Mysteries," at least two of each of these and more, but his voice felt so weak, he could barely speak. He rose from the couch with his wooden rosary beads dangling from his right hand and placed them under his pillow. Then, he laid down on the bed and fell into a deep, peaceful sleep.

When Townsend woke ten hours later, he felt refreshed and rejuvenated beyond reckoning, as if his 58–year–old body had turned thirteen again. He yawned, stretched, smiled and sat up. He wanted to say one more rosary before he took a shower and went down to the dining room, but when he looked under the pillow, Townsend's eyes opened wide with disbelief. He picked up the rosary and held it close to his eyes in the light. The wooden rosary beads had turned to 24–karat gold. God and Mary had indeed sent him a message of truth, and tears of joy welled in his eyes and dropped down his cheeks. Townsend set down the golden rosary on the coffee table next to the opened bible and started toward the bathroom. He smelled the lovely scent of lilac as he walked into the bathroom to shower with renewed purpose.

*

At this point, the only research that mattered to Michael and Linda was to discover what the Urim and Thummim was and where the Urim and Thummim was located. They felt it was best to work independently since two minds were always better than one. Michael utilized the internet and library at Saint Michael's in Lake Geneva where he could stay close to Father Mac in case he had any questions. Linda chose to do her research at Marquette University's library. They would communicate via cell phone.

Michael sat at Father Mac's desk going over everything they had already learned about the Urim and Thummim on the web. He stared at the familiar image of Aaron wearing his ornate breastplate with three rows of four stones totaling twelve. Michael paid particular interest to the twelfth stone, the jasper, the same stone that was used to make bloodstone with the blood of Christ. Again, the number twelve seemed so vital, but he had no idea how "12" would help them find the Urim and Thummim on 01/22/13 or the date they would discover its location.

Michael continued scanning the documents on the Urim and Thummim. The Hebrew translation, "lights and perfections." Another translation, "revelation and truth." Priests used the Urim and Thummim "in the casting of lots." They used it as a medium to communicate with God. A divine oracle. Perfect light. Perfect illumination. Inerrable revelation.

Michael had seen these same definitions in fifty different documents. It was all the same, and he was running out of time. He clicked link after link, but the same texts kept coming up. Michael needed to take a break, so he pulled himself from the computer and stared at the stack of books on Father Mac's desk. His priest friend was an avid reader, no doubt. There were stacks of books on the desk and floor, and floor to ceiling shelves with hundreds of books on those, too. He rose from the desk and walked over to one wall of books and then the other.

Father Mac had rows of theological books. Books on philosophy, anthropology, science, you name it, he had them. Michael noticed fictional books, too. There was Shakespeare, Hemingway, Poe, Austin, Tolkien, and Lewis. He smiled when he saw that Father Mac had Stephen King on one of his shelves, too. Father Mac had his own public library at Saint Michael's Church. Michael walked back to the first set of books, the ones that pertained to theology and one book caught his attention immediately. It read, "Urim and Thummim: A Masonic Legend."

"What is this?" Michael said under his breath. He opened to the index and saw that most of the chapters highlighted the story of how the Knights Templar had recovered the Urim and Thummim, one of the artifacts taken from Solomon's Temple. According to legend, the Urim and Thummim and other recovered treasure were placed back in the temple treasury. Michael had read something about this theory before. He scrolled down the list of chapters with his finger and when Michael saw the last chapter, the title caught his eye. It said, "Urim and Thummim: The Christ Stone."

*

As soon as Michael googled "Christ Stone," a link came up for James Goodrich and a paper he had written called, "The Christ Stone." Goodrich's web address was bibleprophet.com. He clicked on the link and was immediately staring at an image of the "Christ Stone"—a flat rock with a gold lion crouched next to a gold tree with a snake. The lion had fiery, red eyes and looked like he was angrily growling at observers. Michael scrolled down and began reading the introduction:

"The artifact that I have in my possession is a flat oval jasper stone covered on top with a sheet of gold. And on this golden floor springs up the Tree of Life, and in the tree is a Serpent. Next to this tree is the couchant positioned Lion of the tribe of Judah. There are also seven eyes on this stone, including the jeweled sapphire eyes of the Lion."

Michael noticed there was only one date recorded in Goodrich's findings—June 4, 2001. He wondered if the Christ Stone were still in Goodrich's possession after all these years. Michael also saw several references to the meaning of the various symbols of the Christ Stone. Goodrich said that the base was made of jasper because jasper refers to the New Jerusalem of the Book of Revelation. The Tree of Life is also a reference to the New Jerusalem, and the serpent represents Satan who is eventually cast out of heaven. The most important symbol is the golden Lion, the symbol of the tribe of Judah because this is the kingly symbol of Jesus Christ.

Michael scanned down through the scriptural references. As soon as he saw the words, "Urim and Thummim," he stopped and read:

"The artifact that I possess is the Christ Stone of scripture also known in ancient Israel as the Urim and Thummim. It is the Holy Grail of legends. I will provide information regarding the qualities of the Holy Grail. It will become evident from these qualities that the legend involves stone, metal and a tree, all of which are the elements of the Christ Stone."

Michael read through more scripture passages and saw a chart of the comparisons between the Urim and Thummim and the Christ Stone: small object not made with other items of the priesthood; one object made of three components: jasper stone base, a tree and water, which are the two elements that make up jasper, and metal engraving, priestly oracle, gold rampant lion, tree and serpent.

The next paragraph described how the Christ Stone or Urim and Thummim came into James Goodrich's possession in Montreal. Goodrich said the artifact was given to his Canadian grandmother over fifty years ago. The man who gave it to her recognized her bloodline from her surname. She had French Huguenot ancestry and her maiden name was Godric, which means "power of God." The Huguenots created a secret religious organization called "Keepers of the Sacred Secret," and much has been written about the organization regarding the Holy Grail. However, it had never been revealed that the Holy Grail was actually the Urim and Thummim or the Christ Stone.

The last paragraph caught Michael's attention almost immediately:

"I believe whoever it was that gave the object to my grandmother must have known she was from this bloodline of the "Keepers of the Sacred Secret." I am now telling the story of the

Holy Grail to make it publicly known throughout the world. The word "mystery" in the Bible translates to "hidden thing." The hidden thing in the Old Testament was the Urim and Thummim hidden behind the breastplate of the high priest of Israel. In the end times, the Urim and Thummim of the New Testament will become the hidden thing that will be exposed to the just in order to save the world."

At the bottom of the page, Michael noticed one last line. It read, "Not all artifacts are dug out of the earth; some have passed through human hands unknown of their meaning, until the time of their discovery."

At this moment, Michael knew they would look for the Urim and Thummim or Christ Stone in Montreal, and that it had been made in heaven to be used for a miraculous purpose on earth.

CHAPTER THIRTY–FOUR

When Linda Walters left Marquette, it was a cold, windy day. Colder than they'd forecasted for Milwaukee this December. Regardless, she needed some air. She had spent the entire afternoon researching a possible connection between the Urim and Thummim and 1/22/13, but nothing came up. Nada. Zilch. Linda was so frustrated, she felt she couldn't think anymore. She had stared at a computer screen for four hours straight, and her brain felt like it was running on empty.

Linda stepped out onto the sidewalk and walked north toward the center of the city. The wind caught the long, red curls of her hair and flipped them up into the air. She wore a brown, faux–fur coat over an oversized turtle neck sweater, and washed–denim blue jeans with worn, brown cowboy boots.

With every passing block, Linda's mind cleared, and her cheeks flushed rosy from the cool wind that stung her face. She put her hands in her jacket pockets and continued to enjoy the fresh air while she walked.

A half hour later, Linda stood in front of the Cathedral of Saint John the Evangelist on the corner of Jackson and Wells. The aged green hue of the Cathedral dome contrasted with a single, silver cross that seemed to point toward heaven.

"That's it," Linda thought. "I'll go inside for a quick prayer. That'll recharge my batteries."

Linda crossed the street and turned right on Wells to the church's right side entrance. She glanced quickly at her watch. It was just passed three o'clock, which gave her about an hour to get back to Marquette before sunset.

Linda entered the "Domus Dei" door of the Cathedral and saw a large bulletin board on the left side of the vestibule. There were posters of men of all ages studying for the priesthood. The bottom showed a portrait of the men who were most recently ordained through the Archdiocese of Milwaukee.

Linda pushed through the door of the Cathedral and came upon the magnificent crucifix suspended twenty–eight feet above the altar. She walked around to the front and got down on one knee to genuflect.

An older woman with long, graying hair walked in front of Linda as she stood.

"Hello. Is this your first time to the Cathedral?" the woman asked.

"No, I'm a student at Marquette," Linda responded. "But it's been years since I've been inside."

"Beautiful, isn't it?" the woman continued. "They finished the renovation in 2002. See the chairs on the altar? They reconstituted the rose marble from the communion rail to make those. Same thing with the baptismal font in the back. Same rose marble was used there, too."

Linda turned to look at the chairs on the altar and the font in the back. "It is beautiful!" she exclaimed. "The altar is more extraordinary than anything I have ever seen," Linda added as she turned back toward the altar.

A huge crown of thorns hung suspended above Jesus' head. The crown was made of jagged fiber glass clad in copper, and a long copper cross ran diagonally behind Jesus' back. A bronze Jesus was suspended in front of the cross with his arms outstretched and his feet pinned together by the force of the dagger running through them. In fact, there were four large daggers that pointed their sharp spikes into Jesus' body: one in each hand, one in his side, and one sticking up through both of his feet. The five wounds of Christ. A golden dove appeared in Jesus' right hand.

"That dove symbolizes the Holy Spirit," the elderly woman said. "In Saint John's Gospel, the crown of thorns transformed into a crown of glory as Christ, lifted up on the cross, drew all humanity with him into the heavenly kingdom. In death, Christ handed over his Spirit, symbolized by the dove in his right hand in order to establish the Church."

The elderly woman put her hand on Linda's shoulder. "It's nice to see young people in the church again," the woman said. "Go ahead, my daughter, sit here in front of the altar and pray." She gestured toward a seat in the front row and disappeared through the door that Linda had just entered.

Linda sat and reflected on what the woman had told her. She noticed someone sitting in one of the chairs to her right. He looked like a homeless man dressed in black with the hood of his sweatshirt covering his head and face. He was slumped forward resting his elbows on his knees.

Linda continued to pray in front of the altar when she noticed another homeless person to her left. This person was also dressed in black, but was lying down on his side, taking up two or three seats.

Again, Linda turned her attention back to the altar, but she could see more and more homeless people sitting to her left and right out of the corner of her eye. She felt her heart beat faster as more and more homeless people appeared.

Linda felt light–headed, as if the weight of those suffering in homelessness became too much for her. She tried to focus on the crucified Jesus with his arms outstretched holding onto the dove, the beautiful symbol of the Holy Spirit, but the more she prayed, the more it seemed like the large crown of thorns over Jesus' head began to spin. Slowly, at first, but then the spinning was reeling faster and faster.

Linda figured she must be seeing things, so she blinked to clear her vision. When she opened her eyes, the crucifix continued to spin faster and faster. In fact, with every passing rotation, the homeless people appeared to rise from their seats from either side of the aisle toward the altar. Two by two, they climbed the altar stairs and stood underneath the suspended crucifix with its spinning crown. The crown produced a great wind like a large fan suspended in mid–air above the altar, and the homeless stood with their hair blowing in the wind. The revolving crown of thorns was moving so quickly that the sound in the church was like a great typhoon.

Linda placed her hands over her ears to stop the sound, but nothing deafened it. She wanted to run away, but her legs felt like dead weight. She felt paralyzed. The wind became even louder as more homeless people filled the altar space.

Just when Linda thought she might faint, she heard a crack of lightning above her head and a blinding light came from on high. As she held up her arm to shield the light from her eyes, Linda heard a deafening crash that sounded like the altar had just cracked in two. And then there was complete silence.

The church had grown completely dark and all the homeless had vanished, but there was one who remained on the altar. Not a homeless person, however. It was a baby. Linda saw a tiny newborn child lying on the altar with his side pierced through by the point of the crucifix, which had come down from behind Jesus' suspended body. The heavy crown of thorns had stopped spinning and floated motionless above Jesus' body. Now, the only movement came from this injured child who looked as if he were trying to pick himself up from the weight of the dagger–like cross. He made little sounds as if he were suffering. As if he were suffering from the weight of the world in that single dagger.

To Linda's disbelief, the child was able to sit upright even with the weight of the dagger still embedded in his side. He looked directly at Linda and smiled. She could read his mind.

"Do not have pity on me," he said. "Have pity on yourselves."

A drop of blood hung from the corner of the baby's mouth and trickled down his chin. Linda sobbed as she watched the infant in his agony, but he lovingly reassured her.

"Do not weep for me, Linda. Weep for yourselves for the time has come."

Linda felt a tear run down her cheek. She looked down to watch the tear fall, but it turned red when it hit the floor and separated into lighter shades like spattered blood.

When Linda looked back up, the dying infant had disappeared and the crucifix and crown of thorns hung motionless just as they had before. In shock, Linda sat for several seconds before she realized she must have imagined all that had transpired because of stress and exhaustion. She needed fresh air now more than ever. She quickly rose and exited from the back, and wound around to the prayer garden on the other side of the Cathedral.

In the garden, Linda stopped before a large white statue of Blessed Pope John Paul II on her right. All at once, she felt a wave of calm hit her, and she realized how much the strange episode in the cathedral had affected her emotionally. Linda felt her heart slow its pace as she felt peace. She had a duty to help Debbie, and she would not let her down.

Linda felt more resolve than she had in months. She said a quick "Hail Mary" and turned to walk back to Marquette when something caught her attention to her left. Linda saw a man dressed in black standing behind the glass door in the building adjacent to the garden. It was him. The man in black she had feared was following her for so long.

As quickly as possible with no time to think, Linda sprinted out of the garden toward Wells Street. She made a left onto Wells and looked behind her to see the man in black only a block away. Linda increased her pace and crossed over Van Buren just in time to see a black and white striped awning on her left with a sign that read, "Buckley's Kiskeam Inn." She took a chance and ran toward the black painted door to hide among the tavern patrons.

Linda pushed hard against the door and immediately entered into the bar's twilight dark ambiance. It took a couple of seconds for her eyes to adjust and focus. Linda walked up a small flight of stairs past the bar to the back of the room and sat at an empty table in the corner. She could feel her heart racing a mile a minute and her breathing came in heavy pants of air.

"Linda, is that you?"

Linda's head jerked up toward the sound of a familiar voice from Marquette. It was a young man with wavy blonde hair and electric blue eyes she had taken history classes with at school. She felt a sigh of relief as she looked up to see her friend, Blake Baldwin, standing near another table.

"Hi, Blake," Linda said. She looked back toward the door as she greeted her fellow student and noticed the man in black enter the bar. His eyes were darting back and forth as he looked for her. Linda's heart sank as the familiar feeling of fear hit her again.

"You okay?" Blake walked over to Linda and his 6'4" frame conveniently hid her from her perpetrator.

"Not really. Listen, Blake, can you do me a favor and keep standing there? Please, don't look back, but right now a horrible man is following me and just walked in. He's looking for me right now, but you're blocking his view so he can't see me," Linda spoke in a very hushed voice.

Blake leaned in close to Linda, "Do you want me to do something about this, Linda? If you want, I am fully prepared to knock him on his sorry ass." Blake's face was turning red with anger as he spoke.

Linda saw the man in black come up the stairs toward the tables in the back where she sat. He had not spotted her, but it was obvious he was looking for her.

Linda turned back to Blake as an idea quickly hit her. "Kiss me," she said. "Pretend we're making out and kiss me so he doesn't see me."

Blake leaned down and kissed Linda passionately with his left arm around her head to hide the obvious red of her long hair.

To David Bloodstone, it looked like another college couple in need of a real job. "Get a room," David thought as he took in the bar one more time before he turned to leave.

When Blake pulled away from Linda, she looked up just in time to see David exit the door. Blake turned to look, but all he caught was the black of the man's ponytail as he walked out the door. Linda breathed a sigh of relief, and Blake sat down next to her.

"Do you want to tell me what that was about?" Blake asked.

Linda looked at her friend and shook her head.

Blake had never seen this much fear in any person before. "You need a drink," he said and got up and walked to the bar. "Two martinis," Blake said to the bartender. "And make them both doubles."

Blake returned carrying two martinis with huge green olives pierced by little plastic swords. He placed one in front of Linda who sat motionless, her head slumped forward as if she were dazed and exhausted from fear.

Linda looked up at Blake and smiled. "Thanks," she said.

"No problem. You look like you could use a pick me up." Blake leaned forward, his expression a mix of seriousness and concern. "Linda, I know you don't want to talk about who that guy is and what he wants with you, but if you need anything, anything at all, I'm here for you."

Linda took a large sip of her martini, and smiled at Blake. She was finally starting to breathe again. This was exactly what she needed. Normalcy. No more scary, dark men following her trying to hunt her down. No more weird illusions in cathedrals. No more inexplicable bloodstone cameos with magical powers.

Linda took another sip of her martini before she spoke. "Blake, do you remember Debbie Romano? From school?"

"You mean the girl you used to room with, right?" he asked.

"Yes. She had a nervous breakdown not too long ago. Wound up in a hospital and recently went missing. I have reason to believe the tall, scary guy, the one who just left, had something to do with her disappearance. That's why he's after me. He knows I'm onto him."

Blake placed his hand on top of hers. "Shouldn't we contact the authorities?" he asked.

"They've already been contacted. A detailed description of the man was given to them, and they haven't been able to locate him or Debbie."

"We should contact them right now!" Blake exclaimed. "He just walked out the door of a popular drinking establishment in the middle of Milwaukee. That's got to count for something."

"I don't think it will do much good," Linda replied. "Blake, this guy has been like the invisible man. One minute he's here, the next minute he's vanished."

"Come on, Linda. Are you telling me this guy is some sort of ghost? Please. It just sounds like he's had the upper hand for too long, and that won't last. He'll get caught one way or another. One wrong move, and that's that." Blake clapped his hands together as if he were squashing a bug. "Do you know whether Debbie's okay?"

"No. All I know is that man is probably one of the most dangerous men on the planet and Debbie is in with him deep." Linda's eyes welled up with tears at the thought of not knowing whether her friend was dead or alive.

Blake squeezed Linda's hand and smiled warmly. "How 'bout one more round?" he asked and was already on his way to the bar before she could answer.

*

When Linda glanced at her watch, it was already five o'clock and nearing sunset. She thanked Blake and got up from her chair to leave.

"Are you sure you don't want me to walk you back?" Blake asked worriedly.

"I'll be okay. Promise." Linda crossed her heart and smiled. "Thanks for the drinks. I'll see you at Marquette."

Linda reached the door and opened it hesitantly. A gust of cold air hit her in the face and renewed her strength. When she stepped outside, the sun had already begun its descent over Lake Michigan. Linda looked both ways to make sure there were no tall, dark figures in the distance. Seeing no one in particular, Linda decided to venture toward the lake.

"Besides, the Calatrava is supposed to be open late on Fridays, and I'm only a couple of blocks away," Linda thought. "I can always grab a cab back to Marquette later."

The Milwaukee Art Museum, known as "The Calatrava," was named after the famous modern architect, Santiago Calatrava. He designed the Quadracci Pavilion with the Burke Brise Soleil, which looked like a large white metal bird with a Boeing 747 wingspan. The Soleil had two ultrasonic sensors that automatically closed the wings if the wind speed reached more than twenty–three miles per hour in order to keep the Museum on the ground.

Linda had the Calatrava clue in the back of her mind, but the Museum was also scheduled to carry an exhibit of rare historical significance and she wanted to do research for an upcoming "History of Artifacts" class paper. With all of the research she had been doing on bloodstones, she had been slacking in her studies and her grades were beginning to show it. This was exactly the kind of break from reality that Linda needed.

Linda crossed over Marshall and looked over her shoulder to make sure that no one was following her. No one. She crossed over Wells onto Prospect toward the Cudahy Tower. There were glass walls and Linda thought she might have caught a glimpse of a dark figure. She looked again. No one. She must have imagined it.

"Oh, what stress will do to you," Linda thought. "Back to reality and on to the Calatrava."

Linda moved quickly across Prospect and turned right toward the museum. The sun was setting fast now and her pace quickened as she passed the sign for the Juneau Park entrance. She looked back over her shoulder toward the park path and saw a tall, dark figure in the distance. It was him. David stood looking directly at her about a hundred yards up the path.

All time stopped. Linda's fear was so intense that a wave of electricity shot up her back. She wondered if her feet would move or if they would stay glued to the sidewalk. What seemed like hours passed while Linda's eyes met David's. She felt as if she were looking at the devil, himself. This time, a wave of terror ran through her so great that nausea came with it. Linda wanted to vomit, but her sense of survival kicked in first. She ran toward the orange, steel sculpture in front of the Milwaukee Art Museum and the Coast Restaurant in the Miller Brewing Company Pavilion.

Without thinking, Linda turned left and rounded the corner in front of the sculpture. She looked behind to see David closing the gap between the two. Linda made a bolt for the suspension bridge in front of her that led to the Calatrava entrance. She ran as fast as she could over Lincoln Memorial Drive. Linda could tell by the sound of David's footsteps that he was running, too, and his footsteps were getting closer.

Linda reached the glass elevator of the museum and hit the "down" button without thinking. She looked behind and saw David half way across the bridge running toward her. Linda turned back to the elevator. It was directly above her making its way down to her level just as David passed to her side of the bridge. Linda heard the sound of a "ding" and the elevator doors opened before her. She raced inside as quickly as possible and pushed the button for the main floor and the button to close the doors almost at once.

When Linda raised her head, the man in black was only a few feet from the elevator with his right hand raised to stop the door from closing. Out of fear, Linda repeatedly pushed the close door button as she looked into his menacing eyes. The doors miraculously shut just in time, and Linda could see David's fingers through the center opening, but they disappeared as the elevator began its descent to the main floor. Linda felt such relief, her eyes filled with tears.

As soon as the elevator opened onto the main floor, Linda bolted for the women's public restroom next to the museum entrance. She chose the stall furthest from the door and closed and locked it behind her. She threw the lid down on the toilet seat and hoisted herself up on top of the seat into a squatting position so that no one would be able to see her feet under the stall. When Linda heard loud footsteps enter the women's restroom, she stopped breathing so no one could hear her.

"Excuse me!" Linda heard a woman's voice call out loudly from the bathroom entrance. "Excuse me, sir, this is the Ladies' Room. See the sign right here? It says L–a–d–i–e–s' Room?" The woman was chiding the man in black with apparent disdain for the opposite sex.

"Thank God for city women with big attitudes," Linda thought.

"My apologies," David responded to the museum employee. "A friend of mine who's sick just came in here and I was checking on her," he lied.

"I can appreciate that, sir, but rules are rules and you are not allowed in here. I would be happy to check on your friend for you, though. What is her name?" The woman's tone changed from obnoxious to slightly hostile and Linda could tell she didn't believe him.

The man in black responded quickly, "Linda. Linda Walters." David's voice was deep and edgy and a new wave of fear crawled up Linda's spine.

"Linda? Linda Walters?" The sound of the employee's shoes grew louder as she walked toward the last stall. "Your friend is here to check on you. Linda? Are you in here?" The woman stopped just outside of Linda's stall, and Linda stopped breathing entirely deciding that holding her breath was better than being captured by David. The woman waited for a few more moments, but when she realized that no one was in the bathroom other than her, she walked back out.

"I guess you were mistaken," the woman said to David. "She's not here. Now, if I could escort you out of the Ladies' Room, you can look for your friend elsewhere."

Linda waited with baited breath for David to respond. She heard him say, "Thank you," and then heard the click of his boots as he walked out of the bathroom.

A few more minutes passed, and Linda finally allowed herself to breathe again. She quietly sat on the seat of the toilet with her legs against the wall and pulled her cell phone out of her jacket pocket. Linda texted Michael two lines, "SOS. Man in black following me. Meet me at Calatrava, main floor, women's bathroom."

Linda waited for over an hour in the stall. At a quarter past six, she heard Michael's voice call for her outside the bathroom.

"Linda? Are you in there? It's Michael and I'm alone with no one in sight."

"Thank God!" Linda thought. She had been sitting on the toilet seat so long her legs were numb. Linda raced out of the bathroom and the feeling of pins and needles in her feet only quickened her pace.

"Michael!" Linda called as she ran to Michael. She was so caught up in relief, she wrapped her arms around his muscular back and embraced him warmly.

Michael was happy to hug Linda, but after a few moments, he held her at arm's length to get a glimpse of her face. "You okay?" he asked.

"Yes," Linda faltered for a few seconds and then added. "Now that you're here."

"What happened?"

"I was doing research at Marquette and needed a break, so I walked to the Cathedral."

"All the way from Marquette?"

"Yes, I needed the fresh air."

"I'll say," Michael said with great exaggeration.

"When I left Saint John's, I saw him in the courtyard and he started following me." Linda emphasized "him" and "he" with just enough disgust to let Michael know she was talking about the man in black. "I ducked into Buckley's on Wells to try to get away from him and hung out there for an hour. When I left the bar, there was nobody for miles, so I thought I'd walk here to do research. That's when he surprised me by the entrance to Juneau Park. I raced across the bridge and just made the elevator. All I could think to do was duck into a bathroom stall and hide."

"Did he know you were in here?" Michael asked.

"I think so. I don't know. I took the elevator. He apparently took the stairs. He must have seen me run into the bathroom and followed me in. Thank God a museum employee took him on." Linda looked so shaken that Michael grew more concerned.

"Listen, Linda. Let's assume he lost patience and left. He's just trying to scare us into quitting our search for Debbie. Are you hungry?"

Linda shook her head. "But I could use a hot tea. I'm chilled to the bone."

"Good. Let's relax in the museum café over tea. I hear the food is excellent and the prices are really affordable." Michael rolled his eyes and smiled as he put his arm around Linda's back and led her away from the Ladies' Room.

Michael had begun the night afraid, but his fear turned to anger in his quest to protect Linda.

CHAPTER THIRTY–FIVE

Linda Walters and Michael Murray sat in the Calatrava Museum Café sipping chai lattes. They were so busy discussing Linda's encounter with David Bloodstone that Michael had completely forgotten about his Christ Stone discovery.

"Linda, guess what? I found it," Michael announced.

"What? The Urim and Thummim?"

"Yes, except the Urim and Thummim is actually called the Christ Stone."

"You mean it really exists? And someone has it?" Linda was so excited she completely forgot about David Bloodstone.

"Yes, it exists. Yes, someone had it, but not anymore. However, they know where to find it."

"Where?"

"Montreal."

"We have to go to Montreal?"

"Yes."

"I'm game," Linda replied with a smile. "How soon can we leave?"

A half hour later, Linda and Michael walked out of the café when an idea suddenly hit her. "Let's look around for a couple of minutes before the museum closes at eight," she suggested. "I still think the key and address clues were on the Calatrava flier for a reason. Maybe the person wanted us to find something here. Besides, if I ever get back to my schoolwork, I have a paper due on antiquities."

Michael looked at Linda and shrugged his shoulders. "Fine with me," he said.

They went to the admission desk near the collection entrance to pay the fee, but when the employee looked at the clock and saw it was already past seven, he let them in for free. "You guys only have about an hour," he said. "Go ahead."

"Thanks," Michael and Linda said as they headed down the entrance ramp toward antiquities on the main level.

The entire right wall was made of glass, and Michael could see Lake Michigan glistening in the dark. He turned to Linda, "I can't believe how beautiful this place is on the inside. I mean, the outside is spectacular, but so is the inside."

"My favorite part is the location," Linda replied. "The best places are always built next to water."

Linda and Michael came to the end of the ramp and turned right at the Antiquities Exhibit. Before them was a large square exhibit with a glass wall surrounding all four sides. The exhibit was filled with mounds of sand as if they were trying to recreate an excavation site. There were several clay urns lying on top of the sand that looked like they had just been unearthed.

"Looks like a giant sandbox," Michael said with a mischievous smile on his face.

"Not quite. That's a Tophet burial ground. Not exactly a 'play place,'" Linda replied seriously. "Come on. Let's read the description."

Linda walked over to the large, white sign in front of the exhibit. She took a small notepad and pen from her jacket pocket. The title of the exhibit was, "Mexican Archaeologists Unearth Ancient Sacrifices."

"Interesting," Linda said. "It says here that 'objects found in the excavations in Ecatepec, Mexico, by archaeologists in 2004 of an ancient Aztec settlement are some of the first physical evidence to support the gory sacrifices depicted in a centuries–old Indian book of paintings known as a codex.'"

"Codex?" Michael asked.

"Yes. These are most often Indian pictorial texts," Linda replied. "A type of communication using pictures instead of words."

"Okay, but isn't sacrificial stuff just horror movie entertainment?"

"No, it really did exist, but everybody always thought that the Spanish were making the Aztec sacrifice numbers worse to make them look more barbaric and in need of proper Christian instruction."

Linda went back to the description: "In recent years archaeologists have been uncovering mounting physical evidence that corroborates the Spanish accounts in substance, if not number," Linda read out loud. "Using high–tech forensic tools, archaeologists are proving that pre–Hispanic sacrifices often involved children and a broad array of intentionally brutal killing methods. For decades, many researchers believed Spanish accounts from the 16th and 17th centuries were biased to denigrate Indian cultures, others argued that sacrifices were largely confined to captured warriors, while still others conceded the Aztecs were bloody, but believed the Maya were less so. 'We now have the physical evidence to corroborate the written and pictorial record,' said archaeologist Leonardo López Luján. 'Some pro–Indian currents had always denied this had happened. They said the texts must be lying.'"

Linda jotted something down in her notebook and continued, "There is no longer any doubt about the nature of the killings based on these findings. The codices describe multiple forms of human sacrifice. Victims had their hearts cut out or were decapitated, shot full of arrows, clawed, sliced to death, stoned, crushed, skinned, buried alive or tossed from the tops of temples. Children were said to be the most frequent victims, in part because they were considered pure and unspoiled."

"So these Aztecs were cannibals?" Michael asked.

"Yes and no," Linda answered. "I have read of bones discovered with butcher–like cut marks, but these remains were not necessarily cannibalistic. These remains were sacrificial."

Before Michael could ask another question, Linda moved to the next series of descriptions on the exhibit to her left. She took a minute to read quietly while Michael moved behind her to take a look. Linda pointed to some print, "It says here that in December of 2004 at an ancient Aztec site just north of Mexico City, archeologist Nadia Velez Saldaña found evidence of human sacrifice associated with the god of death."

Linda read directly from a quote written by Velez Saldaña: "The sacrifice involved burning or partially burning victims. We found a burial pit with the skeletal remains of four children who were partially burned, and the remains of four other children that were completely carbonized."

Next to the text written by Velez Saldaña, Linda saw pictures of urns that had been excavated at ancient Aztec burial sites. The urns looked like they were stuffed with ashes and small bones.

Linda pointed to the pictures. "These must have been the remains of the children who were sacrificed," she said.

Linda and Michael walked around to the next exhibit and saw similar urns placed on top of the sand.

To Michael, it looked like real ash and bone were contained in these urns, too. "Those aren't real human bones and ashes in those urns, are they?" he asked.

Linda looked carefully at the contents before she answered. "I don't think so. They look artificial to me." She looked again and saw a layer of plastic on top of the ashes and bones. "No, definitely not. See? Those 'urns' are made of plastic. For display only," she answered.

"Good. This exhibit is starting to freak me out," Michael said. He checked his watch. "We should think about leaving soon anyway. Almost closing time."

Linda moved quickly to the last exhibit. "Okay. I'll just make note of this last one."

When Michael reached her side, they saw pictures of ancient Aztec codices on the display. The first picture showed people being held down and burned alive. The second showed human body parts stuffed into cooking dishes with others sitting around eating while a depiction of the god of death looked on. The last picture was of a grotesquely costumed Aztec priest holding a child down to be sacrificed while the child was crying and screaming. The text next to the pictures read, "There is no longer any doubt about the nature of the Aztec killings. Indian pictorial texts known as 'codices' quote Indians as describing multiple forms of human sacrifice."

Linda jotted down some notes and looked up at Michael to let him know she was ready to go. They walked back around to the front of the exhibit toward the exit ramp when something in the sand caught Linda's eye.

Linda noticed a two–foot high block made of stone sticking out of the sand with markings engraved on it. It looked like an ancient burial marker called a "Tophet," but there was a striking symbol engraved in the middle of the marker. The symbol was a truncated pyramid topped with a rectangular bar, over which was depicted the Sun and the crescent Moon.

Linda made the connection almost instantaneously. She had seen that symbol before. "Oh my God," she whispered in shock.

"What is it?" Michael asked urgently.

"See that symbol on the grave marker?" Linda asked.

"Yes," Michael answered with no recognition.

"You've seen it before," she said.

Michael turned to Linda with a blank expression.

"That's the logo for PSI," she answered. "The logo on every

PSI abortion clinic across the country and around the world."

Linda started up the ramp when she heard Michael gasp. "No way," he whispered under his breath. "No way."

*

With the threats from the man in black behind her, Veronica felt less afraid with every passing day. She arranged for Tom to pick up the kids from school so she could visit Rebecca Gomez at Several Sources Shelter. She had purchased little newborn onesies and pajamas for Rebecca and couldn't wait to give them to her.

Veronica closed Turning Point early so she could have time with Rebecca and still make it back for dinner with Tom and the kids. Friday nights were sacred in the Blake home and had become their traditional "pizza nights." Several Sources was located about an hour from Bergenfield. Veronica checked her watch and realized she'd be there by 3:30 with plenty of time to be home by six.

Veronica preferred the Parkway to the Turnpike and decided it would be too early to hit commuter traffic anyway. She pulled out of the Turning Point parking lot and made her way across Bergenfield to Prospect Avenue. Veronica eventually took Oradell Avenue toward Paramus, which was considered the "mall capital" of the state. She saw the sign for the Parkway South and veered to the right to get onto the entrance ramp.

As Veronica drove off the ramp toward the Parkway entrance, she saw Paramus Park Mall on the right. "It's before three and the lot is already full?" she thought.

Veronica sensed a speeding car moving toward her from the side street on her right. She was only about five feet from the toll booth when the same car crashed into her passenger door at full speed. Veronica never expected her Volvo to do somersaults that day, but it did. Fortunately, she wore her seatbelt because her Volvo veered left and did two and a half somersaults just missing the oncoming Parkway traffic.

Veronica's Volvo landed on the shoulder of the highway, and she found herself caught upside down in her car, hanging from her seatbelt by her chest. Her only memory was the man in black walking toward her just before she blacked out.

*

Three months had passed since Cassy fell into a coma, but Drew was anything but depressed. Dr. Andrews saw so much improvement in the past few weeks, Drew knew she was on the verge of waking. In fact, Drew had become so close with Cassy's doctor, he called Dr. Andrews, Steve, and they occasionally lunched together.

When Drew met Steve for lunch the previous week, he was surprised to find out that Dr. Bernard Lanton's body had been discovered floating in the Hudson. Drew knew that he had been missing for weeks, but the fact that Cassy's psychiatrist was murdered never dawned on him.

"You think it was foul play?" Drew asked Steve.

"I don't think it was suicide if that's the other choice," Steve insisted. "I knew Lanton personally, and he wasn't exactly hurting in the egocentric category. Trust me, the guy loved himself."

"Do you think Cassy is in danger, too?" Drew asked worriedly.

"Lanton tried to harm Cassy and Lanton's the one with the enemies," Steve replied. "I think Cassy's been through the worst of it already. Every day's just going to get better for her."

When Drew saw Steve get off the elevator on the way to Cassy's room a few days later, they exchanged pleasantries. Drew spoke of the possibility that Cassy might be awake and healthy enough to go home for Christmas, which was now only a week away. "Wishful thinking is a good thing," he thought as he opened Cassy's door.

As usual, Drew's heart raced when he saw his wife. She was so utterly beautiful, she was almost heavenly. He noticed that her cheeks were rosy with color and her lips particularly red and full. Drew bent down to kiss her. "Hello, darling," he said to her peaceful face.

Drew put his keys in his coat pocket and felt a crumpled piece of paper. When he took it out and opened it, Drew remembered Nurse Bridget had given the note to him the last time he wore his overcoat. He had forgotten all about it.

The handwriting on the note was completely foreign to him, but it looked like it had been written in a man's sloppy script. It read, "Check Leviticus and Kings. Also Zephaniah. Let Elaina know I now have all I need to put the Taninsam ties together." The note was signed, "BL."

Drew's heart skipped a beat when he realized that Dr. Bernard Lanton had written the note and it was meant for Elaina Taninsam, Cassy's biological mother.

"And now Lanton is dead," Drew thought. "There is no way this is just a coincidence. I need a Bible, and I need it now."

Drew hurriedly kissed his wife "Good–bye" and grabbed his coat to leave. If Cassy was in some kind of danger, Drew wanted to find out the what and the who as soon as humanly possible.

*

When Michael and Linda left the Calatrava, they went for dinner at the Coast–A Zilli Restaurant in the Miller Brewing Company Pavilion. It was nearly midnight when they finished. Michael and Linda had spent most of the evening discussing the mysterious link between the Tophet sacrifices and PSI. They made plans to book tickets to Montreal to find the Urim and Thummim or Christ Stone as soon as possible.

There were a few other diners finishing dessert when they stood up to leave, but most of the activity centered around the bar. There was a band playing and several couples were dancing to a slow ballad underneath an illuminated globe.

On the spur of the moment, Michael took Linda's hand and led her onto the dance floor. Linda was tired, but she didn't object. He put his arms around her waist and pulled her close as they swayed back and forth to the sounds of a distant 80's tune. It was the first time Michael had been this close to Linda; the first time they had been anything more than friendly working partners.

When the song finished, Michael took Linda's hand again and led her out into the cold night air. They were caught up in one another, but neither said a word. Both seemed dazed and starry eyed. They were so exhausted they could have fallen asleep at the dinner table, but the attraction between the two was so visible it had become almost tangible.

It was well after midnight, but the two walked aimlessly. Suddenly, it didn't matter that Michael's car was still parked at the Calatrava and Linda's at Marquette. All that mattered was the moment. Ten minutes passed, and Michael and Linda stood before a hotel on the water called the "Hilton Milwaukee River Hotel." They were still holding hands when Michael led Linda to the entrance and inside the lobby. She waited off in the distance as Michael booked a room and handed over his credit card.

Linda felt her heart quicken with excitement and nervousness as Michael turned from the front desk back toward her. She realized, for the first time, how handsome he was: his beautiful, wavy black hair that fell over his big, soft brown eyes; his full lips and straight, white teeth; his broad shoulders and long, slender legs. For the first time since she'd met Michael, Linda realized she might be falling in love.

Michael extended his hand and Linda grasped it and allowed him to escort her to the elevator. She allowed him to guide her down a long hallway to Room 402 on the riverside of the hotel. Michael opened the door with an electronic key and turned on the lights. He opened the curtains to expose a beautiful view of the water from a sliding glass door.

Michael stood behind Linda as they gazed at the starry sky shining above an iridescent body of dark, wavy river water. When Linda turned, Michael pulled her close with a passion and force that was completely new to her. He placed both hands in her hair and moved her lips toward his. The kiss lasted for several minutes, but Michael and Linda needed no oxygen as long as they were breathing in each other.

Michael led Linda into the bedroom, and she allowed him to guide her to the edge of the bed where they stood and kissed passionately. It was as if time and space stood completely still. Linda felt so much love, she thought her heart might burst if she were to continue.

Suddenly with no explanation, Michael felt Linda's shoulders move up and down as if she were crying. He pulled her away and took her face into his hands. She was crying softly and little tears trickled down her cheeks. Michael pushed the tears away with his thumbs and looked at Linda with real concern.

She smiled at him with hesitation. "I can't," she said softly.

"I'm sorry," Michael replied.

"No. I wanted to…"

"What is it?"

"I…I think I'm in love with you," she replied.

"Completely okay," Michael smiled. "I'm in love with you, too."

"I know, Michael. I know. That's the problem." Linda walked into the bathroom and shut the door.

*

When Linda emerged a half hour later, Michael was sitting on the edge of the bed. Linda had never seen Michael look so young and boyish before. He seemed so worried, he looked almost scared. Linda took Michael's hand and led him out of the bedroom and back into the living room in front of the glass door overlooking the river. She closed the open door and motioned for Michael to join her on the couch.

"Michael, I need to tell you something important," she said.

"Okay," Michael said concerned.

"This might seem strange," Linda began, "but I'm still a virgin. I'm sort of saving myself for marriage. I mean, I love you. I really do. I never really thought of it before tonight, but when you rescued me at the Calatrava, my perception of you was somewhat altered. I had always thought of you as a friend. A really good, close friend. We work really well together, but I also looked at you as a "Lady's Man." You know, the kind of guy that plays the field. But then, you rescued me and took care of me. We had that wonderful dinner together, the romantic dance, and holding your hand and kissing you...I'm sorry." Linda looked down at the floor and tears welled up in her eyes.

Michael lifted Linda's chin with the tips of his fingers. "Linda, I love you. Probably since the first time I saw you at Champs, and definitely since you took me on what used to be your dad's boat." Michael took both of Linda's hands in his own. "I might have been a lady's man in the past, but to coin an old cliché, 'there comes a time in a man's life,' well, when a man has to grow up. All I know, Linda, is I love you, and if you want to wait for marriage, I want to wait for marriage right along with you."

What had started as a romantic evening, became more romantic when Linda fell asleep on the bed and Michael on the couch.

Michael dropped Linda at her car still parked at Marquette the next morning. So much had happened the night before, Linda almost forgot about what they had discovered at the Calatrava.

"Michael, I think there's a connection between David Bloodstone and the Tophet sacrificing. I have to admit that this connection is even more frightening than being chased into the Calatrava." Linda was nervously twirling her keys in her hand as she spoke.

"Then it's good we're leaving for Montreal," Michael replied.

"You're right. Let's leave tomorrow," Linda said.

Michael followed Linda back to Lake Geneva suddenly more concerned about his new love than a new lead.

CHAPTER THIRTY–SIX

When Veronica Blake woke up in a hospital bed at Holy Name Hospital in Teaneck, she felt like she could barely breathe and her right arm was in a cast from her shoulder to her wrist. She was trying to remember what happened to her, but when she tried to sit up, her chest and stomach muscles wouldn't let her.

"Why don't you let me do that for you?" Tom asked tenderly.

Tom pushed a button on the remote for the electronic hospital bed, and Veronica felt her body gradually move to a sitting position. He sat beside her while Peter, Grace and Father Raphael stood on the other side of the bed. All four looked so worried and relieved, Veronica felt like she couldn't handle all the emotion at once. She still didn't know why she was beat up and in the hospital in the first place.

"Where am I?" Veronica asked.

"The same place you gave birth to our two beautiful children," Tom replied. "Except this time you're not in the maternity ward."

"Holy Name?" Veronica asked again. "How did I get here?"

"The ambulance took you," Grace answered with tears in her eyes. "Oh Mommy, I'm so happy you're okay." She put her little hand on her mother's wrist as gently as she could.

"Ambulance?" Veronica couldn't remember a thing.

"You were in a car accident," Peter responded. "They found your car upside down. They said if you hadn't been wearing your seatbelt, you would have wound up with more than a dislocated shoulder and broken arm."

"Veronica," Father Raphael began, "a couple from the Marriott next to the mall said they saw the accident. They were the ones who called the police. They said the car that hit you accelerated into your Volvo as if the driver intentionally tried to cause the accident. Do you remember if this was the case?"

Suddenly, the entire accident came rushing back into Veronica's mind at full speed. She had seen the man in black, the same man who had threatened her and her family, come toward her toppled car. She knew who had caused the accident. She knew and she needed to tell Father Raphael and Tom the truth.

*

Jessica met Father Gabe near Fisherman's Wharf next to Ghirardelli Square at a cozy Italian restaurant called Café Pescatore. The Archbishop of San Francisco sat at the bar drinking a cold Sam Adams in his priestly blacks with his white collar loosened at the neck. When he saw her, he shouted, "Jessica!" and gave her a big, burly hug. "Ready for dinner? They just called our name for the table."

Jessica felt oddly relaxed considering she was about to divulge one of the most insidious crimes she had ever heard of, not to mention the man who committed them was her boss.

They sat at a window table overlooking the bay.

Father Gabe smiled, "Can I get you a drink?"

"Yes, thanks. A glass of Chardonnay." She smiled back warmly, dreading what she had to discuss.

Father Gabe ordered the wine, and they both ordered pasta before any conversation began. The friendly priest took another sip of his beer and said in a more serious tone, "So, what's been going on?"

"You sure you want to talk before dinner? This might ruin your appetite," Jessica replied seriously.

Father Gabe smile and patted his expanding waistline. "I need something to ruin this appetite," he said with a smile. "Seriously, Jessica. Whatever you have to say, just lay it on me. I've been around the world and back, and besides, you're a good person and I want to help you. You can trust me."

Jessica shared things with Father Gabe she wouldn't have told Jonathan: her biological ties to Elaina and the Taninsam family; her decision to leave the family to care for Cassy and Debbie; Debbie's adoption by the Romanos; and Cassy's coma coupled with Debbie's disappearance.

Jessica told him about her career opportunity in San Francisco and all of the successful research she had done in the field of adult stem cell research. She suspected Palmer of foul play as soon as she went to him about her research. "Why would a scientist be interested in a dead end field?" Jessica asked.

"Power, money, greed?" Father Gabe asked rhetorically.

"I was blindsided," Jessica responded back. "I was naïve enough to think that scientists were on the side of science."

"In my experience, no matter what the profession, there are the 'Jessicas' and there are the 'Palmers.' I'm also enough of a realist to hope there are more 'Jessicas' than 'Palmers.'"

Jessica couldn't help but chuckle under her breath. "Father Gabe, I need to tell you about a place called the JamBrax Fountain of Youth Spa. It's a luxurious spa located in beautiful Barbados where rich women travel to spend $25,000 for a treatment that consists of liquefied fetal tissues injected into their bodies, so they can feel refreshed and have their libidos enhanced."

A full minute passed before Father Gabe said anything. He rubbed his forehead and took another sip of his beer before he spoke. "This, I did not know," he said.

"The good news is I have all the incriminating evidence right here." Jessica opened up her purse and pulled out the flash drive with Palmer's copied documents on it. She waved it in front of Father Gabe with a smile, and he tried to think of some light hearted comment to come back with, but nothing came to mind. His heart had fallen somewhere into the pit of his stomach.

"That was a first," Father Gabe finally said.

"What?" Jessica asked.

"The first time I ever lost my appetite," he replied. This time, there was no joke intended.

*

The girl with green cat eyes bled for days after her procedure at the Milwaukee PSI clinic. At first, she thought something might be wrong, but when it stopped after a week, she felt better. The clinic told her to get a pregnancy blood test at a hospital a couple of weeks after the abortion. They said this was to make sure that all of the "tissue" had been removed. If the blood test came back negative, everything had been removed. They did not tell her what to expect if the test came back positive.

After her blood was drawn, she waited in a little room with white walls and no windows. She thought about the woman with silver hair. She thought about what it would be like to turn back time to before the procedure. She would have pushed away from the body guard and walked over to the woman. The woman would have embraced her and told her there were other options. Options that didn't involve killing. Options that would have given her a chance at a new life and the life of her newborn child. She would have turned back time to the morning when the silver–winged bird flew into the window. She would have left the sliding glass door open and the bird would have flown right into her bedroom. The bird would have landed on her bed and hopped up on her index finger and it would have let her pet its little silver head.

The girl with green cat eyes looked up from her chair as the nurse came back with her blood test results. The nurse said it was odd that her test was still reading positive for pregnancy. The hormone levels were lower, but she wanted the girl to come back again in two weeks just to make sure. The girl felt a bit shocked that her test still read pregnant. She wondered whether or not the baby was still alive after the procedure. She wondered if the baby was just so strong and healthy that nothing could kill it. This thought made the girl happy. She felt that God might be giving her another sign, another chance.

When she came back two weeks later the nurse drew her blood again. While she waited, she thought again of the silver–haired woman and the silver–winged bird. She was so excited about the prospect of new life still growing inside of her that she began to feel restless as if her heart were soaring. She had not felt happiness like this before. Before the procedure, she had felt only nervousness. Now she felt excitement. She had been given a second chance. The decision would be hers and hers alone. She would make it work.

The girl with green cat eyes heard the nurse coming. She smiled as she waited for the door to open. When the nurse entered the room, she was smiling, too. The nurse told her the results were much better this time. The test was reading negative, and there were barely any pregnancy hormones left in her system. She would not have to return for any more tests. The girl's smile stayed frozen on her face. She felt like her heart had dropped to the pit of her stomach. She found it difficult to swallow, but rose from the chair and thanked the nurse.

When she reached the hospital exit and stepped out into the cold winter air, she felt numb as if she were transfixed somewhere between space and time. She kept her ski jacket open and folded her arms in front of her waist. Her long dark hair flowed evenly behind her as she walked into the wind. She felt displaced like she had nowhere to go and no one who would want her once she got there. She walked aimlessly for over an hour not caring which direction she was going. She had no plan and no particular destination.

The girl with green cat eyes stood on top of the Hoan Bridge, a high rise bridge on 794 in Milwaukee. She felt the wind against her face as she continued to walk to the center of the bridge. When she reached the center, she stood near the edge and looked over the metal railing. She felt nothing except the wind. She climbed over the railing and stood on the edge. She was free. She thought of the silver–winged bird and how it had flown free, gliding through the air with its beautiful colored wings glistening in the sunlight. She spread her long arms wide and felt the soaring of what it must be like to fly like the silver–winged bird. In her mind, her feet became those of the little bird as she pushed off the edge and flew majestically through the air with fearless grace. The girl's mind was soaring high into the clouds while her body plunged to the ground below.

*

When Cassy saw Paolo standing next to her hospital bed, she knew it wouldn't be long before she woke. She saw Paolo through her spiritual realm, but there was very little difference between her perception of the spiritual and physical worlds. All she needed to do was blink her eyes, and she stood before Paolo ready to take flight and embark on another spiritual journey.

"Cassy, this is perhaps the most important journey we will take together before you wake," Paolo said.

"Where will we journey today?" she asked.

"A place we've already been, but one you'll not want to return."

At once, Cassy knew where they were going. She had often returned to it in her sleep, each time the nightmare of it growing like a destructive weed. Cassy had remembered the sight of it, the sounds of it, and the smell of it, so vile had it been. As Cassy remembered, the smell of burning flesh came flooding back into her mind.

Cassy would have preferred to remain airborne forever when they flew toward their destination. They landed and she stood on the dry and barren terrain trying to find her courage. Cassy did not need to be told where she had been taken. She saw the tall, bronze statue in the center of a great field with dry sand blowing in the high heat of a desert sun. The statue's hands extended out with its palms up and its arms sloped down toward the ground. The little fires on either side of the statue looked like low pits, and this time she knew what the fires consumed.

"Baal Hammon," Cassy said as she watched the sacrifice ritual from afar.

"Yes," Paolo replied sadly.

Cassy watched in horror as an infant slid down the arm of the bronze god. She winced as the child slipped into the fire pit below to his death.

"Child sacrifices to Baal Hammon, their god, and Tanit, their goddess," Cassy said.

"Yes," Paolo replied again.

When Cassy looked back on the scene, the father of another child ceremoniously handed his offspring to the waiting priest. Immediately, the child screamed and cried in the priest's arms. The priest chanted something, placed his thumb in a nearby urn, and painted colorful chalk on the child's forehead. The child was placed on the hand of Baal Hammon, and the sound of his cry filled the air with grief as he fell down into the waiting pit.

"Today, I will learn how Moloch, the god of death, was given life," Cassy said.

"Yes."

"Moloch collected sacrifices for himself in order that he might have human life. That is how Moloch became David Bloodstone," Cassy stated.

"Now you will witness this for yourself," Paolo said as they walked toward the pit.

*

This was the closest Cassy had ever come to the statue of Baal Hammon. She was surprised at how tall it stood, glaring down at her from more than twenty feet above. The immense bronze structure had the head of a bull and the body of a man. Inside the hollow statue was a large fire that made Baal Hammon appear to glow red.

Cassy watched robotically as infant after infant was ceremoniously placed on the hand of the statue and slid down screaming into the flames below. She felt like screaming herself, but she stayed strong and took a deep breath.

"He is Baal Hammon. The sacred bull," Paolo said.

"Why the head of a bull?" Cassy asked.

"Moloch took many forms as the 'Prince of Hell,'" Paolo replied. "He was a demon who found pleasure in making mothers weep and specialized in stealing their children."

Cassy looked at the statue and noticed that the eyes of the bull glowed green as the body glowed red with fire and burnt offerings. "Why are the eyes green?"

"The eyes are made with counterfeit bloodstones from the blood of Simon."

"The same Simon I saw perish when he fell to the ground in front of Nero and Peter and Paul?"

"Yes, those counterfeit bloodstones are becoming more powerful with each sacrifice. They have been sacrificing children to their false god all day, and the counterfeit bloodstones are almost powerful enough to bring Moloch to life."

"Moloch is about to come to life?" Cassy asked frightened.

"Do you see how the eyes glow more green with each sacrifice?"

"Yes, they are glowing stronger now than the red of the body."

"Exactly. It will not be long now. Prepare yourself, Cassy, this will not be easy to witness. You will be shocked at what you are about to see."

Cassy readied herself for the worst as the sun set and the light of day gave way to looming darkness.

With each infant sent into the flames of Baal Hammon, the glow of the bull's green eyes shined brighter and brighter. Suddenly, Cassy saw fumes of green gas escape from the bull's eyes and circle around its head into the air. She was so frightened, Paolo held her hand for support.

"Remember Cassy, we are not visible here. No one can harm you," Paolo said reassuringly.

Cassy looked back at the statue with the gleaming green bull's eyes. The wind was picking up and the green fumes were turning to mounds of smoke so thick, she could barely make out the image of the bull's head. It was as if a giant green cloud hung in the air with two intense rays of green light submerged within. The wind was blowing so hard now, Cassy felt her hair whipping around as she squinted her eyes to see. She gripped Paolo's hand tighter and tried to steady herself against the wind.

The people around the statue began to scream and moan. The painted priests who placed the infants on the sacrificial hands of Baal Hammon knelt in the wind and bowed down before their false god. They uttered loud incantations in a language Cassy could not understand. Those who beat drums during the sacrifices beat them louder and louder.

The mixture of incantations, screaming, drums, high winds, and green fumes became too much for Cassy. She wanted to cover her ears, but she did not want to lose her grip on Paolo's hand.

Suddenly, when Cassy felt she would not be able to endure one more second, the winds and fumes dissipated, and she thought she glimpsed a man floating above the bull's head. The man's arms were extended out to either side and his head hung down in sleep as he seemed to float on air. Cassy could see the man through the green mist. He was tall and handsome with long black hair. The man wore no clothes at all, as if he had just been created or born through the power of the sacrifice of innocents and the counterfeit bloodstones.

"Moloch, in human form?" Cassy asked.

"Yes," Paolo replied.

"Who...?" Cassy asked even though she knew his name.

"David Bloodstone," Paolo answered.

Just then, Moloch's body descended to the ground. When his feet touched the earth, he opened his eyes and smiled devilishly. Cassy felt her heart stop with terror. Moloch's eyes were glowing bright green, and he stared forward as if he were looking directly at her.

"Paolo..." Cassy began as she felt the terror shoot up her legs.

"He can't see you," Paolo answered quickly. "He is looking through us toward his mate. She is behind us."

Cassy turned her head and saw a beautiful woman walking past her from behind. The woman had long black hair and wore a long sheer black dress that blew behind her in the wind. Cassy could not see her feet, but she assumed the woman was barefoot as she moved toward Moloch.

All of the people were silent in shock and awe. They appeared dumbfounded. Should they rejoice in their god, now human, or should they cower in fear?

Neither seemed necessary since Moloch had every bit of his attention fixated on the woman moving toward him. The woman, too, seemed not to notice the people around her. Her eyes were on Moloch and Moloch, alone.

When she reached him, the woman stood before Moloch completely motionless in surrender. He took her in his arms so passionately it seemed he would devour her like an animal. The woman leaned backward and allowed Moloch to seduce her as he held her in his arms. She bent down to lift her dress and her long black hair fell forward onto Moloch's legs. When her dress came up, the woman did not have feminine legs at all. She had grotesque, hairy legs like a mule. Her legs and feet were like those of a dragon, and she possessed a long tail that moved at will as if it, too, had a mind of its own.

Cassy's stomach revolted as she watched the beastly woman remove her dress. She felt her mouth go dry as she tried to force a question out of her mouth. "Who is that?" Cassy finally managed to ask Paolo.

"Lilith, Queen of the Night, the Mother of Demons, and the Wife of Satan," Paolo replied. "Lilith and Moloch, or should I say, Lilith and David came together to produce an offspring of witches—witches who would one day be known as the Taninsam witches."

Cassy could feel herself lose consciousness in the spiritual realm. Her body fell backward and Paolo moved quickly to catch her.

It seemed no time had passed at all. Cassy was back on her hospital bed.

To Paolo, Cassy looked anything but peaceful, but he thanked God for the steady beat of her heart flashing across the monitor. For the first time in a long time, Paolo felt genuine fear. The shock of discovering her true ancestry had been too much for Cassy—too much for her frail body to handle. She had no idea what was still expected of her. She had no idea how vital a role she would play in the destruction of the bloodstone curse.

"Rest, dear one," Paolo whispered as he placed his hand on Cassy's forehead. "There will be one last journey, and then you will awaken with newfound strength."

CHAPTER THIRTY–SEVEN

Debbie Romano woke up in an expensively decorated apartment in Manhattan. She didn't know how long she'd been kept there against her will. David had come for her at the hospital in Milwaukee, but she remembered very little since. It seemed like weeks had gone by since her last recollection of consciousness as "Debbie Romano." This scared her beyond anything else. If she had become "Deborah" because of David and her bloodstone cameo necklace, she had no memory of it. She had to find out where she was and how to get out of there as quickly as possible.

Debbie lifted herself off the double bed of the guest room, but she was so nervous about whether David was in the apartment, she could hear her own heartbeat thumping through her nightgown. Debbie put her ear against the bedroom door and listened for noises outside. Nothing.

"Thank God," she thought.

Debbie waited until she finally had the courage to open the door. She walked out into a large living room with high ceilings and tall windows trying not to make a sound. Debbie inspected the kitchen, study, bathroom and master suite and realized David was nowhere to be found. She breathed a sigh of relief.

Debbie searched the apartment suite for clues before David

returned. She chose the master suite first and looked around the bedroom. The first thing she noticed was how clean and perfect everything appeared. Apart from her bedroom, it looked like the rest of the apartment was completely untouched, as if no one else had slept there. The marble tile in the master bathroom sparkled with cleanliness. There was nothing out of place as Debbie searched, so she crouched down to check underneath the king–sized bed.

Something white immediately caught Debbie's eye. She got down on her hands and knees and stretched forward to retrieve a small white piece of paper that looked like it had fallen off the night stand. She snatched up the note. It was written in David's script and read: "Tophet Exhibit–MOMA."

"Looks like a good place to escape to," Debbie said under her breath.

Half running back to the guestroom, Debbie dressed and walked out the front door with the only thing she possessed—the clothes on her back. She said a quick prayer that she would make it to the MOMA safely. Once there, she would call her family for help.

*

When Drew arrived home with the note he found in his coat pocket from Nurse Bridget, he immediately read it again just to make sure he knew exactly which Scriptural passages he needed to research. "Check Leviticus and Kings. Also Zephaniah. Let Elaina know I now have all I need to put the Taninsam ties together." Again, the note was signed, "BL."

"What happened to Dr. Lanton?" Drew asked himself as he searched for his Bible. "Did Elaina have anything to do with his death?" A pang of fear hit Drew's gut so hard, his hand started to shake. He had to stay focused on the task at hand. The only way to help Cassy was to figure out what Dr. Lanton's note meant.

Drew sat at his desk with his Bible and read Leviticus and

Kings to see if there were any connections between the two books. The Book of Leviticus was a book of laws for the Israelites, and there was an entire section entitled, "The Book of the Law," within 2 Kings.

Drew concentrated on these similarities first. Since the 2 Kings section was shorter, he read that first. It was predominantly about the reign of King Josiah, but what stood out most to Drew were the apparent ritualistic sacrifices of children done in honor of the false god, Moloch.

The passage from 2 Kings 23:10 read, "He also defiled Topheth, which is in the valley of the son of Hinnom, that no man might make his son or his daughter pass through the fire for Moloch." There was a notation at the end of the passage that pointed to Leviticus 18:21, the very same book that was mentioned in the note. This passage read, "Do not give any of your children to be sacrificed to Moloch, for you must not profane the name of your God. I am the Lord."

Drew turned to the Book of Zephaniah to see if child sacrifices to Moloch were mentioned there, too. It didn't take long to find what he was looking for. In Chapter One, Drew saw the name Moloch mentioned again. The passage from Zephaniah 1:5 read, "For they go up to their roofs and bow down to the sun, moon, and stars. They claim to follow the Lord, but then they worship Moloch, too."

"Who was Moloch and what did he have to do with Elaina?" Drew thought. If it meant saving his wife, Drew was going to find out fast.

Drew would call his friend Father Raphael at Saint Mary's in Dumont where he and Cassy had been married. If there was anyone who knew about this "Moloch," it would be Father Raphael.

*

When Drew woke the following morning, he felt like he hadn't slept at all. He had vivid dreams of Cassy being hunted down and sacrificed to Moloch all night. Drew left a message for Father Raphael and decided to visit Cassy at the hospital. He had such a foreboding fear, he needed to check on her to make sure she was okay. Drew folded Dr. Lanton's note with the three biblical passages and put it in his pocket before he left the house.

When Drew reached the hospital, Cassy was sleeping peacefully in her room. He breathed easier and realized that last night's dreams were just dreams and nothing more. Drew kissed his wife and sat next to her closely. He wondered whether he should go to Father Raphael or wait for him to call back.

"He'll probably think I'm going crazy," Drew thought. "Afraid of some Biblical character from thousands of years ago. Totally ridiculous. Maybe I'll wait for him to call back. Then I'll have more time to sort this out."

A half hour later, Drew grabbed his coat and kissed his wife "good–bye" before he headed to the elevators. As he walked down the hall, Drew saw a very tall, thin man with a long, black pony tail come toward him. Without explanation, Drew's heart skipped a beat from fear, but there was no explanation. To Drew, the man looked strange and out of place, but he felt badly that he had made a judgment of someone he did not know based solely on appearance.

"Now, my bad dreams are making me paranoid," Drew thought as he reached for the button next to the elevators. He looked behind him while he waited and realized the man had already disappeared. For a split second, Drew thought he saw the door to Cassy's room close as if the man had just entered.

"Is this paranoia, too?" Drew asked himself. "It can't hurt to check on her one last time before I leave."

David Bloodstone entered Cassy's room. He had come for her, and he had brought Cassy's bloodstone cameo necklace with him. David took the necklace from his coat pocket and raised his hands to slip the necklace around her neck. His hands were directly above Cassy's head when he saw a blinding white light from over his right shoulder.

Paolo had come to protect Cassy, but David did not want to fight. David vanished from the room.

Paolo heard footsteps come toward Cassy's door. He vanished, too.

When Drew walked into his wife's room, there was no one there. "Yes, Drew, you have now reached a completely new level of insanity," he thought and walked back out toward the elevators.

*

As soon as Jessica showed Father Gabe the files from Palmer's computer regarding JamBrax's Fountain of Youth Spa, she and Jonathan booked a flight to Barbados where the spa was located. Posing as Mr. and Mrs. Smith, a wealthy couple who were there to enjoy the amenities of the spa, they spent one evening at the JamBrax Spa. This turned out to be more than enough time to obtain substantial evidence against Palmer.

Jessica scheduled a massage, facial and a special anti–aging treatment. The treatment involved lying on a cot while the contents of an IV bag coursed through her veins.

"I do not feel comfortable with this," Jessica told the woman in the white lab coat. "Am I allowed to know the contents of the liquid in that bag?" Jessica asked pointing to the IV.

The woman smiled professionally before responding. "Absolutely," she answered. "For all intensive purposes, this is a mixture of the essential nutrients that provide optimum healing and energy for the body."

"What exactly are the essential nutrients?" Jessica asked again.

"The essential vitamins and minerals from the best, most soluble sources: vitamins A, B6, B12, C, D, E, K, calcium, magnesium, iron, phosphorous, potassium, zinc, gingko biloba, aloe vera, ginseng, pepsin, selenium, germanium, algin, kelp kombu, kozu and nori...and, of course, there is one secret ingredient. We are the only spa with special access to this ingredient. The only ingredient designed to turn back the hands of time. The only ingredient designed to make you young forever."

"What is that ingredient?"

"That ingredient, Mrs. Smith, is one that I cannot reveal," the woman answered with a professional smile. "Otherwise, every spa in the world would want it."

At that moment, the door buzzer sounded and the woman excused herself. She opened the door to Jonathan who looked frantic.

"Yes, Mr. Smith?" the woman asked.

"Sorry to interrupt," Jonathan began, "but I think there might be a problem with one of your other clients in the next room. I think I heard screaming." Jonathan was playing his part perfectly.

For the first time since entering the room, Jessica saw the woman's smile fade. "Yes, thank you," she said hurriedly. "I'll be right back."

As soon as the woman left, Jessica detached the IV bag from the hook and stuffed it into her purse. "Let's go," she said to Jonathan, and they both exited the facility using the back door.

Jonathan had already packed their bags and loaded their rental car. Their bill had already been paid in cash so that there would be no trace. The total was $25,250.00.

When they returned to San Francisco, Jessica and Jonathan took the contents of the bag to someone they knew who wasn't connected with USF. The results were exactly as they had anticipated—no vitamins, no minerals, no super–nutrients. It was just straight liquefied fetal remains.

When Jessica and Jonathan gave the evidence from the IV bag to Father Gabe, the Archbishop knew it was a closed case. He took it to the police station, and Palmer Braxton was arrested that afternoon. His bail was set at half a million.

Palmer was given one phone call, and he called Elaina Taninsam. She had her lawyer bail Palmer out, but it wasn't for his sake. She was concerned about PSI's reputation. Palmer would have to destroy any evidence that linked JamBrax's Fountain of Youth Spa to PSI or she would have to notify David Bloodstone. A dangerous prospect for Palmer. A prospect that Palmer could not bring himself to even fathom.

*

Marie and Doc Murray had always been "early–to–bed" and "early–to–rise" people. In fact, there were many days when they rose so early, the sky was still pitch black.

This morning, Marie and Doc lay in bed and stared at the ceiling unable to fall back to sleep. It was only 4 a.m. They held hands and talked until 4:30 while Doc drummed his right hand on his chest through his v–neck T–shirt.

"What's say we go for a little breakfast this morning at Mo's?" Doc was looking over at his wife with a grin on his face and a twinkle in his eyes. He knew Marie couldn't resist the grin and the twinkle.

"Why not?" Marie asked in return.

"Okay, let's get to it," Doc said with a hint of surprise in his voice. He knew Marie didn't usually like to go out to eat. She didn't like to spend money on food she could make at home.

By five o'clock, the Murrays sat at a booth opposite a long line of bar stools next to Mo's counter where he made all conceivable breakfast combinations known to man.

Mo's was a classic greasy spoon diner set up in an old railway car in Fontana, Wisconsin. By greasy, Mo made everything with heaps of butter he kept stowed in a giant aluminum tub next to the griddle. If Mo made eggs, a big glob of butter went on first. If Mo made pancakes, the batter would spread out and push the hot butter all around the sides. Even if Mo made bacon or ham, loads of butter kept the griddle slippery, so it didn't stick.

"What can I get you for?" Mo asked Marie and Doc from over the heads of the counter diners.

"Eggs, sunny side up with rye toast, light on the butter, and coffee," Doc said. "Marie?"

"Mo, what kind of bread do you use for the French toast?" Marie asked.

"I don't know. That thick doughy stuff that Itchy buys."

Itchy was Mo's wife whose real name was Donna. She had earned the name "Itchy" because she was so allergic to dogs. In fact, Itchy knew more about how to combat allergies than anyone. She was always on some new allergy medication, decongestant or antihistamine, but no matter what she swallowed, sprayed or rubbed on, she was always itching. Itchy must have been head over heels for Mo to put up with all those allergies and itching. Everyone assumed that Mo couldn't live without his dogs, and Itchy couldn't live without Mo.

"French toast, please, light on the butter. Decaf coffee," Marie said.

"Right–ee–o!" Mo yelled from the counter as he scooped two big heaps of butter onto the griddle.

Marie saw Itchy clearing dirty dishes off the furthest booth in the back. "Itchy, is that a Journal on the table?" she asked.

Itchy looked down at the newspaper and picked it up to read the front page. She was looking through pink rimmed spectacles that were dangling from the end of her nose and connected to a pink and silver glitter chain. She itched her right arm while she answered Marie, "Yeah, honey. Do you want it?"

"Yes, please. I'll get it." Marie stood up to get the newspaper and tucked it under her arm as she picked up the mugs of coffee that Mo left on the counter for her and Doc. "Which one's the decaf?" she asked Mo.

Mo looked inside both cups and pointed to the one in Marie's left hand.

"How can you tell?" Marie asked.

"Decaf's lighter," Mo replied.

Marie sat back down opposite her husband and handed Doc the sports pages. She opened up to the front page story as Doc started trading Packer scores with Mo. The headline caught Marie's attention right away. It read, "Girl's Picture Taken As She Jumps From Bridge To Her Death." Marie quickly turned to the inside page and what she saw shocked her enough to make her hands shake as she held the newspaper.

The picture of the girl with green cat eyes looked almost eerie as she appeared to gaze directly into the telephoto lens of the camera that happened to catch the girl jump at the right time. The person had been taking pictures of the bridge from below for a grad school project and had caught the girl throwing herself over the side.

Marie stared at the face of the girl she had made eye contact with at the Milwaukee abortion clinic. She had wanted to speak with the girl and she was sure the girl had wanted to speak with her, but now she knew that the girl had gone through with the abortion.

As Marie read the article, she thought about someone else who had committed suicide after an abortion. This girl had gone back to a clinic for a follow–up after an abortion and was in the bathroom for so long that someone had to go in and check on her. It turned out the girl had slit her wrists and bled to death in a shower stall.

Marie finished the article about the girl with green cat eyes who had decided to end her young life. She looked back up at the girl in the photograph and decided to tear the picture out of the newspaper so she could keep it. She was folding it when Doc looked up from his football scores.

"Someone you know?" he asked.

"Yes. Someone I met the other day that I wanted to pray for," Marie answered. The lump in her throat had become so large she felt she might not be able to swallow. She had wanted to do so much for that girl and her unborn baby. She had been so close to being able to help her.

When Marie put the picture in her purse, her eyes were so filled with tears she knew she wouldn't be able to hide them from her husband.

"Doc, your eggs and French toast!" Mo distracted Doc long enough for Marie to wipe away the tears before Doc could return with their breakfast plates from the counter. They were both drenched in pools of hot butter.

Marie picked up her fork and played with the butter long enough for Doc to take notice.

"Lose your appetite?" he asked.

"No, just thinking," Marie said.

"About what?"

"Just life," Marie answered. "You ever wish you could turn back time?"

"I'll leave that up to God," Doc said.

"Time?"

"Life."

CHAPTER THIRTY–EIGHT

Paolo knew there wasn't much time before David would come again for Cassy, so he had to work fast.

Cassy had witnessed Moloch's "birth" into the human world when he became David Bloodstone. She had seen David unite with Lilith, the Mother of Darkness, to form the Taninsam family of witches. She had discovered that her ancestry was linked to the largest abortion chain in the world so that David could retain his human form by feasting on the blood of the innocents.

Cassy had been through so much Paolo hated to put her through anymore, but he knew that her sacrifice would save lives. She only had one more journey to make, and this would be her last. Cassy would learn the secret to defeat David and his family of cursed Taninsam witches.

Paolo placed his right hand on Cassy's forehead and her eyes immediately opened. She looked uneasy at first, as if someone might be there to harm her, but once she saw Paolo she smiled and sat up. Cassy reached out to Paolo, and he took her hand and brought her to her feet.

"Cassy, we've run out of time. David is coming for you. He is coming for you and Deborah and he is trying to keep Jessica from interfering with his plans. We must now travel to the deepest and darkest of all places, but there is a power which exists and comes from God that can destroy all the terrible things that have come to be. This power comes from the heavens and with it all darkness will turn to light and all death will turn to new life."

*

Cassy trusted Paolo and knew that he would keep her safe no matter what happened. She knew that it was up to her and her sister, Deborah, to defeat David with the help of her Aunt Jessica. Whatever fear she felt, she had become a true soldier of Christ, and her love of God through her spiritual journeys with Paolo had given her the grace to fight evil no matter what the consequences.

Cassy took Paolo's hand, and they began their last flight into the spiritual realm. Normally, Cassy felt as if she were soaring up to the heavens. This time, the opposite was true. The instant Cassy took Paolo's hand, she felt as if they were falling through the floor feet first. She was reminded of a roller coaster ride she had taken when she was a child. The roller coaster had plunged down several stories so quickly she thought her stomach had been pulled into her chest. This experience was similar, but she felt no sickness. She felt only despair. She knew where Paolo was taking her, and she didn't want to go.

Cassy and Paolo fell as if an inner drive were pulling them down and as they descended, the depression and despair grew worse. Cassy could feel a great amount of heat work its way through her body, radiating an electric charge of desperation so severe she felt her heart and soul might be entirely consumed by fire. Cassy felt she couldn't withstand the temperature any longer, but Paolo squeezed her hand, and she knew they were close to their destination.

Whenever Cassy had thought of the place called, Hell, in her childhood, she had thought of red devil costumes with long, pointed tails and pitchforks. The place she and Paolo stood in now was nothing like she had ever imagined. There were no costumes. Just ordinary people lurking about with no purpose. Cassy noticed quite a few of these people—too many to count.

As she looked into their faces, Cassy thought she recognized some of them, and a terrible feeling came into her heart. It was not the look of them that made Cassy feel so uneasy. It was the feeling of the place that was so terrible. Yes, it was horribly hot just as the "fires of hell" would lead one to think. But it was more than this. It was a feeling of despair and despondency beyond any she could possibly fathom.

Around her, there was no life, only a feeling of death and destruction. Around her, there were no dreams, only lost hope and disheartenment. There were no musical nuances, only loud cries of pain and anguish so great, Cassy felt like a 250–pound weight had been laid on her chest. She felt she couldn't breathe.

"This is Hell?" Cassy asked Paolo.

"Yes. Satan's domain. He's been able to draw many souls to himself, especially in the last hundred years," Paolo responded.

"Why?"

"Lack of faith, no belief in God, conceit, hedonism, genocide, abortion…"

"Do these people have a chance to leave this place?" Cassy asked again.

"No, Cassy. That's why our choices in life are so important. Every day of our lives we have the power to choose eternal life or eternal damnation."

"But I thought God was merciful?" Cassy could not contain her grief for those around her who had chosen such horrible fates for themselves.

"God is merciful, but God is also just," Paolo responded. "Trust me, Cassy, the Heavenly Father weeps for these people more than you know, but He entrusted free will and they chose to ignore what is good and right. Their evil was not done in ignorance. It was done with full knowledge and consent. When an abortionist kills a baby inside or outside the mother's womb, you are crying for him now. When a senator vetoes a bill to protect an infant who is born alive after a botched abortion, you are crying for him now. When a priest proclaims that abortion is not a sin, you are crying for him now."

Suddenly, Cassy heard loud wails come from somewhere around the corner. With these wails, came gnashing of teeth, which Cassy had never heard before. "Please, Paolo, please take me away from here. I cannot endure their pain any longer."

Paolo took Cassy's hand, and they ascended quickly and effortlessly. They reached a second destination within seconds. This place was filled with sadness and isolation, but there was something drastically different than Hell.

"Where are we now?" Cassy asked quickly, breathing much easier.

"A place called Purgatory," Paolo explained. "Purgatory is not Hell. Purgatory is not Heaven. It is a place somewhere between."

"Why do I feel so much better now?" Cassy asked innocently.

"People do not remain in Purgatory forever. They have a chance at Heaven," Paolo answered. "Most come here when they die."

"How long do they stay?"

"That depends on the person. The more good the person does on earth, the less time in Purgatory. The less good the person does, the more time in Purgatory. It's a purification process that takes as long as needed."

"But one day they will enter into Heaven?"

"One day they will come face to face with Love Itself."

Paolo took Cassy's hand, and they ascended to their third and final destination—Heaven. Cassy knew in her heart that she was not ready or worthy to meet her Lord and Savior, Jesus Christ, but it would be her goal for the rest of her life once she had awakened from the coma. Cassy knew there must be another reason for Paolo bringing her here.

Heaven was as magnificent as Cassy would have expected and

an infinite amount more. It was more than the opposite of Hell, too. Heaven was love, happiness and fulfillment all at one time like a great team of people who were ever victorious in winning the game of life over and over. Cassy could hear beautiful and angelic music playing in the distance and the fragrance of flowers permeated the air. She looked around her and saw an eternal communion of people existing in love and harmony forever. It was like getting goose bumps over something wonderful that keeps repeating. This place was life's greatest achievement; the place Cassy yearned to one day enter.

"Do all people go to Purgatory first or do some go directly to Heaven?" Cassy asked.

"Some go directly to Heaven."

"Who?"

"Saints."

Paolo took hold of Cassy's hand and this time he led her to an altar more magnificent than she had ever seen on earth. The altar was dedicated to "Our Lady of Guadalupe," when Mary, the Mother of God, had appeared to Saint Juan Diego in Mexico. There were mounds of red roses around the fantastic and colorful image of Mary, and the sweet smell of roses was so fragrant, Cassy felt as though every portion of her being had been awakened. A beautiful and gleaming gold box stood on the altar directly in front of Mary's image.

Paolo gently opened the box and a great stream of light filled the altar with a rainbow of colors that hung in the air. He carefully placed his hands inside the box and took out a small statue made of jasper stone covered with gold. On top of the gold was the couchant positioned Lion of the tribe of Judah and the Tree of Life with the Serpent entwined in the tree. Cassy counted seven jeweled eyes on the stone, but the jeweled sapphire eyes of the Lion gleamed most. At once, Cassy saw a ray of brilliant light shoot out of the inner chambers of the statue. She felt the need to shield her eyes from the intensity.

"What is it?" Cassy asked.

"The Christ Stone," Paolo replied. "It was fashioned in Heaven and houses the one true Bloodstone made of the blood of Christ. This is the one Bloodstone that can defeat David. Cassy, when we return, you will awaken, and you will need to locate the Christ Stone. I will help you, but only a Taninsam can wield its power against David."

*

When Debbie Romano walked out of the Manhattan Center, she discovered that it was connected to the New Yorker Hotel. She did not want to make a call from this location because she wanted to get as far away from 34th and 8th as possible before David returned. She would make the call at the Museum of Modern Art on 53rd and 5th. Debbie started uptown toward the MOMA with three things on her mind: get out of this area, call her family, and find out what she needed to discover at the MOMA as quickly as possible. It was freezing cold, but Debbie felt nothing. She was too intent on what she needed to accomplish.

Debbie continued north on Eighth Avenue and checked her watch. It was half past noon and there was a good amount of traffic, which made her feel safer. An hour later, she entered the MOMA and paid the entrance fee with cash she had found in a drawer in David's apartment. Debbie looked around for a pay phone and spotted a museum employee handing out maps just inside the entrance.

"Excuse me, can you tell me where there's a pay phone?" Debbie asked.

"Second floor. Just outside the restrooms," the employee answered as he handed Debbie a map to the museum.

"Thanks." Debbie found the elevator and took it to the second floor. She quickly dialed her parents' number.

"Hello?" It was Debbie's mother, Lucia.

"Mom? It's Debbie. I'm okay."

"Thank God!" Lucia wept into the phone as soon as she heard her daughter's voice.

Debbie explained everything she could remember to her mother as quickly as possible. Lucia told Debbie that she, Pietro and Father Mac would immediately catch the next flight to New York and meet her at the MOMA.

Before she hung up the phone, Debbie realized there was one important question she forgot to ask. "Mom, what's the date?"

"January 5th," Lucia replied.

Two months had passed, and Debbie didn't even know what had transpired during that time.

*

Debbie sat in the MOMA cafeteria staring at the note she had found under David's bed. She had eaten most of a roast beef sandwich with mayo, but she felt so nervous the last bite seemed to be lodged somewhere in the back of her throat.

"Tophet Exhibit, here we go," she said as she rose from the table and checked her map. "Fourth floor."

Debbie got off the elevator on the fourth floor and followed the signs to the exhibit she was inexplicably fearful to see. In fact, the closer she got, the more her legs felt like heavy cement poles keeping her from getting to her destination. When she was just short of the exhibit, Debbie felt loathsome to round the corner, as if her fear kept her glued to the floor. She had to force every step.

When Debbie finally came face to face with the Tophet Exhibit, she saw that it was enclosed by glass on all four sides. Mounds of sand filled the giant glass box all the way to the top with tipped clay urns lying on top of the sand as if they had just been unearthed at an excavation site. Debbie read the words, "Tophet Burial Ground," written on a white card in large print on each side of the glass enclosure.

Debbie walked around the recreated excavation site and saw that it was actually a Mexican archeological site unearthed in 2004. The site provided physical evidence of ancient Aztec sacrifices. Debbie noticed that children were the most frequent victims because they were considered pure and unspoiled, a better sacrifice to their pagan god, Moloch. The urns were filled with recreated skeletal remains of children who were either partially burned or completely carbonized.

As Debbie made her way around the replicated display reading the details of the excavation, she began to feel faint. It was as if she existed in a state of semi–consciousness that was separate from reality. Debbie could hear the sound of a distant drum beat grow louder with every passing step. She felt the heat of fire on her face, as the smell of something burning and vile filtered into her nostrils. The drums became horrifically loud as her mind spun out of control. Suddenly, the screams and cries of dying children hit Debbie like a bolt of lightning striking deep in her soul.

"Are you all right, Miss?" One of the MOMA guards had come up from behind Debbie and placed a comforting hand on her back.

"What?" Debbie asked still in the fog of her dream.

"You screamed like you just saw the 'boogie man,'" the guard said.

Debbie saw that some of the museum patrons were staring at her like she was crazy. "Oh, yeah. Thanks. I'm fine. I…ah…tripped and almost fell. Sorry," she lied. "New shoes," she said with an uncomfortable smile.

"Okay, then. Just making sure you're all right," the guard replied before leaving.

"Thanks, again," Debbie called after him as she walked around the corner of the display to finish reading about the excavation.

When Debbie saw the last wall of the display, she became so frightened, she wished the guard had remained to help her. Debbie recognized the engraved symbol on the Tophet burial marker. She would have recognized it anywhere. The sun. The crescent moon.

The upside down pyramid.

Debbie looked at her watch. Only three o'clock. She had plenty of time to get to the New York Library and back to the MOMA to meet her parents and Father Mac. Debbie had important research and it couldn't wait.

*

When Elaina Taninsam bailed Palmer Braxton out of jail, he wasn't worried about a criminal record. He wasn't even worried about money or his reputation. He was worried about saving his life and he knew he needed to hide.

Palmer decided to leave the country as soon as possible. Other than the United States, he knew Barbados like the back of his hand. He had spent many months researching the island before he built JamBrax's Fountain of Youth Spa.

Palmer would leave everything in the States untouched. Where he lived. Where he worked. What he owned. Didn't matter. He would begin anew with a whole new life. A whole new identity. Palmer had taken great pains and resources to acquire a new identity, so that when he arrived at San Francisco International Airport, his first class ticket was under the name of John Reginald Miller and not Palmer Braxton.

Palmer sat at the gate waiting for the plane bound for Barbados to arrive. He wore tinted sunglasses and a baseball cap when his cell phone rang unexpectedly. It was Elaina.

"Stay calm and act like everything is normal," he thought before he hit the call button.

"Elaina," Palmer said faking confidence.

"Palmer, I hope you destroyed any tainted embryonic stem cell research that might be linked to my company," Elaina said in a steely tone. "Because if even the tiniest bit of fabrication gets out, it could lead to PSI's destruction."

"Not to worry, Elaina, not to worry. I'm about to board a plane to Barbados as we speak, and it was my every intention to destroy any and every link that exists." Palmer felt like he believed his own lie, he was playing it so well.

"I hope so, Palmer, because if you fail, it will be your reputation and not mine; your ass behind bars, and not mine; and if the authorities don't get you, David will."

Palmer heard a faint click and pressed the button to end the call. He tried to ignore the looming premonition that his days were numbered. Palmer hoped that changing his identity to John Reginald Miller might add on a few more years.

*

Father Gabe Sanders checked his messages at the rectory and disappeared into the Cathedral to pray in front of the Blessed Sacrament before dinner. He was thinking a lot about Jessica and Jonathan and what they had discovered in Barbados regarding Palmer Braxton. The Archbishop wasn't just worried about unethical science. He was worried about the killing of unborn children, and Father Gabe suspected a dark and demonic force behind the whole operation.

The Archbishop rose from the kneeler and walked over to the Shrine of Our Lady of Guadalupe. The shrine was one of four, each weighing over one and a half tons, and they were attached to the walls in each corner by structural supports to create a "free–flowing" effect.

Father Gabe gazed at the colorfully animated image of the Mexican Mary and noticed a small piece of white paper underneath a glass vase filled with beautiful red roses. He lifted the vase and grasped the note. "Who is she that comes forth like the rising dawn fair as the moon bright as the sun," it read. Father Gabe was a bit perplexed that this Scriptural passage had been left underneath the vase and written by hand in black script. He also noticed the emblem, "KofC," printed at the bottom of the note. "Knights of

Columbus," Father Gabe thought. He placed the note in his pocket for safe keeping.

The Archbishop decided to make sure his vestments were ready for the weekend's Masses before he left. When he reached the sacristy behind the altar, what he saw made his gut revolt, and he had to swallow hard to keep from vomiting. Blood was dripping from the walls so severely that he thought it smelled like stale meat in a butcher's shop. There were pentagram symbols everywhere, and each pentagram contained a smeared, bloody handprint in its center. The word "Reign" was written above the pentagrams with red dripping blood.

Father Gabe immediately called the police, and they examined the handprint inside the pentagrams with a magnifying lens. There was a tiny word written inside each handprint where the blood was not able to stick to the wall. To Father Gabe, it looked as if the word were written in an ancient biblical language.

The police officer turned to Father Gabe as soon as he saw the word. "What language is that?" he asked.

"Hebrew," Father Gabe answered.

"What does it mean?"

"Moloch."

CHAPTER THIRTY–NINE

Michael Murray and Linda Walters arrived in Montreal to meet with James Goodrich regarding the Christ Stone. James and his grandmother shared a flat in Old–Montreal on Saint Paul Street East, which was very close to the Notre–Dame–de–Bon–Secours Chapel. The historic chapel was built in 1655 in Montreal, the city originally dedicated to the Blessed Virgin Mary.

Michael and Linda rented a car at the airport and drove to Le Glamour Cosmopolitan Hotel on Rue St–Denis in the Latin Quarter of Montreal. They hadn't had a chance to brush up on their French when they stepped into the quaint entrance and realized that no one was speaking English. The concierge was very pleasant, though, and spoke English as soon as she knew they had come from the U.S.

The travelers checked in and climbed a corner staircase where they shared a room on the second floor with two bedrooms and one adjoining bath. The decorations in the hotel were contemporary and elegant with pictures of Audrey Hepburn hanging above the queen sized beds in both bedrooms. There were chandeliers and black art deco furniture with hints of red, white, and black zebra print.

The drive to Old–Montreal was beautiful and scenic, and

Michael and Linda were struck by how close the water was to Saint Paul Street. The weather was cold and overcast with a mist in the air that hung like thick fog. As Michael and Linda drove over cobblestone streets, they felt like two people out of time who should have been seated on a horse instead of in a car. They parked at a meter on the street and walked to a series of aged brownstones that fit perfectly into the historical setting.

When they found the address, Michael walked up the stone staircase with Linda close behind and rang the buzzer. A young and frail man answered the door almost immediately.

"Michael Murray?" he asked timidly.

"James, good to meet you." Michael offered his hand for James to shake, and James took it hesitantly. Michael stepped to one side. "This is Linda Walters, my...associate. Thank you so much for taking the time to see us. May we come in?"

"Yes, of course." James cleared the way for Michael and Linda to enter. He led the two into a small study with a sliding glass door leading to a terrace off the back. The décor was elegant and quaint with dark taupe walls and beautiful red floral curtains that draped long windows on either side of the sliding glass doors.

There was an elderly woman seated in a rocking chair with white hair done in a bun and piercing blue eyes. When she saw her grandson accompanied by guests, she lit up like a firefly.

"Bonjour," she said softly.

"Grandmother, Michael Murray and Linda Walters." James addressed his grandmother in English with a slight French accent. "They are here about the Christ Stone."

James' grandmother's expression changed from delighted to despondent in three seconds when she heard the words, "Christ Stone." There was an awkward silence before she said, "Please, sit down," indicating the brown leather seats across from her.

"I'm Marguerite Goodrich," she said. "Can we get you something? Tea?"

"No, thank you," Michael replied instantly. He didn't want to cause the woman any trouble.

"It's no trouble at all," Marguerite Goodrich said right on cue as if she had heard his thoughts. "James?" she instructed.

"Yes, Grandmother." James disappeared to fetch the tea.

"Now," Marguerite turned her attention back to Michael and Linda. "How did you find out about the Christ Stone?"

Michael and Linda looked at one another, and Michael decided to go first. "I'm a journalist and was hired to do a story on a young woman named Debbie Romano. Her original name is Deborah Taninsam. In our research, we discovered that the Taninsam family has ties to an organization that performs abortions worldwide. Our research has led us to situations that have been unnatural and possibly even supernatural. To be frank, we've had to deal with supernatural instances that have been...well...somewhat demonic in nature. Our research led us, first, to the Urim and Thummim and here to the Christ Stone."

"Mrs. Goodrich," Michael continued, "Linda and I have been followed, harassed, and almost murdered twice since we started on this assignment, and we were told that the only hope we may have is in the Christ Stone."

Mrs. Goodrich sat attentively listening to Michael's entire story, but remained silent when he finished.

Just then, James entered the study carrying a silver tray with tea kettle, cups, milk, sugar and little white napkins with a thin, gold trim.

"Ah, James," Marguerite Goodrich exclaimed joyously. "Thank you, dear."

James took it upon himself to pour the tea asking Michael and Linda whether they wanted milk or sugar.

Marguerite held her tea cup with her pinky daintily pointed up and sipped the sweet hot liquid delicately and deeply. She set down her cup and said, "Now, please allow me to tell you my story."

"My grandson, James, was not the only 'James' in the family. He was named after his father, James, who was my son, and his father, James, who was my husband. I would say that all three of them had as much fascination with the Christ Stone as you two, isn't that right, James?"

"Yes," James replied with guilt.

Marguerite continued, "It turns out there have been many names for the Christ Stone: the Scepter of Righteousness, the Ancient Secret, the Hidden Thing, the Urim and Thummim, the Holy Grail, the Stone from Heaven, the Agate Urn, the Foundation Stone…the Christ Stone. No matter the name, the fascination for my husband and son became a matter beyond obsession. It became all–encompassing for them."

"How did your family come to possess the Christ Stone?" Linda asked.

"The Christ Stone was given to my husband over sixty years ago because of his French Huguenot ancestry. The original name of his family was 'Godric,' which means 'power of God.' The name is derived from the Old English 'God' combined with 'ric,' which means 'power' or 'rule.' Eventually, his name became 'Goodrich.' You see, the Huguenots created a secret religious organization called 'Keepers of the Sacred Secret.' I'm sure the two of you have heard of this organization and all that has been written concerning the Holy Grail?"

Both Linda and Michael nodded their heads.

"It has been written that Canada was settled as a direct result of the Holy Grail in order to create the prophesied 'New Jerusalem' in the New World. Even Samuel de Champlain, the explorer and founder of the Quebec colony, was said to be a secret agent for the Grail Dynasty. In 1654, the Grail was moved to Montreal by a mysterious secret society called the Compagnie du Saint Sacrement. In 1670, the Grail or Christ Stone was buried in a secret vault underneath the little statue of Notre–Dame–de–Bon–Secours Chapel by Saint Marguerite Bourgeoys. Before she died, she asked the Keepers of the Sacred Secret to hold the stone until the day that the rightful family inherits it."

"How did they determine the date?" Michael asked.

"Saint Marguerite said the day would be determined when the family of 'God's power' married a woman with the saint's own name. She also prophesized the chapel's destruction in a fire that would consume everything except the wooden statue of Notre–Dame–de–Bon–Secours Chapel, the same statue that housed the vault of the Christ Stone."

"Marguerite and James!" Linda exclaimed.

"Yes, James received the Christ Stone as a gift at our wedding. Some years later, he was instructed to take the Christ Stone to Italy to consult with Saint Padre Paolo. At that point, it went back in the vault underneath the statue at the chapel."

"Is that where it's located today?" Michael asked.

"I don't know," Marguerite replied sadly. "When my husband returned from Italy, he took the Christ Stone back to the chapel, but he was hit by a car and killed on the way home. My son went to the chapel to find his father and the stone, but he was killed, too. That stone has caused only heartache for me. Now, my grandson is all that I have left."

*

James Goodrich volunteered to show Michael and Linda the vault underneath the statue at the chapel. Marguerite stayed behind and wished the young couple good luck, but warned them of the danger they might face from the "enemies of the stone." James was very quiet as he led Michael and Linda down the cobble–stoned street to the Notre–Dame–de–Bon–Secours Chapel.

When they reached the chapel, a feeling of nostalgia came over Linda—almost as if she had been there before. A great light seemed to emanate from within the chapel as the darkness of fog and mist turned to the light of holiness and grace. The walls were white and beautiful chandeliers hung from the ceiling.

James led them to the altar, and Linda and Michael were

amazed at the simplicity of the statue of Notre–Dame–de–Bon–Secours. A wooden statue of Mary, the Mother of God, and her infant child stood before them; the only ornaments, Mary's crown and Jesus' halo, both made of gold. The regal nature of the statue was not in its material, but in its imagery where both mother and child stood ready to save the world.

As soon as they reached the altar, James turned to Michael and Linda quickly and unexpectedly. "I must tell you that the Christ Stone is not here. It was removed by my father and brought to New York. He said it was imperative. That it would be used for spiritual warfare. He believed that the Christ Stone was the greatest weapon known to mankind—the only weapon that could possibly defeat the devil."

"Why didn't you tell us before?" Michael asked skeptically.

"My grandmother doesn't know. My father never had the courage to tell her. He thought she would think he was insane. She never believed my grandfather, so my father knew she would never believe him either."

"Why?" Linda was suddenly very curious about James' openness.

"My grandfather thought that the stone had come down from heaven itself." James looked at the floor of the chapel out of embarrassment.

"Did your father believe this, too?" Linda asked again.

"Yes. He felt it was a complete and utter fact."

"What do you believe, James?" Linda asked.

"There was never any doubt in my mind."

"How do you know for sure?" Michael's curiosity was getting the best of him.

"My grandfather went to Padre Paolo in Italy to consult him about it. This was back in 1960. Padre Paolo told him exactly what it was and where it came from. My grandfather knew that he would have to sacrifice much in order to bring the stone safely back to Montreal."

"What do you mean?" Michael asked.

"My grandfather knew that he would have to sacrifice his life."

"He was able to return the Christ Stone back to the chapel and then he was killed?"

"My grandfather had already been mortally wounded on the trip back to Montreal. He made it to the airport where my father met him to pick him up. My grandfather died in my father's arms. It was my father who returned the stone to the chapel."

"Do you know who caused your grandfather's death?" Linda asked gently.

"Agents of the devil." James spoke so matter–of–factly, no one would have questioned his answer.

"But your father? He was also killed on his way to New York? Did these same 'agents of the devil' kill your father, too?" Michael asked.

"I don't know. I saw him off at the airport. My only memory is that he was accompanied by a priest. They were apparently going off on this mission together—this mission to New York. That was the last time I saw him."

Michael and Linda drove back to the hotel with only one thought on their minds.

"Next stop New York," Michael said.

Linda nodded her head in agreement.

*

When Debbie Romano entered the New York Public Library on Fifth Avenue, she was completely amazed by the immenseness of it. It was so grand, she almost forgot the serious nature of why she was there.

"First step, first," Debbie thought.

Debbie approached the Information Desk and asked if she might be able to utilize a computer for internet research. She explained she was a History Major at Marquette University in Milwaukee.

The librarian gave Debbie a broad smile and showed her to a computer in the main room of the Research Library. Librarians usually had a soft spot for fellow academicians.

As soon as Debbie sat down, she googled the description of the Tophet symbol with the sun, moon and converse pyramid. The symbol came up immediately as the logo for PSI, the very same organization owned by her biological mother, Elaina Taninsam.

"What connection does PSI have to David Bloodstone?" Debbie thought.

Debbie brought up everything she could about the company and its origin. A recent web page included a picture of the Abortion Rights' Alliance and National Organization for the Reproductive Rights of Women. As she stared at the photo, Debbie was sure she recognized David in the picture. He stood next to Elaina dressed in a dark suit with his long, black hair slicked back in a ponytail. It was definitely him.

Next, Debbie's research brought her to PSI's development in the sexual revolution of the 1960s. At this point, the company was owned and operated by Elaina's mother, Madeline, Debbie's biological grandmother. Debbie managed to find a photo of Madeline with some of her employees at a women's rights' conference in Los Angeles. Her heart raced when she saw David in this photo, too, except he hadn't seemed to change physically. He appeared exactly the same age, this time wearing a low–cut blousy black shirt with gold chains around his neck and his hair down and long hanging around his face. Debbie knew she had to find more pictures, but the internet photos didn't go back beyond the sixties.

Debbie asked the librarian if there was any data on microfiche and was led to a special room where the microfiche data had been loaded onto computers. Debbie sat down to research PSI in its original stages. There were many articles written by her great–grandmother, Alexandria Taninsam, under the name, "Women's Birth Control Review." These articles were written sometime between the early to mid–1920s. There was also a book called, "A

New Civilization," written by Alexandria. The articles together with the book led to the creation of the first Parenting Services International in New York City.

There were quite a few New York papers that carried headlined articles about the newly formed women's health clinics. Alexandria was pictured with the mayor and several women who staffed the clinic. Debbie almost stopped breathing when she saw David standing next to Alexandria in a black pin–striped suit. His black hair was shorter and slicked back from his face, but he looked exactly the same with no difference from year to year at all.

Debbie smiled coyly as if she had just unearthed a deep, dark secret. She continued to stare at David Bloodstone in the photo and saw a man timeless and frozen, as if time meant nothing to him, as if he were beyond normal, earthly rules.

"Was David even human at all?" Debbie thought as she folded the three downloaded pictures and put them in her pocket.

Debbie thanked the librarian and started back toward the Museum of Modern Art to meet her family.

*

Cassy knew that something had changed. She was still in a coma, but it felt like she was finally coming to the water's surface after swimming in the deep for months. She had seen light on her journeys with Paolo, but the light of a distant reality was showing itself on the other side of her vision.

Cassy could make out voices on the other side. She thought she heard Drew, her beloved Drew. He was saying something to Dr. Andrews. Cassy could sense excitement in the room. She could hear Nurse Bridget murmuring joyfully as if there were a party in her hospital room. She could almost make out faces through the heavy fog of half–open eyelids and the sleep that had lasted for months.

Cassy felt her hand being lifted and held warmly. She blinked and tried to let her eyes function again. In her semi–consciousness, she swam hard and came so close to the surface that she could see air bubbles form from her nose and mouth. An upward and luminous motion led Cassy back to the physical reality she had yearned for so long.

Drew sat next to her and held her hand as Dr. Andrews and Nurse Bridget clapped and laughed, the four all together like long lost friends.

Drew spoke in a shaky, emotional tone. "Cassy," he began. "I've missed you so much. Thank God you're back."

Cassy found it easy to smile, but difficult to speak. She was so thankful, yet she had forgotten how to form words. She wanted to tell Drew how much she loved him and missed him, too. They waited silently as Cassy tried to utter unrecognizable sounds.

Drew gently squeezed Cassy's hand as she continued to stammer unsteadily until she felt comfortable enough to form words again. "How…did…you know…I was…waking?" she finally asked.

Dr. Andrews spoke first, "Bridget came into your room to check on you, and she saw your eyelids fluttering. She immediately called me, and I called Drew."

Cassy smiled and tried to sit up on her own; she was so excited to be with those she loved. Dr. Andrews pushed a button on Cassy's bed, and her body was elevated to a sitting position.

"Thank…you," Cassy said exhausted from trying to sit up and all the excitement. Her body had slept for so long, she wasn't used to being awake.

Dr. Andrews and Nurse Bridget excused themselves and left the room so that Cassy and Drew could be alone. They would come back later to run tests.

Drew pushed the button again so that Cassy could recline back. He ran his hands over her forehead to make Cassy more comfortable. She let out an exhausted sigh as she allowed her head to sink back into the pillow. She was still so tired. Drew kissed her forehead a few more times, and Cassy slowly wrapped her arms around her husband realizing again how much she had missed him.

Suddenly, Cassy pulled herself up using Drew's shoulders for support. It was as if Cassy's strength had come back in a single second.

"What's wrong?" Drew asked.

"We need to contact Father Raphael right away," Cassy said.

"Cassy, are you okay?"

"Yes, I'm fine, but we need Father Raphael's help as quickly as possible."

CHAPTER FORTY

As Debbie walked back to the MOMA to meet her parents and Father Mac, she felt like the central character in an episode of "The Twilight Zone." What did PSI have to do with ancient sacrifices? How could David exist without aging? Nothing made any logical sense. Debbie needed her parents and Father Mac now more than ever. She needed rational people who could make sense of what was happening around her.

Debbie entered the MOMA and showed her ticket to the guard at the top of the stairs. She looked up at the clock and was surprised to see how much time had passed since she left the museum. Debbie was supposed to meet her parents and Father Mac at the entrance, but they had not arrived yet and it was already seven o'clock. The museum was only open for one more hour.

Debbie went back to the Tophet Exhibit to study the PSI symbol again to see if there was any information she was missing. She would check back at the entrance every fifteen minutes.

As Debbie walked to the glass enclosure of the exhibit, she saw the Tophet marker looming in the distance like a tombstone in an abandoned graveyard. Suddenly, David lunged toward her and grabbed onto her wrist. It hurt so badly, she had to stifle a cry or she knew that he would tighten his grip.

"Are you curious how I found you?" David said under his breath.

"Nothing about you surprises me anymore," Debbie retorted coldly. She was so scared, she was almost crying, but she didn't want David to know.

"Then it won't surprise you to know you're coming back with me and won't be leaving for a very, very long time." David's eyes were so menacing, they looked like they were glowing green.

"Where are we going?" Debbie asked even though she knew he was taking her back to his apartment. That was David's lair.

"Your new home," he replied with a cold smile.

David took Debbie by the arm as nonchalantly as possible to the MOMA exit. They passed by the entrance where Debbie was supposed to meet her family, and she dropped a New Yorker Hotel card on the ground just inside the door. It was the only thing she could think to do to let her family know where they could find her.

*

By the time David and Debbie made it back to his apartment, Debbie knew the best way to buy time was to act like she was Deborah again. The last thing she wanted was to have him control her again with her necklace.

David shut the door and pushed Debbie into the foyer. She used the opportunity to act like the force of his push had made her fall. When Debbie got up from the floor, she used whatever acting skills she possessed to become Deborah.

"David, my love, how long have you been gone?" Debbie walked toward David, her words delivered in a low, seductive growl.

"Deborah?" David asked, genuinely surprised.

"Yes, darling, it's me." Debbie put her arms around his shoulders and down his back. Her hands rested on the back of his jeans, and she felt a small piece of paper sticking up from one of his back pockets.

David grabbed Debbie hard and kissed her forcefully with a rough and ravenous passion. After several seconds, he pulled away from her skeptically.

Debbie held onto the paper as she released her arms and hid it in her left hand.

"One minute, darling," David said and walked into the master bedroom suite.

Debbie grabbed an umbrella and hid it behind her back like a sword.

David came back clutching her bloodstone cameo necklace. "Yours, darling," he said and held the necklace up to her.

Debbie screamed and pulled the umbrella out to strike David, but he was too quick for her.

David grabbed the umbrella in one hand and grasped her around the throat with the other. He beat her effortlessly and mercilessly. When he was through, Debbie was left sprawled on the floor like a limp, rag doll. David tied her to a chair with rope and slammed the door as he stormed out of the apartment.

Debbie was left barely alive sitting in the foyer of David's apartment, tied to a chair. She had been stranded again, but this time she knew who her captor was, and she was scared for her life.

*

Father Raphael arrived at Valley Hospital and said a special blessing for Cassy. She remained weak, but seemed to find renewed strength from the blessing. Cassy asked Drew if she could speak with their priest friend alone.

"Of course. I'll be downstairs getting coffee," Drew replied lovingly. He winked at Cassy and closed the door behind him.

Cassy turned back to Father Raphael, "Father, what I am about to tell you may seem inconceivable, but I need to share it with you. It's something very important that happened to me while I was in the coma."

"Try me," Father Raphael replied.

Cassy told Father Raphael about every spiritual journey she had taken with Paolo. She told him about what she had learned about her Taninsam ties, David Bloodstone, and most importantly, the one true Bloodstone that existed within the protection of the Christ Stone. Cassy told Father Raphael about her new mission, the mission she needed to fulfill with her sister, Debbie, and her Aunt Jessica. This mission had become Cassy's purpose in life and would ultimately save the lives of millions.

When she finished, Father Raphael, stood up, squeezed her hand and kissed her on the cheek. He walked over to his attaché case, the one he always carried, and gave her a small statue of Saint Michael, the Archangel.

"Cassy, I want you to keep this with you at all times from now on. Just as Saint Paolo was your protector during your spiritual journeys, Saint Michael will be your protector now. You have been blessed with a great task, but this task may seem like a heavy burden. Christ's cross was a heavy burden, but the cross leads to salvation. Crosses become our transportation to heaven."

*

After meeting with Cassy, Father Raphael drove back to Saint Mary's and stopped in the church to pray. He genuflected in front of the tabernacle and knelt before the shrine he had constructed for Our Lady of Guadalupe. The colorful shrine made of a bright mosaic pattern of stones reminded Raphael of his Mexican roots.

Underneath the mosaic, there was an assortment of different colored vases filled with fresh red roses. For one split second, Raphael thought he saw a piece of white paper sticking up underneath one of the vases. He had just knelt in prayer, but his curiosity got the best of him, and he stood up to retrieve the paper.

"Like the rainbow gleaming among luminous clouds like the

bloom of roses in spring," the paper read.

"Just like Our Lady of Guadalupe," Father Raphael thought as he noticed the golden "KofC" emblem at the bottom of the paper. The priest assumed it must have been written by a fellow member of the Knights of Columbus and folded it twice before he placed it in his pocket. Raphael knelt again to pray for Cassy, but he jumped up immediately when he heard a loud scream from inside the sacristy.

Father Raphael ran into the sacristy and saw Kevin Dennis on his knees crying into his hands. The priest was about to ask the boy what happened when he witnessed the tragedy himself. Someone had broken into the sacristy and vandalized the sacred space with large, grotesque handprints. From a distance, it looked like they had used red spray paint, but as Raphael came closer to the wall, he realized it was not paint at all, but blood. Father Raphael's heart plummeted to the pit of his stomach as tears rolled down his cheeks.

The blood was smeared in thick sheets across the wall. Most of the bloody marks looked like pentagrams, and some had the word, "Reign," written in the center. Other pentagrams had large handprints smeared into the center. When Father Raphael looked closely, he could see a tiny word written in Biblical Hebrew. It looked like "MLK," but he knew what it meant without having to translate: "Moloch, the god of death."

Father Raphael studied the bloody symbols and noticed that the blood seemed to get thicker the closer he came to the sink. The priest thought he saw little skeletal body pieces stuck into the gobs of blood.

What the priest saw when he finally reached the sink made him cry out loud as he clutched his mouth in horror. There, in the sacristy sink, was the mutilated body of a fully–developed and aborted baby, her little body covered in the same red blood as the walls.

Father Raphael went to Kevin who was still quietly crying on the floor. The priest would call the police, but not before he had comforted and protected his sacristan.

*

When the Romanos and Father Mac reached the Museum of Modern Art in Manhattan, it was only minutes before the museum's closing. They had no way of knowing that David had roughly escorted Debbie back to his apartment in the Manhattan Center only ten minutes before. The three searched everywhere for Debbie and asked the security guards on duty whether they had seen her from a photo Lucia carried in her purse. Only one guard remembered seeing her, but that had been hours before.

When Father Mac exited the MOMA behind the Romanos, he saw a small white card lying on the ground and picked it up. It was a New Yorker Hotel card; the same hotel Debbie had told Lucia about on the phone; the same hotel Debbie had been held against her will by David.

"Lucia? Pietro?" Father Mac called as he held up the hotel card to Debbie's parents. "David's got her again."

When the Romanos and Father Mac checked into a suite at The New Yorker Hotel, they immediately began a search for Debbie, but days passed without any luck. The police and hotel staff assisted them to the best of their abilities, but Debbie could not be located anywhere. It was as if she and David did not exist.

*

When the plane began its descent into LaGuardia International Airport in New York, Linda's mind was racing out of control. She and Michael received a message from Father Mac when they returned from Montreal: Debbie had disappeared again, and their only clue was a New Yorker Hotel card. The Romanos and Father Mac were staying at the hotel, but they couldn't find Debbie anywhere. Linda and Michael would meet them there and help with the search.

Linda looked at Michael who sat next to her on the plane. He had fallen asleep. "Poor thing," she thought. Their wild goose chase had made it impossible to get a good night's rest, and they were both exhausted.

Linda figured if she couldn't sleep, she might as well go over her research. She took out her notebook. First, they would check into The New Yorker Hotel and reconnect with Father Mac and the Romanos to compare notes. Second, they would visit Saint Patrick's Cathedral, the cathedral that housed the Archbishop of New York, to find possible leads to the Christ Stone and the mysterious death of James Goodrich's father.

Linda flipped to the next page of her notebook and saw the Calatrava flier that was left inside her back door the day of the boat accident on Lake Geneva.

"After all," Linda thought, "That flier had a Manhattan address on it and there was a key taped near the address." She sat back in her seat and thought about the address.

"Wait a second!" Linda looked back at the address on the flier. It read, "311 West 34th Street." The New Yorker Hotel was also located on 34th Street.

Linda looked through her notes for the confirmation e–mail. The hotel was on 34th Street and 8th Avenue; the same address as the hotel where Debbie was being held captive and the same address as the Calatrava flier with the key.

*

When Cassy woke in her hospital bed in the middle of January, it was as if the coma had no effect on her body at all. She had a mission, and by the grace of God, she had been given all the energy she would need to fulfill that mission.

"Drew, this may sound unbelievable, but I feel completely

recovered. I have a strange feeling that I'm needed in New York, and I need you and Father Raphael to come with me."

Cassy's husband let go of her hand as soon as she mentioned leaving the hospital. "Cassy, it's only been two weeks since waking from months of being in a coma. You can't be serious."

"I am more serious about this than I have ever been about anything else in my life."

"I know, Cassy. I know," Drew replied. "You're serious and, frankly, I've become more serious about it, too. Ever since I found the note from Dr. Lanton. Father Raphael feels it, too. Something is happening, something huge, and I have a feeling we're right in the middle of it. I'll get the doctor."

When Dr. Andrews and Nurse Bridget followed Drew back into Cassy's hospital room, Cassy was already dressed and ready to leave.

"Cassy, what are you doing?" Steve Andrews asked.

"Dr. Andrews, we need to leave. You've checked my vitals. You know I've made a complete recovery. Drew and I need to leave." Cassy looked at both the doctor and nurse with the kind of pleading that comes from complete desperation.

Steve Andrews walked over to Cassy and gave her a hug. "Cassy, I trust you. If you feel that you're ready to leave, I'll sign you out immediately."

"Thank you, Dr. Andrews." Cassy walked over to her nurse. "And Nurse Bridget," Cassy said as she hugged her, "thank you for everything."

*

When Father Raphael received a call from Cassy and Drew about New York, the first person he thought of was Veronica. She had been discharged from the hospital the day before Christmas and had spent the week between Christmas and New Year's recuperating.

Veronica had gone back to work, but Father Raphael kept in constant contact because he was worried about her safety. "Veronica, I know that all of these things are related: the vandalism at the church, Cassy's spiritual dreams, her mysterious visitor, a man named David Bloodstone, even your accident. Cassy and Drew want to leave for New York right away."

Veronica sat at her desk staring at the statue of Saint Michael she had received from Father Raphael. "How long will you be gone?" she finally asked.

"I don't know. A week or two? I told the parish I'd be gone through January, just in case. I have the feeling I'm about to embark on something really important. Like a crossroads where the forces of good and evil come face to face. It's like we've always talked about, Veronica. A great spiritual battle that's been brewing for decades about to come to fruition."

"Well, you had better be careful, Obi–Wan Kenobi. I don't want Darth Vader and the Death Star taking you down." Veronica was more serious than sarcastic.

"Hey, I've got something mightier than a light saber on my side," Father Raphael replied.

"What's that?"

"God, the Father; Jesus Christ, His Son; and the Holy Spirit, my Sanctifier."

"I know, I know, but I can still worry," Veronica said seriously.

"Don't worry, be happy. And pray," Father Raphael replied paternally.

"I will. I will. See you in a couple weeks?"

"Si, adios."

"Yeah, adios to you, too. And Father?" Veronica asked.

"Yes?"

"May the force, and I mean the force of God, be with you."

CHAPTER FORTY–ONE

Michael and Linda met Father Mac and the Romanos in the lobby of The New Yorker Hotel. The lobby had high ceilings, a large low–hanging crystal chandelier and polished marble floors that reflected light like a glowing pool of water. Michael and Linda ran up to their three fellow "cheeseheads," but Father Mac looked unusually depressed, and the Romanos were so crestfallen, it looked like they had been grieving for days.

"No news yet?" Michael asked though he already knew the answer.

"Not a one," Father Mac replied sadly.

"Well, we have some," Linda said optimistically. She suggested they all meet in the Romanos' suite as soon as possible.

Linda took the Calatrava flier with the key and address out of her notebook as soon as she and Michael walked into the Romano's room. "This address is not sheer coincidence," she said. "Someone wanted us to find this place."

"Now, we just have to find the lock that fits that key," Michael added pointing to the Calatrava flier.

"Where do we start?' Father Mac asked.

"The concierge," Michael replied.

"You think the concierge can help us find our daughter?" Pietro

Romano asked.

"I think the concierge can give us a tour of the hotel," Michael answered with a wink and a smile.

"Michael, I don't think concierges give tours of private property," Linda said.

"But I'm doing a story...on the beautifully renovated New Yorker Hotel," Michael responded pulling out his press pass.

*

Michael walked up to the concierge and smiled handsomely at the cute young girl in her twenties. "This out to be easy," he thought.

"Can I help you?" she asked pleasantly.

"Yes, Michael Murray," he replied as he shook the concierge's hand and showed her his press pass. Michael told her he was doing a story for "Travel and Leisure" and needed a tour of the hotel.

"I'd be happy to show you the hotel," she said grandly, excited about the possibility of getting exposure in a magazine. "I'm actually studying to be an actress," she said. "I just do this job to pay the bills."

"Yeah, you and every other pretty young head in New York," Michael thought as he exclaimed, "Great!"

Lucy, the concierge, was eager to show Michael every nook and cranny of the hotel. He carried along his camera for authenticity and snapped pictures every few minutes, even taking some of Lucy in different locations to gain "brownie points." Michael received a tour of the lobby, the restaurant, the café, the diner, the ballroom, the convention center and one of the hotel's suites on the penthouse floor, but nothing stood out or looked any different. If Debbie were being held captive somewhere in the hotel, there was nothing obvious to indicate it.

Outside the penthouse elevators, Michael asked Lucy how many suites and hotel rooms there were in the hotel.

"Twelve suites and 680 rooms," she replied.

"Are there any rooms that are ever rented or leased for longer periods of time?" he asked again.

"No."

Michael and Lucy walked into the elevator, and he watched as Lucy hit the "L" button for lobby. There was no button for the eighth floor, which seemed odd.

"What happened to the eighth floor?" he asked.

"That floor is used by the Manhattan Center."

"What is the Manhattan Center?"

"That's where they have concerts and such. The eighth floor has business offices that are used by the Manhattan Center."

"Is there a way to go back and forth from The New Yorker Hotel to the Manhattan Center?" Michael asked as if this might pertain to his article.

"There's a glass door on the eighth floor that leads to the Manhattan Center, but only authorized personnel of the hotel have key cards for that door." It was obvious by Lucy's expression that she did not have a key card for the door.

"I see," Michael said trying to sound as disappointed as possible.

A smile crossed Lucy's face. "I do know where we can get a key, though," she said.

"You do?" Michael flashed her a smile a mile wide.

"One of the security guys has been trying to get me to go out with him for weeks," she said laughing. "He'd probably give me the keys to his car if I asked him."

Before Michael knew it, he was walking toward the glass door on the eighth floor with Lucy and the security guard. The guard took the key from his pocket like he was the President of the United States and when Michael heard the lock click open, Lucy decided to stay behind with the guard. She didn't want to get in trouble if someone saw her in an unauthorized area, and she needed to get back to work. The security guard was happy to escort her back down alone.

Michael continued along the corridor of Manhattan Center's business offices. There was a difference between the hotel ambiance and the corporate world, but it didn't seem like these offices were actually leased or owned by businesses. They were too empty and quiet for business activity.

Michael rounded the corner and saw what looked like a suite at the end of the hallway. The door was too ornate to be someone's business door. Michael stopped at the door and put his head against it to see if he could hear anything inside. He thought he could hear a muffled voice on the other side of the door.

Linda had been smart enough to give Michael the mysterious key just in case. He took it out of his pocket and stopped to think about whether he was doing the right thing.

"I made it this far, so why not?" Michael thought. He stuck the key into the door suddenly anxious about running into the man in black who had now become everyone's enemy. The lock turned instantly, and Michael stepped inside of the suite before he could stop himself. He immediately came upon a grand foyer with luxurious and expensive furniture. A girl with long black hair sat in a chair in the center of the foyer with her back to him. Her hands and feet were tied to the chair, so she couldn't move.

"Debbie?" Michael asked as he walked around to the front of the chair.

Debbie looked up at Michael, her mouth gagged with a long white scarf.

Michael knelt in front of Debbie and untied her mouth gag and her hands. She looked incredibly weak, but she was holding a small piece of paper in her fist for Michael to take. For all he knew, Debbie could have been holding that piece of paper for days. Michael gently took the paper and opened it. It read, "01/22/13."

Michael didn't stop to ask questions. He could do that later. For now, his only priority was to get Debbie to safety.

*

Archbishop Gabriel Sanders and Father Derek Ekwonye had worked with Catholics United for Life since the beginning of the new millennium. They worked with Father Frank Pavone, the President of Priests for Life, and Father Shenan J. Boquet, the President of Human Life International, to uncover the numerous unlawful practices of PSI and other abortion chains that received government funds through tax dollars.

The latest scandal involved a female college student who worked undercover for Catholics United for Life posing as an underage pregnant teen at a local PSI clinic. She told a PSI employee that she was raped by her 35–year–old boyfriend, and the employee told her on tape that she could hide that information from her parents and local authorities. At another PSI clinic, a male student posed as a hustler who was involved in sex trafficking of minors. This PSI employee told him on tape that "his girls" could get easy abortions and still work the streets as soon as possible.

The four priests and their pro–life organizations had caught these PSI employees red–handedly, but nothing seemed to stop pro–choice politicians and abortion lobbyists from continuing tax–funded government money to big "non–profit" abortion businesses.

However, when JamBrax's corrupted research on embryonic stem cell experimentation came out as linked to PSI, the negative press hit the streets from both sides of the fence, and even the pro–choice bureaucrats were silenced.

Elaina and David were furious over the news: Elaina knew it could hurt profits; David knew it could lessen the number of abortions performed; and both knew that Archbishop Gabe Sanders and Father Derek Ekwonye were behind the revelations.

Murder was the only thing on David's mind when he left Elaina. He would not send for anyone else to take care of this for him. This, he would take care of himself.

*

Father Gabe, Father Derek, Jessica and Jonathan felt exuberant when they came back from the local pizzeria in the Italian section of San Francisco right around the corner from Saints Peter and Paul Church. They had unearthed enough corruption between Palmer and PSI that it looked like the abortion empire was about to implode. To celebrate, Father Derek promised to show them his magnificent "Italian Cathedral of the West."

As the four walked through the city park toward Saints Peter and Paul Church, Father Derek told them stories of the bombing of the original church building back in 1926. "The bomber struck four times before they finally nabbed him," the priest animatedly recounted the story to his listeners. "The police were set up all over the place in disguise every night from 11 to 5 because that's the time he always struck. One night, he came up with a package and laid it close to the entry wall. He bent down to strike a match to light the fuse, and...BANG! The pitiful guy's standing before the Lord in Judgment. Have mercy on his soul, Lord. Have mercy on his soul." Father Derek made the sign of the cross as he spoke.

"Why would someone do that?" Jessica asked. "Did they find out why?"

"Just some raving wild–eyed sidewalk preacher who patronized the bars on Third Street," Father Derek answered.

"You'd think that would be the last place someone would want to bomb," Jonathan interjected. "God's house, I mean."

"Unfortunately, not everyone believes in God," Father Derek replied.

"Unfortunately, some people believe in the opposite of God," Father Gabe added. "Like only seeing the negative image of a photograph."

"You mean turning light into darkness and darkness into light?"

Jessica asked.

"I mean some people work for Satan," Father Gabe replied. "Some people work for him and they don't know it, while others work for him and they know exactly who they work for."

"Who would want to work for Satan intentionally? Don't they believe in Hell?" Jonathan asked.

"You'd be surprised. They're all around us. You see them every day, but you don't know. Sometimes you know. Like with Palmer and Elaina. But most of the time you don't know. There are so many lost souls who risk damnation for all eternity."

"What can we do?" Jessica asked.

"Pray."

*

Father Derek entered Saints Peter and Paul Church with the Archbishop of San Francisco and Jessica and Jonathan close behind. They walked along the bright red carpet toward the altar, which was made of white marble with gold trim that gleamed like the eternal kingdom. There was a large mosaic of Jesus holding the Bible with one hand and gesturing a sign of the cross with the other above the altar. Jesus wore a red cloak, and the letters, "IC," "N," "K," and "XC" appeared in red above his head.

"What do the letters mean above Christ's head?" Jessica asked.

"They mean 'Jesus Christ conquers,'" Father Derek answered.

"Conquers what?" Jonathan asked.

"Evil," Father Derek responded again.

Father Gabe stepped forward, "Conquering evil was so essential to Jesus Christ's mission Saint John said, 'The reason the Son of God appeared was to destroy the works of the devil."

Suddenly, they heard a horrible and deep cackle that seemed to come from the depths of the church. They could feel the floor shake as if a seismic earthquake were penetrating the floors of Saints Peter and Paul Church at that very moment. The floor in front of the altar split in two forming a long crevice with large pieces of marble on either side. They were separated with Jessica and Jonathan on the left side and the two priests on the right.

Jessica gasped for breath as she saw green smoke rise from the crevice in the floor. A tall man with long, black hair rose through the floor amid the green smoke. He stood among them and smiled menacingly, his eyes green and glaring with rage.

"You want evil?" the man asked in a low growl, his teeth like the fangs of a wolf and his eyes seething like those of a vicious cat on the attack. "I'll give you evil like you've never seen before!"

The man in black grew to a monstrous size and hovered over them from the frescos of the ceiling. The marble columns that held up the altar shook from the force of the evil perpetrator, and Jonathan saw one of the columns directly above the two priests start to fall.

"Watch out!" Jonathan yelled as he leaped over the cracked floor and raced to Father Gabe and Father Derek. Jonathan made it just in time. He jumped up and pushed Father Gabe onto his back and out of the way of the column.

Jessica and the two priests breathed a sigh of relief until they realized what had happened. Jonathan had been crushed by the column in his attempt to save Archbishop Sanders. Jessica let out a shriek and leaped over the cracked marble floor to Jonathan's side as he lay cold and still underneath the column.

The monster–like figure that had killed Jonathan went to strike a different column to bring down the two priests, but Jessica witnessed a great white light flash above Jesus' mosaic head where the dove of the Holy Spirit was painted. She looked back to make sure the two priests were still unharmed. When Jessica turned back to the menacing creature, he had disappeared. A holy man dressed in white had come to conquer the evil one.

Jessica looked upon him thankfully. She needed no introduction. "Paolo," she thought as her hand rested on Jonathan's slain body.

*

When Michael knocked on the Romanos' door, he felt a surge of emotion run through him at the prospect of reuniting Debbie with her parents. Pietro was the first to open the door and see his daughter alive and free. Debbie was weak and famished, but Michael held her up so she could stand.

"Oh, my dear God!" Pietro exclaimed as he held his daughter in his arms.

Lucia ran forward, tears running down her cheeks, and the three embraced warmly for several minutes.

"Praise and glory be to a gracious and loving God!" Father Mac shouted from inside the room as Michael pulled the door shut.

Linda, who had not seen her best friend in months, came forward to give Debbie a long and tearful hug.

Debbie was too weak to stand, so Pietro helped her to the bed while Lucia ordered room service for her. Debbie realized how wonderful it was to have her mother and father there to take care of her again. It was more important for her to get back on her feet before she would tell them what she had discovered at the MOMA or what she had found out about David.

Michael and Linda decided to search David's suite before his return, but Michael knew that it might be difficult to get Lucy's help again. He thought it might be best to try to enter the eighth–floor suite from the Manhattan Center entrance instead. Father Mac wanted to join them to give Debbie a chance to reconnect with her parents alone.

It was freezing outside, but they hadn't thought to bring jackets. They made their way out of the hotel and quickly walked against the wind to the Manhattan Center entrance. It was only four in the afternoon, but it was already after dusk. They walked inside and saw a large African–American man seated at a security desk just inside the lobby texting someone on his iPhone.

"Can I help you?" he asked politely looking Father Mac up and down in his priestly garments.

"Yes," Michael came forward immediately with his press pass. "We're here from Saint Patrick's Cathedral. The office of Archbishop Timothy Cardinal Dolan. He's planning a conference here and wants us to check out the facility."

Father Mac and Linda looked at Michael curiously and immediately nodded their heads as if this were the most important assignment of their careers.

The security guard looked at Michael's press pass and again at Father's Mac's attire. He shook his shoulders, "No problem, the concert hall is on the second floor. Do you need someone to show you around?"

"No, thank you," Michael replied innocently. "We'll find our way."

"Elevator's straight ahead," the guard said and went back to his iPhone.

They walked to the elevator and hit the "up" button. It was unused and immediately opened in front of them. They walked in and Michael pressed "8." When they got off, Michael took the key out of his pocket while Linda and Father Mac followed close behind. They walked around the corner from the elevator, and Michael breathed a sigh of relief when he saw that the suite door was still closed at the end of the corridor.

When they reached the door, Michael placed his ear against it to make sure there was no one inside. He inserted his key. The door opened easily, and Linda and Father Mac followed Michael inside. The chair still sat in the center of the foyer with loosened ropes.

"Poor Debbie," Linda said.

"Thank God she's safe now," Father Mac added.

"Let's look for clues," Michael interjected. "I don't feel like facing Debbie's abductor."

"Good idea," Linda agreed.

There was a large living room with high windows, a kitchen,

study, guest room and master suite. Father Mac took the living room and kitchen; Linda, the study and guest room; and Michael, the master suite. Everything was so ornately decorated, the search for clues seemed like it would take all night.

After an hour, Father Mac and Linda felt there wasn't anything unusual. In fact, it didn't look like anyone lived there at all. The guest room, kitchen and foyer had been used by Debbie, but nothing else looked like it had even been touched.

Michael had been searching the master suite and, again, nothing appeared unusual and everything seemed untouched. He couldn't help but notice the expensive paintings in the room. They all appeared to be originals, and he realized how wealthy David Bloodstone must be.

Michael walked to the king size bed and saw an original Monet hanging above the headboard. He touched the ornate, gilded frame and pulled it back to see what an original looked like from the back. Michael couldn't believe his eyes. There was a safe built into the wall behind the painting.

"I found something!" Michael called to the other two.

"What is it?" Linda asked as she ran into the room with Father Mac right behind her.

"Look! Help me get this down." Michael and Father Mac climbed onto the bed to take the Monet off the wall. They laid it carefully on the end of the bed.

When Michael turned back to the safe, he realized that it was a combination lock. The key was only good for the front door.

"Michael, unless you or Linda is a professional burglar, I don't think we're getting in there," Father Mac said under his breath.

"Wait...I just may have something." Michael retrieved the crumbled note Debbie had given him from his pocket.

"What is it?" Linda asked.

"A note with a date on it that Debbie gave me when I rescued her," Michael said.

When Michael punched in the six numbers of the date, a

familiar "click" could be heard as the lock opened.

"You've got to be kidding me," Father Mac whispered as Michael opened the door of the safe and quickly withdrew its contents.

There was a small stack of papers—no stocks, no bonds, no jewelry, no money—just papers. The first was an old, yellowed original copy of an article on the front page of The New York Times dated January 22, 1973 entitled, "High Court Rules Abortions Legal the First 3 Months."

Underneath was a promotional folder from Parenting Services International with a printout of the number of abortions performed per year by each state since 1973 and the number of abortions performed per year by each country that had legalized abortion.

Underneath the PSI folder was an aged black and white photo of a beautiful woman with an exquisite cameo on the nape of her neck. She wore a low–cut black silk dress and had long, black wavy hair with intense black eyes.

Father Mac thought she looked like someone he had seen before. Perhaps an actress from years ago. He couldn't remember.

At the bottom of the pile, there was a picture of Saint Patrick's Cathedral and a recent newspaper clipping from the March for Life in Washington D.C. with a date scrawled in thick black ink that read, "01/22/13."

"The date on the paper Debbie gave me," Michael said. "The date that opened the lock."

"What happens on January 22nd, 2013?" Linda asked Father Mac.

"The date for the next March for Life in Washington D.C."

"Why would David care so much about the March for Life?" she asked again.

"I doubt he's going there to pray," Father Mac responded back.

"No, I think he has something planned that's a little less peaceful," Michael interjected. "Father, how many people were at the March for Life last year?"

"Almost five hundred thousand, but you'd never hear it from the major media. They like to pretend that no one goes or that it doesn't happen at all."

Linda's eyes widened as she gasped. "Michael, you're saying that David might be trying to wipe out a half a million people on January 22nd? That's only a week away!"

CHAPTER FORTY–TWO

If Palmer Braxton thought relocating to Barbados and taking up a new identity as John Reginald Miller was going to protect him from David Bloodstone, he was sorely mistaken. David had many demon spirits working for him and they had human contacts in every corner of the globe, including Barbados.

Palmer was only "John" for about a week when David's cohorts found him deep–sea diving off a rented boat on the Caribbean. It was very simple. David waited for Palmer to emerge out of the water and tied him to a seat. Then, David rigged a bomb and blew up the boat. David also blew up JamBrax.

No Palmer. No JamBrax. No evidence against PSI.

*

Michael, Linda and Father Mac carried the contents of David's safe back to the Romano's suite at The New Yorker Hotel. They figured the "cat was already out of the bag" since David would discover Debbie missing anyway. He'd be livid at that discovery alone.

Before leaving David's apartment, they closed the safe and placed the Monet back on the wall. There was a chance David wouldn't even know the safe's contents were missing. He'd be more interested in Debbie's location. Besides, they knew their only chance of survival was to locate the Christ Stone, and the information in the safe might provide a clue to its whereabouts.

When Pietro answered the door, he seemed relieved that they were safe and that it wasn't David Bloodstone who had come knocking. He said that Debbie had eaten a full meal from room service and had fallen asleep in her mother's arms.

Michael showed Pietro what they had discovered, and they rifled through David's papers in the living room of the suite. If each were a piece of a puzzle, they all seemed to go together. Everything except the picture of the woman with the cameo and the picture of Saint Patrick's Cathedral.

The group decided that Father Mac should stay at the hotel with the Romanos to find out the identity of the woman in the picture while Michael and Linda travel to Saint Patrick's Cathedral.

"We'll meet back at the hotel for dinner. By then, Debbie should be awake and we can find out what she knows, too." Michael spoke as he and Linda made their way to the door. "In the meantime, make sure you check the door before you answer it. Next time we meet up with 'you know who,' I want to be prepared."

*

Father Mac went to the hotel's business center to research the mysterious woman in the picture whom he knew he had seen before. He ascertained, first, that the woman was not a famous movie star. His second theory was that the woman could have been a Taninsam family member or an employee of PSI, but these theories proved to be futile.

Father Mac knew he had seen the woman before. He knew that he had seen her image recently. He had not seen her on television or in person. He had seen her in a picture.

Suddenly, he knew exactly where he had seen her picture: Rabbi Levine's office. That was it. The picture of the woman his friend had loathed as much as anyone could loathe Satan. It was Lilith. Father Mac knew that the picture he and Michael had discovered in David's safe was a picture of Lilith.

*

Linda and Michael hailed a cab and arrived at Saint Patrick's Cathedral just before 5:00 p.m. They walked into the vestibule in the back of the Cathedral and were immediately transformed by its holy and peaceful aura. There was a slight fog of incense still hanging in the air, and the intricate Gothic design produced a feeling of mysticism that neither had experienced before. Linda took Michael's hand and he immediately squeezed it as if no words were needed to convey what they both felt: a love not only for one another, but for God and His Church, as well.

One of the two guards on either side of the center aisle smiled at the couple and nodded. Michael and Linda walked slowly up the aisle toward the magnificent altar in front of them, their hands still united as one. Thoughts of holy matrimony came into their minds as they proceeded forward. When they reached the altar, Michael and Linda kneeled and genuflected with a sign of the cross.

"Should we check out the small chapels behind the altar, first?" Michael asked as he turned to Linda.

"Yes, that seems like the best idea," Linda responded as if she were just coming out of a dream. She let go of Michael's hand and tried to get her mind back on the job of finding the Christ Stone.

They walked up the stairs to the left and passed by each chapel as quickly as possible once they saw who the saint was and whether or not that particular saint seemed likely to lead them to the stone. In the back of their minds, they knew that the most probable chapel would be one associated with Mary. After all, "through Mary to Christ." Directly behind the altar in the center of the chapels was one of the most beautiful chapels Linda and Michael had ever seen. It was the only chapel that was protected by glass doors.

The two smiled at one another and stepped inside hoping that this chapel would provide at least a clue to the whereabouts of the Christ Stone. There were about forty seats with kneelers in front of a large, white statue of Mary standing on a marble altar. A golden tabernacle with a lit candle sat to the right of Mary to let people know that Jesus was indeed present.

Michael and Linda walked to the front pew and kneeled down to pray. If they were going to find the stone that would defeat David Bloodstone and his evil plans for January 22nd, 2013, they needed to pray first and discover clues later. Ten minutes passed in silence.

When Michael raised his head, Linda looked at him and smiled. She felt suddenly overwhelmed with the urge to kiss him. Michael could sense what she wanted and as he leaned toward her, a shuffling noise came from somewhere behind them. They turned and saw an elderly man who worked for the Cathedral changing votives at the back of the chapel.

The man smiled kindly at the young couple and went back to his work. He had a glove on one hand and a metal tool in the other using the tool to take out the hot wax and the glove to place it in a box filled with sand.

Michael and Linda rose from the kneelers to search for clues in the chapel. They didn't want to touch anything they weren't supposed to touch, and they didn't want to appear conspicuous, so after walking around the chapel a couple of times trying to find something obvious, they realized there was nothing there and decided to move on. The two walked out of the glass doors and exchanged pleasantries with the man before making their way toward the other chapels. Again, there were no saints that stood out who might have held clues to the Christ Stone.

When Michael and Linda walked down the stairs toward the

altar, they noticed a beautiful shrine on the Saint Joseph side dedicated to Our Lady of Guadalupe. This was another altar dedicated to Mary, and more importantly, the only apparition of a pregnant Mary.

"Could it be possible that Our Lady of Guadalupe would lead them to the Christ Stone?" Michael thought.

As soon as he and Linda picked up fliers on "Our Lady of Guadalupe: Celestial Patroness of the Americas, Empress of the Americas, Star of the New Evangelization," the man who had been replacing the votives came toward them.

"Are you looking for the Christ Stone?" he asked.

Michael and Linda almost dropped their fliers, they were so taken aback by the man's question.

"How did you know?" Linda asked startled.

"Saint Padre Paolo told me you would come," he answered.

"Yes, we are looking for the Christ Stone," Michael replied as if he knew the man were speaking the truth. With everything he and Linda had been through so far, he was now quite comfortable with the phenomena of the spiritual world.

"You won't find it here," the man replied.

"Where can we find it?" Linda asked.

"The United Nations," the man answered hesitantly. "Monsignor John Crawford brought it there."

"Do you mean the priest who traveled with James Goodrich?" Michael asked.

"Yes."

"Do you know what happened to James? His son is hoping that his father might still be alive," Linda said.

"James is dead," the man replied sadly.

"Do you know how he died?" Michael asked.

"All I know is Monsignor Crawford wanted him out of the way."

"Do you know where we can find Monsignor Crawford?"

"He's in his office, but he won't see you if he knows why

you're here. Tell him you're with the media. He likes to see himself on television. Just out the doors on the left and in the building on the right."

"Thanks!" Michael and Linda both called out to the man as they rushed out of Saint Patrick's Cathedral.

*

Michael and Linda were buzzed right through to Monsignor Crawford's office as soon as he knew they were there for an interview. They said they were there to discuss the historical artifacts of the Cathedral, and Michael showed the Monsignor his press pass. Monsignor Crawford was in his early fifties, but he looked more like forty when he flashed his pearly white veneered teeth. He had perfectly combed dyed black hair and a fake spray-on tan that looked almost orange in the fluorescent office lights.

Michael, Linda and the Monsignor were discussing the first-generation relics located in the Cathedral, and Linda looked like she was taking very detailed notes as she repeatedly scribbled "Christ Stone" in her notebook.

"Your knowledge of these saints' relics is incredible," Michael said. "Saint Patrick's is fortunate to have you."

"I have a doctorate in church history," Monsignor Crawford replied.

"You know, I was recently commissioned to do a story on a mythological artifact called the Christ Stone," Michael began. "Of course, everyone knows it doesn't really exist, so there was very little information of value. If I had been able to discuss this topic with someone of your background and credentials, I probably would have been able to write a much more interesting piece." Michael looked over at Linda, his good and faithful assistant, who willingly nodded in mock agreement.

Monsignor Crawford's face turned a shade of red that made his fake orange tan look almost genuine. He quietly cleared his throat to regain his composure and shook his head back and forth as if he had never heard of such an artifact.

Michael continued, "Linda, I have never seen such humility in all my life. The Monsignor clearly has knowledge of the Christ Stone, but he doesn't want to appear like an expert in all fields. Please, Monsignor Crawford, you are clearly the most humble expert in the field of church artifacts that we have ever met."

As Monsignor Crawford sat in his chair looking at Michael and Linda, it became evident that he was struggling with how much information he should divulge about the Christ Stone. Talking about it should have been against his better judgment, but in the end, the Monsignor's ego won out. "I not only know of the Christ Stone," he said all too eagerly, "I have actually possessed it for a time."

"You mean it actually exists?" Michael asked overly incredulous.

"Yes, the Christ Stone exists," Monsignor Crawford replied with a slow smile.

"Can we see it?" Michael asked innocently.

"Off the record?" the Monsignor asked.

"Strictly, off the record," Michael replied.

"Yes, but it's not here."

*

Monsignor Crawford agreed to meet Michael and Linda at the United Nations building the next morning at 10 o'clock. The time worked well since Debbie needed the rest. She had not woken all afternoon or evening, and everyone assumed it would be better to discuss things with her the next day.

When Michael and Linda entered the United Nations' lobby, it would have been a lie to suggest that they were not absolutely thrilled to stand in one of the most important buildings in the entire world. Every single world leader had stood where they stood right now and it made them feel important.

At precisely ten o'clock, Monsignor Crawford greeted Michael and Linda and led them up a flight of stairs toward an elevator shaft at the end of a hidden hallway. It appeared to be a high security area, and the Monsignor had to hit some special code before he had access to the "up" button next to the elevator. The three stepped into the elevator when it arrived and Monsignor Crawford hit floor "10." When the doors opened onto the tenth floor, Michael and Linda were surprised to see a security guard seated at a table almost directly in front of the doors.

The Monsignor greeted the guard, showed a special I.D., placed his index finger on a special finger print screening device, and filled out a form to show name, signature, date, and time. Michael and Linda had to fill out the same form as Monsignor Crawford's guests. Then, they were led to a special room where Monsignor Crawford was given his lock box by the security guard who closed the door and left.

With great formality, Monsignor Crawford pulled out a small gold key and inserted it into the lock on the box. Before opening it, he said, "Again, Michael and Linda, what I am about to show you is 'off the record.'"

The Monsignor opened the lock box and pulled out a small black velvet pouch. He took a small jewelry box out of the pouch and announced, "Michael and Linda, I give you the Christ Stone."

Monsignor Crawford opened the box, but when he looked inside he became horribly alarmed.

"What's wrong?" Michael asked.

"It's gone! The Christ Stone is gone!" The Monsignor looked like his face was turning blue with anxiety.

To Michael and Linda, it looked like he wasn't even breathing. They began to fear that Monsignor Crawford was on the verge of a heart attack.

"What do you think happened to it?" Michael asked again.

"You think I know? Security! I am calling security

immediately!" Monsignor Crawford ran out to get the security guard and slammed the door behind him.

Michael and Linda were left alone staring at the empty Christ Stone box.

"Oh, my God!" Linda exclaimed as she picked up the box half thinking the Christ Stone would appear at any moment.

"What is this?" Michael asked noticing a small, white note sticking out of the black velvet pouch. He quickly pulled out the note. "From the land of the Aztec to the Queen of the New World. From East to West and back again, she seeks to protect life, liberty and happiness where they would no longer have her." Michael saw a small emblem at the bottom of the note that read, "KofC," with the date, "12/12/12."

They heard loud footsteps coming toward the door, and Michael shoved the note into his pocket as fast as possible.

When the door flew open, Monsignor Crawford entered looking like the poster child for Post-Traumatic Stress Syndrome. The security guard followed close behind looking almost as stressed as the Monsignor.

Monsignor Crawford picked up the box and held it out for the security guard. "You see? You see? Where is it?" he screamed. "This is a breech in national security, and I will have your badge if you do not locate this precious stone immediately!"

*

When Debbie finally woke, she told her parents that she needed to see Father Mac, Linda and Michael as soon as possible. She had discovered important information regarding David Bloodstone and PSI that she needed to share with them that was linked to the next March for Life. Pietro and Lucia recommended that she try to eat something to regain her strength first. Debbie managed to eat breakfast and shower. Afterward, she felt like she was almost back to her old self again.

Father Mac knocked on the Romano's door and told them there was a surprise waiting for them in the lobby. Debbie's eyes opened with fear at the thought of seeing David again, and Father Mac tried to calm her. "No, Debbie. It's not who you think. This is a good surprise," he said.

When the priest led the Romanos down to the lobby, Cassy, Drew and Father Raphael were waiting just underneath the chandelier. As soon as Cassy saw Debbie, she ran to her and embraced her warmly. They had not seen one another in years, and the sisters were both openly crying. It had been so long since they had been separated, neither wanted to let the other go.

Cassy and Debbie were both full–grown women now, and neither Elaina nor David would come between them again. Suddenly, they felt invincible, as if nothing could destroy their bond.

Pietro, Lucia, Drew and the two priests left Cassy and Debbie on the lobby couch and went to the front desk to get rooms for Father Raphael, and Drew and Cassy. When the group turned around with the room keys, the two sisters were so engrossed in one another, they hadn't even noticed they were left alone.

*

Jessica knew there was no use staying in San Francisco. Not without Jonathan. Her heart had been broken into a thousand pieces, and she felt like she couldn't breathe. Jonathan had saved the life of Archbishop Gabriel Sanders, but it had cost him his own.

The police had come to Saints Peter and Paul Church to file a report. There was no logical explanation for the crumbled marble floors and fallen columns than to say that the church had suffered a severe earthquake. There was no rational reason for Jonathan's death than to say that he had been killed because of a natural disaster.

Father Gabe had placed his arms around Jessica as Jonathan's body was taken from under the collapsed column and carried out of the church. Nothing else could be done. They were priests, not miracle workers. Jonathan was not coming back to life.

In that instant, Jessica realized there was important work to be done, and no amount of evil, no matter how powerful, was going to keep her from it. She knew in her heart that she was meant to go to New York. There, she would unite with Cassy and Debbie. There, she would discover what she needed to accomplish with the help of Father Gabe and Father Derek. If the three had any fear of David before, it was lost after Jonathan's death.

CHAPTER FORTY–THREE

Father Mac made sure that Father Raphael and Drew were settled in their rooms before he left the hotel to take time to pray before the Blessed Sacrament. On the spur of the moment, he checked a map for the closest Marian church he could find, which was near Gramercy Park in the Flatiron District of New York City. He bid farewell to Cassy and Debbie, who still sat chatting on the couch in the lobby, and hailed a taxi to Saint Mary's Church on East 15th Street.

When Father Mac stepped out of the taxi, he marveled at how modern the church looked from the outside. It was nestled on the corner, immersed with the other Flatiron buildings, but it stood out because of its glass façade. There was a tall steel cross sticking out of the furthest corner and a large, beautiful image of Christ on one of the outer walls.

Father Mac entered the church and gravitated to the altar dressed in his blacks looking like he was preparing for Mass at his home parish. He knelt in front of the tabernacle and said special prayers for Debbie and the Romanos, as well as Cassy, Drew and Father Raphael. Father Mac knew they were all in danger, but with the grace of God, everything good would prevail. Mass was about to begin, and Father Mac knew it must be a sign from above that he had arrived just in time.

After Mass, Father Mac noticed a beautiful shrine dedicated to Our Lady of Guadalupe near the back of the church. He knelt in front of Our Lady of Guadalupe and prayed for the unborn and an end to abortion. He prayed that God might help him on his mission to build a culture of life in the United States and all over the world.

"People need to believe in the beauty of all life," Father Mac thought. "And the belief starts at the point where life begins. Please, God, help them to believe."

When Father Mac rose from the kneeler, he saw a small piece of white paper lying underneath one of the smaller statues of Our Lady of Guadalupe. He stooped down to pick it up. The note was written in cursive. It read, "Count the caps that pay tribute to Mary, the Virgin, the Mother of God, and Queen of the Universe." There was a KofC emblem on the bottom of the note, and Father Mac knew right away that it must have been written by a member of the Knights of Columbus.

"Interesting," Father Mac thought. He put the note in his pocket and left the church to hail a cab back to the hotel.

*

Michael and Linda had to wait at the United Nations building until a detailed report of the missing Christ Stone was completed by the police before they were permitted to leave. They had never witnessed someone come so close to a heart attack as Monsignor Crawford had that day.

When the Monsignor realized the Christ Stone was missing, he turned beet red, and when he came back with the security guard, there were little droplets of sweat dripping from his forehead. By the time the police arrived, the Monsignor's collar was soaked with perspiration and his face looked like a blotchy sponge.

After the police searched the room with the lock box, velvet pouch, and black jewelry box, they were taken to another room where Linda, Michael and the Monsignor were searched again. However, no Christ Stone was found. The report was made and they were finally left alone several hours later.

"I can't believe it!" Monsignor Crawford was pacing back and forth in the little room, still bright red with anxiety and acting as if Michael and Linda had already left. "I always knew some little 'right–to–lifer' was going to come for it…that's why I took it to begin with…to get it out of the hands of the enemy. I took it and put it in the safest location I knew, and they still got their grubby little hands on it and stole it!"

"You mean you know who stole it?" Michael asked deciding to test his luck and see if he could get Monsignor Crawford to continue talking.

"No, I don't know who stole it! I know what stole it! Those pesty little Knights of Columbus maggots and their ridiculous anti-abortion agenda! Always poking their noses into my business at Saint Patrick's! I knew what they were after! They don't care if this whole planet gets polluted! No, they don't care if families have twenty kids each.

"If it weren't for programs like the United Nations Population Fund providing birth control and sterilization, where would we be? I don't care about forced abortions in China or Africa or any other place where the government tries to get a little control over its people. Why do you think the United Nations helped me hide the Christ Stone in the first place?

"I will not let the hindrance of too many people destroy this planet, and I don't care if half a million right–to–lifers have to die in Washington! As far as I'm concerned, they deserve it!"

For one split second, Monsignor Crawford realized he had said too much. Whatever made him open his mouth to spill everything, made him close his mouth just as quickly. He realized Michael and Linda knew too much, and they could tell in an instant that the Monsignor was now deciding what to do about them.

Michael knew he couldn't wait for the angry Monsignor to

decide. They were in great danger. Before he could think, Michael jumped up and threw his right fist into Monsignor Crawford's jaw as hard as he could. The Monsignor was thrown to the floor long enough for Michael to grab Linda's hand and pull her up and out the door as quickly as possible.

They could hear the Monsignor moaning in the background while they half–ran to the elevator that would take them back down to the floor above the lobby. Michael prayed that they would not need the same pass code to descend that Monsignor Crawford used to take the elevator up. When Michael and Linda reached the elevator, they could already hear security guards running to the room where they had left Monsignor Crawford.

"Please, God," Michael said as he reached out to hit the "down" button. Mercifully, the elevator door beeped and opened in front of them. They got in and hit the button for "2" as quickly as possible. For Michael and Linda, it was as if every floor were passing in slow motion; the elevator could not move fast enough.

When the doors finally opened on the second floor, there was a red alarm flashing and beeping as Michael and Linda ran to the escalator and rode down to the lobby. People in the lobby looked around to see what was wrong, and Michael and Linda tried to appear as nonchalant as possible, as if they were just other people trying to figure out the problem.

They hurried through the lobby, out the United Nations building, and climbed down the stairs to a line of waiting taxis on the street. Michael opened the door and grabbed Linda's elbow to help her in as he scooted in just beside her and closed the door.

"Thirty–fourth and eighth," he said to the cab driver as he handed him a fifty. "As fast as you can get us there."

Michael and Linda looked up toward the United Nations building and saw two security guards sprinting down the stairs as the cab screeched out into the city traffic.

Michael placed his hand on Linda's knee to try to calm her, but the tears were already rolling down her cheeks.

"He knew!" she cried. "He knew!"

*

Jessica knocked on the Romano's door with Father Gabe and Father Derek standing on either side of her. Cassy and Debbie had already made their way up to the large suite to join the rest of the group. When Pietro and Lucia opened the door, they were in complete shock to see Jessica. Regardless of the seriousness of the situation, both Cassy and Debbie ran to their aunt and the three women embraced with tears of joy. At long last, they were together and they knew no amount of evil could ever tear them apart again.

After Jessica introduced Father Derek and the Archbishop of San Francisco to the group, Cassy knew it was time for her to tell her story, the story Paolo had taught her through her spiritual travels. She gathered the group together, and everyone sat down to listen.

Cassy recounted what she knew of the counterfeit bloodstones and how they were created with jasper and the blood of Simon, the messenger from hell. She told them of the Aztec sacrifices to Moloch, the god of death, using the counterfeit bloodstones. Cassy saw the counterfeit bloodstones become powerful enough to turn Moloch "human." She told them that Moloch had become David Bloodstone.

Cassy had seen David unite with Lilith, the goddess of death, to form the first of the Taninsam witches, the same family of witches who were the bloodline of Jessica, Cassy and Debbie.

Cassy noticed that Debbie had begun to cry, so she took a moment to console her sister. The rest of the group seemed as if they were in shock, as if what she were saying couldn't be true. Everyone except Jessica. Jessica already knew.

Cassy told them that through PSI, the sacrificing to Moloch was allowed to continue. She said this was the only way David could remain "human."

"There is a way to defeat him," Cassy interjected. "To defeat David."

Cassy told them of the creation of the one true Bloodstone formed from jasper stone and the blood of Christ. The one true Bloodstone could destroy the god of death.

"I saw Aaron's breast plate and the power of the twelfth stone made of jasper," Cassy said. "I witnessed Aaron as he hid the Urim and Thummim in his breast plate, and I watched it being passed from King David to King Solomon. And I know that the Urim and Thummim was not made of this earth, but of heaven. I know all these things because of my great protector and spiritual guide—the man who taught me all these things so that I could bring them to you in order to defeat David."

"Who is your protector?" Father Gabe asked.

"Saint Padre Paolo," Cassy answered.

"You know Saint Padre Paolo even after his death?" Father Mac asked.

"Yes, and he is connected to each one of us in a very special way. You see, this has been planned for a very long time."

*

When Cassy finished her story, Father Mac told them about the information that Michael and Linda had found in the safe in David's apartment where Debbie had been held captive. Father Mac held up each clue to the group.

First, he took out the old, yellowed New York Times' article from January 22nd, 1973, entitled, "High Court Rules Abortions Legal the First 3 Months."

"Pretty obvious why he kept that one," Father Gabe said.

"Big party for David and PSI that day," Father Derek added.

Next, Father Mac showed them the PSI promotional folder with the number of abortions per year since 1973 and the number of abortions per year by each country that had legalized abortion.

"What's the total number of abortions worldwide since 1973?" Father Raphael asked.

"About two billion," Father Mac answered.

The whole room was silent for several seconds before anyone spoke.

Father Mac continued, "We also found this black and white photo." He held up the photo so everyone could see the picture of Lilith wearing her bloodstone cameo. "I did some research in the business center downstairs. Turns out this is Lilith, David's bride, and the mother of the Taninsam witches."

"Is that a bloodstone cameo necklace made from the counterfeit bloodstones around her neck?" Father Raphael asked.

"Yes," Father Mac replied. "It seems that every female member of the Taninsam family has bloodstone cameo necklaces made for them. The images of the women carved on the bloodstones were exact images of the women wearing them."

"Who made them?" Father Gabe asked.

"David? Lilith? Black magic? Your guess is as good as mine," Father Mac said.

"I think I might be able to answer that for you," Jessica spoke up for the first time that evening. "My brother, Samuel, was Elaina's husband and Cassy's and Debbie's biological father. He was the first Taninsam, as far as I know, to question the family's practices. My brother believed in the value of life, and for this he was killed.

"I never spoke of this before, but I know my brother discovered many secrets. These secrets were linked all the way back to the beginning of the Taninsam family...to the time of Moloch and Lilith when David first came to be. I can also guarantee that bloodstone cameo necklaces were never made. They were born just as the female infants were born. The necklaces appeared on the necks of the Taninsam baby girls as soon as they were delivered from the womb, and they can never be destroyed."

"What happened to our necklaces, then?" Debbie asked.

"I don't know," Jessica answered. "My brother discovered a secret incantation that would allow the Taninsam witch to be separated from her necklace. That's the only reason you and Cassy and I have not had to endure the burden of wearing them any longer. And only David has the power to bestow the necklaces on us again."

*

When Father Mac pulled out the newspaper clipping from the March for Life in Washington D.C., everyone in the suite knew that January 22nd was only two days away. He held the clipping out for everyone to see and pointed to the thick black ink scrawled along the article that read, "01/22/13."

"So, David's got big plans for the March for Life?" Father Gabe asked.

"Wouldn't the 'March for Death' be more up his alley?" Father Derek countered.

Father Raphael snickered sarcastically. "What would David want with the March for Life?" he asked.

"To kill the marchers," Father Mac responded seriously. "If he gets rid of the marchers, he gets rid of the pro–lifers."

"How many attended last year?" Father Derek asked.

"Almost five hundred thousand," Father Gabe answered.

Pietro rolled his eyes and shook his head. "Oh, my good and gracious God."

"Cassy, you said the only way to defeat David was to find the Christ Stone, right?" Father Gabe asked.

"Yes, that's right," Cassy answered. "Paolo entrusted this last mission to all of us."

"How close are we to finding the Christ Stone?" Father Gabe asked again.

Father Mac took the last clue out of the pile of documents—the picture of Saint Patrick's Cathedral. He held it up. "This was the last thing in David's safe. We think it might be a clue to the Christ Stone's location."

"How do you know?" Drew asked.

"Michael and Linda were sent from Montreal to New York to find the Christ Stone. They met with a priest at Saint Patrick's Cathedral yesterday, and they're meeting with him again today."

"At the Cathedral?" Cassy asked.

"At the United Nations," Father Mac answered.

*

There was such a sharp bang on the Romano's door that everyone literally jumped in their seats.

"I'll get it," Father Gabe said as he got up from his seat. "If it's David, I'll punch his lights out."

"I've got your back," Father Derek said from behind.

When Father Gabe opened the door, Linda and Michael were standing there in complete bewilderment and out of breath. They figured either they had the wrong room or Lucia and Pietro had hired a couple of priestly linebackers as bodyguards.

"What's going on?" Linda asked.

"You must be Linda," Father Gabe said with a big smile. "And Michael." Father Gabe shook Linda's and Michael's hands, and they entered the Romano's suite to join the rest of the group. Everyone stood while the San Francisco trio was introduced.

"Did you find it?" Father Mac asked Michael and Linda.

"Yes…and no," Michael replied. "It was stolen from the United Nations by someone from the Knights of Columbus."

"The Knights of Columbus?" Father Gabe questioned bewildered.

"We think so. Why? Do you know something?" Michael asked.

"As a matter of fact, I found this note, and it was written by someone from the Knights." Father Gabe took the note he had found near the shrine of Our Lady of Guadalupe out of his pocket

465

and held it up for everyone to see.

"My heavens!" Father Mac exclaimed.

"Holy Mary, Mother of God!" Father Raphael said at the same time.

Father Mac, Father Raphael and Father Gabe all held up their white notes simultaneously.

"Paolo," Cassy thought to herself.

*

After dinner, the group sat in the Romano's suite for hours trying to see if they could make any sense of the four clues written on the Knights of Columbus letterhead. They knew they had less than 48 hours to find the Christ Stone and get it to D.C. before the March for Life began.

When the notes were placed together, the one that seemed to trump all the others was the one discovered in the black velvet pouch in Monsignor Crawford's lock box at the United Nations. It read, "From the land of the Aztec to the land of the New World. From East to West and back again, she seeks to protect life, liberty and happiness where they would no longer have her."

"Why would the Knights of Columbus leave a clue for the Christ Stone at the United Nations if they didn't want Crawford to have it in the first place?" Drew asked.

"They wanted someone to find the clue to the Christ Stone. They just didn't want it to be Crawford," Father Mac replied.

"Why?"

"I think we can answer that," Linda said looking at Michael. "Before we found out about Monsignor Crawford, we met a man who worked at Saint Patrick's Cathedral who asked us if we were looking for the Christ Stone."

"Right out of the blue?" Father Mac asked.

"Yes," Linda responded without hesitation. "He said Saint Padre Paolo told him we would be coming."

Everyone looked at Cassy who smiled and shrugged her shoulders. "Sounds like Paolo was giving clues to members of the Knights of Columbus," she said.

"Why didn't the Knights want Crawford to have the Christ Stone?" Drew asked again.

"Crawford wasn't exactly a good guy," Michael answered this time.

"What do you mean?"

"First, the man who traveled with Crawford from Montreal to New York with the Christ Stone is no longer living. Second, Crawford referred to the Knights of Columbus as 'pro–life maggots;' and third, Crawford thinks the Right–to–Life Marchers deserve death."

"And he was made a monsignor?" Drew asked surprised.

"Kind of a reversed conversion experience," Father Gabe said, and everyone in the room chuckled. "The important thing is that Saint Padre Paolo wanted us to find the Christ Stone and knew we would find the note."

"Let's take the clue that Michael and Linda found in parts," Father Mac said as he looked at the note. "Father Derek, can you take notes for us?"

"Absolutely," Father Derek replied taking out a small notebook and pen.

Father Mac continued, "First, 'From the land of the Aztec…'"

"Mexico," Father Raphael said quickly.

"Yes, good," Father Mac replied. "'To the land of the New World…'"

"Would that be Canada?" Linda asked. "I mean, the 'New World' where the Christ Stone was taken after Jerusalem."

"In this instance, I think 'the land of the New World' is the United States of America," Father Derek answered.

"Makes sense," Michael added. "Canada was considered the 'New Jerusalem' when the Christ Stone was moved from Jerusalem to Montreal. The 'New World' is the U.S."

"What went from Mexico to the U.S.?" Cassy asked.

"Our Lady of Guadalupe," Father Raphael answered.

"Our Lady of the Immaculate Conception," Father Mac corrected.

"But, both Mary, the Mother of God, regardless," Father Gabe interjected. "In one instance, the Mother of the Americas. In the other, the Patroness of the U.S."

"Father Mac, let's continue using 'Our Lady of the Immaculate Conception,'" Father Derek said as he was taking notes. "'From East to West and back again.' Was it possible that the Christ Stone was moved from East to West and back again?" he asked.

"As far as we know, the Christ Stone was moved from Montreal to Saint Patrick's Cathedral to the U.N. in New York, and that was it," Michael said looking at Linda for agreement.

"That's it," Linda confirmed.

Father Mac had all four Knights of Columbus' notes lined up in a row. He had been playing with the order and moving around the notes as people spoke. Suddenly, he sat straight up. "What if the clue has to do with the order of the notes themselves?" he asked.

"You mean, 'From East to West and back again?'" Jessica asked as she sat between Father Gabe and Father Derek.

"Yes," Father Mac answered. "Think about it. Father Raphael found his note on the East coast. Father Gabe, on the west coast, and then I just stumbled upon another note at Saint Mary's Church in New York."

"Father Raphael, what is your parish called in New Jersey?" Father Gabe asked.

"Saint Mary's," Father Raphael answered.

"That's our Mary!" Father Gabe exclaimed. "Saint Mary's Church in New Jersey, Saint Mary's Cathedral in San Francisco, and Saint Mary's Church in New York. 'From East to West and back again.'"

"Now we have our order," Father Mac said excitedly. He placed the notes in order from left to right. "Now, the last part, 'She seeks to protect life, liberty and happiness where they would no longer have her.'"

"Well, the first part's easy enough," Debbie said. "Mary is obviously protecting 'life, liberty and the pursuit of happiness' as in the Declaration of Independence."

"Very good, Debbie. That has to be it," Father Mac said. "But what about 'where they would no longer have her?'"

"Same place," Debbie answered quickly looking around the room as everyone sat silent. "You know, separation of church and state, the line the government always uses out of context. The founding fathers used Judeo–Christian principles to set up the U.S. government to protect 'life, liberty and the pursuit of happiness,' but they never took God out of the equation. They just wanted to make sure that the people had freedom of religion and there was no one government religion imposed. Washington D.C. is the one that would no longer have her."

Everyone in the Romano's suite at The New Yorker Hotel knew Debbie was right. The Christ Stone was somewhere in the nation's capital.

CHAPTER FORTY–FOUR

When the group finished in the Romano's suite for the night, everyone knew the location of the Christ Stone. Washington D.C. Same place as the March for Life. They had narrowed their search for the Christ Stone to a little over 68 square miles.

They said, "Good night," and went to their own rooms for much needed rest.

Everyone except Michael. He knew he wouldn't be able to sleep. The burn was on. They were almost there. They were so close to figuring out the location of the Christ Stone.

"You okay?" Linda asked as they walked to their separate, but adjoining rooms.

"I'm going to spend a little time in the business center before bed," Michael replied holding his notepad and pen. He had every single piece of information from beginning to end in that notepad including all four Knights of Columbus notes. Father Mac had kept the originals. Michael had copied them verbatim.

"Do you need me to tag along?" Linda asked exhausted.

"No, you get some rest. I won't be long."

When Michael sat down at the business center computer, the entire conversation in the Romano's suite replayed in his head.

"What did Father Raphael say about Mary and Mexico?" he

thought. Looking at his notes, his eyes were drawn immediately to the reference, "Our Lady of Guadalupe."

"Are there any churches in D.C. with that name?" Michael thought. He googled it and saw only references for books, schools and the shrine in Mexico City.

"What did Father Mac say about Mary and the U.S.?" Again, Michael checked his notes. "Our Lady of the Immaculate Conception." When he googled this, he smiled and nodded his head.

Michael came face to face with the "Basilica of the National Shrine of the Immaculate Conception," the largest Catholic Church in the U.S., and the tallest habitable building in Washington D.C., second only to the Washington Monument.

"If I were a Knight, that's where I'd hide the Christ Stone," Michael thought. He scrolled down through images of the interior of the Basilica, but when he saw the altar dedicated to Our Lady of Guadalupe, a chill ran up his spine.

The date of the feast day of Our Lady of Guadalupe was December 12, and the last celebration of the feast day was held on 12/12/12, the same day the Christ Stone was stolen from the United Nations. That was the significance of the number "12." They would find the Christ Stone at the largest Catholic Church in the country at the Shrine of Our Lady of Guadalupe, the only pregnant apparition of Mary, whose feast was celebrated on 12/12/12. They would find the Christ Stone on 01/22/13, the date of the next March for Life and the national day of prayer for the unborn.

"That's it!" Michael exclaimed.

*

The next morning, everyone seemed in good spirits. They had found out about Michael's discovery, and all four priests agreed that the altar to Our Lady of Guadalupe at the National Shrine was the most likely hiding place for the Christ Stone. Father Gabe had visited the Shrine so many times before, he knew the Our Lady of Guadalupe altar well. He also knew that the Knights of Columbus had contributed money to build the famous blue fresco dome of the Immaculate Conception.

The group had only 24 hours to find the Christ Stone before the March began, but what seemed impossible the night before was now highly plausible. The plan was to check out of The New Yorker and get to D.C. as quickly as possible. They had arranged to take a train to D.C. from Penn Station.

After breakfast, they met in the lobby of the hotel.

"Are we all here?" Father Gabe asked after check out.

Everyone looked around to check.

"Has anyone seen Debbie?" Lucia worriedly called out in the distance. It was obvious she was thinking the worst.

"She was just beside me!" Pietro exclaimed.

"Debbie? Debbie?" Cassy and Drew called throughout the lobby.

Jessica walked around to the elevators to see if Debbie was still there. She came back alone and very upset.

"We'll check upstairs!" Michael said taking Linda's hand.

"Father Gabe, you and Father Derek, check the first floor," Father Mac instructed. "Father Raphael, you and Jessica, the stairwells. I'll take the elevator and remaining floors. Pietro and Lucia, let the hotel know we have a missing person."

Two hours passed and Debbie was still missing, but the group knew what they had to do. They had to return to David's apartment. If he had taken her again, she would either be there or in D.C. with David.

Father Mac led the group to the entrance of the Manhattan Center. He turned to them before he entered. "Just follow my lead," he said.

The same security guard sat at the desk as before, and Father Mac recognized him immediately. The guard was texting on his iPhone, and Father Mac felt like he was having a "déjà vu" moment.

"Excuse me?" Father Mac asked the guard. "I was just here the other day checking on the facilities for Archbishop Timothy Cardinal Dolan? I need to let the rest of the staff see it before we can make a decision."

The guard took one quick look at the four priests and the rest of the group, and shrugged his shoulders for them to pass.

"Thank you," Father Mac replied as if this were the most important decision the security guard would make all day.

The group assembled inside the elevator and Father Mac hit "8." It was snug, but they all fit and ascended to the eighth floor without any interruption. When they got off the elevator and rounded the corner, the amount of foreboding felt by everyone was so intense it was tangible.

They reached the door to David's apartment, and all was quiet. Father Mac turned to Michael who produced the key and stuck it into the lock. It turned easily and the door pushed open. They walked into the empty apartment and closed the door behind them.

"Debbie's not here," Lucia said in dismay.

"Let's check the rooms just to make sure," Father Mac replied. "David might be hiding her."

Linda and Michael checked the study. Jessica, the kitchen. Lucia and Pietro, the living room, and Cassy and Drew, the guestroom. Father Mac led the other three priests into the master suite.

After a quick search, they met up in the master bedroom to report that Debbie was nowhere in the apartment.

"Father Mac, where is the safe in the wall where the documents were found?" Father Gabe asked.

"Right here." Father Mac climbed on top of the bed and pulled down the painting that hid David's safe.

"Do you still remember the combination?" the Archbishop asked again.

"Of course, Michael?"

Michael jumped on the bed in front of the safe and stood next to Father Mac who was still holding the painting. "The combination is '012213,'" Michael said as he entered the numbers to unlock the safe. It clicked open, and Michael pulled open the door. The safe was still completely empty. He closed the safe again, and Father Mac hung the painting back on the wall.

"Interesting," Father Gabe said as he walked around the room analyzing the other paintings. There were three more in the master bedroom. One hung directly across the room from the bed, and the other two on the left and right walls. They were all original Monets.

Father Gabe walked to the left wall and lifted the painting to look behind it. No safe. Next, he walked to the right, and still, no safe. When Father Gabe walked to the far wall, there was a beautiful painting of a woman holding an umbrella in a colorful garden. The painting was large and quite long.

Father Derek moved forward to help the Archbishop lift the painting from the wall. Suddenly, the group saw a long, silver vault with another digital lock.

"Holy Toledo!" Father Raphael exclaimed.

"Good work, Father Gabe!" Father Mac added.

Michael shrugged his shoulders and looked at Linda. "I can't believe we missed it," he said.

Father Gabe smiled cunningly, "Should we try the same combination for this one?"

"Can't hurt," Father Mac replied. He looked at Michael who punched in the same numbers. There was no click or green light to show that the lock had opened.

"Any other ideas?" the Archbishop asked again.

"Can we use numbers for letters like a phone pad?" Cassy asked.

Michael nodded, "My assumption is yes, as long as it's still six digits."

"Try 'Moloch,'" Cassy said.

"Perfect, considering his large ego," Jessica added.

"That's '554513,'" Michael said as he punched in the numbers for "Moloch."

Everyone waited with baited breath for the safe to open, but there was no click and no green light.

"What about 'Lilith?'" Cassy suggested again.

"'434373,'" Michael said as he punched in the numbers. This time, a loud click sounded, and the door to the vault opened in front of their eyes.

The eleven people crowded around David's vault gasped at what they saw. On the floor of the vault were millions of dollars in bundles of money—one hundred dollar bills packaged neatly in large blocks and piled up high in long, neat rows. There was expensive jewelry, too, on the floor of the vault lying on top of the blocks of money. It looked as if they had just unearthed the wreckage of a pirate's ship filled with treasure.

The top shelf of the vault was lined with black velvet and it caught everyone's attention even more than the millions in cash and jewels. There were three exquisite bloodstone cameo necklaces lying side by side, each with images eerily resembling Debbie, Cassy and Jessica. The necklaces sparkled so severely, it was obvious there was a dark magic about them.

Before anyone could utter a word, the door to David's apartment opened and slammed shut. They turned to see David clutching Debbie from behind.

Debbie screamed, but David held his hand over her mouth to stifle her cry. There was no time to think. It all happened so fast, they would later feel that they had only blinked, and Debbie, Cassy, and Jessica had disappeared. A great whirlwind of darkness had descended upon them, and the three women who stood among them only seconds before completely vanished.

*

"Jessica and Cassy and Debbie," Father Derek began. "They're gone."

"David…took them," Father Gabe added.

"He's taken them…all three of them," Father Mac repeated stunned.

Father Raphael peered into the empty vault. "And their necklaces…they're gone, too," he added.

"Oh, my God. I can't believe I let him get away with it." Drew was so devastated, he could barely speak.

Lucia buried her face in Pietro's chest to hide her sobbing.

"Try not to grieve," Father Raphael said trying to console them. "I know we'll be able to find them if we put our heads together."

"You're right," Michael added. "We already know where David's taking them."

"That's right, Michael," Father Gabe replied with renewed confidence. "David's headed to Washington D.C., and we'll be right there to meet him."

"And we'll have something David's not expecting," Linda added. "The Christ Stone."

*

For Cassy, David's abduction was similar to the spiritual journeys she took with Paolo, but there were also significant differences. In many ways, this out–of–body experience was completely opposite. Where there was light, this led to unending darkness; where there was freedom, this felt like perpetual captivity; and where there was joy, this produced a feeling of depression so severe, she felt she no longer had control of her own emotions.

Cassy flew through blackness for what seemed like hours. She could not see Debbie or Jessica anywhere. She knew that David had taken them to this dark place, but she couldn't see him either.

Cassy's mind was playing tricks on her in the darkness. Sometimes, she heard evil cackling around her, and then it would suddenly disappear. Other times, she heard Paolo's voice calling to her to let her know he was there to protect her, but then there was only silence.

At some point, the blackness seemed to lessen, as if the dark of night were turning into the hazy gray of an overcast day. There was no sun in this place, though. No light at all. Just shades of gray as if no oxygen existed in the air.

Cassy felt her body touch down onto a gray and barren terrain. She walked as if there were some destination she would reach in all the gray.

Cassy eventually found her voice. She called to Debbie and Jessica even though she knew from the depths of her soul that this was pointless. She was present in some alternate realty that had no relationship to time and space as we know on earth. She was present somewhere non–existent. Somewhere between heaven and earth. Somewhere never realized or created.

Cassy hastened her pace as if walking faster might get her to a place that actually existed. Occasionally, she could see dark figures peering at her eerily. She felt frightened when she thought she saw David come toward her, the darkest figure of all. She could see the evil in his eyes. They were glowing with a greenish hue and burning into her soul. David held up his hands, and Cassy saw that he was holding a bloodstone cameo necklace out toward her with her image. She began to fight when he tried to place the necklace around her neck. She would do anything to keep him from controlling her with that horrible, unholy stone.

Cassy prayed as if her life depended on it. The more she prayed, the more David's image began to fade. It was as if every word of her prayer kept David further and further away. Cassy felt emboldened by prayer, and when she couldn't see David any longer, she prayed for Debbie and Jessica, too. It was the most liberating and empowering experience of Cassy's life, and she began to feel invincible.

Suddenly, Cassy saw Paolo run toward her through the gray haze with a strong light blazing behind him. When she ran into his arms, they grasped one another electrified by a powerful bond of love for God and life. Cassy let go of Paolo and saw Debbie and Jessica run toward her in the distance. The three women embraced with a love that went beyond mere blood relations. They had a common purpose, and nothing could stand in their way.

Paolo told them to follow the light, the same golden–white ray of light that had radiated behind Paolo. They looked for the light, but there was no sky and the tunnel of gray seemed to go on forever.

"Have faith, trust in God and follow the light," Paolo said. He pointed to the end of the tunnel, and the three women saw a distant and subtle light. They turned back to Paolo, but he had already mysteriously vanished.

They were left alone, but safe from David. Cassy, Debbie and Jessica began to walk toward the light.

CHAPTER FORTY–FIVE

By the time the four priests, the Romanos, Drew, Michael and Linda reached Washington D.C., it was late in the evening the night before the March. Exhausted, they spent the night at a hotel near the National Shrine of the Immaculate Conception.

Early the next morning, they decided that half the group should try to locate the Christ Stone at the Shrine, and the other half should wait in the Mall for Jessica, Cassy and Debbie at the March for Life. If the prediction were true and David was trying to wipe out close to half a million people, it would take place at the Mall.

They were absolutely positive that the Christ Stone would be discovered at the National Shrine of the Immaculate Conception, the largest Catholic Church in the Americas. The Christ Stone would be discovered at the chapel dedicated to Our Lady of Guadalupe. They would use the Knights of Columbus notes found by Father Gabe, Father Raphael and Father Mac as clues to find the Christ Stone in the chapel.

Michael, Linda and Father Raphael were chosen to locate the Christ Stone at the National Shrine. Father Mac, Drew, and the Romanos would travel to the Mall where they hoped to find Cassy, Debbie and Jessica. Father Gabe and Father Derek were scheduled to speak in the Mall before the March for Life began. The

Archbishop of San Francisco knew that he would be an excellent decoy for David should he try to intervene in their search for the Christ Stone.

*

Father Raphael, Michael and Linda entered the Basilica of the National Shrine from the rear of the crypt level. When Father Raphael swung the door open, he sensed something trying to slow him down. He felt lightheaded, as if his head were spinning and his mind were racing all at once. The priest held the door with one hand and placed the back of his other hand on his forehead as if he were faint.

"Father, are you all right?" Michael asked with concern.

To Father Raphael, it felt like Michael was speaking through an old walkie–talkie; his voice was slow and distorted as if it were in slow motion. The priest needed to get control of himself and push forward no matter what was trying to hold him back.

"Yes, yes. I'm fine," Father Raphael replied. "Thanks, Michael. Let's get going."

As soon as they walked through the door, they saw a book store on the left and a large cafeteria with wood tables on the right. There were still some marchers lingering about, but many had already made their way to the Mall to hear the speakers before the March began.

Michael noticed that many of the people were in high school or college, much younger than even he and Linda or Father Raphael. There were people from all walks of life: religious pastors, priests, brothers and sisters; families with young children; students on class trips; prayer groups from churches; and elderly people in wheelchairs. Some attendees were gearing up for the March; they put coats and hats on and readied signs that read, "I regret my abortion," and "Life begins in the womb."

Michael looked down at his watch. It was 9:35. He knew the

speakers would begin at noon, but David would not wait until 1:30 when the March began. He would kill the marchers when they were still huddled together in the Mall listening to the speakers. This meant they had roughly two and a half hours to find the Christ Stone and get it to the March.

They continued down a long corridor and saw a tall marble statue of Mary in the distance. Just after the book store, Father Raphael spotted an information booth and stopped to get directions to the Chapel of Our Lady of Guadalupe.

"Excuse me?" he asked with a big friendly smile.

"Si?" A small Hispanic woman smiled up at the priest making no attempt to conceal her obvious attraction to Father Raphael's good looks.

"We need to locate the Chapel of Our Lady of Guadalupe. Can you help us?" Father Raphael spoke with urgency, and the woman quickly pulled out a small map.

"Si." She pointed to number "47" in the upper church. "Past the statue of Mary, take the stairs on her left, make a left at the top of the stairs and go to the fourth chapel on the left." The woman spoke very quickly in Spanish as if she knew that Father Raphael's life depended on it.

"Gracias," Father Raphael said as he took the map and started back down the corridor.

Michael and Linda tried to keep up from behind.

"What did she say?" Michael asked.

"Left, up, left," Father Raphael replied.

Michael and Linda exchanged surprised looks as if to ask, "It takes that much Spanish to say that?"

As soon as Father Raphael reached the statue of Mary and made a left to get to the staircase, he saw a band of invisible demons lurking on several stairs trying to scare them off. They looked like evil ghosts floating in a cloud of mist. Suddenly, Father Raphael felt the same pulling force, as if something were trying to hold him back from ascending the staircase.

"In the name of Jesus Christ, be gone!" the priest said sternly and pushed his way through the unseen forces. They vanished immediately.

Michael and Linda had not seen anything in the stairwell, but they knew that Father Raphael must have seen something very frightening. At this point, Michael and Linda would have believed anything. Since the bloodstone mystery began, nothing surprised them anymore.

They took the stairs quickly. When they reached the top, they were fully immersed in the magnificence of the Basilica. The floors were made of marble with ornate, marble columns throughout. The ceilings were painted with spectacular frescoes and domes in blue illustrated biblical characters and scenes.

As they rounded the corner toward the fourth chapel on the left, Father Raphael began to feel like the marble floor was moving. He quickly stopped to regain his balance and extended both arms out to make sure that he would not fall to the floor.

Linda reached out to take the priest's right hand and called out to him from a seeming distance. "Father? Don't worry. I've got you," she said.

Michael took Father Raphael's left hand, and the priest felt as though he could walk forward once again, as if his mind were clearing and focused. Michael and Linda held Father Raphael's hands trying to keep him from collapsing while they walked as quickly as possible. To the March–for–Life onlookers, they must have looked like three over–aged lunatic children running uncontrollably down the great Basilica's halls. They passed the Saint Vincent de Paul chapel, the Miraculous Medal chapel and the Saint Louise de Marillac chapel until they finally reached the chapel they were yearning to see.

The Chapel of Our Lady of Guadalupe was more magnificent than they had anticipated. The entire chapel was decorated in a brightly colored mosaic that made the hue of the stones sparkle with celestial wonder.

The image of Our Lady of Guadalupe was spectacularly colored depicting Mary in a long blue shawl as she stood pregnant bearing the baby Jesus. It is the only apparition of Mary in which she is "with child," signified by the band above her waist. The name "Guadalupe" is a Spanish transliteration of the name the Virgin gave to Juan Diego in his Nahuatl tongue, which means "the one who crushed the serpent."

As Michael entered the chapel, he saw that Mary was standing on the head of Satan, crushing him with her sandaled feet. There were large, red roses strewn beneath her, and she was surrounded by a golden glow. The roses came from Juan Diego's cloak as he knelt before her with his arms outstretched in gratitude and awe.

On both the left and right walls were numerous images of people who had come to pay homage to Mary when she appeared to Juan Diego on Tepeyac Hill outside of Mexico City in 1531. Michael felt as if he were part of the procession of mosaic figures coming from North, Central, and South America with lighted candles to pay tribute to the Virgin.

Linda still held onto Father Raphael's hand when Michael let go and walked into the chapel to take in its beauty. Michael turned around to check on them and saw that Linda was having a difficult time leading Father Raphael into the chapel. It seemed as though the priest was in considerable pain as he strained to push himself forward and into the chapel. Linda tried with all her might to pull him forward, but something was holding him back.

Michael stepped forward and grabbed Father Raphael's arm. In an authoritative voice he said, "In the name of Christ Jesus, stand aside, and let this holy priest enter." As soon as Michael said this, whatever was blocking their entrance gave way, and all three were thrown into the chapel with the force of Linda and Michael's pulling.

Father Raphael was flung forward, but another force seemed to break his fall. Suddenly, he found himself kneeling in front of Our Lady of Guadalupe on a velvet–cushioned kneeler with a prayer in

English and Spanish encased in glass.

The priest looked up at Linda and Michael who stood on either side of the kneeler visibly concerned. "Thank you," he said. "We are well protected inside this magnificent chapel from the apparent evil that was trying to keep us out."

Linda and Michael breathed a sigh of relief.

Father Raphael looked back at the prayer in front of him and began to read it in English:

> *Dearest Lady of Guadalupe, fruitful Mother of Holiness,*
> *teach me your ways of gentleness and strength.*
> *Hear my prayer offered with deep–felt*
> *Confidence to beg this favor…*
> *O Mary, conceived without sin, I come to your throne of grace*
> *to share the fervent devotion of your faithful Mexican children*
> *who call to you under the glorious Aztec title of*
> *"Guadalupe" the Virgen who crushed the serpent.*
>
> *Queen of Martyrs, whose Immaculate Heart*
> *was pierced by seven swords of grief,*
> *help me to walk valiantly amid the*
> *sharp thorns strewn across my pathway.*
> *Queen of Apostles, aid me to win souls*
> *for the Sacred Heart of my Savior.*
> *I plead this through the merits of your merciful Son,*
> *our Lord, Jesus Christ.*
> *Amen.*

"Do you think the prayer might be part of the clue?" Michael asked.

"I don't know," Father Raphael answered. "Let's take out all the Knights of Columbus notes before we make any deductions."

Michael took out the notes and placed them in order on a bench near the right wall. "From East to West and back again."

Raphael rose from the kneeler to take in the rest of the chapel. He saw phrases printed along both sides of the mosaic walls on either side of the image of Our Lady of Guadalupe. They were written directly underneath the figures that were lined up to process their devotion to Mary.

Father Raphael read the phrases on the left and right walls aloud: "Who is she that comes forth like the rising dawn fair as the moon bright as the sun," and "Like the rainbow gleaming amid luminous clouds like the bloom of roses in the spring."

"Those are the phrases on the first two notes!" Linda exclaimed. "From East to West."

"Our first two clues," Michael added.

"Yes, if there were any doubts of finding the Christ Stone here, they have now been eradicated," Father Raphael responded. He walked over to the third clue, the "back again" Knights of Columbus note that Michael had placed on the bench. Father Raphael read the note out loud, "Count the caps that pay tribute to Mary, the Virgin, the mother of God, and Queen of the universe."

"There's a lot that pays tribute to Mary here," Michael said.

"That's for sure," Linda added.

Father Raphael continued to walk around the chapel taking in every single picture and prayer. He pulled the rosary beads that he always kept with him out of his pants' pocket, so he could hold them while he walked.

"'Count the caps' means we're supposed to be looking for capital letters, right?" Michael asked.

"The phrases underneath the people on either side only have capital letters in the first words of each phrase," Linda answered.

Father Raphael was still taking in every word and image in the chapel. There were the phrases on the walls and the prayer on the kneeler. Phrases and prayer. Two separate entities.

Could one lead to the Christ Stone? What about the other? Could they be used together to determine the Christ Stone's location? Or were they to be used separately for two different purposes?

"Phrases and prayer," Father Raphael said as he walked around the chapel in deep thought. "Let's assume that the phrases underneath the images and the Guadalupe prayer are supposed to be used separately in order to find the Christ Stone. In fact, let's start with the phrases." Father Raphael turned back to the left wall, "Who is she that comes forth like the rising dawn fair as the moon bright as the sun?" he asked.

"That's easy. Our Lady of Guadalupe," Linda answered pointing directly in front of her at the mosaic image of Mary in Mexico.

"Absolutely," Father Raphael answered. He walked to the right wall, "Like the rainbow gleaming amid luminous clouds like the bloom of roses in the spring?"

Michael looked for a rainbow in the mosaic pattern and found none. He looked for clouds, too, but found none of those either. Then the word "roses" jumped out at him as he realized the obvious pattern of roses that appeared on the wall underneath the image of Our Lady of Guadalupe.

Directly to the left of Mary was the image of Juan Diego kneeling before her with his arms outstretched holding his cloak open to show something of intense value. There were beautiful, red roses falling out of the cloak and cascading across the mosaic underneath Mary. A pattern of roses led Michael's gaze to a small alcove in the wall to the right of Mary. The roses stopped once he reached the alcove. There was a lush, tropical plant with a beautiful fuchsia flower on the shelf that hid something inside the alcove.

"Wait a second…" Michael moved toward the plant in the alcove and climbed two stairs to the right of the altar. He removed the plant and saw a magnificent single rose that was illustrated in mosaic in the middle of the alcove.

"Roses in the spring!" Father Raphael exclaimed as he made his way to the alcove next to Michael.

"That's it!" Linda called out from behind.

"May I?" Father Raphael asked Michael before he touched the

beautiful mosaic rose hidden by the plant.

Michael nodded excitedly as he looked around the chapel to make sure that no one could see them.

As soon as Raphael touched the rose, the mosaic image mysteriously pushed back and slid down to reveal a secret compartment with a numeric digital lock.

"Oh, my God, the Father, the Almighty!" Father Raphael exclaimed before he could stop himself. He made a sign of the cross.

"Father, do you think the Guadalupe prayer will help us figure out the code?" Linda asked.

"Yes, of course! Phrases and prayer! Good thinking, Linda!" Father Raphael walked back over to the last note on the bench and picked it up. "Count the caps that pay tribute to Mary, the Virgin, the mother of God, and Queen of the universe."

"Father Raphael, I remember seeing large capital letters written into the prayer of Our Lady of Guadalupe," Linda said. "Look over here." She walked to the kneeler and pointed to the prayer written in English. "Counting the 'caps' has to mean counting the capital letters."

"That's it!" Father Raphael shouted out without caring whether anyone could hear.

Michael took the small notebook and pen out of his jacket, and Linda knelt at the kneeler to recite every capital letter, line by line.

"D, L, G, M, H, H, O, M, I, M, A, G, V. That's the first paragraph," Linda reported.

"Q, M, I, H, Q, A, S, H, S, I, S, L, J, C, and A are the second paragraph."

"Got them," Michael said.

"Okay. Here we go." Raphael was so excited, his hand was visibly shaking while he read the note. "'Count the caps that pay tribute to Mary, the Virgin, the mother of God, and Queen of the universe.' So, we're supposed to count capital letters, but how many?" he asked Linda and Michael.

"Father, can I see the last Knights of Columbus note again?" Michael asked.

"Yes, of course." Father Raphael handed Michael the note.

Michael studied it, and his eyes lit up. He had discovered something. "There are distinct capital letters in this clue, too," he said. "M for Mary, V for Virgin, G for God and Q for Queen."

"Four capital letters for a four–digit code!" Linda exclaimed staring back up at the lock now completely visible in the alcove.

"Excellent," Michael replied quickly as he noticed two marchers come toward them deep in prayer. They were trying to look over Linda's shoulder to read the prayer of Our Lady of Guadalupe.

"Oh, I'm sorry," Linda said and stood up to get out of their way. One of the marchers nodded gratefully and knelt before the mosaic apparition.

Linda, Michael and Father Raphael huddled around the bench in front of the lock in the alcove, and whispered so that no one could hear them.

"Michael, walk over and count the M's." Father Raphael seemed excited enough now to burst.

Michael walked back over to the Guadalupe prayer and stood directly behind the marchers to count the M's. He walked back to Father Raphael and Linda. "Four M's," he said.

"V's?" Father Raphael asked again.

Michael walked back over to count and returned. "One," he said.

"G's?"

He went back and forth again. "Two."

"Q's?"

Michael went back and forth one last time feeling like the two praying marchers must have thought he looked like a neurotic psycho. "Two again," he answered.

"4122," Linda said aloud, and all three looked up at the lock eager to try to open it.

Before they went to the alcove, they checked on the marchers to see if they looked like they were ready to leave. They did not want to attempt to open the lock in front of others. The marchers had switched places at the kneeler, but they were still praying.

"Father, we can't afford to wait," Michael said.

"You're right, Michael," Father Raphael answered. "I'll think of something."

Father Raphael approached the marchers. "Excuse me, I was just about to hear these dear young people's confessions, and I was wondering if you needed too much more time?"

"No, Father. Go right ahead. We were just finishing. No problem," the two marchers spoke at once, glad to be of service to a priest.

"God bless you," Father Raphael said as the marchers left the chapel. He turned back to Linda and Michael with a wry smile. "Aah! The magic of wearing a collar!" he exclaimed.

"Do you want me to give it a try?" Michael asked.

"Absolutely!" Father Raphael replied.

Michael turned to the lock and pressed "4122" and "enter" on the key pad. They could hear a little puff of air as the door gave way. When Michael opened it, the jasper and golden Christ Stone sat inside looking oddly unremarkable, but incredibly holy. He took the Christ Stone out and gave it to Father Raphael as Linda watched with wonder.

Father Raphael held out the sacred stone, and a gleaming light shone forth that connected the Christ Stone to Mary's pregnant womb. In one instant, they knew that this object could defeat any evil.

CHAPTER FORTY–SIX

There were almost 500,000 people gathered in the Mall waiting for the March for Life speakers. Hundreds of buses had come from all across the country filled with grade school, high school and college students all set to make their stand in defense of life. Families with young children congregated on the lawn to make sure that children's coats were buttoned and hats and gloves put on correctly. Religious priests, sisters, brothers and deacons, young and old, were assembled among the crowd.

People from all across the country, from all walks of life, from all different religions, and all ages were turned out to stand up for a common goal that united them in spirit and fundamental goodness.

Drew, Father Mac and the Romanos stood by the stage waiting to catch a glimpse of Debbie, Cassy and Jessica who they thought might appear at any moment with David while Father Gabe and Father Derek stood on the podium with the other speakers waiting to speak.

Marie and Doc Murray and their group from Wisconsin waited by the stage, too. They were not aware that their son, Michael, was fighting for their very lives in his quest for the Christ Stone. Veronica and Tom Blake stood in the crowd with Peter and Grace, and Veronica smiled at Kay and Kevin Dennis even though she was worried about Father Raphael because she hadn't spoken to him in days. A much happier Dr. Albert Townsend stood among the sea of pro–lifers wondering if he would ever be called upon to speak about his conversion, and Evee Ekwonye stood waiting for her brother, Father Derek, to speak.

Everyone was excited for the March for Life to begin. Everyone, except Elaina. She was waiting in the background with some of her employees. She had no idea of David's plans, but she knew he was there somewhere.

*

"Ladies and gentlemen, I give you Archbishop Gabriel Sanders from San Francisco!" Father Derek stepped aside from the podium mic on the stage in the center of the Mall to make way for Father Gabe, the last speaker at the March for Life 2013. Father Gabe's pro–life reputation preceded him and thunderous applause and cheers were heard throughout the entire Mall.

Father Gabe stepped up to the mic and greeted the hundreds of thousands of people cheering in the Mall. "Thank you, good people of Washington D.C. and this great and free nation we call the United States of America! I traveled from the sunny state of California, but despite the cold January temperatures, there is no place I would rather be than right here with you all!"

Again, the crowd applauded and cheered for the Archbishop.

Father Gabe looked out at the young people in the audience. "To all of the young people here today from grade schools, high schools and universities all across this country, may I say, God bless you! And to families, young and old, may I say, God bless you! And to every heritage, culture and religion, may I say, God bless you! Isn't it fantastic to be part of the majority of this great and free country who considers themselves 'pro–life?'"

The speakers standing on the platform could feel the energy and excitement of the audience as they cheered and chanted, "Pro–

Life! Pro–Life! Pro–Life!"

Father Gabe continued, "My pro–life brothers and sisters, once upon a time, there was a dark day in the history of this great nation when African people were kidnapped from their homes and sold into slavery, but the light of God shown from above and the slaves were set free!

"My pro–life brothers and sisters, once upon a time, there was a dark day in the history of this great nation when our Jewish brothers and sisters were taken from their homes and killed in concentration camps, but the light of God shown from above and the Jews were set free!

"My pro–life brothers and sisters, forty years ago on January 22nd, 1973, there was a dark day in the history of this great nation when our Supreme Court decided that our unborn children could be legally murdered in their mothers' wombs, but the light of God shown from above and we are standing here today united in the name of life!

"A great pro–life man once led this great nation. In 1984, President Ronald Reagan wrote a book called, 'Abortion and the Conscience of the Nation.' I would like to read an excerpt from his book right now:

"'Make no mistake, abortion–on–demand is not a right granted by the Constitution...Nowhere do the plain words of the Constitution even hint at a 'right' so sweeping as to permit abortion up to the time the child is ready to be born. Yet that is what the Court ruled. As an act of 'raw judicial power,' the decision by the seven–man majority in Roe v. Wade has so far been made to stick. But the Court's decision has by no means settled the debate. Instead, Roe v. Wade has become a continuing prod to the conscience of the nation. I have closely followed and assisted efforts in Congress to reverse the tide of abortion—efforts of Congressmen, Senators and citizens responding to an urgent moral crisis. Regrettably, I have also seen the massive efforts of those who, under the banner of 'freedom of choice,' have so far blocked every effort to reverse nationwide abortion–on–demand.

"'Despite the formidable obstacles before us, we must not lose heart. We know that respect for the sacred value of human life is too deeply ingrained in the hearts of our people to remain forever suppressed. What, then, is the real issue? When we talk about abortion, we are talking about two lives—the life of the mother and the life of the unborn child. Anyone who doesn't feel sure whether we are talking about a second human life should clearly give life the benefit of the doubt. Scientific evidence proves that the unborn child is alive, is a distinct individual, and is a member of the human species.

"'The real question today is not when human life begins, but what is the value of human life? The abortionist who reassembles the arms and legs of a tiny baby to make sure all its parts have been torn from its mother's body can hardly doubt whether it is a human being. The real question for him and for all of us is whether that tiny human life has a God–given right to be protected by the law—the same right we have. Every legislator, every doctor, and every citizen needs to recognize that the real issue is whether to affirm and protect the sanctity of all human life, or to embrace a social ethic where some human lives are valued and others are not.'"

Father Gabe looked back up from his notes. "My pro–life brothers and sisters, just as the great President Ronald Reagan said, let us 'affirm and protect the sanctity of all human life!' My pro–life brothers and sisters, today we are here to make history! Today we are here to let the light of God shine through each of us so our unborn children are set free! May I say, with God's help, let this be the last year we have to March on Washington to let the voices of the unborn be heard! May I say, with God's help, let freedom reign, today and forever! Amen!"

*

When Father Raphael, Michael and Linda found the Christ Stone at the National Shrine, they felt its power and thought they would be magically transported to the March for Life, but this was not the case. Reality came back hard and fast. They needed to take the fastest transportation means possible to get the Christ Stone to the March for Life.

Michael gave the Christ Stone to Father Raphael and closed the compartment in the chapel's alcove. The priest put the Christ Stone into a special pouch and tucked it safely in his right hand. Father Raphael held it so tightly someone would have had to cut off his hand to get the stone.

When they left the chapel, they turned back to Our Lady of Guadalupe and saw a brilliant halo of light shining above her head. It was unmistakably miraculous, and they left feeling energized by her spirit.

They exited the same way they entered, ran down the road to Catholic University of America, and took the Metro from Brookland to the Smithsonian. As they rode the Metro, they could hear Father Gabe speaking as if they were actually standing in the Mall with the rest of the marchers listening to his speech. Linda, Michael and Father Raphael knew this was physically impossible, but they also knew that nothing was impossible with God.

God was with them as they made their way to the Mall.

*

When Cassy, Debbie and Jessica neared the end of the tunnel, they could hear a massive crowd cheering in the distance. Father Gabe was speaking, and they could hear the deep resonance of his voice inspiring the crowd. He was coming to the end of his speech, and every phrase seemed to bring greater applause.

Just as Father Gabe spoke his last sentence, the three women found themselves standing on the back of the stage where Father Derek waited with the rest of the speakers. It was as if the light at the end of the tunnel had led them directly to that moment in time.

Father Derek was surprised and elated to see them and gave each a great bear hug. "You're all right!" he said joyfully. "Praise be God, you're all right!"

When Father Gabe finished, he walked to the back of the stage to see what was going on and saw Jessica and her two nieces standing next to Father Derek. "What took you so long?" the Archbishop joked. They hugged and laughed heartily despite the circumstances.

Cassy immediately decided to warn the marchers of impending danger. It was only a matter of time. She led the group to the mic at the front of the stage.

When Father Mac, the Romanos and Drew caught sight of them, they all breathed a sigh of relief.

"Marchers and fellow pro–lifers," Cassy shouted into the mic as the crowd stirred with enthusiasm and applause. She tried to quiet them by holding up her hand. "Please, I know this may sound unbelievable, but we have reason to believe that someone who is not a friend to the pro–life movement is trying to harm all of you. Please, try to remain calm and carefully begin to exit the Mall."

When Cassy finished, she spotted David in the crowd a great distance away and pointed so the others could see him. Through supernatural powers, it only took David a second to near the stage, and he immediately raised his hand with a force so great that Debbie was picked up from the platform and suspended into the air.

David lowered his hand and Debbie dropped into his arms and fainted. He threw her over his shoulder and carried Debbie into the middle of the square where marchers screamed and cleared the way. David raised his arm again and invoked a wicked incantation with a loud cry.

Immediately, a great wind rose up as the crowd of marchers screamed and ran from the scene. The Mall became rampant with pandemonium, and the wind escalated to a force so great, the marchers had to hold their signs and hats so they wouldn't fly away. They screamed and cried as they tried to hold down strollers with infants.

Cassy, Jessica, Father Gabe and Father Derek ran down off the stage with the rest of the speakers to find safety from the winds. They joined Drew and Father Mac, and Jessica put her arms around Pietro and Lucia to comfort them. The winds became strongest in the center of the Mall, and a great cyclone formed and spiraled up toward the sky. All at once, David walked into the cyclone and disappeared with Debbie.

*

Father Raphael, Michael and Linda reached the Smithsonian stop on the Metro and ran off the train and up the escalator to the National Mall. They did not get very far, though. They could see the great cyclone in the distance coming from the center of the Mall.

"Oh, my God!" Linda shouted.

The local traffic had come to a complete stop and pedestrians were standing and staring at the unbelievable scene before them. There were sounds of police sirens everywhere, and some people were on their cell phones taking pictures and sending images of the catastrophe to everyone they knew. Local news vans were out with reporters and cameras broadcasting the apparent "Attack on Washington D.C." to viewers.

The threat of the looming cyclone and the chaos around them forced Michael, Linda and Father Raphael to slow down as they made their way through the catastrophic scene. The closer they came to the Mall, the more they could hear the screams of the marchers. Father Raphael had to tighten his grasp around the Christ Stone even more to make sure it remained safe through the wind and turbulence.

When they reached the center of the Mall, they came as close to the force of wind as possible and Father Raphael took the holy stone from the pouch in his hand. The priest held it out toward the fierce wind tunnel. Immediately, a secret compartment in the bottom of the stone opened, and the brilliance of the one, true Bloodstone shown so brightly Father Raphael had to shield his eyes.

As soon as the priest held out the Bloodstone, David emerged from the cyclone violently grasping Debbie around her waist. "I will kill her this very moment unless you destroy that horrid stone!" David screamed as he raised his hand over Debbie. She began to choke and pulled her hands up to her neck as if she were being strangled by some unseen force.

"No!" Elaina came up from behind David to try to protect her daughter. She gripped David's neck from behind, but he was too powerful for her. David grabbed Elaina by the arm and threw her into the cyclone.

Debbie was still struggling to breathe, and Cassy and Jessica ran over to her along with the rest of the group. David threw out his hand to keep them at a distance.

"Debbie will perish unless you destroy that hideous stone now!" David hissed at the group.

Debbie was on her knees gasping for every breath while everyone remained paralyzed and unable to intervene. Suddenly, a clap of thunder sounded from directly above and a white light blinded them with a powerful flash.

Miraculously, Paolo stood before the group between the cyclone and David, and Debbie stood up, freed from David's grasp. Paolo smiled at Father Raphael who immediately handed him the Christ Stone. When Paolo held it out to Jessica, Cassy and Debbie, they realized their mission and extended their hands to grasp the Bloodstone together with Paolo. At once, the Christ Stone illuminated a bright and iridescent light that retracted the sunlight and transformed it into a beautiful golden arch.

David screamed uncontrollably and disappeared back into the

cyclone.

When Cassy, Debbie and Jessica let go of the Bloodstone, Paolo mysteriously rose into the sky with the Bloodstone still gleaming in his hands. He landed on top of the Washington Monument, and there was a spectacular symmetrical cross pattern of light beaming across the sky. When the saint disappeared, the Christ Stone continued to shine above the cyclone from the Monument.

Cassy gazed at the distant stone and was reminded of a time when she was a little girl, and she had so desperately tried to rid herself of the Bloodstone's opposite. One holy and one evil. One, a culture of life, and one, a culture of death.

When the wind from the cyclone died down until there was no wind at all, the Christ Stone was left where the cyclone had been. The Christ Stone was completely closed now, hiding the one, true Bloodstone inside. It had served its purpose and saved many lives. It had become a symbol of truth.

EPILOGUE

Cassy, Debbie and Jessica remained with their hands tightly entwined when the cyclone disappeared. Every marcher who attended the March for Life 2013 stood in a state of shock and awe at what had just transpired. They tried to catch a glimpse of the three women who had saved them from the cyclone.

Cassy, Debbie and Jessica had accomplished what they had set out to do. They smiled at one another and squeezed each other's hands before letting go. It was time to go, and there was hope that a new day would dawn in the battle for a culture of life.

Debbie walked over to the Christ Stone and picked it up. She studied it in wonder that so small a thing could make such a difference. When Debbie held it up, she accidentally pushed a button and the secret compartment opened again to reveal the one, true Bloodstone. A ray of light flashed brightly, and Debbie dropped the Christ Stone. The crowd had to shield their eyes from the great light, but Debbie stood transfixed and fell backward as if she had suddenly fainted.

Michael ran forward to close the secret compartment of the stone and quiet the brightness of the light. He gave the Christ Stone to Father Raphael who placed it back in the pouch he still carried. Michael bent down to check on Debbie, and Cassy and Jessica ran to Debbie's side. Lucia, Pietro and Linda stood by as

Michael placed his hand on Debbie's forehead. He moved the long black hair from her face and tried to revive her.

When Debbie opened her eyes, she smiled cunningly at Michael. He had seen that look before. He had seen that look in Deborah. Michael felt fear shoot up his legs as he saw David's face in hers. He saw the counterfeit bloodstone cameo hanging around her neck and knew that David had given her the necklace in the cyclone before he disappeared. She had been overcome once again by its power. In the end, Debbie had been taken by Moloch, and the sacrificing would continue.

AUTHOR'S NOTES

The Bloodstone Legacy is the first novel of a trilogy of pro–life suspense thrillers that links demonic witchcraft to the abortion industry. The second novel, *The Rise of Moloch* continues the fast paced Bloodstone saga and is set to come out in 2014. The third and final novel of the trilogy rises to its greatest heights in the epic, *The Carousel Master*, set to come out in 2016.

The events and characters depicted in this trilogy are fictitious. Any similarity to actual persons, living or dead, is purely coincidental.

ABOUT THE AUTHOR

Lesa Rossmann resides in New Jersey with her husband, Charlie, and their four children: Xavier, Blaise, Jude and Seraphina. Lesa is the owner of Lux Caelestis Media LLC and holds a Masters in Systematic Theology from Seton Hall University's Immaculate Conception Seminary School of Theology in South Orange, New Jersey. _The Bloodstone Legacy_ is the first novel of a trilogy. You can visit Lesa online at www.luxcaelestismediallc.com.

Made in the USA
Lexington, KY
12 March 2013